The
Missing Years

Also by WALTER LAQUEUR

COMMUNISM AND NATIONALISM IN THE MIDDLE EAST

YOUNG GERMANY

RUSSIA AND GERMANY

A HISTORY OF ZIONISM

CONFRONTATION: THE MIDDLE EAST AND WORLD POLITICS

DICTIONARY OF POLITICS

WEIMAR: A CULTURAL HISTORY

THE ROAD TO WAR

THE FATE OF THE REVOLUTION

GUERRILLA

TERRORISM

Edited by Walter Laqueur

FASCISM: A READERS' GUIDE

THE GUERRILLA READER

THE TERRORISM READER

The
Missing Years.

a novel by

WALTER LAQUEUR

LITTLE, BROWN AND COMPANY · BOSTON · TORONTO

Contents

The Interview

John Masterman III had been highly recommended by his professor, who spoke of him as one of the most gifted graduate students who had ever come his way. John Masterman was now writing his dissertation on a neglected subject of much intrinsic interest and any help given to him would be much appreciated. The next day – it must have been June or July 1971 – John Masterman III phoned; I told him that I would see him for an hour but was not too encouraging: I doubted whether I could be of much help. I have been visited by too many students of late who for reasons unknown to me had come to believe that Thomas Mann had been a close friend and Brecht a patient of mine, that Einstein used to discuss the theory of relativity and Fritz Lang his cinematic problems with me.

John Masterman III was a tall young man in his early twenties, bespectacled, with blond hair, intelligent and exceedingly serious. He came with a young lady whom he introduced as a fellow student and who was quite obviously his girl friend. She was pretty in an unobtrusive way and very poised; both were very polite. When I told them that I had a strong aversion to tape-recorders they agreed to make notes.

They looked briefly at my books and pictures, and I gave them tea; he began questioning me almost immediately. Unlike some others who had come to see me they had done their homework; when John III opened his case I saw among his papers xerox copies of various articles and extracts from books I had written many years ago.

'Have you read all this?'

'Yes, of course. . . .'

'I am greatly flattered, but this is surely not your field of specialization?'

John agreed that some had been heavy going, but how could he possibly ask meaningful and relevant questions if he did not know about my background?

'But you are not writing about me, I am just a source, not a central figure. The little you need know about me you could have found in a reference book.'

Sure enough, John III took out a copy of my entry in *Who's Who* and said that he was aware of this, but the entries were usually sparse, and sometimes positively misleading. A good write-up would make a genius of a very modest talent, and vice versa.

I had to agree with him, and so we went over my entry. 'Born Mariabronn, south-west Germany, 1898.' He had never heard of it, was it a big town? No, it was not.

'Younger son of Louis Lasson and of Jenny Lasson née Colmar.' How many brothers and sisters did I have? Had my parents been the main formative influence in my years in Mariabronn? Could I tell them a bit more about my mother? I answered briefly.

'Military service 1916–1918.' Had I actually served in the front line? Had I been wounded? What was the impact of the war on me? Had it made me a pacifist? He then went on to 'Studied medicine: Heidelberg, Freiburg, Munich, Berlin 1919–24', and said he would like to come back later on to this period in my life; he would be most interested to have more details about student life at a time of great political upheaval and runaway inflation.

'It says here you were head of the department of internal medicine at St Carolus Hospital, Berlin, 1929–33, and honorary chief consultant to the main Jewish hospital; and that you came to the United States in 1946. Quite a few years are missing. Surely this is a misprint and should be 1936? Or did you go to England before the war and came to the US only after it had ended?'

I said that the entry was quite correct; I had left Germany in 1946. He thought I had not understood and repeated the question. I repeated my answer.

He said: 'Forgive me, but I thought you were of Jewish origin....'
'I am.'

At this stage the girl friend, hitherto silent, joined the conversation: 'But this is impossible. Most Jews left, and those who stayed behind were killed. If you had stayed on in Berlin....'

'I would not be here now' – I completed the sentence. John Masterman III slightly resented the intervention of his girl friend, but agreed with the substance of her remarks.

'Am I right in understanding that you were in the German capital throughout the war?' 'Yes.'

'But this is extraordinary ... Were you the only one?'

'No, there were a few others.'

They were still incredulous. Could I please tell them more about it? How did I survive?

'I hate to disappoint you, but this is not a matter of public interest.

2

As far as the topic of your dissertation is concerned, what you call the missing years are not really relevant and meaningful.' (Why did I have to poke fun at these nice young people by using their atrocious terminology?) But they were not offended. They had suddenly become quite agitated, both were talking at the same time; John gesticulated and spilled the tea in his excitement. They did not accept my refusal but tried to return to the subject time and again, directly and in a roundabout way. But I was adamant, and in the end they had to settle for a few anecdotes about some famous contemporaries of mine, which, I am sure, can be found in the books but seemed new to them.

At the end of an hour I indicated that I had another appointment. They thanked me profusely, though the interview had clearly fallen short of their expectations. As they were about to leave the girl stopped in the hall: 'Forgive us our insistence, it isn't just idle curiosity ... I hope you will tell the story one day.' I said that at one time I had thought I never would, that my resolution had weakened of late, but I was not quite ready yet. I then went back to my study to work on the manuscript which for almost three years had been the central occupation in my life.

A Family Reunion

It all began on that evening in 1968 when we had our family reunion in the Berceuse. This is one of the old-fashioned French-Italian restaurants on Fifty-sixth Street which provides reasonably good food at prices that are not exorbitant. The distance between the tables is such that one can talk without being constantly overheard. For special occasions there are a few smaller rooms; these were known in my youth as *chambres séparées*, and have unfortunately become quite rare of late. It was early July, and it was as hot and oppressive as only New York can be. Half the inhabitants had left town and those remaining in this giant oven were reluctant to leave their air-conditioned rooms, bars or cinemas. Everyone seemed to be bad-tempered; it was not an aggressive mood, for there was not enough energy left to be aggressive. It took me a long time to get a taxi and the driver seemed to regard my hiring him as an imposition. He kept up a monologue while we drove down Fifth Avenue, expressing doubts about his own sanity: what was he doing out in the streets in this weather driving around some useless jerks instead of retiring to his home in Queens with a cold beer and watching a ball game?

Luigi, the doorman at the Berceuse, was the only man in New York not too dispirited that evening. 'Dottore,' he cried, 'where have you been all these days? Why do you boycott us? Don't they give you good food? Has anyone offended you?' This was Luigi's idea of a joke: I had been to the Berceuse the previous two evenings, a fact that had not escaped his attention; he had a prodigious memory. I had known him since he had joined the staff and on one occasion I had been able to do him a little favour. If one listened to him, one would think however that I had saved his life and that of his family several times over. Perhaps he liked me because I know a little Italian, perhaps he felt protective towards a man getting on in years. But I was clearly one of his favourites, and I had to think of new excuses all the time not to have dinner with his very considerable family, a dinner which, he assured me, would be incomparably better than anything I was likely to get in the Berceuse.

Luigi told me that he had taken good care of the members of my family who had already arrived. 'Your sons, Dottore,' he said, 'they look

4

very much like you, I recognized them immediately. And the ladies, very nice, very beautiful – maybe a little skinny,' he added as an afterthought. 'And the bambini – very nice, very sweet.' Luigi, the old rascal, tried to live up to the image of a stage Italian on every possible occasion. It appeared that one of the bambini had already managed to spill a carafe of red wine, but Luigi told me not to give it another thought. It happened every day and the Chianti was nothing to write home about in any case.

I passed the bar and entered the general dining area; in a little room at the far end a table had been set. I shivered, the air-conditioning was on full blast. Everyone held in his hand a drink of sorts, and the children looked bored (already?). I greeted a cousin of mine and his wife, nice people and faithful friends; but I shall say little more about them, for the party was not for them but for two out-of-town visitors, Erich and Peter, my sons, with their wives and children. (They are now almost as old as I was when the Second World War broke out, which is to say that I have to get rid of the habit of calling them 'boys'.)

Erich went to America soon after the war; he had to struggle at first but eventually graduated in chemistry and now heads a pharmaceutical laboratory in California. Peter lives in a collective settlement in Israel; he was sent as an emissary for two years to help coordinate cultural work in the Jewish communities of New England. I have visited Israel a few times and knew his wife Rina, a Sabra, but the two brothers had met only once in twenty years, and their families were total strangers to each other. It had not been at all easy to have this family reunion, what with Erich out west, and Peter and me on the east coast. After a few months planning we had at last found a date convenient to all of us.

Now that the festivities were about to start, I felt ill at ease. So, I am certain, did everyone else in the room, though long experience has taught me to dissimulate perhaps a little more effectively. The conversation was anything but animated and so I asked the waiter to give us more drinks; we worked our way through the antipasti, the various lasagnas and risottos, and after half an hour the ice had been broken (a singularly inappropriate metaphor considering the heat outside) and everyone seemed on moderately friendly terms with everyone else.

Peter and Erich were talking about old days and common friends, and what had become of them, and also a little about their present preoccupations. I was at the head of the table; next to me were Rina and Joyce, Erich's wife, a redhead, with, I suspect, the temperament said to go with it; Rina is dark and has beautiful eyes. I believe the girls liked each other, though communication was not easy, Rina's English being rudimentary. But Joyce tried hard and so I had a little time to observe the younger generation around the table.

With them the language problem was very real; the three Israelis having arrived only a few weeks before had only a smattering of English. Peter's oldest, who was about to join the army, was the most fluent. He tried to talk to Erich's girls about sport, a subject in which they quite obviously had no interest. Later he was more successful with a thorough survey of the international pop scene. Still it was heavy going, especially for the two younger ones; I was a little sad watching cousins meeting for the first time in their lives, not even having a language in common.

They seemed to be quite normal children living up to the national stereotypes: Erich's girls were rather loud, uninhibited and a little ostentatious, the Israelis were self-conscious and aggressive. Like their mother they were evidently overwhelmed by New York, but unwilling to show it. They tried hard to impress on their cousins from California that most things at home were done differently and presumably better; I overheard Peter's boy trying to explain to Erich's all-American girls that every educated person should know long sections of the Old Testament by heart – in Hebrew, of course. It was a little ridiculous, but they were in a strange country so much bigger and richer, and they had to assert themselves.

Observing my family, I was neglecting my duties as a host. When we had the main course behind us, Erich said: 'You are not very talkative tonight. What is it?' Erich has always been a good observer. I confessed that for no obvious reasons I had been reminded of the golden wedding of my parents, his grandparents, in 1931. There had been some fifty people, all close relations. We had celebrated it in a Berlin restaurant; Erich and Peter had been present, the one aged six, the other four. They had been the youngest people there, and spoiled by everyone. It was, to the best of my recollection, the last time all of us had been together. Erich and Peter claimed that they remembered most vividly every little detail which, of course, was sheer nonsense. Peter said that the chocolate ice cream on that occasion had been fabulous. ('Vanilla,' said Erich; 'Chocolate,' said Peter, and so it went on for quite a while.)

The others were now listening to our conversation. One of Erich's girls asked, 'How far can you trace the family back?' 'Well, I remember my grandfather when I was very small and he was quite old. He was born around 1830, and he had some letters in his possession written by his

6

father and grandfather, which takes us back into the eighteenth century....' 'And on Grandma's side?' 'Even longer,' I said, 'to the Middle Ages.'

The Israeli boy said: 'But why didn't all of you leave Germany in 1931?' There seemed to be no good reason, I answered, we were born there, we were part of the country. German was our language and anyway we had no other home. He persisted: 'But you should have known. . . .' 'No,' I said, 'I didn't and cleverer people didn't. Every fool knows what happened yesterday, but even the greatest genius cannot tell you what will occur tomorrow. Looking backwards, everything usually seems inevitable: it happened, because it was bound to happen.' 'Only blind people could not have seen. . . .' 'Well, we were not blind, and yet we did not see, and nothing was bound to happen. If Hitler's plane had crashed in 1930, the Nazis might not have come to power, and there would not have been a world war, and, among many other things, you would not be in this restaurant in New York eating scampi and escalope Milanese.' The boy persisted: 'But some people went to Palestine even then. . . .' 'Yes, a handful, and they did not go because they thought that their life was in danger.'

One of Erich's daughters wanted to know about the house in which her father had grown up. Her younger sister asked whether it was really true that we had two Alsatians at the time. The Israelis asked whether there were any other relations left whom they had not heard about; where did they live and whàt did they do? It became a bit of a question-and-answer session: I described the house in Dahlem and the garden, the street in which we had lived and the neighbours, as well as I could. I confirmed that at the time we had two big dogs. There were some first and second cousins dispersed over half a dozen countries. 'Can't we have a general meeting one of these days?' Erich's elder girl asked. 'That would be complicated,' I said, 'there hasn't been much contact for years. I do not even know whether some of them are alive. And how is your Spanish and German? Don't you have enough of a problem with your Israeli cousins?' 'No problem,' she said, 'I think we should have a reunion.'

It was touching; but how much of it was just idle curiosity? When I was their age – and indeed for many years after – I took very little interest in family affairs, nor, to the best of my knowledge, had my sons ever shown any pronounced inclination in this direction. I asked for an explanation, and Erich told me that there had been a change, perhaps because so many of us had disappeared prematurely. Peter said

7

that archaeology was the most popular hobby in Israel, and what was this but yet another manifestation of the quest for roots? People were looking for old coins and pieces of pottery, they wanted to know where they came from and where they were going.

I was not at all convinced; there was something unnatural in this preoccupation with the past on the part of young people, and I told them as much. Not that they should grow up ignorant of their origins, but a wise man had once said that even God could not change the past, but man could shape the future – up to a point, at any rate.

'We still have some business to transact,' Erich said. 'What business?' I asked. 'As if you did not know,' Joyce smiled. They began to sing 'Happy birthday to you'; I was given a very nice repeater watch, a beautiful piece of French origin, circa 1880. 'You had one back home,' Erich said, 'it impressed me no end when I was small. We know you lost it. This is the best we could do – I hope you'll like it.' I looked at the watch; I looked at them; I was moved. I also got an album with photographs, in which everyone was represented, and not just once; two tins of Qumquat preserves from Israel, an old map of the Ottoman empire – there was no end to the presents.

'I hope you do not expect a speech,' I said. 'I am very, very grateful. You shouldn't have. . . . At my age one doesn't celebrate birthdays.' 'But this is a special occasion,' Rina said. 'I feel like Hans Sachs in the *Meistersinger*,' I said. 'It is easy enough for you. You make it very difficult for me.'

'But we have a request too,' Peter said. 'Did you ever think of writing your autobiography?' 'Yes, when I was very young, and there was nothing to write about.' 'I mean more recently?' Erich said. 'You are not that busy these days.' 'Whether I am busy or not has nothing to do with it,' I said. 'There is nothing of general interest to be told; I hope you do not want to blackmail me.' 'Peter is right,' Erich said. 'Others will judge whether it is of interest or not. And if you have such doubts about your own life, why don't you write also about the rest of us?'

I tried to tell them that only people who had been somewhere in the centre of the historical stage, or had at least rubbed shoulders with those who were, should put their recollections on paper. 'I couldn't agree less,' Peter said. 'In any case, your story and ours was not an ordinary one.' I explained that they were obviously not aware of the difficulties involved in any such endeavour. We had been separated for many years; I knew in broad outlines what had happened to them, but this was certainly not enough. Erich said: 'We shall sit down and write, so you'll have all the source material you need. Can you think of any other excuses?'

I told them that the whole idea was perfectly ridiculous, nobody would be interested in the fate of three people out of as many millions. An account of this kind should have a unifying theme, it should have conflicts, tensions, drama. 'I could think of at least one unifying theme,' Peter said. 'We survived.' 'This,' I said, 'is a fortunate circumstance, but it does not make a Tolstoy or a Balzac out of me.' Erich said, 'You have a duty, you know,' and the others echoed him. Joyce said that in her family there was one of those old Bibles in which the births and the deaths of several generations had been recorded. We had not even this, and anyway, mere dates would not be sufficient in our case. There was an account to be written, and surely our conversation that evening had shown how much interest there was. 'Do promise you will try.' And she kissed me. 'Promise,' said Peter and Rina and Erich and the children. 'I do not promise anything,' I said. 'It is preposterous, I am not unemployed. If you feel so strongly why don't you write your own stories? Writing is an art, I never mastered it, and you can't teach an old dog. . . .' 'Promise,' said Rina; 'Promise,' said the others.

Foolishly I said, 'I'll think it over,' hoping that this would be the end of the conversation and that they would forget in due course. We talked about a great many things that evening, and when close to eleven o'clock I paid the bill and we had stepped outside, searching for taxis in a city which had hardly become any cooler, I felt that the evening had not gone too badly.

One morning in early 1969, I went to see Frederic in Mount Carmel Hospital. We had been friends and colleagues for a great many years. He had been one of New York's great surgeons in the post-war period; he could have been the very greatest but for his many outside interests. Now he was semi-retired, having handed over the department to a man who had once been his star pupil. Twice a week Frederic and I would go for a walk and review the events of the past few days. At the end of one such walk I had asked him for the name of a reliable doctor; I had not felt well lately. He said that he would be glad to be of assistance, if I still trusted the judgment of an old hand, and he would consult one of the more gifted and trustworthy younger people in the department, if necessary. I had seen him twice since; there had been a battery of tests, and now I was to get the verdict.

Frederic's room was on the top floor overlooking the river. He was quite relaxed, and in no hurry to discuss the business at hand. We had been to *Elisir d'Amore* at the New York City Opera the evening before; both he and I were great Donizetti fans. There was a great deal to say about Beverly Sills and the other star performers. After having briefly surveyed the political situation, he commented on the changes that had taken place in the hospital management during the preceding few months. Then he looked out of the window; it was a rainy day and quite dark.

When I asked him at last whether the tests were now complete, he said after a slight hesitation that the results were neither as good as one could hope for, nor as bad as might have been feared. This was one of his standard phrases which I had heard him use a great many times when conveying findings that were not very pleasant. 'Which is to say that it is a malignancy.'

'Possibly,' he said. Correcting himself immediately, 'Probably. You neither want nor need our professional sales talk. We are not absolutely certain; for this, some exploratory surgery would be needed which is quite unnecessary since the treatment will be the same in any case. I don't expect a rapid deterioration. You know as well as I do that at our age these things usually take a long time. You have been living with it for years without even knowing it. It does not seem in an active phase just now. So the bottom line is this: we shall do what we can, which, as you know, is not too much – unlike the man selling the "Elisir d'Amore" who had a panacea for everything' – he hummed the aria 'Udite, udite, o rustici . . .' – 'The chances are about even that you will not die of this at all. Neither of us will die young; come to think of it, I have not been feeling too well of late either.' He went to the cupboard where, strictly against regulations, he always kept a bottle of bourbon and a box of cigars. We had a drink and went on chattering for quite a while. Before entering the corridor I carefully extinguished the cigar.

That evening in my apartment, I again looked at my will, decided that no changes were necessary and, at that late hour, began to write the account which the family allegedly so much wanted. Erich and Peter, much to my surprise, had been as good as their word; their recollections of the years during which we had been separated had arrived that very same day.

I did it out of a sense of duty, without any enthusiasm whatsoever. I did not make much headway at first, partly because the treatment was unpleasant and debilitating, but mainly perhaps because I was no longer accustomed to writing. I had difficulties with the English language and the organization of the material. I had to make frequent visits to the New York Public Library and the Leo Baeck Institute to look up old books and periodicals and refresh my memory. But then, gradually, I got into my stride; I became interested in the subject, my writing improved and became, in fact, my main preoccupation.

In the spring I went for a month to the Virgin Islands, and there amid palms and sweet-smelling bougainvilleas made good progress. I found it very restful to look out from my room overlooking the harbour, watching the tourist steamers coming in. During my stay there, I read in *The Times* that Dr Frederic Ream, the well-known surgeon, honorary member of countless scientific institutions, had died following a stroke.

I returned to New York and had a little relapse, but after a while they let me travel again. I went to Europe, and shortly after my arrival in the old hotel in the rue Jacob, where I had lived as a student, a cable reached me in Paris announcing that a boy had been born to Erich and his wife, another grandchild. I decided to dedicate the book to him, in the unlikely event of it ever being finished. And I went on writing.

One day that summer I had a call from Robert who was passing through Paris. I took him for dinner to one of the small places in rue Bonaparte, opposite the Arts school, which had changed little since my student days; there are not many of them left now in Paris. Robert will reappear in my story but only much later and he ought to be introduced: I had met him first in Berlin in the early nineteen thirties but came to know him well only in New York in 1947. He belonged to that overwhelming majority of German-language writers who never quite made it in the United States. Unlike Thomas Mann and Brecht, Doeblin and Feuchtwanger, he was young enough to switch to English, and he had written during the war two long novels which were well received by the critics but did not sell at all. Together with Heinrich Mann and a few others he was invited to return by the East German government in 1947. Heinrich Mann died before he could return; Robert went, only to realize that man does not live by bread alone, or to be precise, that the preferential treatment given by the government to writers was bought at a heavy price, and that it was not just a matter of a few ritual genuflections before Stalin and Ulbricht. Robert stuck it for eight years. Then, after Khrushchev's speech at the twentieth Party Congress, he and his family left the villa in Karlshorst, the domestic servants, garden, pictures and all, and crossed the border, which was not at all difficult in those pre-Wall days. He settled in Munich.

I had read and liked the two historical novels he had written since his departure from New York, one on the German peasant war during his East Berlin period, the other on Beethoven, in his Munich years. These were fine books, the one on Beethoven, I believe, even sold well. But they were highly impersonal works by an excellent craftsman; cautious books, all too obviously the work of someone living in internal exile, careful not to reveal too much about himself. The books were very different from the intense, passionate man I had known.

I remember having long talks with him the winter before his departure: I had been greatly impressed by his integrity, his immense erudition, his insight. He disliked America, and was very bitter. He had given me chapters of an autobiographical novel on which he was working at the time. I read it in one go; it was a fragment from the great novel of our generation, but it remained a fragment. As Robert wrote in one of his infrequent letters: 'This kind of novel can no longer be written.'

He did not feel at home in West Germany either. They made him a member of various academies and suchlike institutions, but as far as the German public was concerned he was a historical relic, one of the few remaining from the Weimar period. Although he had published only a few essays before Hitler took over, it was quite true that he did belong to a bygone period. The style had changed and also the intellectual climate; he had nothing in common with the leading post-war writers in the Bundesrepublik, nor did he belong to any of the literary coteries. He was frequently invited to give memorial lectures of various kinds; the critics did not quite know what to make of him. Obviously he was an important writer, but even more obviously he was so much out of touch with the Zeitgeist as to be wholly irrelevant. During a trip to Germany a few years earlier I had mentioned his name to some German acquaintances; most of them thought he had been dead for a long time.

But he was very much alive and he was the first person outside the family in whom I confided. I told him that the writing was going better in some ways than I had expected, but that I was dispirited by various problems that had arisen. Should I use the first person in my account, or should the story be told by a narrator? There was much to be said in favour of a third person, simply because some of the events I had not witnessed myself. And there were others in which I had been very much involved but which even today, after so many years, I found painful to relate. I would certainly feel more at ease if the story could sometimes be told in a more neutral, detached way, but was it permissible to mix two totally different approaches?

Robert smiled, quite unmoved by my predicament. A wise old American, he said, had once told him that there were twenty-two different ways to skin a bear, or had it been another animal? Each was right. He had read many a book by writers who stuck to all the rules in the textbooks and who had failed nevertheless. And he had read others violating all known rules who had emerged triumphant. It did not matter, he said, whether one jumped on occasion from the past tense to the present, or by whom the story was told – for every situation there were a variety of approaches. I was a lucky man if these were my main difficulties.

I had to admit to my old friend that there were indeed other, more serious ones. I had become dissatisfied with what I had written and tried to tell him why. It was not too difficult to describe events, but once I tried to catch a glimpse of human nature, to explain in detail emotions and motives and what it meant to be alive at a certain period, I was bound to take liberties with reality. But what was reality? What I had felt then, or what I was feeling now?

'You are discovering America,' Robert said. 'There is a basic difference between the historian and the writer of historical novels. We novelists study human relationships, portray living characters, try to show that each human being is somehow unique. We need a plot where everyone and everything is accorded a certain role so as to make the whole picture convincing.'

'Precisely,' I said, 'and I have not one plot, but many plots; frequently there is no beginning and no end. It is like watching the traffic in front of a railway station; people put in an appearance, good and evil, interesting and boring people, but quite often they disappear in the distance, out of our life. So there is no happy end and no sad end, only loose threads, and this is not very satisfactory. I read the other day in Carlyle that history if rightly interpreted is grander than fiction. An interesting observation, no doubt, but not much help to me in my predicament, for history is not only immensely rich but also quite chaotic. And how can one bring order into this chaos?'

Robert said that I was making mountains out of molehills; no one could possibly ever depict the whole reality, nor was it desirable. After all, historians too were selective, concentrating on what seemed significant and important. Was I perhaps overambitious; was I trying to present the panorama of a whole age? 'No,' I said, 'definitely not. I am trying to write about myself and those who were close to me, and at the beginning this was plain sailing. But then I reached a point when the discrepancy between the individual's thoughts and emotions on one hand, and the enormity of the general tragedy on the other, becomes so palpably obvious that I find it well-nigh impossible to write about the uniqueness of human beings and the relationships between them. Our bodies and minds continued to function, we had sex, we experienced fear and sorrow and sometimes even joy. And yet what did it matter, in the face of a catastrophe of this magnitude....

'Let me provide an illustration: in 1943 after an air raid I happened to walk through the streets of Berlin. There I was, witnessing the last days of German Jewry, arrest and deportation, with background music, so to speak, provided by explosions and fire and the wailing of sirens. There were no poetic images and no symbols and the voice of the individual was no longer audible in this deafening, horrible noise....'

'But you are not doing badly,' Robert said. 'Forget the hidden recesses and the twilight regions of the mind, forget all you read about *angoisse* and the human condition. Forget Proust and Kafka, forget even Tolstoy – he wrote about a different age and another kind of war. Can you imagine the likes of the Rostovs and Pierre Besukhov in 1943? You are not going to write the great novel of the Second World War; that will probably never be written, much less the great novel of the nuclear age.' 'In short, I am trying to do the impossible?' 'Not at all,' Robert said. 'Tell in your own words what you saw, simply, artlessly, do not psychologize, be yourself, do not be self-conscious. Do not try too hard to play the detached, inconspicuous observer; when Flaubert advised writers to efface themselves completely before their subject (I think Ranke gave the same advice to historians), he did not think of you. You are a reticent man in any case, and a clinical observer by training and profession. Don't worry, your story will not be too subjective.'

Robert's advice was welcome; it helped me in an hour of doubt. Perhaps I had been unduly concerned about reviewers and my non-existent readers. My ambition, after all, was not to arouse curiosity. I was writing for myself and those few who had expressed interest. We paid the bill, and went for a long late stroll along the quays of the Seine, recalling our first visit to the city of lights and the changes that had taken place in the many years since.

Part One

Peace and War and Peace Again

1. Small Town Childhood

I was born in a little town in south-west Germany, in the year America and Spain went to war and Bismarck died. Mariabronn is in a valley, not far from the Black Forest; on a clear day one could see almost the whole mountain range from the top floor of our house on the outskirts. The town had been founded more than a thousand years ago; it had prospered in the Middle Ages, but fallen on evil days following the war and turmoil of the seventeenth century. There was a steady exodus from our region following epidemics and bad harvests, and the town began to recover only when the railway reached Mariabronn. The medical spas in our neighbourhood had been known since Roman days, and there was an unsuccessful attempt to make Mariabronn a second Baden-Baden. But agriculture prospered again in the area, and since ours was a market town, it benefited from the general upsurge; further-more, some enterprising citizens began to set up workshops which in time became small factories.

Mariabronn counted some thirty thousand inhabitants when I was born, which, if one has to live in a town, is perhaps the optimal size. One was bound to meet friends and acquaintances in the street at almost any time of the day; it was a good-natured town and citizens took a great deal of pride in it. On the other hand, it was big enough to afford several good schools, a theatre, a first-rate library and even a newspaper.

Mariabronn was an attractive town. Many of the houses still had gabled roofs; they had been built by leading members of the guilds and well-to-do merchants. In the centre there was a massive cathedral whose spire could be seen from miles away. Above all, it was the river, dividing it down the middle, which gave Mariabronn its particular character. It was not a town of extremes: winters were not very cold – a vine grew in our garden – and the summer was never unbearable. There were few, if any, very rich families, but nor was there grinding poverty. There were no big buildings, no big shops; even our local railway was tiny, the object of many jokes.

Mariabronn was predominantly Catholic, but there was a sizeable Protestant minority, and a small Jewish community, counting perhaps 300 souls, when I was born. Jews had lived in this region since Roman days. It was, in a way, a historical city, for the medieval Reichstag had once been in session there for several years, an important battle had been fought at a river-crossing in the immediate neighbourhood in Napoleon's days, and our greatest poet had fallen in love with a local girl, and dedicated to her some of his finest poems; she was flattered but married a parson. Mariabronn attracted many tourists, but there was only one major hotel in town and most of the visitors came just for the day. Tourism could have been developed, but the local people, however friendly, did not want to see too many strange faces, and no attempt was made to build more guesthouses and eating-places.

Mariabronn was what sociologists of a later age would call a face-to-face community. On fine summer evenings father used to take me and my elder brother for a walk. Usually we crossed the bridge to the park in front of the railway station, and as we walked he had to lift his hat several times a minute, greeting passers-by to the left and right. It would have been easier to leave his hat at home, but this, of course, was simply not done in those days. We traversed most of the town on a walk like this, yet it took little more than half an hour – unless, of course, we had to stop for father to talk to an acquaintance. There was not much excitement; the marriage of the daughter of a prominent citizen or the arrival of a new teacher in the local high school were events of major importance. No one had been murdered in Mariabronn for a decade or more and there were few thefts. The local police force was small and the station closed at seven in the evenings except on Saturday nights, when a few drunks had to be taken care of.

The Lassons, our family, were well known in town. My paternal grandfather, a tailor by profession, had settled there as a young man and my mother's father, who had died before I was born, had been a miller in a nearby village. My father had wanted to study, but there was not enough money; after graduating from high school with the much coveted school leaving certificate, the Abitur, and after one year of army service, he went as an apprentice to a big firm of textile wholesalers in Frankfurt. His great ambition was to become independent as soon as possible, but not because he was particularly eager to make a lot of money. He regretted to his last days that for want of money he had never been able to study, to travel as much as he wanted, to buy all the books he liked. He thought that with a little luck he could earn the money he needed and then retire at forty-five to devote his time to the things he really wanted to do in life.

He was lucky: a little inheritance, the money my mother brought into the marriage and a loan from a wealthy friend in Frankfurt enabled him to open a textile factory in Mariabronn. Everyone warned him that the time was not right; there was much competition and industry as a whole was threatened by a recession. But father had done what would now be called his market research. He bought modern machinery, concentrated on the production of certain specialized items and established connections with prominent wholesalers. After an uncertain beginning and certain perhaps inevitable setbacks, the factory began to expand.

When I was born father was almost forty, and by the standards of the time and place quite wealthy. But our lifestyle was not different from that of our neighbours. We lived in a big comfortable house, but so did most people we knew. Neither father nor mother spent much money on clothes, and there were few, if any, luxuries. Holidays were spent in the neighbourhood; we did not live that far from the French and Swiss borders but a trip abroad was still a rare occasion. The idea of buying a car – the first of them appeared in our town when I went to elementary school – would have struck my father as a wild extravagance, since almost any place he would want to visit in town could be reached within a few minutes. For trips out of town there were hackney cabs and for greater distances our little railway. Mother had two women to help with the domestic chores; Bertha was the cook and nurse, and had been with us as long as I could remember, and a younger girl from one of the neighbouring villages tidied the house and took care of the garden.

Father was a man of medium height, quick intelligence and a quick temper. He dearly loved his family, but sometimes I got the impression that he loved his music and his books at least as much, and from time to time he would get depressed because his dream of retirement at forty-five was not going to be realized after all.

Mother was still very much a country girl; she had grown up in a village, and spoke the melodious dialect of our region as well as most natives. She had been to a boarding school in Frankfurt, run by the widow of a minor diplomat. The girls were taught French conversation, some English, visited museums and the theatre, and could take either piano or singing lessons. They were also taught etiquette, how to make small talk, how to plan a meal, how to enter a room more or less gracefully, how to greet strangers, how to prepare their trousseau. It sounded rather funny, yet mother had actually liked it, and said she found much of it of considerable use in later life. She kept in touch with some of her teachers for many years after, and she used to write and get letters from several friends she had made at boarding school even after her children had grown up. A great deal of nonsense has been written about teachers before the First World War: later generations have come to believe that all teachers were little despots taking sadistic pleasure in driving high school students to suicide. Nothing could be further from the truth.

Whether the years in Frankfurt made a great deal of difference as far as her intellectual development is concerned is a moot point. Mother was not uneducated, and she was anything but stupid. Her intellectual interests were certainly limited and she read few books, but she was clever and she had the kind of instinctive wisdom that cannot be learnt from books. When father was seriously ill and had to stay away from the factory for several months, she ran the place without any prior knowledge or preparation; after he returned to work, he admitted, somewhat reluctantly, that she had shown astonishing competence and that in some respects her judgment had been better than his own. She was very ambitious for her sons and her one major weakness was her intolerance. She either loved her fellow human beings or she hated them, there was little in between.

She had met father, when she was nineteen and he twenty-five, at one of those chaperoned, much-maligned dancing lessons. After three months they were engaged; there was some resistance to the marriage on the part of her family. They said she was too young and insisted on a cooling-off period, hoping that she might do a little better. But she was a headstrong girl and usually got what she wanted. The wedding photo was in our dining room. It showed a radiant very young woman with black tresses, smiling mischievously, not at all overcome by the solemn occasion. Like father she had a quick temper, and there were frequent quarrels when the children were believed to be safely in bed. Both were energetic people with firm convictions about most things in life and for all I know they needed these quarrels. But there was no nagging; the storms blew up suddenly, never lasted long and I don't think they ever quarrelled seriously. There were three children; a little girl died at the age of two, then came my brother, and after an interval of seven years I made my appearance. Every year on the day our little sister had died we used to visit the grave; the cemetery was not far from our house, it was a friendly place with a lot of trees, shrubs and flowers, unlike some of the graveyards I saw later in life.

Most of my recollections of our small town are pleasant; could it be that my memory is at fault, that it has become selective, that in retrospect everything appears in a bright light? But however much I try, my memories are still those of a beautiful little town and friendly people. Of course there were tragedies in the little world of a young boy; a quarrel with a friend, bad marks in school, the death of my dog run over by a carriage. There was the boredom of family visits in our Sunday best. Father was an only child, but mother's brothers and sisters were dispersed all over the region, and since she was the youngest, there were also nephews and nieces to visit.

I think I was never really unhappy in my boyhood. I had the good fortune to be born – just – in the nineteenth century, a fact which has given me considerable satisfaction. It was a much better century, on the whole, than the one that succeeded it, and certainly more humane. Even those born ten years later no longer knew what it meant to grow up in a world that was more or less intact, in which there was little fear, few unforeseen perils, in which people were, on the whole, confident; perhaps they had fewer expectations and were therefore reasonably happy. There were no modern amenities or wonder drugs and the standard of living even of wealthy people was lower than of poor people today. There was sickness and poverty in our little town, and in the slums of the big cities there was drunkenness, ignorance and brutality; some people lived in conditions unworthy of human beings. Yet by and large it was a better time to be alive than the present century which has brought so much technical progress but little peace of mind, let alone happiness.

I am told that what I am saying may be correct for a small number of privileged people but not for the rest, the great majority. But this is not how I remember it: I was not an over-protected child, I kept my eyes open, and I am fairly convinced that my impressions are at least as correct as those of the young historians who have analysed all the statistics about the world before 1914 and read all the records of poor-houses, prisons and hospitals.

I grew up a country boy, unlike most of the friends I made in later years. Nature in those days was never far away. The paved street in front of our house turned into a footpath just behind the cemetery two hundred yards further on, and then it stopped in the middle of a meadow. Later, when I had a bicycle, it took exactly five minutes to reach the nearest forest; after another ten the sights and sounds of civilization had disappeared altogether. There were wild flowers, berries and animals, and I learned how to fish at an early age.

During the long holidays I was sent off to stay with the people who had bought grandfather's mill. The first day I was deeply unhappy, longing to return home. The second day I watched the peasants bringing in the corn, and was fascinated by the working of the grinding mill. I was given an old black horse at the age of ten; it had seen more of the world than I had and was of infinite patience, tolerating stoically my attempts to saddle and mount it. Gradually I came to know the peasants and their families, and to understand their work. My efforts to assist the miller were enthusiastic but insubstantial. I helped to replace the sacks into which the flour was filled, I went to buy beer in the inn, and acted as messenger boy. Seldom did I return from one of these missions without a little present – a piece of cake or some apples or pears or even peaches.

In the forest there was an unending variety of mushrooms and berries; if one knew the right place one could collect more than one could carry in a few minutes. Mother was a great mushroom expert and she tried in vain to teach me the difference between those which tasted good and others which were just barely edible. I did know in the end the poisonous mushrooms; one had to steer clear of *Amanita phalloides*, which were quite deadly, the red toadstool and a few others. To be on the safe side I concentrated on the *Steinpilz* which, as it happened, I also very much liked to eat. All others I treated with great respect, whereas mother knew exactly which mushrooms could be eaten only when young, which were edible only in part, and she had a sixth sense for discovering them beneath several inches of fallen leaves.

I did not 'love' nature any more than I loved sun or rain or snow; it simply was part of our life to a much greater extent than it is now and I tried to understand some of its mysteries. And there were a great many mysteries, such as the birds coming and going, building their nests and breeding. There were constant surprises in the forest, and when I came home, rather late, usually dirty and sometimes very wet, father usually made signs of disapproval. But he did not ask me to change my ways; he was a believer in authority, but on the other hand an agnostic as far as the value of education was concerned. I have great sympathy for his views. Mother, on the other hand, followed the doings of her little savage with much sympathy; it was more or less the way she had grown up herself.

Later on, about a couple of years before the outbreak of war, I became a great reader. But I still preferred to read outdoors, and I had my favourite camping site on a nearby hill conveniently near a cave, providing shelter. I used to take a piece of bread and sausage and read for hours. From time to time I would put the book aside and observe the larks, the thrushes and the blackbirds, the little railway in the distance slowly making its way along our river, the locomotive blowing hard. Skiing in winter was not yet fashionable, but there was much ice-skating on frozen rivers and lakes, and everyone had a toboggan. Further up in the mountains big horse-drawn toboggans were used. The trees were snow-covered and the total silence was interrupted only when the wind blew the snow from the upper branches.

Like most boys of my age, I wanted to be an Indian chief or at least a brave; I doubt whether they could have taught us much woodcraft. For we could shoot with bow and arrow and carve wooden flutes; there was so much fish in the river that one could catch them, if necessary, with a big handkerchief. My friends were boys from the neighbourhood and, of course, my classmates. With them I collected butterflies and beetles, went fishing, played football, read travel stories, and dreamed about adventures in far-away countries.

Once a year a photographer with an enormous camera came to our school; the poor man always needed a long time to set up his apparatus and found it next to impossible to keep thirty boys reasonably quiet and in their places. When I look at the photographs, I remember most of the faces even though I have forgotten the names. Two I do remember.

Hans-Juergen was the son of the editor of the local newspaper. His father had a big library and in later years used to lend me books; he was guiding my first steps in German and world literature. With some amusement he watched the enthusiasm of a boy discovering the great nineteenth-century novelists. He was also the head of the liberal party in town, and his position in a predominantly Catholic neighbourhood was not at all easy.

He was a highly educated man and his Sunday editorials were widely discussed in town; sometimes they were even quoted in the national press in the big cities. After his death, his family had a collection of his articles published; the other day, by pure chance, I found a copy in the New York Public Library. These editorials were written in curiously antiquated language; like a sermon in church they usually took some quotation as a starting-point, only it was not from the Bible, but more likely from Schiller or Horace. They were quite remarkable essays in some ways, outspoken and sometimes prophetic, warning against the likely consequences of the arrogance that was so typical of the style of our government in foreign and domestic policy alike.

Karl Heinz was the son of an army officer from Northern Germany, who had married a local girl, and by good luck had been stationed ever since at the local garrison. His paternal grandfather too had been an officer, and in the long corridor of their apartment there were crossed swords and various other militaria, including two Iron Crosses and other orders, and pictures of Vionville, Mars la Tour and other battles of the war of 1870–71. Karl Heinz would follow in the footsteps of his father and grandfather; we envied him because he had fencing lessons. His parents were perfectly civil people, but it did not take me long to realize that my welcome in their home was a little less warm than elsewhere. I mentioned it once to father, and he said he was not surprised. It was some time before I understood that there was no personal animosity; they simply kept somewhat aloof or, to be precise, they had their own little circle, to which we did not belong.

I did mention that there was an old Jewish community in town; a few generations earlier it had been somewhat bigger. Services in the synagogue were conducted by old Rabbi Singer, a village Jew like my mother, and thus very much part of the local scene. The community was too small to afford a full-time rabbi; but there were many Jewish families scattered in the villages in the neighbourhood, and Rabbi Singer served the whole district. He would visit them in an old-fashioned one-horse vehicle, circumcising the newly born males, confirming them at the age of thirteen, marrying and burying them. His learning was a little uncertain – only a few rabbis were university graduates in those days – and his Hebrew, I am sure, was shaky. But he was very much a man of the people with a great deal of common sense; Jews and non-Jews alike would look for advice to this small and lively man with his white beard, on matters which had nothing to do with religion whatsoever.

When he helped me to prepare for my Barmitzvah he would invite me sometimes to accompany him on his vehicle, and I would recite the lesson I was eventually to read out in synagogue. Old Singer, usually half asleep, mumbled 'Very good', 'Go on, continue', 'I hope you understand what you are reading'. Needless to say, I hardly understood a word.

Singer had a friendly word for everyone, inquiring about the health of children and parents, about the harvest and the animals; he would be asked to taste the new wine, to accept eggs and vegetables as a token of appreciation; he would even be offered a freshly shot hare, and have to explain that his religion unfortunately forbade the consumption of certain food. His help would be asked as an arbiter to settle quarrels, as the peasants were most reluctant to go to court. His wisdom on matrimonial affairs, and even on medical problems, was taken for granted. Singer was on excellent terms with the local clergy, Catholic and Protestant alike; sometimes, on a summer evening, I would see him taking a walk with a local priest, immersed in animated conversation, and it was fairly obvious that they were not engaged in theological disputation.

The community, it seemed, consisted of a few big families, or clans, such as the Blums and the Kahns and Weils and Dreifuss; this, of course, was an exaggeration, but not by very much. Families were much bigger in those days (mother, for instance, had three brothers and three sisters) and much more closely knit. Three of the doctors in town were Jewish, and two of the lawyers; there were a dozen Jewish shopkeepers and an equal number of artisans, and they, with their dependents, broadly speaking constituted the community. There was some intermarriage, but this was a recent phenomenon.

None of the local Jews took their religion seriously; I met my first Orthodox Jew only years later. Some members of the community would turn up in synagogue only on the Day of Atonement. Old Singer gently chided those that were remiss from time to time, but certainly did not threaten them in the style of the Old Testament prophets. There had been one conversion when I was a boy, but as it concerned a family of newcomers no one was greatly upset and it was a cause of amusement rather than resentment.

I cannot remember any open manifestation of antisemitism, except once or twice from a drunken peasant, and once in school. If there was vicious anti-Jewish feeling, I certainly did not come across it. A man might be called 'the Jew', but there was no malice in such a designation, he was still 'our Jew', different, but equal. Jews belonged to all civic and public associations, and would be asked to contribute to church collections. In some other parts of Germany the state of affairs was less satisfactory, but our region had a tradition of tolerance; our Grand Duke had a Jewish doctor and a Jewish lawyer, and there were even some Jewish officers, much to the disgust of the Berlin authorities. Our region, meaning a hundred miles west and east of a line between Strasburg and Basel, is commonly believed to have been the cradle of European civilization: the tolerance was part of the Allemanic inheritance and the local Jews had been thoroughly assimilated for many generations.

They still had certain specific characteristics of their own, but it is not at all easy to define them or to assess their importance. In later years, after I moved to another part of the country, I realized that the differences between the native Jews and the local population were of no great consequence any longer. Yet why was there not more inter-marriage, and why were Jews more often than not on intimate terms only with other Jews? I do not have an answer. Perhaps it was just because they were as conservative in their habits as the rest of the population.

When I grew up, Mariabronn was in a state of transition. This was no longer the age that Spitzweg had painted: the quaint, narrow streets and shops, populated by apothecaries or antiquarians smoking enormous spills, all this had already disappeared. The romantic period had given way to the modern age, streets were broader and kept in perfect con-dition, street lighting was introduced, the night watchmen were no longer making their rounds, the motor car made its appearance. When I was ten I was taken to see a nearby air show; there were a few planes, and they actually succeeded in taking off.

But life was still unhurried, everyone went about at a measured pace like a British policeman. People worked long hours, but it is also true that at almost any time of the day the benches in the park would be occupied and it was always difficult to find an empty table in the two coffee houses in the market square. There were two big events in my childhood: one was the flood of 1910, when part of the population of the lower city had to be evacuated. For a week we had many guests in our house; I thought it great fun, but I am not sure whether mother found it equally hilarious, and certainly the guests did not. But such mutual help was utterly taken for granted, and I am sure we too would have found shelter in similar circumstances.

The other event was the death of a neighbour, the owner of the biggest bakery and pastry shop in town. He fell from the roof of his house while trying to do some repair work. I was playing in the street; we ran to assist him to get up. But he was beyond help. It was the first time I saw a dead man and I did not sleep well for some nights thereafter.

At the age of twelve we were, of course, all young militarists. Once a week Bertha's younger brother came to our house, and I became very friendly with him. He was doing his military service, and he taught me how to stand to attention and march like a soldier; he let me play with his side arms, much to the annoyance of his sister. A cavalry regiment was stationed in town; we would watch it leaving for manoeuvres, with Karl Heinz's father in command. On festive occasions their brass band played marches by Fucik and Lincke in the market square. The trumpets and the big tuba, the Sousaphone and the silvery drums were most impressive; everyone hummed the marches. There was nothing particularly aggressive in these exercises; they were an integral part of the pre-war scene. No one seriously thought that the dragoons would one day be used for something other than manoeuvres and parades and playing the 'Glow-worm Idyll'.

A small boy is seated on a foot-stool in the corner, dreaming, perhaps half-asleep, in the flickering gaslight. His father and the other men pay no attention to him; they are playing and their music is filling the room. What does he think or feel, what makes him stay? The name of the composer means nothing to him; he knows the instruments, but certainly not the difference between an adagio and an allegro. But there is a magic in this music, a magnetism, something that irresistibly attracts him, even if those who perform are, at best, gifted amateurs. Music expresses a mood and it creates a mood, merry or solemn.

This scene is one of the most vivid recollections of my childhood. When I think of events that happened a long time ago, or of persons, why is it that these thoughts are so often accompanied by a melody? When I underwent psychoanalysis many years later, I found that the free association of words did not come easily to me, but I had no difficulty associating tunes, and these would almost invariably lead me on to people or events. Even now, when I am humming a tune, I find upon reflection that it is a symbol standing for someone or something. There are leitmotifs which are easy to place, but at other times a day may pass or even a week before I remember.

I grew up in a family in which music played a central role, and this was quite customary in those days. I do not wish to imply that more people went to concerts, and of course with the invention of the radio, the gramophone and the long-playing record, classical music is now reaching more people than ever before. But I believe that there was then more active participation, nor was the love of music and its appreciation restricted to what would now be called the intelligentsia.

Father played the violin and (not very well) the piano. Mother had studied the piano during her years at boarding school. Two evenings each week were devoted to music; father's quartet met on Tuesday, and on Thursday he would practise or play some of the new sheet-music which had arrived. I was permitted from an early age to stay up on Tuesday evenings, provided that I was neither seen nor heard and withdrew silently at nine. Later on I was allowed to turn over the pages of the music. My father, as I said, played the violin; Traub, a local music teacher, the cello. I do not remember who played viola and double bass; there were frequent changes. I remember a student of theology, very young, very shy but the most gifted musician of them all, or so they said, and I also dimly recall the figure of one of our doctors – usually a late arrival, always likely to be called away at short notice.

The group met regularly up to the outbreak of war, and, less frequently, after 1914 as well. They would gather for a light meal, but they would never know in advance whether there would be three or four or five of them that night, and on this, of course, the choice of the repertory would depend. Their range was limited to Haydn and Mozart, Beethoven and Schubert, nor would they try Beethoven's late quartets which they found too difficult, or Schumann, let alone Brahms or Dvorak. I think they liked Haydn more than any other composer, perhaps because there was so much to choose from. For Haydn more than any other composer the quartet had been the favourite mode of expression.

My own taste was, of course, altogether unsophisticated – I liked the melodious works – as I do to this day. My favourite pieces were Haydn's op. 76 No. 3 with variations on 'Gott erhalte Franz den Kaiser' in its slow movement, and Schubert's Quintet in A Major op. 114 – the Trout. Later I learnt to appreciate the three Razumovski quartets and Schubert's No. 29 in A Minor, in which the Andantino from 'Rosamunde' reappears, and Beethoven's op. 18 No. 4 in C minor.

It is a truism that men of my age find it much easier to recall scenes of their youth than events that have taken place quite recently. And so I have only to close my eyes for the scene in our parlour to return. A winter evening, snowflakes falling in the street, the great tiled stove exuding pleasant warmth and four bearded gentlemen seated in a half-circle fiddling away – sober, unromantic, yet faithfully rendering the joy and the sorrow, the sweetness, the solitude, the resignation, the happiness, the lyricism and the cries of anguish, sometimes even the exotic character of these creations. I cannot say how accomplished their technique was, but I am fairly sure that no one could teach them much about the spirit and mood of the pieces – they knew that by instinct.

I had no inclination whatsoever toward the theory of music, but became very interested in the life of the great composers. But I was soon disappointed: Haydn had led a quiet and relatively happy life (except for his marriage); Beethoven was not exactly a romantic hero; true, he had suffered a great deal, but this did not make him any more likeable; and Schubert – poor Schubert, assistant school-master, pure and innocent, the 'most modest and sympathetic of friends', no one could help liking him. And then there was Mozart, about whom Richard Wagner had written that he was the greatest and most divine genius. But how is one to define and explain genius? The question has pre-occupied me for a long time and I am no wiser now than I was when I was young. Hazlitt, in an interesting essay, once asked whether genius was conscious of its powers, and reached the conclusion that he or she acted unconsciously and that those who have produced immortal works have done so without knowing how and why. Our greatest composers certainly did not know why.

At the age of nine I had my first piano lessons. The teacher was a surly elderly lady who had instructed several generations of children. I was a most unsatisfactory pupil – there was, as I saw it, so little in common between the music I liked and the endless finger exercises. My teacher certainly lacked youthful enthusiasm and could not convey any to me, but I should not look for excuses: I was simply not very eager to learn. After a year or two of little progress and many admonitions she talked to my parents, and my lessons were discontinued. In later years I very much regretted that I had not persevered – one of many regrets.

At the age of fifteen I began to attend opera performances fairly regularly. My father, like so many of his contemporaries, was a fanatical Wagnerian. To me the great master appealed much less; I preferred Mozart, Italian opera from Bellini and Donizetti to Verdi, at that time rather neglected in Germany, and also the German Romantic opera which, with the exception of Weber's *Freischütz*, had never had the success it deserved outside Germany. Almost all these operas had highly unsatisfactory libretti, and quite frequently even the best among them were based on perfectly ridiculous plays. Wagner, to be sure, was not ridiculous, but the pathos sounded false to me, however theatrically effective: I could not possibly enjoy the unending recitation. I always looked upon Wagner as a sinister genius lacking inner harmony and I have not changed my views.

My reflections on these subjects are of no public interest, except that any record, however superficial, of these years, would be incomplete if no mention was made of music. Whether 'music doth change nature' I do not know; whether the man or woman who hath no music in himself is bound to be a villain, I doubt. I do know however that my life would have been poorer but for my immersion in music, high and low, from an early age.

At the age of six I went to a private school, which prepared male children of middle-class families for entrance to the humanistic Gymnasium. The four years there passed uneventfully; I had no particular difficulties in learning to read and write, to add and subtract. My handwriting was not too good from the beginning, and since my teachers were not willing to accept this I spent many hours copying pages from the text-book. At the time I took a dim view of these restrictions put on the free development of my personality; in later years, having been exposed to the illegible handwriting of colleagues, I had some sympathy for my teachers who after all had the unenviable duty of reading my essays in class and my homework for the subsequent twelve years.

If classes in the preparatory school had been small and informal, secondary school was big, and indeed overwhelming, at least at the beginning. It was located in the town's biggest building. An impressive gate led to a big staircase; if one turned to the left one ended up in the director's office, the teacher's common-room, and the other offices. To the right there was the big hall, the *aula*, in which the whole school assembled on special occasions. The origins of the school went back to the seventeenth century, when it was sponsored by the church. It was inordinately proud of its tradition, and this pride and a certain *esprit de corps* was inculcated in all the pupils; on the first day they were told that they were greatly privileged to be allowed to sit on the very benches on which generations of outstanding men had been educated, men who had rendered important service to the state and society, to science and the arts; we should try to emulate their achievements even though we could, of course, never equal them. That some of these great men had been by no means outstanding students was not mentioned.

School began at eight in the morning and went on till one, six days a week; there were breaks of ten to fifteen minutes after each lesson.

We had Latin lessons from the day we entered; from the age of twelve there was French, and a year later Greek as well. Great emphasis was put on the study of our native language and literature and, of course, history. There were a few science lessons, but the topic was not thought to be of paramount importance, or, to be precise, there were other schools, including one in our town, which specialized in these subjects. On the whole, a 'humanistic' education was thought to be vastly preferable to one emphasizing natural science. Our director and most teachers were certainly convinced of the advantages of a classical education, and the response of the pupils was one of tired resignation: we did not question their judgment but failed to share their enthusiasm. Ovid and Horace were often incomprehensible, and Homer and Sophocles exceedingly difficult to understand even with the help of a dictionary. Literal translations of these and other authors could freely be ordered in the bookshops; for convenience's sake they were printed on very thin paper and in small format. Thus without fear of detection one could put them in one's pocket and consult them under the table, or in the toilet, a practice which was, of course, strictly forbidden.

The study of Latin and Greek grammar and the works of the great writers was a tiresome duty; one hardly ever had the feeling that these subjects had any bearing at all on the real world as we knew it. But many generations had been educated on these lines, and what had been good enough for Goethe and Schiller clearly was good enough for us.

I remember little of what we learnt in those years, except perhaps a rudimentary knowledge of Latin, and of Roman and Greek history, a few sayings such as 'fiat justitia', 'Navigare necesse est' and 'Errare humanum est', the stories of Ulysses and the Trojan war. In retrospect, I am inclined to take a more lenient view of the value of these topics as a medium of education for young boys. Having been in touch with subsequent generations of students who were taught subjects far more 'relevant', and having seen the result, I came to realize that it does not really matter that much what children are taught at ten.

Only a small fraction sticks to memory, in any case, and the gifted will make headway anyway, provided they can lay their hands on a few good books. Much depends admittedly on the personality of the teacher, who can make an interesting topic boring, or generate, within limits, enthusiasm even for boring subjects. Most of our teachers had never been taught how to convey their knowledge to others; the younger ones perhaps found it a little easier to communicate with us, but this was by no means universally true. There was an aged Greek teacher, who had been the star pupil of one of the great classicists of the period but who, for one reason or another, had not chosen a university career. (According to rumour this had something to do with his marriage, many years earlier, to a young lady who was not accepted in society.) When he was in the right mood, he would forget his audience and its intrinsic lack of interest in the subject, and would treat us as intellectually curious adults, and describe in vivid detail the great splendour that was Hellas. We understood little of what he was saying but instinctively felt that he was an inspired man of extraordinary knowledge and that the subject was of importance. A hush would descend on the class as he described Schliemann's findings and how he had for a few months participated in the excavations; he would explain to us what a palimpsest was, and how palaeography and textual criticism had developed. He almost made it seem like a detective story, and this was many years before the popularizers ever thought of making Greek and Latin culture accessible to the millions.

Our German teacher was also a gifted man in his way, but his home life, according to rumour, was not too happy. He too was near retirement, and frequently he would go for a few drinks to a nearby pub for consolation and inspiration. Sometimes he would fall asleep after his return, sometimes he would be merrier than usual without obvious reason, once or twice he started weeping. We guessed the reason and felt uncomfortable but no one made a joke. At other times the boys were admittedly cruel. One of our teachers tended to be sarcastic; the pupils did not mind being upbraided or punished for lack of preparation, laziness or bad behaviour in general, but reference to the innate stupidity or certain immovable personal characteristics offended the sense of justice and fairness of young people and provoked a vicious reaction. This teacher had no easy life at our school; he was subjected to all the torments schoolboys could think of and in the end, I believe, he asked to be transferred.

Our headmaster believed in an authoritarian approach and deliberately cultivated the image of a dour, forbidding personality; to be seen by the director was the ultimate punishment. He never beat a boy nor did he raise his voice, but he was so awe-inspiring that many of my contemporaries would have greatly preferred almost any form of corporal punishment to crossing the threshold of his office. I met him a few times in retirement, many years later, an old man with an ingratiating smile, great tact and altogether a most pleasant personality. When I told him that we had seen him in a very different light, he said: 'You were not that much mistaken. The boys would have torn me apart if I had shown any sign of weakness.' It made not the slightest difference if the offender belonged to an influential family; the headmaster was a believer in equality before the law, and the law as far as the school was concerned was himself. There was a story, perhaps apocryphal, that one of the highest officials in the land, who had come to intervene on behalf of his son about to be expelled, had left the director's office precipitately and with a very red face. True or not, the story made the rounds, and never thereafter was the attempt made to influence a man who was clearly as incorruptible as Cato.

The senior teachers of the main subjects had the title 'professor', but this did not of course apply to such marginal and relatively new subjects as the arts, music or gymnastics. Marks were given for general behaviour and religion, and the pupils were seated in the classroom more or less according to their achievement – first was the 'primus'; the system was not foolproof because the primus was not necessarily best in all subjects. There were few extracurricular activities, other than a rare performance of the school orchestra playing inevitably Mozart's 'Kleine Nachtmusik'. Class excursions were quite unknown, and membership in youth groups such as the *Wandervogel* was discouraged in our part of the country. But in the streets and in public places we had to wear our school caps and behave as befitted junior members of an institution of such distinction.

In short, we were expected to behave like grown-ups; youth was considered an inevitable transitional stage of no particular merit; the century of the child and the adolescent had not yet been ushered in. Young people, it was assumed, knew little, tended to behave irresponsibly and were therefore of little use to society. If this was the general philosophy underlying education, most teachers remembered, however dimly, that they too had been young at one time, and they tended therefore to make allowances for minor breaks of discipline. If, on the other hand, the transgression was too blatant, it could not, of course, be tolerated. Was there an official school 'ideology'? Yes and no – the Emperor's birthday was celebrated, and also the anniversary of the battle of Sedan and the day in 1871 on which the empire had been established. But patriotism was dispensed in moderation, perhaps because in south Germany memories of our own traditions were still very much alive and pan-German enthusiasm less widespread than in Prussia.

School, in short, was part of the process of growing up, sometimes painful, sometimes interesting; there was an *esprit de corps*, but not too much of it, and a certain cameraderie. No one loved school, few found it intolerable. In later years I read much to the effect that this had been the period of the identity crisis, of the torment of puberty, of pupils' suicides, of the breakdown of communication between the generations; Wedekind's *Fruehlings Erwachen* had been written in the previous decade. But that is not the world I knew. School and education, as I recollect it, did not make that much difference; the young people I knew were inclined to be rather robust and 'normal'. Perhaps this made them a little philistine and boring; it was certainly not a sentimental period. If any of my contemporaries systematically cultivated or analysed their emotions, this escaped my attention. I had some friends and comrades among my classmates, but these relationships as a rule did not last; as we left school we drifted apart. A few of them I met in later life; we usually had an interesting half-hour talking about the old days, and what became of whom.

In the long summer vacation of 1913 my parents took me for a trip abroad. I had been with them to Switzerland the year before, and to Heligoland in 1911, but that hardly counted. There was a great deal of *Reisefieber* at home; even my unemotional father was infected. Travelling to see distant countries was the great dream of my childhood; from an early age I collected brochures of the big shipping companies such as HAPAG and North German Lloyd, advertising trips to places such as Las Palmas, Puento Arenas, Colombo and Yokohama. I wanted to be an explorer or at least a world traveller, and spent long winter evenings studying railway and shipping timetables. At the age of eleven I could have acted as adviser to Phineas Fogg in planning his trip around the world in eighty days. Thus the prospect of seeing Paris and even London preoccupied me for many months before.

The railway station had always been a magic place for me. To this day I associate the idea of travelling with going by rail; I still find flying an unsatisfactory mode of transport, suitable only for people who have to arrive quickly and who do not enjoy travelling. Travelling involved, for me, the smells and the sights of a railway station, looking out of the train window, immersing oneself in the surrounding landscape, studying and absorbing it. Going by rail had more style than jet-age travel, and people were far better prepared for the trip. Who would have dared to go to a foreign country without acquiring some basic knowledge about the places to be visited? Who would not have familiarized himself with at least a few phrases in the local language?

34

There was much excitement at home for weeks prior to our departure. New travel bags of heavy leather were bought, father wrote letters to business associates in Lancashire whom he wanted to meet, reservations in hotels were made, an English phrase-book for travellers and Baedekers were ordered at the local bookseller. Everything was planned to near perfection.

Father had been to Paris a few times, but always on business trips, or so he claimed, and he admitted that he knew little of the city. My older brother was at the university at the time and had to prepare for an examination; we were to meet him in Paris later on. And so the three of us left Mariabronn on a fine July morning, changed trains twice, and arrived in Paris late at night. All I remember about the trip from the station is that there were still a great many people milling about in the streets well after midnight; the boulevards were decorated, the city wore a festive air, there was music and people were actually dancing. Never had I seen anything like it, and my first impression was of a very happy city. I thought that the good people of Paris made dancing in the streets a daily practice. Only the next morning did we realize that it had been Bastille Day and that the Parisians were no more prone to dancing in the streets than the inhabitants of Stockholm or Moscow – I should have said St Petersburg, to be precise.

Pre-war Paris has been described thousands of times by both visitors and natives. What impressed me were the conventional sights – the broad boulevards, the Eiffel Tower, the bridges over the Seine, the great state buildings, the colour, the liveliness, the whole ambiance. Father had prepared a very full programme for us, which included all the obvious museums, walking along the Champs Elysées from the Place de la Concorde to the Arc de Triomphe, Versailles of course, and many other places. Mother wanted to see some of the famous shops and to watch the passers by on the Grands Boulevards. So we did a bit of everything which, I suppose, was as well.

The hotel was comfortable and the food excellent, but these were not the main attractions for a boy of fifteen, who did not even pay much attention to the elegance of the women in the Luxembourg and the Bois de Boulogne. I do remember, however, that people were talking more loudly than at home, gesticulating and expressing their emotions freely: some laughed, some wept and no one seemed very self-conscious, certainly not the young couples walking in close embrace along the quays of the Seine. They were actually kissing, and no one seemed to mind.

35

One evening leaving a restaurant in Montmartre I saw two men fighting with knives and a great many onlookers calling for even more dramatic action. Father explained that these were the famous Apaches, and that the scene, more likely than not, had been staged for the benefit of foreign tourists. For it was quite obvious that the gendarmes present in force had no intention of intervening.

Dutifully I went with my parents to watch the performance of a seventeenth-century tragedy, of which I understood next to nothing. We went to a bal musette which was more lively; and an open-air concert given by a military band in the Jardin du Luxembourg on a Sunday afternoon reminded me of similar occasions at home. On another day we saw thousands of workers waving red flags on the Place de la République; they were carrying banners, calling for a general strike and possibly even for revolution. I had never seen anything like it. My brother told me that the speaker was Jean Jaures, that he was the greatest orator of the day, but that the call for revolution was not to be taken quite literally. I accompanied Hans to some of the bookshops and art galleries in the rue Bonaparte; he wanted to buy some contemporary pictures, but then even the post-impressionists had already been 'discovered', and the time to buy them cheaply had already passed. But he persuaded father to go to an auction, and they came home with a Seurat which I still have; the yearly insurance premium, needless to say, is now far in excess of what he paid.

The streets of Paris were full of motor cars large and small, some open, some clumsily constructed, some very elegant – there was an infinite variety of makes. For those accustomed to small-town traffic, even crossing a big Paris street was a major challenge; the policemen would wave us on impatiently, Paris was clearly not a city for provincials. But there were also many quiet parts, only a stone's throw away from the main streets. There were people in Paris who neither hurried nor shouted.

We took the obligatory *bateau mouche* trip on the Seine and watched the fishermen, the artists and the crowds in front of Notre Dame. In the evening we gazed for a long time from Sacré Coeur at the sea of lights that was Paris – truly this was the capital of the civilized world. Father said that I was very fortunate indeed to see all this at such a young age; he had not had such good luck and only hoped that I would appreciate it.

The trip to London was something of an anti-climax. We arrived with the boat train at Victoria station, and if I had been overwhelmed by the size of Paris, the size of everything in London was on yet another, bigger scale. But there was also something disturbing in this greatest of all cities; perhaps it was the lack of harmony, the contrasts between wealth and poverty, between beauty and ugliness. I had some difficulty in understanding the natives unless they belonged to the educated classes; the common people in this country, so it seemed to me, not only looked different but also spoke a language which was altogether incomprehensible. In the East End I saw slums for which I was equally unprepared: not only was it a dismal sight, there was a strong smell of poverty about these endless grey, sad, rundown streets. But the ugliness was in some ways fascinating, and this was true even with regard to the slums and the drunken people on Saturday nights.

There were, of course, other aspects to this majestic city, which strongly impressed themselves on my adolescent consciousness: the bustling crowds, the enormous traffic jams in the Strand, in Piccadilly and Regent Street, the double-decker buses, the shops, and the port of London. Fairs and giant sales were going on in some of the big shops. Soldiers were very little in evidence, much less so than in Germany and France. It was explained to me that there was no obligatory military service in Britain. In the East End I heard much Yiddish; there were theatres and newspapers, as well as billboards with announcements in this language.

We had relations in London, who lived in a well-to-do suburb called Dulwich and who were clearly very English. They were second-generation British, and though we were received cordially enough, I felt that our hosts were torn between their obligations towards us and the desire not to be reminded of their non-English origins. I found their attitude strange at the time. They had absorbed the self-confidence, and to a certain extent also the arrogance, of the British upper-middle class: there was only one right way to do things and this was the English way. There were two boys of my age in the family; they went to a public school, behaved very politely, with great ceremony and, I thought, with great affectation. They were quite willing and even eager to show me the London they knew and were proud of. They had not the slightest interest in anything I could tell them.

From what I have reported so far it might be supposed that I did not like England, but this would be far from the truth – I simply had mixed feelings. England, or as it was then called, Great Britain, at the height of its power, was certainly a most impressive country. But I also found it a puzzling country, more remote from my experience than

France, which was no doubt why my parents' generation, and also my own, were drawn to Paris rather than to London, culturally as well as in most other respects. One admired the sterling qualities of the British, but felt little desire to live among them for any length of time. I found them strange, and I did not like their attitude towards foreigners. It was never rude, but usually patronizing.

Our relations were well-connected people. One afternoon they took us to a great horse-race about an hour's drive from London, I forget whether or not it was Ascot. It was a most splendid occasion. A slight breeze was blowing over a gently rolling landscape in bright sunshine. Many impressive gentlemen and elegant ladies were pointed to us as they arrived. We watched the royal enclosure; Mr Balfour was there, Mr Asquith, Curzon, Churchill and Haldane and Grey and Lansdowne, countless dukes and earls with their families, Kitchener and many generals and admirals in their resplendent uniforms; tall English beauties in their summer dresses and the most amazing hats I had ever seen. I remember nothing about the race, but everything about the picnic, which we had seated on folding chairs. There was smoked salmon and champagne and strawberries and cream. Years later this scene came to my mind when reading Burke's elegy about the sweetness and joy of life before the outbreak of the French revolution. True, the English royal family has not fared that badly, and I believe there still are such races and even a royal enclosure. But I also suspect the splendour has never been quite the same since 1914.

I remember another scene, some time after; father had gone on business to Lancashire, and mother and I, following the advice of the family, went to Cowes on the Isle of Wight to watch the royal regatta. Again we were extremely lucky; there was not a cloud in the sky, many hundreds of white boats were sailing to and fro in the Solent, and in the distance, majestically ploughing the sea, were the great battleships of the Royal Navy. The King was there and the Queen and many countesses, and there was a great deal of pomp and circumstance. There were so many different classes of boats, small and big, open and closed, 'Dragon' and 'Star', as to make it quite impossible for the non-expert to understand who came in first, and who last. But did it really matter? It was an overwhelming spectacle, all the more impressive because it was so effortless, unplanned, there were no commands, orders were neither issued nor obeyed, unlike at the parades I had seen at home.

Back in London I walked the streets for hours; my lunch consisted of mussels or jellied eels which I bought from street vendors. When I got tired I sat on a bench in Hyde Park. There were many people riding and they all seemed to know each other. Nannies in a sort of uniform were pushing baby carriages, older children were accompanied by their governesses. Had these poor children been orphaned? I was reassured that this was not the case; the British upper classes believed that father and mother ought not to be involved in the details of education.

One evening after dinner father and his British cousin were discussing politics: they agreed that the German Emperor was a loudmouth, an arrogant fool, but the war was still most unlikely. Too many people had a vested interest in peace and the pursuit of business; modern war had become too expensive, it could not last longer than a few weeks. This even the generals knew; any future war was now bound to affect all European countries and would bring about their common ruin. Was it worthwhile courting disaster for some lousy Balkan principality or even for Alsace Lorraine? Clearly not. For this reason world peace was in no danger, even though there would be, no doubt, periodic crises. Our British uncle said that at one time there had been much competition in trade between his country and ours, but this was no longer so. The United States were now Britain's main competitor, but countries no longer went to war because they competed in exports. England had built quite a few new warships in recent years; her supremacy at sea was not imperilled.

The English branch of our family was still nominally Jewish, but they lived, thought, and felt like other middle-class Englishmen. What kept these people from converting? Jews were accepted almost everywhere in society and in business. The King had many Jewish friends, a fact which had not escaped the cartoonists. There were even Jewish cabinet ministers. On the other hand, in England it was customary to 'belong', and Jews who wanted to 'pass' as non-Jews would be suspected of opportunism, of lack of loyalty and integrity. And so the Jews continued to stick to their ancient faith, or at least professed to do so. A few times a year they would go to their synagogues; it did not mean much, they went far more often to their clubs. The claim that the Jews were a separate people struck them as preposterous; for if there were some cultural distinctions between them and their fellow Englishmen, these were surely rooted in the past and thus became of less importance with each generation.

The situation of the new immigrants from Eastern Europe congregating in the East End was different; they had to stick together for protection in a strange new country; alone, clearly, they would have been utterly lost. But ultimately they too would become fully-fledged Englishmen. In later years these assimilated Jews were bitterly attacked by the Zionists, who called them renegades to their people. This I always failed to understand, for surely one cannot betray something one does not believe in.

All this became clearer to me only in later years and it applied, of course, to Germany and France as well. Antisemitism did raise its head on occasion, Jews were discriminated against, but on the whole there was good reason to believe that such prejudice would gradually disappear. Thus the assimilation of Jews seemed a perfectly natural process; to reject it made no more sense than rejecting rain or snow or wind or any other natural phenomenon. These questions did not at the time cause me any sleepless nights.

I try to think of myself as a sixteen-year-old boy: how much does one see at this age, how much does one know, how much does one understand? One's faculty to observe, I suppose, is perhaps better developed than at any other age; as for one's judgment, this is a different proposition. By an incredible chance some letters of mine written between 1912 and 1914, and also parts of a diary, have come into my possession during the past year. I was surprised and pleased to find that I did keep my eyes open, even at that early age. But I was acutely embarrassed by the arrant nonsense I put on paper with so much certainty and conviction, uncritically repeating views which I had heard or read. I could have sworn that I had never written such things – but here it was, in my own handwriting, which has not changed that much over the years.

One afternoon in early May 1914 I was waiting in a queue in front of the municipal theatre. A famous orchestra, with an even more famous young conductor, was to perform that evening; there was a limited number of cheap places available and a few hundred predominantly young people were competing for less than a hundred seats. Behind me there was a girl my age whose face seemed vaguely familiar. I very much wanted to talk to her, but this was 1914, we had not been introduced, and I was at least as awkward and gauche as the average boy of my age. I looked at her, but when our eyes met I quickly turned away. The sales office was to open only in half an hour; she had brought a book and started reading. Someone inadvertently pushed her from behind and she dropped the book. I quickly picked it up and dusted

40

it with my handkerchief, which gave me a good chance to see what book it was; by good luck her name was inscribed in it too. I overcame my shyness, and after a few minutes we were engrossed in an animated conversation.

When the sales office opened it became apparent that our prospects were very dim. When my turn came, the old man behind the cash register bellowed 'Last one'. There was a groan of disappointment from the young lady behind me. And then I had a sudden brainwave. I recalled that everyone in the queue had the right to buy two tickets. I bought two and was rewarded by a very nice smile. By that time I had gathered sufficient courage to ask my pretty neighbour whether we could perhaps meet half an hour before the performance to continue our conversation. She hesitated, but being indebted to a fellow music-lover, she eventually agreed to meet me in front of Café Birnbaum on the market square, where young men and women in Mariabronn have met since time immemorial.

And so we met half an hour before the performance, and for a great many hours in the weeks after. We had various intellectual interests in common, but I am fairly sure I would have been very much attracted by Margarete in any case. I thought that she was the prettiest girl in the world, and that I was quite unworthy of her; I was walking on a cloud and wrote bad poems. The story has neither beginning nor end, and it has been told a million times. My experience with girls was virtually non-existent, I had no sisters, and there was, of course, no co-education in those days. To talk to them did not come easily; there seemed to be no middle ground between worshipping from a distance and treating them like boys.

But the difficulties were not unsurmountable. Much has been written about the great sexual repression of that period, about the strict conventions ruling middle-class life in this as in other respects. This was, I suppose, largely true; but then I am hardly in a position to judge, for my knowledge of that world was strictly limited, and by the time I had grown up it had ceased to exist. There was a façade of respectability, but we can all surmise what went on behind the façade. Nature was stronger than the conventions, and Margarete and I spent our time not only in listening to Schubert and reading romantic poetry.

It would be tempting to write that the object of my first love was a banal little girl, neither particularly good-looking nor clever, but this would be quite untrue. She was a pretty, gifted and vivacious girl; she married during the war, but her husband was killed. She studied medicine, as I did, and her second husband became burgomaster of Mariabronn. We drifted apart, but many years later, suddenly and altogether unexpectedly, she was to reappear in my life. The story will be told later on; words cannot express my gratitude to her. She is still alive, still practising medicine; I think she had a very happy life, there is much to be said in favour of not moving around too much in the world as I did.

I have every reason to remember the summer of 1914. I recall, in particular, an excursion; the long summer holiday had recently started and the two of us took an early train to Meersburg on Lake Constance, a little town with medieval gates and old houses on a vine-clad slope. The ways of providence are clearly unfathomable for Lake Constance too is to feature again in my story, and very prominently at that. But this was 1914: we took a steamer to the island of Mainau, a lovely place with woods and a big park. The ship was full, most of the passengers were excursionists, there were some families, but most were young people like us. A group of students were singing loudly if not very melodiously.

It was a fine day; how good it was to be alive! At noon it became quite hot; we rested under the trees – Margarete picked a few wild flowers and made a little garland. I was lying on my back, watching the swallows in the skies. There was no sound but the rustling of the leaves above us; we talked about the future. There were some rumours of war, but then there always had been, especially in the Balkans, and this was of little concern to us. We swam in the lake and returned in the late afternoon, sunburned, tired and happy. It was 3 August 1914, and at the railway station they sold a special edition of our local paper, an 'Extrablatt'. It contained only a few lines: war had been declared on France, and German troops had entered Belgium.

It was the first 'Extrablatt' I ever saw, and there were many more to follow. I had only the haziest notion of what war meant, but so, I suppose, had everyone else: guns firing and soldiers marching, acts of bravery and some unfortunate people getting killed on the field of battle. Wiser people than I did not believe for a single moment that this was the end of the world we had known and the beginning of a not very happy new era.

During the next few weeks there were many special announcements: Liège had been taken, Mühlhausen was liberated, German troops entered Brussels, German troops advanced deep into France, all within the first month of the war. A decisive battle had been fought against the Russians at Tannenberg and they had been completely routed. The war would be over, everyone agreed, by Christmas at the latest. We all became amateur strategists, drawing maps, looking up exotic places in the atlas. Our gallant Austrian allies had triumphed at Zamosc Komatow and Limanowa. It sounded most reassuring even though no one knew what it meant. No one doubted the necessity of the war; it had been imposed on us by envious Frenchmen and devious Britons.

I was sixteen years old when the war broke out; there were two more years to graduation. A few of my classmates were talking about volunteering, but I doubt whether they were serious. Everyone knew, of course, that sixteen-year-olds were not taken; they could have lied about their age, but perhaps their honesty prevailed over their patriotism. Little changed in school at first, except that those in the top grade, the *Oberprima*, had to enlist; a few were not taken, probably for reasons of health, and they returned shamefacedly to school. Some of the younger teachers joined reservist units such as the *Landwehr*. Once a week we were convened in the big school hall and, following some major battle, were subjected to patriotic speeches. At the end of the second such meeting the speaker announced that he had the sad duty to inform us that a member of the top form of the school had been killed in action in northern France. He conveyed the school's condolences to the bereaved family, which would find comfort in the knowledge that their son and brother had been chosen to make the ulitimate sacrifice for his country. And we should feel pride in the privilege of having had such a young man in our midst. As Horace said, 'Dulce et decorum est pro patria mori'. We would always remember him. A memorial tablet was to be affixed to the wall in the entrance hall, but the local stone-masons were busier than usual in those days and by the time the tablet was ready, three more names had to be added. By the end of the war the list had grown to thirty-five, including two teachers.

I am not aware of any major changes in our home life during the first year of war. There was enough to eat, though we had to forego, of course, the more exotic imports. Father experienced some difficulties in his factory, for raw materials were in short supply almost from the beginning and he was ordered to adjust production to the requirements of the army. In 1915 shortages began to appear as far as essential goods were concerned; the quality of leather and textiles deteriorated, and to get a new pair of soles was virtually impossible. There were enough potatoes and sugar beet, but no white flour, and coffee was replaced by chicory and later by a brew of acorns. Everyone had to sign various war loans, and gold watch-chains were surrendered for iron ones bearing the inscription 'Gold gave I for iron'. Since I drank no coffee at the time, had no money to give away and not even a gold watch-chain, all this hardly affected me. The food situation became really critical only during the winter of 1916–17, and was even worse the winter after, but by that time I was no longer at home.

I doubt whether our region was even remotely as much affected by the food shortages as the big towns. We were, after all, in the middle of a rich agricultural area, and almost everyone had friends or relations among the peasants in the neighbourhood. My parents certainly had, and vaguely familiar faces would from now on appear in our home after dark. What went on behind closed kitchen doors I do not know, but there was meat and eggs and cheese, fruit and even wine. Nor did our neighbours starve, though everybody of course complained about the hardships – or alternatively declared how they were only too willing to make these sacrifices for the war effort and for victory.

My brother had joined the army early on; he served in northern France and was wounded in early 1915. The news reached us a week later. Hans was not however seriously injured, and after his release from hospital he appeared at home for a short leave, his one and only during the war. We had never been very intimate; the reason was not a mutual dislike but simply the fact that seven years are an enormous gap when one is young – it spans almost a generation. For him I was no more than a boy, and he seemed to me closer in age to my parents than to myself. The fact that he was now a soldier who had seen battle, whereas I still went to school every morning, put an even greater distance between us. I was proud to walk the street of Maria-bronn with him, but he certainly did not confide his innermost thoughts in me.

I do recall however that the stories he told me about life in the trenches were quite different from what I read in the newspapers or heard in the speeches in school. He thought that the war would go on for years and that its outcome was uncertain. He had become a fatalist; perhaps he would make it, perhaps not. One day when I helped him dusting and rearranging his old books, he quoted Lamartine to me:

> Je suis déjà solitaire
> Parmi ceux de ma saison...

He was alone among his contemporaries not from choice, but because so many had been killed.

On the evening before his departure he took me aside and told me that though we had never been particularly close, my chances of survival were better than those of his remaining friends. He handed me a parcel which was to be opened if he did not come back. This was the last time I saw Hans. My brother was mortally wounded in action in late May 1918 in the last German offensive between Soissons and Rheims. I was in the trenches at that time and the news reached me only weeks later. I was thinking of my parents and wished I could have been home, even though there is nothing to be said when death strikes, all words of comfort are false and of no avail. But I felt that my presence would have made some difference as far as mother was concerned. After my brother had died, she became firmly convinced that I would not survive the war either. She had always been a great letter-writer, and waited eagerly for the postman each morning. She now closed herself in her room at nine when the postman usually called and only hesitantly emerged at ten, refusing to look at the mail; if there was a letter marked 'On Active Service' father had to read it out to her. Years later she told me that after many a bad night her instinct had told her that she had lost her one remaining son. Fortunately, even a mother's instinct is sometimes mistaken.

I opened my brother's little parcel after my return in December 1918. It included some love letters, several poems and an unfinished novel, quite obviously autobiographical. I sent the poems to a literary magazine in the late 1920s; they attracted some attention and have been put in various anthologies. The other day I was surprised (and gratified) to find a reference to Hans in a history of German literature in the twentieth century. The author referred to him as one of several young poets who died before their talents had fully matured.

The last years in school were very boring. If the purpose of studying Greek and Roman authors and similar subjects had not been obvious before, they now seemed altogether irrelevant. The teachers showed little enthusiasm, their pupils were lethargic. But both sides had to go through the motions even though no one, however incompetent or lazy, would be permitted to stay down in school. 'Abitur', the graduation examination, was advanced by six months, so as to coordinate it with our induction into the army. Patriotic speeches became less frequent and less intense. Occasionally a teacher would tell us that we should make greater efforts so as to be qualified for the challenges that would face us in later life; this struck me as funny, for it was uncertain whether there would be a later life, nor was it clear in what way Tacitus would help me to meet its challenges.

Finally, one morning in the late autumn of 1916 I appeared in a black suit together with some twenty classmates to submit ourselves to the written and oral examinations that were to prepare us for the future. I wrote an essay comparing Uhland and Moerike, two nineteenth-century poets who were born and lived in our region; I translated some verse from the Odyssey (Ulysses' homecoming as a beggar), and in the oral examination I answered some detailed questions about the wars between Frederic II the Great of Prussia and Maria Theresa. This I passed with flying colours; but for indifferent results in mathematics, I would have got the overall mark of 'very good' instead of 'good'. I was not, however, much perturbed, and neither were my parents or teachers.

One morning a week later all of us, together with our parents, met in the school's great hall for the last time. The head of the school said that fate had decreed that we were to graduate at a grave moment in world history. He quoted from one of Horace's Odes,

> Si fractus illabatur orbis
> impavidum ferient ruinae

which has been translated as:

> If the round sky should crack and fall upon him
> the wreck will strike him fearless still.

Heroism was still the commandment of the hour. He said that school had done what it could, and that we were soon to face a greater test which, he hoped, we would pass to everyone's satisfaction, including our own. We then repaired to the pub opposite, to drink beer legally for the first time in our lives.

But to the best of my recollection everyone was in a sombre mood; no one got drunk on this occasion. How often had we talked about the great day when the torture of school with its iron discipline and intolerable pressures would be behind us. The great day had come and gone and it now seemed, alas, a very unimportant date indeed. For even the dimmest among us was aware that he had graduated from one school only to enter another in which there would be infinitely more exertion and suffering, in which punishment was usually very severe, and would be distributed quite indiscriminately. For as a great poet

46

who was born in our neighbourhood – Friedrich Schiller – had written, Patroclus, the bravest of the brave and Achilles' closest friend, lay buried in front of Troy; whereas Thersites, the coward and demagogue and the most repulsive man in the Greek camp, returned home safely. This was 1916, and all of us understood that we were about to participate in a compulsory lottery in which there would be many losers and no winner.

2. War

I attended an international medical congress in Brussels in the late summer of 1960. It was one of those mammoth affairs with banquets, excursions and obligatory lectures in which no one is really interested; the real work is always done in sub-groups and committees. I chaired one of them and, over several luncheons and dinners, I became friendly with Dr Verschoylen from Ostend, a quiet and very pleasant man some ten years my junior. I mentioned in conversation that I had known Ostend and its vicinity quite well at one time in my life, whereupon he insisted that I should be his guest for a few days and that we should tour west Flanders together, where he had grown up. My plans for the week after the congress were vague; I was to meet friends in Switzerland, but this was only towards the end of the month. And so after the last session we went by car to Ostend where my good friend had a splendid house overlooking the sea on Zeedijk, which is another name for the King Albert Promenade. My reception by his wife and their two daughters could not have been more cordial. It was as if I were an old friend of the family and not a perfect stranger.

It was a very warm day quite untypical for this part of the world and we took a long walk along the sea front, passing the Kursaal, the Royal Palace, and the jetty. We sat down for a few minutes on the sandy beach where a great many people were enjoying the evening sun – families from Brussels, young people playing energetic ball-games. I mentioned to my friend that it was most pleasing to see so much life in a city which had been quite dead when I visited it last. We had an excellent dinner *en famille* and the conversation went on for some time after.

I was tired but sleep did not come to me. I looked out of the big window, taking in the lights and noises of a fashionable seaside resort. I had every reason to feel at peace; I was among friends and I had been received as an honoured guest. But there was a disquiet, very real, if difficult to explain; a free-floating fear, remembrances of things long forgotten, ghosts that I thought had been laid to rest. I thought again of 1917, of living people and of the dead, of the noise and of the mud of Flanders, of soldiers with whom I had fought, of the times I had waited or hidden during the shelling. I had not thought of Flanders for a very long time, and no doubt for good reason: the instinct of self-preservation which had guided me during the war made me forget these scenes. One cannot constantly relive moments of great danger, of suffering and deprivation, if one wishes to remain sane. But one cannot entirely forget either. I did not fall asleep until the early hours of the morning, when a cool breeze began to blow from the sea.

Next day was again fine and we had a massive breakfast in the garden. The ladies provided us with food and drink as if we were about to leave for a distant desert, and there were reminders from Mrs Verschoylen, who also hailed from west Flanders, not to forget to call on an aged aunt in one place, and a cousin in another. At last we left Ostend; driving leisurely we crossed canals and little rivers and arrived in Dixmuide in no time, and then drove on to Ypres. Even before we had reached the town I had begun to recognize a landscape that had once been all too familiar to me; to refresh the memory there were the road signs saying 'Bikschote' and 'Prolkapelle' and '3 Kilometers Langemarck'.

Parts of this road had been the no man's land between the German and the Allied front lines for four years, and the fields left and right had been all too often no-man's-water that could be crossed only by boat. These were very ordinary roads lined with poplar trees, neither broad nor narrow, and once upon a time a million men in grey field-coats had walked these roads from west to east, and from east to west; British and Irish, Canadian and French and Australian, Prussian and Bavarian soldiers had passed here, not to mention howitzers, cavalry units, cyclists and even motor cars. They had marched in rain and sunshine; in the beginning they had been singing, but soon they had become silent and stolid columns.

We drove beyond Ypres to a hotel on Mount Kemmel owned by a friend of Dr Verschoylen's. During the next two days we toured the neighbourhood, as far as Armentières to the south, whose Mademoiselle had acquired as much fame in the First World War as Lili Marlene in the second. We passed dozens of cemeteries, some well kept and almost elegant, others quite simple with wooden crosses and slabs of concrete. We passed remembrance blocs and signs 'Here was the invader stopped', crossing the Lys and the Yser and the Denle, and half a dozen forests. The great British military cemetery at Tynecot provided a fine panorama over what had once been the Ypres salient. Now it was a most peaceful landscape, with many farms and cows and little lakes, high trees, orchards, all of it bathed in brilliant sunshine, with hardly a cloud in sight.

49

This then had been the site of one of the biggest battles in history, with hundreds of thousands of young people killing and maiming each other in an attempt to seize a road-crossing or a little canal. What struck me above all was how close to each other the places were; the distance from Langemarck to Passchendaele is about three miles, and it is about the same to Ypres; a child could walk the distance in an hour and it took us four minutes by car. But for the Germans Ypres remained an elusive goal for years; it took the British four years to reach Passchendaele, and in the end there was no longer space to bury those who did not make it.

I arrived on the Western Front in November 1916 after three months in a training camp. The division to which I belonged was part of 'Army Group Crown Prince Rupprecht' – which, in turn, consisted of four armies, the First, the Second, the Fourth and the Seventh, all of them sadly depleted. Rupprecht was the heir to the Bavarian throne, a middle-aged gentleman who survived not only this war but also the next and who, as it subsequently emerged, by late 1916 no longer believed in a German victory. But the fighting had acquired a momentum of its own; it went on quite irrespective of what even the commander might think or feel. The Fourth Army faced the Ypres salient, my new home for the next two years. It was commanded by another Prince, Albrecht of Wurtemberg, who was replaced subsequently by General Sixt von Arnim.

How did so many German and Allied soldiers come to be bogged down in this part of Europe, and why was it the scene of such ferocious fighting? During the very first weeks of the war there had been a race for the sea; Dunkirk and Calais remained in Allied hands but Ostend and Zeebrugge did not, and these naval bases threatened Allied connections with England. From October 1914 almost up to the end of the war, the front line ran southwards from a point on the coast about ten miles west of Ostend, almost at a right angle. Most of the fighting took place at the Ypres salient: there was one major battle for Ypres each year of the war. Usually after a month the fighting died down, and then it would transpire that the front line had moved west or east some five or six miles, and sometimes even less than that. Yet the attacks continued with great vigour and the defenders showed equal determination. The German strategists argued that Ostend and Zeebrugge were important naval bases and that an Allied advance of even a couple of miles would bring them under constant heavy artillery fire, so that they would no longer be able to function.

When I arrived at the front there were only a few survivors of the early battles of 1914. My regiment had originally consisted mainly of volunteers, but most of them had been killed in the famous storming of Langemarck in November 1914. Two years later Langemarck was, just, in German hands, which is to say that not a stone was left of the village, and that some 50,000 young people, many of them students, had been killed. By 1916 the positions of the German troops were purely defensive; there was much trench warfare, accompanied by artillery fire which, from time to time, became very heavy indeed. The German positions had the advantage of height, but this was by no means a decisive advantage; they could be easily spotted and were subjected to systematic shelling by heavy guns and, more erratically but also more dangerously, by heavy mortars. There were three lines of trenches. The company to which I belonged was stationed in the first line some miles south of Ypres between the so-called great and little Bastion and the famous Hill 60. About a mile behind us was the second line of defence, and at Hollebeck, another two miles further back, the third line.

Life in the trenches has frequently been described. War is usually hell; but as there are various degrees of heaven, so there are various kinds of hell, and Flanders was certainly one of the worst. According to the Army Field Manual, a trench should be at least four to five feet in depth, but in this part of Flanders it was futile to dig, for even at one foot one invariably reached subsoil water. The army architects had reached the conclusion that the troops should be positioned in massive concrete dugouts. But these were soon flooded too, especially during the rainy season; they had to be located on high ground, could be easily spotted, and were under constant shelling. The choice was, broadly speaking, between water-filled shell-craters and damp concrete pill-boxes and other such structures, where a direct hit was even more likely. During the first three or four months of my time in the front line there was fairly massive shelling during the day and patrol activity during the night. The German artillery was quite noticeably weaker than the British, and our first line was very weak indeed; apparently it was assumed that in the case of a major attack this line could not hold in any case.

Our advance posts and those of the British were just a hundred yards apart. I located the place where I had been stationed in early 1917 without much difficulty, for there were some obvious landmarks. It was on the left bank of the Ypres-Lys Canal, to the south of a little forest. At a distance of several hundred yards a railway line passed. In front of us was the Zillebeck Zee and to our right Hill 60, the artillery observation post. By 1917 all the farms in the neighbourhood had been destroyed, the railway, needless to say, did not run, and the landscape consisted mainly of water-filled craters. It would never have occurred to us that one day human beings would again work and live in these places. Yet great is the persistence and ingenuity of men and women in times of war and peace alike; forty-five years later, the traces of war had been almost entirely erased but for the occasional pill-box along the canal, which had apparently become tourist attractions. There were farms and houses everywhere; on Hill 60 boys were flying their kites and on the Zillebeck Zee they were angling and sailing.

When I think back to 1917 the glue-like mud of Flanders comes to my mind, the constant rain, the lack of sleep, the dirt in the trenches, the vermin, the insufficient food. All this has been described very often. No one was prepared for this kind of life, no one would have thought that human beings could possibly exist in these conditions for any length of time. Yet survive they did, after the initial shock, and gradually they became masters in the art of survival. They became inured to suffering and death, almost insensitive to hardship. There was no heroism, no spirit of sacrifice: few volunteered for night patrols. No one thought about the future, even the coming day seemed an eternity away. There was no indoctrination of the troops; there was nothing left to be said, and by 1917 few believed in victory any more.

My platoon commander was a student, one of the few survivors of 1914. From time to time, in a quiet interval at nightfall, he would open up and hum an old Landsknecht song about death riding on a pale horse through Flanders; he would tell me that for better or worse people had always been fighting, it was part of the human condition; and that nowhere had people been killing each other more obstinately than in Flanders, where Marlborough and Napoleon had fought. He said that there was every reason to assume that the British suffered as much as we did, and that the stalemate would eventually lead to an honourable peace. Germany had to survive, even if we did not return. About his own chances of survival he was sceptical. He was killed during the very last German offensive of 1918.

With all the ugliness, the stench and the hardships, there were hours of satisfaction and even enjoyment. Every new day was a present, a warm meal became an event, hot coffee or tea an occasion to celebrate, and a bottle of wine a major holiday. I was familiar with the landscape of Flanders in more peaceful days from Coster's *Ulenspiegel*, a book which I greatly admired, and also from the pictures of Peter and Jan Brueghel, of Teniers and of Brouwer. And even with the ravages of war something of the charm of this landscape remained. Never before or after have I seen the stars in the sky so clearly. There were some trees left, and on a cold January morning their crowns were covered with hoar frost. During intervals in the shelling some of us would hunt ducks and other water-fowl, strictly against orders of course, but men likely to be killed at any moment were not overawed by instructions issued by some *Etappenschwein*, a staff officer in Brussels perhaps. The local commanders closed their eyes to such infringements of discipline.

During March and April 1917 British activity in the air increased and the shelling was intensified. More British divisions were concentrated opposite our positions, and since our reconnaissance was also more active, it seemed that there might be another offensive. The German High Command assumed that Flanders would be only a sideshow in 1917, that the main direction of the Allied thrust would be further south, towards Lille or Arras. If there was increased activity in our sector, perhaps it was just a diversion, to induce the German command to withdraw some divisions from France where they would be most needed in the months to come. The French, furthermore, needed some respite. In May 1917 France faced a major crisis; whole regiments mutinied, Nivelle was replaced by Pétain, there was the danger of a collapse of French morale.

And so the British decided to come to the help of their French allies, and from early May on the German positions came under heavy pressure. British superiority in the air was almost absolute, and while aerial bombing was not very dangerous in those far-away days, no one liked the visitors in the skies above us, for they helped to guide the enemy artillery. They did their job well: every row of trees, every hedge behind which a single machine gun could be concealed was systematically shelled, as were all the roads in the rear. For two weeks we had no hot meals, no change of clothes, the wounded could not be transported to hospital, and those in the rear got little more rest than we did. At night there were frequent raids, some of them quite fierce, with Allied units cutting their way through the barbed-wire entanglement in our forward line. This intensive shelling lasted for seventeen days, and then on 7 June 1917 the battle began. At our section south of Hill 60, twelve British divisions faced five German; nowhere had there been up to this date such a heavy concentration of artillery.

By now the German command took the offensive seriously, and even guessed correctly the direction of the British attack. This was not too difficult because conditions in Flanders were such that one could stage an offensive only in certain places. One obvious place was the rising ground north and south of Wytschaete, and the famous Messines ridge. (Wytschaete was a little village about three miles to the south of the position of my regiment.) But guessing the direction of the offensive was not much help, for the German command had few reserves in men and even less in material. Even in those days, well before the Americans appeared in strength on the Western Front, the superiority of the British augmented in this sector by Canadian, Australian and New Zealand divisions was quite remarkable. The Allies seemed to have an almost limitless supply of ammunition, whereas German artillery had to economize strictly. The Allies also had more tanks, and many more trucks and cars.

On the eve of the battle my own division the 204th (Wurtemberg) was about the only one in this sector still up to more or less normal strength. All the others had suffered heavy losses in the previous two months and were scheduled to be replaced. But there was yet another element which worked in favour of the Allies: surprise. But could there have been any surprise if the two enemy camps had been facing each other for almost three years at close quarters? The answer, very briefly, is that while the German command closely observed enemy preparation on the ground and in the air, it had forgotten that there was yet another dimension, below ground. The British had been digging galleries and tunnels for a year and a half, trying to reach our forward position. Our engineers had watched these activities with some amusement: it was obviously one of those typically English eccentricities. The Germans were firmly convinced that the digging operations were futile, for the very same reason that it had been impossible to build effective trenches – the high water-level.

From time to time the German artillery would shell the entrance to the British tunnels; the German engineers would listen with some giant stethoscope, and then they would shake their heads and report their findings to their chief, a lieutenant colonel named Fuesslein. Fuesslein, a competent engineer, told the generals that some subterranean activity was still going on but that owing to the German countermeasures some of the mining had been stopped, and what had been overlooked could not possibly be of much importance. Fuesslein did not realize that the tunnels which the German engineers had intercepted were mostly

54

feints, and that the British were digging on an even lower level. British mining engineers had been mobilized, and they had somehow solved the problem of the water – something which Fuesslein had thought impossible. And while the German engineers tried to listen with their stethoscopes several hundreds of tons of explosives had been deposited under the German first line.

The great attack began shortly before dawn on 7 June, and as fate had it I had been ordered during a lull in the shelling, the evening before, to accompany a small group of injured soldiers to hospital in Comines, a little town about five miles behind our lines. The river Lys runs through this little industrial city; in more peaceful days it had been the border between France and Belgium, with the river dividing the northern (Belgian) and southern (French) part of town. I was billeted in the old customs building on the southern bank. With its red-brick houses, many of them damaged, Comines was anything but a pretty city, but to those returning from the front line it was paradise. One could get a drink, some of the shops were open and one even saw a few girls in the street.

It was a warm night; the customs house was fully occupied, but there was some room immediately below the roof, where I took my mattress. To say that I slept well would be an understatement. But around four in the morning the big British guns opened up and some of the shells fell uncomfortably close to the outskirts of Comines. A few minutes later there was an air-raid warning; no one took it very seriously, for it was an unusual hour for British aircraft to appear over the German lines. Yet a few moments later there was an enormous explosion, and then within a few seconds there were a dozen more: altogether, it later appeared, there had been nineteen, but some of them coincided. We were later told that they had been heard on the south coast of England as well as in the Rhineland, and I am perfectly willing to believe it.

I watched the spectacle from the roof of the customs building, and these were certainly the most impressive fireworks I had ever seen: giant carmine-red mushrooms were slowly rising, reaching from the vicinity of Hill 60, where my regiment was stationed, to Ploegsteert forest in the south – a distance of seven or eight miles. The earth was shaking; there was a muffled roar, and pillars of fire, enormous smoke clouds, and objects large and small were hurled into the sky. No one had ever seen anything like it, and if we at a distance of several miles were shaken, it was easy to imagine the effect on those closer to the scene.

Large sections of the German first line were effectively destroyed, but the psychological effects were even greater. The survivors retreated in almost total disorder, and the connection between front line and field command was cut. The British swiftly overran the first two lines of defence, and at the end of the day they were threatening the third and last line. The only section of the front in which the British did not make major progress on that first day was the one held by my Wuertemberg division. There were only two explosions in this sector – a major one about hundred yards to the west of the railway line, and a smaller one about the same distance to the east of the railway. But eventually this division too had to be withdrawn; there was a danger it would be outflanked from the south, and the German command badly needed it to defend the new lines of defence hastily established in the rear. At the end of the third day it was clear that the second British army under General Haig had succeeded in its immediate objective of seizing the high ground near Messines. The only question remaining was whether this had been the ultimate objective or whether the British divisions would press further on.

It soon emerged that the British aims were limited. The battle for the Wytschaete salient lasted for a week, and resulted in a better starting position for the battle of Flanders planned by the Allied forces for later that year. The British and their allies lost 28,000 men, the Germans 25,000. These figures are small in comparison with Verdun or the Somme, but such comparisons are of little interest to the soldier in the front line. All we knew was that from the nine companies of the regiment stationed to our left not a single man came back, and of another regiment, one officer and four orderlies returned. The explosions I had heard and witnessed that morning from the customs house in Comines had been the biggest in the history of the war, indeed, in the history of all warfare up to 1945, and the psychological shock on the German side was immense.

There were no major operations during the subsequent nine or ten months, which is not to say that life in the trenches became more pleasant or the shelling less dangerous. There was another winter in the mud of Flanders, more suffering, and it seemed that the war would go on for ever. Then in late April 1918 there was a great German offensive; a dozen German divisions were concentrated to storm

56

Mount Kemmel, a few miles west of Messines, where much of the fighting had taken place in June 1917.

Mount Kemmel rises to about two hundred metres above the plain; it is not a giant among mountains, but it does offer a good view in all directions. I have mentioned the Hostellerie Mount Kemmel, a fine little hotel on top of the wooded hill in which we stayed for the night; all the major battlefields of Flanders can be seen from there without the aid of binoculars. In 1918 the English and French units which had been sent as reinforcements were afraid that a German advance of even two or three miles could endanger their whole network of communications, and consequently every square yard was defended; there was bitter fighting which went on for days. Again whole divisions faced each other within the most narrow confines – a few hundred metres at most.

On 27 April I received a battlefield commission; for some time I had been the senior non-commissioned officer in my battalion, and since in the fighting that day most junior officers in my unit had been killed, the colonel summoned me and, in a ceremony lasting about thirty seconds, pronounced me a second lieutenant in the Imperial Army. I was more than a little surprised, for while promotions up to the rank of sergeant could be made by the regimental commander, the promotion of an officer, even the most junior, was a most elaborate affair – it always came from the Ministry of War and I believe it had to be signed by the Emperor himself. But during the last year of the war even the Imperial Army could no longer stick to its time-honoured customs, for by that time it had lost some 50,000 of its officers. And so, later that year, a week before the Armistice, I duly received my officer's 'patent'; it was the last letter I received from anyone during the war. I never got my uniform, my epaulettes or my sword, which was no great loss: the sword would have looked out of place in Flanders in the autumn of 1918. I did get the Iron Cross, first and second class, as well as some South German orders; I kept them in my desk in Berlin but eventually they were lost.

The German units held Mount Kemmel for about four months, and then, in the last days of August 1918, the British counter-offensive started and the German army slowly withdrew. By the end of October the British had reached Courtrai, about twenty miles to the east of Ypres. But then the German defences crumbled, and the slow, orderly retreat became a stampede. One week after the Armistice had been announced I was on a train entering Cologne railway station. There was a field kitchen on the platform providing hot meals of sorts; few officers were to be seen, and no military police. There was the same sour smell of sweat, leather and black bread of inferior quality. No sighs of relief were heard, the shock had been too great, the blood-letting too large.

I went through the war without a scratch. I doubt whether in all the years that have passed since I have written more than a few lines or talked for a few minutes about it. Many years later I read an essay by Walter Benjamin in which he noted with evident surprise that hardly any of those who returned from the war had a story to tell. Was it just poverty of feeling, or had their inner selves not been affected by the war, or had they on the contrary been overwhelmed, numbed by the shock? It is certainly true that most literary accounts of the war appeared only a decade later, when there had been time to reflect and to digest. Benjamin, I am sure, observed correctly; most of those who came back had no story to tell except perhaps some anecdote about a patrol or some other adventure, or about the quality of the food or the rats they had killed – stories totally disproportionate to the enormity of what they had undergone. I know this from experience: when asked, while on leave, by parents or friends about life in Flanders all I said was: 'We were shelled. Sometimes we shot back. It is wet, the food is lousy, one doesn't sleep much. People get killed.'

What was there to say? How could we describe the noise, the dirt, the moaning of those hit by a bullet, the look or the stench of bodies in the process of decomposition? Walter Benjamin was a clever man but also very naive, like some of my New York friends, and he spent the war years in the rear and later in Switzerland. He did not miss anything of importance. The trenches were not a place for people of great sensibility; they would have lived there in a state of even greater agony than the rest of us. And so one spent much of the time dulling one's feelings, and it usually proved easier than one thought.

I have read some of the war books, good, bad and indifferent. But even the best have a tendency towards distortion, attributing qualities and motives such as heroism or cowardice, where there was in the end only indifference. Soldiers reacted instinctively, mechanically most of the time. Life in the trenches was a primitive existence, centering around such basic human needs as eating and sleeping and defecating. A great deal of poetry was written about the war, but almost all either in the very first weeks or months, or in places far away from the trenches. To survive in the trenches one had to get hardened, and hard people seldom write poetry. Those who did not get hardened broke down, collapsed, suffered from shellshock, and some went mad. I came across such cases as a medical student and as a doctor in later years.

But these were few; and it is in many ways more interesting to realize that the great majority remained more or less sane and went on functioning year after year in truly inhuman conditions. I have been pondering this, and while I have found some explanations I have not been altogether happy with them. The young men on both sides were patriots; they truly thought that their country had been attacked by enemies out to destroy it. They had been educated to accept authority, and while after a year in the trenches no room was left for heroics, something of a team spirit had grown or been inculcated, and it seemed wrong to let down one's comrades-in-arms. Discipline was not questioned, and while in the front line there was at least a chance of survival, a deserter or mutineer was certain to be executed. And so the German soldier in Flanders could be relied on to hold out, except, of course, when the odds against him became overwhelming.

I distrust the war books for yet another reason: war is a time of total confusion. Tolstoy noted it of Borodino, every soldier before and after knew it, and it was also true in 1914–18. (The situation has somewhat changed since, what with the advances in electronics.) Our field telephones did not work much of the time; messengers had to be dispatched, but quite often they did not reach their destination, and even when they did the situation had changed in the meantime. Even high commanders in the field were in the dark much of the time and the sodier in the trench knew nothing at all, except what he saw with his own eyes. Nor was he curious; everyone in the trenches had learnt within the first few days the elementary rule – not to see and not to be seen: slow learners did not survive.

I have described very briefly the events of 7 June 1917 as I saw them. I had a grandstand seat, but this was a rare exception; normally I would not even have known what day of the week it was. Had I been in the trenches, I would have felt a big bang; this might have been my last impression. But if I had survived, I would probably have followed the example of my neighbours to the left and right and worked my way back to the rear, jumping from shell-hole to shell-hole. All this was done by instinct; cavemen, I suppose, reacted the same way. Guns were fired, hand-grenades were thrown by instinct, one ran and jumped by instinct, but there was no time for mature reflection. I have read the war letters of students who were killed in the war – there have been several such collections. What high-flown phrases; and yet how typical these letters are of the psychology of the new recruit. There was little hate for the enemy, but a great deal of pathos about the necessity of sacrifice so that the fatherland could live. How horrible it all was, and how beautiful, and what totally different human beings they had become. Most of these letters date from 1914, or were written during the first weeks spent at the front. The pathos did not survive long in the trenches, nor did the sentiment.

For my generation the war was the great school, but the lessons, alas, were almost entirely negative; most of us tried to forget the war years completely. A few, it is true, made a cult out of the war; they joined veterans' associations and celebrated all the remembrance days. For them these had been the finest years in otherwise drab and uneventful lives. Some continued to believe that there must have been a deeper meaning to the slaughter with its hecatombs of victims. They went on extolling the spirit of 1914 – sacrifice, discipline and soldierly virtues. This went on for some twenty years, and with the nationalist wave in the 1930s these slogans again became popular, at least in Germany.

When I came home in 1918, hungry and tired, my intellectual education had been set back by years. But I had been exposed to life, and even more to death, and was mature, as the saying goes, beyond my years. Politically I was still quite innocent, but no great sophistication was needed to understand that the war had been a gigantic blunder, totally unnecessary, that all the sacrifices had been in vain, and that it was very doubtful whether Europe would ever recover from the effects of this civil war. That it would never be the same again was taken for granted. As the years passed it became clearer that the main lesson the strategists had learnt was purely technical: not to repeat the mistakes of trench warfare.

How could one go back from the hell of Flanders to peaceful pursuits, a normal civilian existence, to learning, following a profession, enjoying oneself, making love, getting married? The transition was not easy, but one could, and one did. Of the erstwhile innocence not much remained: the veterans were thoroughly disillusioned, and those who turned to active politics quite frequently became the standard-bearers of Fascism. Human life had become cheap during the war years; there were no longer many believers in the goodness of man and humanist values.

I had grown up in a small town where all classes of the population mingled. But in the trenches I experienced a revelation, and not a pleasant one. One met, as everywhere, some fine people and some objectionable characters, but what struck me above all was the almost universal dislike of educated people, which frequently turned into anti-semitism. Most young Jews had gone to the war in 1914 with an enthusiasm equal to that of Protestants and Catholics, but they soon realized that however ardent their patriotism and exemplary their behaviour, there was far more antagonism towards them than they had ever imagined. This apart, they perceived, much to their surprise, that they were indeed different in some ways in their thinking and feeling, and that the fact had not escaped others, even if they themselves had been largely unaware of it. And in any case, they were not liked.

Every Jew had non-Jewish friends, and they would defend him against criticism and attack. But Jews in general had few friends: they felt isolated and branded when in 1916 all Jews serving in the front line were suddenly counted by special order of the government – even though the intention allegedly was 'to correct malicious rumours'. I was less shocked than others, simply because I was already more familiar with the widely prevailing anti-Jewish feeling. I frequently passed as a non-Jew, comrades spoke to me uninhibitedly, and I am ashamed to say that I did not always make it immediately known that I was Jewish.

Thus I learnt at a comparatively early age that one should not have illusions about human nature; the war was a good school precisely because all tensions and conflicts were aggravated and one could watch mankind in the raw. Many became openly cynical; few, if any, committed suicide because of their disappointment with human nature. Few decided to leave Germany after the war. For after all, the war years had been untypical, years of enormous strain; and just as individuals are not normally judged by what they would say or do in a state of advanced intoxication, it was widely believed that there was no reason for despair, that in normal circumstances people would behave differently, and that in any case civilization would gradually reassert itself.

I spent three days with Dr Verschoylen touring west Flanders, and I came to admire his tact and patience. He had been a child when the war broke out; he had just a few dim recollections of occupation and widespread destruction, an unhappy episode in the history of his people. Yet he showed no boredom as I went from one hill to the next and, immersed in my thoughts, fell silent for long periods. We saw more visitors than I had expected – old people who went straight to the

61

cemeteries, classes of school-children shown around by their teachers. In Ypres, in the evening, beneath the Menin Gate, a big war memorial, we witnessed the Last Post ceremony; we were told that it took place every day of the year.

At the end of the third day my curiosity had been satisfied. The experience had been more unsettling – even at this distance in time – that I had ever thought possible. Verschoylen who had watched my moods closely decided that a visit to Bruges would do us good. And so we went off to the canals and bridges and gabled houses and museums of Bruges, less than an hour away by car. This made me think of Burgundian dukes and Flemish burghers, of Alba, the lords of Orange and Egmont. We even went to that little place Damme, on the outskirts, where Ulenspiegel was born; and I thought of him and of Lamme Goedzak, their asses and their dog whose name was Titus Bibulus Schnouffius.

3. Old Heidelberg

Peace has come and war is over. The soldier is home again like millions of others; he left a schoolboy and he has come back a man. He is not yet of age in the eyes of the law, but he has been to a cruel finishing school, he has undergone a test of nerves which should prepare him for most situations likely to face him in civilian life. He left a world that was more or less intact, in which young men and women could plan their future with reasonable certainty, provided they were in good health, in which authority was obeyed, in which there was not much violence; not a very exciting world admittedly, but one in which there was security and hope.

Now a new world had come into being, full of excitement but with no more certainties, no authority, no undisputed beliefs and values. Even the value of money, it was soon to appear, can no longer be trusted. Those who have come back are confused about their own future, that of their country and of mankind. Who is there to advise them?

Our soldier has returned to Mariabronn. He enjoys sleeping in a soft bed, and though there is not much coal, he freezes less than in the trenches. The Spanish flu has bypassed him and his family. There is not much to eat, but his mother is spoiling him and he is grateful for her attention and kindness. But already, after a few days, he is becoming restless; what is he doing in the room in which a small boy grew up? He dearly loves his parents, but they have aged, and they think of him still as the eighteen-year-old who needs their advice. He sees some well-known faces in town, but even they have become strangers; they have followed their own pursuits while he was away and an eternity divides them from him. The town is no longer sleepy and romantic, it has been affected by the bad mood engendered by the general predicaments of age. Mariabronn is no longer a cheerful place, even the children hardly smile. But then there is not much reason to smile.

The time has come to leave home, the sooner the better; but where will he go, and what will he do? In the long nights in the trenches he sometimes thought about life after the war. He reached no firm conclusions. He is interested in literature and history, but these subjects can be of no earthly use to him, unless he wants to teach – which he doesn't. Perhaps he should not go to university at all, for it will mean four more years (and possibly much longer) of dependence on his parents. He feels in some ways very old; a year in the trenches, they said, counts for ten. He had to waste some of the best years of his life, can he afford to waste any more? But what future is there is store for him unless he studies? And other considerations apart, he is genuinely eager to learn, to know more, he is aware that he has no general education. He could follow in his father's footsteps; though the subject has never been discussed, he feels that the father would only be too happy if the son were to continue his life-work. But he does not want to be a merchant or industrialist or banker, he lacks interest and ability. He has no gift for a technical or a strictly scientific career. He had long discussions with another lieutenant in his company, a few years older, who had just started studying medicine in 1914. This friend is firmly convinced that the doctor's profession is the only worthwhile one in the world and his enthusiasm is infectious. The infection is a mere accident; the soldier might have chosen the law if he had encountered someone equally confident about the superiority of the legal profession. Such accidents are frequent in life and no apologies are needed.

In January 1919 he leaves home. Mother is very sad. She behaves as if she is about to lose her youngest son for ever, though he will be in the neighbourhood, in Heidelberg, only an hour or two away by train. Most weekends (he promises) he will come home. The old people need him.

'Alt Heidelberg', what magic the name exudes:

Old Heidelberg, dear city, with honours crowned and rare
O'er Rhine and Neckar rising. None can with thee compare!

This is the city everyone knows: duelling-places and taverns along the river, students with coloured caps, students with enormous beer mugs singing 'Gaudeamus Igitur' and flirting with the local girls. It is familiar from countless songs, novels and musicals; even Mark Twain was attracted by Heidelberg. It is still a fine city, with its castle, and bridges, and the old narrow houses squeezed between Castle Hill and the Neckar. Just outside the city there is the Molkenkur with its view of the castle, and the Philosophenweg, the beautiful walk with a panoramic view over the whole city and well beyond it. In the centre of town there is Ruperto-Carola University, the oldest in Germany proper – only Vienna and Prague were founded even earlier. The medical institute and the university clinic are on the banks of the Neckar, near the Roemerbruecke.

Nothing has changed: the elderly professors who were teaching here during the war are still around. There are the same garden restaurants, there is a cable railway, and motor boats to Heilbronn. Everything is the same and everything is different: four out of five students are former soldiers and they have no money. This seems an unnecessary statement, for students never have money. In the old days even the very richest young men sometimes had to cable home before the end of the month requesting first aid. But it is different now. Then there was just the inconvenience of sending a cable, and the likelihood of being told off for overspending: they knew that there was money and that it would be sent. Now there is none; the students know it and prefer starving to begging from their families. They managed without their parents' help during the war, they cannot go back and depend on them now. Some have no hot meals for weeks, some have contracted tuberculosis, still a killing disease. They work in unheated rooms in the university, they sleep in cold and damp bedrooms. Many come to lectures in their old army coats and frayed suits. No one gets drunk, and no one has fought a duel; they have had all the fighting they wanted.

The purchasing power of the German Mark is now one tenth of what it was before the war, but the student can count only on 500–600 Mark each month. The situation of the student has deteriorated both absolutely and relatively: in 1914 the student had three quarters of what an unskilled worker earned, now he is left with merely one quarter, and this is far, far below the bare minimum needed. The sons and daughters of the middle class can no longer afford to study. But they still go on studying, even if their prospects of employment are dismal. In fact they constitute now the overwhelming majority of the student body.

How do they make ends meet? Most have to look for work to earn extra money. In the old days they could always give private lessons, but the demand was always limited and it is even more limited now, for only few can afford to pay. Some work as waiters, some wash dishes, some have become commercial travellers, some work on building sites, some in factories, some as messengers, some do odd jobs, some allegedly work as gigolos. But there is not much industry in Heidelberg, not that many dishes have to be washed in the Restaurant Perkeo, and there are no known gigolos in town. The situation is very bad; and yet, seen in retrospect, 1919 was quite tolerable, perhaps because everyone suffered at the time, and the main problem facing students was to find a roof over their head. But the state of affairs continued to deteriorate and 1923 was the worst year by far. The song 'O alte Burschenherrlichkeit wohin bist du verschwunden?' (Old glory of studentdom – whither hast thou disappeared?) has assumed a new meaning.

Most of the students are former soldiers; they are in a hurry and want to finish their studies as quickly as possible. Our soldier – or should we say our student – is also in a hurry, but he still finds time to attend some of the lectures and seminars in philosophy and literature, in sociology and history. Some of the lecturers in Heidelberg are men of world fame; for decades to come people in many countries will talk with awe of these argonauts of the spirit, of these giants of modern thought; their seminars have entered the annals of modern intellectual history. But their fame does not always survive exposure at close quarters. Some, our student thinks, are mere speechifiers and empty babblers, some may be great men in their field but lack the gift of conveying their knowledge to others. Some are too obscure for him, but there are others who greatly impress him and he will be for ever grateful for the opportunity to have sat at their feet for a little while. How could all these activities be crammed into a working day? In later years he will be at a loss to explain it. The war had been a good trainingground; one had to keep awake for many hours in difficult conditions.

After a year our student moves on to Freiburg, and then after two more semesters to Munich, where he will stay for two years. It was customary in those days as it was in the Middle Ages to move from one university to another. The practice has much to recommend it. Munich was less expensive in those far-away days; it is a much bigger town than either Heidelberg or Freiburg and there are more possibilities of finding work and earning money. Our student distributes newspapers in the morning and helps to remove furniture. But he still would not have been able to continue his studies but for a *deus ex machina* in the form of one of his father's cousins.

This black sheep of the family had been dispatched to the United States thirty years earlier, and had built up a small business in the Middle West. He wrote a letter to Mariabronn early in 1920 saying that he had been reading about the sorry plight of people in the old country, and could he perhaps be of some help in some small way? Father had replied that he did not need anything, but there was the case of a deserving young man trying to continue his studies against

66

heavy odds. Ever since, a small dollar cheque would arrive at the beginning of each month. It was a tiny cheque, minute, almost microscopic, but oh, how he looked forward to that cheque! For when our soldier first entered university in Heidelberg a dollar had been just 8.60 Mark; at the end of the second semester it had jumped to 52 Mark. In November 1920 it went up to 87 Mark, in November 1921 it had risen to 272 Mark, in November 1923 it was worth 4,200 billions. Our student had become a multi-billionaire; but so, alas, had everyone else.

But he was lucky compared with many others, as he had been lucky during the war. During the most difficult time he not only had enough to eat, and a room which could sometimes even be heated, but he could buy the books he needed for his studies. And he could even buy some of the books he did not need for his studies, laying the foundation of what later became a sizeable library. He did not have to engage in barter, nor did he have to hitch his services to the price of a kilo of butter as many professional people of his acquaintance did. His problems are of a different nature: they may appear funny in retrospect, but they were not at all funny at the time. Occasionally those who printed the money would go on strike, and then our student would walk the streets of Munich with a dollar bill which no bank could change, like the hero in O. Henry's story; truly a case of starving in the midst of plenty.

It was a fascinating period in every respect, and Munich was one of the main centres of action. Bavaria was on a collision course with the Berlin government, and in addition there was a curious home-grown movement of fanatics in the capital of Bavaria shouting 'Death to the Jews' and 'Down with the November Criminals' – meaning those who had replaced the Emperor and signed the Versailles Peace Treaty. They met in the beerhalls, shouted, roughed up their opponents and had a sizeable following. They were led by a rabble-rouser named Adolf Hitler, who was not even a German citizen. In November 1923 the Nazis became over-confident and staged a rising which was suppressed without difficulty.

But the demonstrations and the meetings and the parades continue. There are barricades in the street, people are killed and wounded in clashes and ambushes. Thieves are no longer after money, for even the seizure of a five-ton truck of money would not be rewarding; they dismantle door handles, church bells, and even the lids of the sewers in the street and bronze statues in the parks, for metal is in great demand.

The French occupy the Ruhr, and then leave again. Duisburg and Gelsenkirchen are not the most beautiful of cities at the best of times, and they are in even worse shape now. The French do not enjoy their stay. There are strikes and the unemployed demonstrate.

While all this goes on, the student and his colleagues are taught the essentials of anatomy and physiology, pathology and bacteriology; they then proceed to dermatology and surgery, venerology and anaesthesiology, otorhinolaryngology and proctology and many other subjects. He has to know a little about the urinary tract and more about the respiratory tract, he has to have a smattering of dentistry and even of psychiatry. A great deal of chemistry and biology is taken for granted, much more than he was ever taught in his school with its emphasis on a classical education. He has to make this good in his spare time. He spends many hours in laboratories acquainting himself with instruments and methods. He memorizes the most important drugs, and some which have been long out of date and which he will never use; he picks up some gynaecology and obstetrics – after all, he has to be able to deliver a baby without help.

There are many, far too many, lectures, but as the years go by the emphasis shifts to clinical work. With a little group of fellow students he follows the professor on ward rounds; at night he is attached to a senior colleague at a first aid station. He is mortally afraid in the beginning; how can he possibly cope with the unlimited number of contingencies that may face him? There is so much to learn, a whole lifetime will not be sufficient. His colleagues in other faculties worry whether they will ever find work; a mathematician has calculated that the average arts graduate will have to wait twenty-five years for a job.

His chances as a doctor are better, but he still does not know whether he should be a general practitioner or specialize. Nor is he sure whether he will be a competent physician. On a recent visit to Mariabronn he had a long conversation with the old doctor who delivered him and who has known his family – and many other families – for so many years. The old doctor has been out of touch with modern medical thought for decades and he has long given up following professional literature. But he has seen in his time thousands of sick people, he has much common sense and even more experience, and he knows that with all the recent advances, the powers of nature are still greater than the knowledge of the physician. This old doctor has told him that like every physician he will make mistakes in the years to come, and that in a few cases these may be fatal mistakes. But this has been so since the

68

beginning of medicine. A good doctor should appear confident towards his patient, and sceptical and questioning towards himself: a self-satisfied doctor should always be distrusted.

Fifty years have come and gone, and the student of 1920 no longer feels patronizing towards the old village doctor who gave him this advice. In fact, he would use similar words when addressing young colleagues. The new generation know so much more, they have learnt about diseases and conditions which they may never meet. But quite frequently they do not have sufficient insight and empathy as far as the patient is concerned. The medical curriculum is admirable, but there is no room in it for experience; perhaps rightly so, for every new generation has to make its own mistakes and there is no known way of bequeathing experience except by trial and error.

The years of study are years of great turmoil in the history of his country. A democratic republic has been established, the first ever, but it is not yet widely accepted, it has no roots in the popular will; economic crises and social tensions make it seem unlikely to last. The student of the early 1920s could not live in an ivory tower even if he wanted to; at every step he confronts the harsh realities of life. As he studies the tibia and the os calcis, shots are fired outside the clinic, as he dissects a corpse, a few more are brought in from the street. Like other students he visits political meetings and for a little while becomes involved with one of the many factions of the extreme left. He does not tend towards extremism and the people in that group attract him more than their ideas. Among them he finds true idealists, those putting the cause of humanity above their personal ambitions and their career. They are also among the most consistent opponents of war and militarism, and this is the thing about which he feels perhaps most deeply.

But idealism and the willingness to make sacrifices do not *per se* sanctify a cause; they can be also found among the men on the extreme right. There is an arrogance and fanaticism in these admirable men and women which repels him; they seem firmly convinced that they have the revealed truth and therefore have the right, however few of them there are, to dictate to the many. He is told that a free and just society can only be built by a ruthless dictatorship. The student has not much sophistication and experience yet, but he instinctively feels that this is a dangerous argument and may cause untold misery. The philosophers, he is told, have only interpreted the world in different ways, it is the commandment of the hour to change it. Well and good, but what if those changing the world are not clear in their minds about what can and what should be changed? They talk for ever about rational thought, but they have the zeal and the intolerance of deeply religious people, and in the last resort they are true believers. And so with all his sympathy for their enthusiasm to build a better world, he withdraws from their circle.

Little has been said so far about the private life of our student. Is it all work and no play, has he no feelings, has he not been in love, is he not feeling sorrow or anger? It is not an easy question to answer, for our student is not an extrovert, and there are very few who know him well. He has learnt to control his emotions, he needs friendship and love, but he is afraid of being disappointed and hurt, and so will seldom make the first move. Outwardly he is a reasonably polite young man, seemingly self-confident, stable and composed, not very talkative, a young man who knows where he wants to go and who, his friends and teachers think, may go far. There are quite a few who are more intelligent than he is, or more widely read, but he has a creative mind and sometimes an astonishing intuition; sometimes he will suddenly come up with the right answer to a problem which has preoccupied or misled better minds for a long time, and he will not even be able to say how he reached the solution. Above all, as has been noted, he is a lucky young man.

But the image from the outside is incomplete, and in some respects it is misleading. The student is a constant worrier about himself and about others. He has not accepted himself – the way he looks, the way he behaves, the way he is constituted. He is immodest, he has an inclination to boast. He knows his weaknesses, but it is one thing to analyse the self and another to come to terms with it. He does not live at peace with himself, and in his edition of Pascal the words *Le moi est haïssable* are underlined.

But then there are days when he thinks that this refers to others rather than to himself; and on some rare occasions it seems to him that, all things considered, the world is not such a bad place, and that no one is really hateful. In short, our student is a moody young man, and while his outward equanimity may fool many, it will not mislead a close observer.

He is now in his fifth year of studies, and on his calling card it no longer says 'stud. med' but 'cand. med'. It is the last day of the old year; a few weeks ago the Mark was stabilized. With some friends he has been for a short walk in Munich's English garden and then in the

Hofgarten. It is bitterly cold, but thousands of people are still up – they want to usher in the New Year out in the streets. The student and his friends find a table, not without difficulty, in the Café Luitpold, where generations of students and their elders and betters have sat and drunk and talked. It is a luxury they can now ill afford, but this is a special occasion; no one knows where the next New Year will find them. They hope it will be a better year, which is not an unreasonable hope, because 1924 cannot very well be worse than 1923, which was abysmal. As the clock of the nearby Theatiner Church begins to strike midnight, and the chimes of the bells are taken up by a dozen others from near and far, our student has another of his premonitions – that the coming year will be a decisive one in his life. At his age every year is decisive, but this one, he feels, will be more decisive than others.

4. Grand Hotel

I am writing these lines on a summer evening in the garden of the Grand Hotel, Interlaken. A high hedge divides the garden from the Hoehe Weg, the main street, and in the distance looms the Jungfrau massif, covered in snow. There is a great deal of noise from the street and I am too often distracted. It has been a warm day but it is getting chilly now; soon I will have to return to the main building. There is still a lot of movement in the street outside – hikers with their knapsacks returning from a mountain excursion, tourists strolling about, looking at the expensive watches in the shop windows.

I arrived here the day before yesterday and found the place less changed than I had expected, though prices have soared and as a result this hotel, as most others, now has to rely on the package-deal market. It is difficult to imagine that today's guests would have been welcome here back in the 1920s. I do not regret the change, in fact I find it interesting: young people from Japan, Israel or Spain, loud and badly dressed, the young men frequently ill-mannered and the young women moving about less than gracefully. But they laugh a great deal, and when they come into the dining room the place comes alive.

Yesterday I went to Grindelwald and from the terrace of a coffee house in the main street I looked at the Eiger for a long time. Today I took a guided tour to Kandersteg; but for a few showers and the indifferent jokes of the guide, it was a most enjoyable experience. The dinner tonight was excellent; I feel reasonably content, and hope I will be able to make some progress with my writing during the next few days.

Having spent many nights in modern American hotels, I have a weakness for old ones. This sounds snobbish, and it is of course quite true that most European hoteliers could learn a lot from the amenities provided in even second-rate American motels. But there is something inimitable in the atmosphere of a European Grand Hotel, even the shabby ones: the long corridors with old furniture, the old pictures, the quaint staircases, the palm courts without palms, in which once upon a time orchestras used to play. The Interlaken Grand Hotel is very much in this tradition. It was founded back in the 1830s by an enterprising young shepherd who had migrated to Interlaken from the Unterland. He opened an inn which later expanded; his son further enlarged it and got one of the best-known French architects of the day to construct a new building. In 1882 it was the first hotel in this neighbourhood to introduce electric light.

Who were the tourists in those days? Enterprising Germans and Englishmen, no doubt. There was no mass tourism as yet; the first tour organized by Thomas Cook was in the 1870s. But Interlaken had always been an ideal base for excursions to the mountains; situated between two major lakes, it is ringed with mountains and forests. Weber and Wagner had been here, Mendelssohn and Brahms, to rest or to look for inspiration.

And so the Grand Hotel went from strength to strength and in the first decade of this century it finally acquired world fame. On 1 September 1907 a young well-dressed lady approached an elderly gentleman at lunch, and shot and killed him from short range. There was a big commotion; she was arrested, and it emerged that she was a Russian student, the daughter of a former general and high Tsarist official. She had intended to assassinate Durnovo, minister of police and one of the pillars of the regime, who had indeed stayed in the hotel. She killed an elderly French guest, a retired businessman from Paris.

I do not know how the hotel survived the First World War and the Second, when tourism was at low ebb. But survive it did, and according to all indications it is now doing well. Most of the waiters are foreigners – Yugoslavs, Spanish, Italians, a few Germans from the Lausanne hotel school. The chief cook is German; the pastry cook, a great artist in his field, is an Arab. Only the head porter speaks the local dialect. He is an oldish man, probably about to retire. I became friendly with him – I find head waiters and concierges highly intelligent people, usually very charming and always most helpful. Their knowledge of human nature is immense; many of my professional colleagues could learn from them.

He took the initiative. On the evening of my arrival, when I was leaving the hotel for a short walk, he addressed me as I was about to hand in the key: 'Welcome back, Herr Doctor.' I turned around. 'Thank you – but are you sure this is not a mistake?' 'I am not sure,' he confessed. 'It was a shot in the dark. We see thousands of people each year. Once my memory was infallible. I am getting on and sometimes these days I mix up names and faces. But I still think we had the pleasure of seeing you here. Was it perhaps during the war?' 'No,' I said, 'try again.' The man in the queue behind me made impatient noises. 'You do not mind, doctor, do you?' said the concierge smilingly.

73

'Not in the least,' I said, 'but I still think you are mistaken.' 'Perhaps so,' he said.

The next morning when I sat at the breakfast table, reading what is known locally as the 'Zürcher Zeitung', my new friend came up and said:

'Forgive me, I was racking my brain; it was a real challenge, I could not sleep. And then suddenly I did remember. But I still was not altogether certain, and so I went to the basement and looked up some old registers, and now it has all come back. It was my first year at work, as a junior messenger, on the lowest rung of the ladder. And this is probably why I remember. . . . Do you mind, Herr Doctor, if I tell the management? I am sure they will be greatly honoured.'

I told him that I was more than happy to renew our acquaintance, but that I would be most grateful if he would keep his knowledge to himself. In any case, it was hardly a matter of public interest and I was sure he would sympathize with me and keep my little secret. If one had lived as long as the two of us, one knew that to bring up memories from the distant past always involved a measure of pain and sorrow, for it made one only too aware of those dear to us, who are no longer among the living. I had a drink with the concierge that night after he had finished work, and in one hour I learnt a great deal about aspects of modern tourism, social change in contemporary Europe and the economy of Switzerland, not to mention the history of the Grand Hotel in the twentieth century.

I now have to go back in time. In 1923 I graduated in medicine; the examination took several weeks, and the oral test in particular was severe and thorough. In my main subject I was interviewed by two leading authorities who asked and listened for hours on end. Such a procedure would be quite unthinkable now with the much larger number of students. I wanted to specialize at the time in internal medicine and applied for a position as voluntary assistant – the very lowest, in the Berlin clinic of Professor Riemwald. He was one of the leading cardiologists of the day, certainly the one most in the public eye and in demand, which was surprising because he also had the reputation of being the rudest doctor in Berlin. Much against expectations I was accepted; and again, much to my surprise, after some weeks of totally ignoring me, Riemwald actually talked to me. With the reckless confidence of youth I had published an article in a leading medical journal about the psychological relationship between doctor and patient, and its effects on the prospects of recovery. The article had found its

way to Riemwald's desk. And so the following discussion developed:
'I have read your article. It is based, no doubt, on your experience
with several thousands of patients.' 'Well, Herr Professor,' I said, some-
what subdued, 'I was really concerned with the theoretical aspects. . . .'
'Theoretical aspects my foot,' he shouted. 'What infernal impertinence.
This is the kind of article great doctors write at the end of their career.
And you thought this could be a subject for theoretical speculation. . . .
I do not want whippersnappers around here who make this clinic a
laughing stock.' And he left the room in a huff, slamming the door.

I started packing my few belongings, assuming that my Berlin career
had come to a rapid and inglorious end; but just as I was about to
leave, the Geheimrat half-opened the door and said: 'Let it be a lesson
to you. By the way, some of your formulations were not bad. Come to
dinner tomorrow night.' This was not an invitation but a command.

Next evening I turned up at his villa in the Grunewald, on foot needless to say. The other guests had come in chauffeured Horchs and
Maybachs. The dinner was excellent, but I felt out of place between
the great and famous of politics and economics – with a sprinkling of
writers and well-known actors. Riemwald introduced me to everyone
as his most successful assistant. 'Would you believe it,' he said, 'this
young genius is twenty-six years old but he already had thousands of
patients. Ask him, if you are interested in the details. . . .'

A kindly-looking, fat, elderly man who saw my embarrassment took
pity: 'Don't take it so hard, you know the Geheimrat, he obviously
likes you, this is his particular way of showing affection. Tell me
about yourself – have you been with him for long?' I told him the little
there was to be told and, for reasons I no longer remember, concluded
with a long and detailed survey of Germany's foreign policy problems.
My new friend, whose face looked vaguely familiar, drew me out; I
went on and on. When I got up to the League of Nations he interrupted me and said: 'This is most illuminating. Have you ever thought
of politics as a career? But you'll probably do even more good in
your present profession.' He introduced me to his wife, a kind elderly
lady and it was then that I realized that I had made a fool of myself
for the second time that evening, for I had been talking to the man
who had been Foreign Minister until a few months previously. His
name is remembered to this day – I shall call him Bornemann from
now on.

One morning a few weeks later I was called urgently to see Riemwald
in his office. He told me that he had an assignment for me which I

would surely not refuse. A highly placed patient of his who was quite seriously ill needed a long holiday. But he was not willing to go on leave unless a personal physician would travel with him, for he was also a bit of a hypochondriac. It soon emerged that the patient was Bornemann, who had in the meantime again become Foreign Minister.

I said I would love to accept the job, but how could I bear the responsibility in view of my lack of experience? What would I do in an emergency? Riemwald said that he had never thought too highly of my intellectual faculties in the first place and that he was by no means certain that I would ever be a doctor to whom one could safely entrust a patient. But, as he raised his voice, there was a limit even to stupidity, and that I was about to exceed the limits: 'Of course you couldn't do a thing if he gets another attack, but neither could I nor anyone else; the man has had several massive attacks, and it is touch and go whether he will survive the next.' 'And why me?' 'Because he asked for you,' Riemwald said. 'He did not remember your name but mentioned the young man who had given him that interesting lecture over dinner about the conduct of German-French relations. And who could this have been but you?'

Riemwald said that I would be given detailed instructions, but these were not too explicit: I was to take care that my patient did not over-eat, take his pulse and blood pressure once a day, give him a sleeping pill at night and administer injections in the event of an attack. I gladly accepted the assignment, and my colleagues envied me. I was to leave almost immediately with Bornemann and his wife and we were to spend four weeks in a hotel in Interlaken. I had not had a holiday since I went to Paris with my parents more than ten years earlier. During the inflation Germans could not even dream of a trip abroad and even now, a year later, a holiday outside Germany was a rare event.

We went by train. It was a long trip, and I tried to get accustomed to my new responsibilities. This was not easy, because while I had to be constantly in attendance I wanted also to be inconspicuous. I do not remember much of the trip, except that Bornemann said that I was of no use to him because I was quite hopeless as a card-player. He was smoking too many strong cigars and, worse still, was eating too much between meals. Wherever the train stopped more than three minutes I was commissioned to get him a pair of sausages, and since the train made a major stop almost every hour, the intake of sausages was very substantial. When I raised some mild objections I was told that he would not die a young man in any case, and that sausages were one of the few things in life he still enjoyed. The only result of my interventions was that later on, in Interlaken, he would no longer ask me, but send out a messenger boy, or he would slip out for a few minutes, and return quite obviously a happier man. Mrs Bornemann watched, saw everything and suffered. And I felt quite churlish for trying to deprive him of something he enjoyed so much.

The next weeks were delightful. For the first time in years I was in no hurry, there was no tension, no challenge, no worry; it was quite unsettling at first. In the beginning I felt a little awkward to be in the company of someone who was the object of general attention. Bornemann was at that time one of Europe's leading statesmen. He was constantly approached by journalists, and when we entered the lounge or the dining room or any other public place everyone would look in our direction. But one became accustomed to it, and after a few days it did not bother me any longer.

Bornemann had made it clear that he wanted to see me for a little while in the morning, during or after lunch and for an hour in the evening; the rest of the time I was free to do what I liked. In the evening we walked slowly along the rapid Aare just behind the hotel; every few minutes he would sit down on a bench breathing heavily. 'I do not know why I am doing this. . . . The least you can do is to entertain me during this unnecessary exercise.' His curiosity for a man in public life was very great indeed. He wanted to know all about my parents, about school, about my years in the army. He had risen from very small beginnings; his father, I believe, had worked in a post office. He had worked his way up, and while he was a man of the right, he had nothing but contempt for the traditional right-wing establishment.

The Bornemanns had no children, and I suppose they liked to have a younger person around. They certainly took a parental interest in my well-being. He was as far as I could judge a man of real kindness of heart, polite, always willing to help, who in private life would not have touched a hair on anyone's head. But he was ruthless in politics, completely cynical and, on occasion, even immoral. I was by then already aware that the morality of the Sermon on the Mount does not apply in public affairs. But I was still shocked, and I am sometimes surprised even now, by the different standards of morality applied by politicians in public and private life.

Sometimes, when he felt not too well, we would take a horse-drawn cab and drive along the main street, passing the Kursaal, watching the mountains in the peculiar reddish evening light. But Bornemann was not really interested in the marvels of nature, and excursions were in any case ruled out. He just wanted to rest, which he did after a fashion sitting in an easy chair in the garden, humming and hawing, complaining, watching people walking on the promenade, and devouring countless daily newspapers which poor Mrs Bornemann or myself had to buy at the kiosk opposite.

Never in my life had I eaten so well or been waited upon so much. Coming from a country in which the after-effects of war were still palpably noticeable, the wealth and abundance of goods displayed in the shops was overwhelming. I could not absent myself from the hotel for too many hours, and this precluded a visit to the Jungfrau. But I made it by rail to the Jungfraujoch, and on another day I went to the glacier near Grindelwald.

Bornemann and his wife were genuinely concerned that there would not be sufficient entertainment for me. During dinner on the first evening, Bornemann looked around and said: 'Well, my boy, this does not look promising.' Almost all the guests were in their sixties or seventies; and there was the King of Afghanistan, or his brother, with a very considerable retinue. I said that there was no danger that I would be bored, and that in fact I would be only too happy to get a little rest. He replied that there was time enough to rest in Berlin, that he too had been young once upon a time; and then suddenly, watching the door: 'I say.'

An old lady had entered, very erect, very haughty, obviously accustomed to be recognized and fussed over, accompanied by a very young, strikingly pretty girl in a dark green dress. They were greeted by the maître with great deference. The old lady was carrying an old-fashioned handbag, a pompadour, as if to express her contempt for the twentieth century. She took a seat, and then began to study the enormous menu through her lorgnon. The younger lady smiled and said something, but the grandmother – or was it the great-aunt? – did not respond. She examined with evident disapproval the people at the neighbouring tables.

The meal went on for a long time, and the Bornemanns and I tried to guess who and what the other guests were. His guesses about country of origin, profession and so on seemed to me quite preposterous. Later I found out that he had almost invariably been right; he had an uncanny gift of observation.

There was a notice at the door announcing that there would be a small dance for hotel guests that night, and that everyone was cordially invited. I told Bornemann that I was a little tired and would go to bed after our walk. He replied that he was obviously out of touch with the younger generation; did they have any interests at all? Did they still know how to enjoy themselves? Or were they perhaps sexless? I would do him a personal favour if I would go to the dance at least for a while and report to him the next morning whether there was anyone of interest among the other guests. I told him I was one of the world's most awkward dancers ('It cannot possibly be worse than your card-playing') and that I hoped he appreciated the extent of my sacrifice.

The dance was a dismal affair; the smallest of orchestras played the hits of 1924. But 1924 was not a vintage year; there was 'Fascination', and 'Destiny', and a nice little song about the sweet girls of Paris, which is still remembered because some years later it became the theme song for René Clair's *Sous les toits de Paris*. There were a few tourists from other hotels, but most of those in attendance were there like myself out of curiosity or boredom. An elderly couple was half-heartedly dancing a slow foxtrot.

I was about to leave them when, somewhat hesitatingly, the young lady in green entered. She must have felt as lost as I did, and this helped me to overcome my shyness; I went up to her and introduced myself. She smiled. After the second dance I apologized for my clumsiness and suggested a little walk; it was a mild evening, no coats were needed. I was elated. Amor, as the ancients would have said, inspired my speech; I listened and I looked at her and I took her arm – O youth, O transport of delight, O blissful state – I have not the faintest recollection what I said that night, or where we walked. All I know is that I felt drawn as if by a magnet to the young lady at my side. She looked even younger than her age; she was twenty-three, her name was Elizabeth von Arnsburg, and she was the fourth and youngest daughter of a family of the lower aristocracy.

She spoke with detachment and utter frankness: the family had seen better days, her parents had become bitter, the atmosphere at home was oppressive. She had left home to work as a companion to wealthy elderly ladies, so as not to be a burden to her family and to escape the sadness and recriminations at home. It was not always a pleasant occupation, but the only one she could do with reasonable competence. She had not wanted to study; she was interested in music, literature and the arts, but these were unprofitable subjects. Now she travelled with Countess Donner von Donnerstein, the widow of the Silesian industrialist and landowner who had been one of the richest men in

Wilhelmian Germany; half the property had been lost during and after the war, but it was still immense.

The horrible old lady was not her great-aunt, as I had thought, but her employer. My knightly instincts were awakened and I blurted out: 'But this must be horrible, can I help you to get away?' Elizabeth was greatly amused: 'Why should I leave? You've got her all wrong: she just likes to play the dragon, but she really is a sweet old lady, and very well educated, much better than I am. She is a bit eccentric, but I am not exploited nor oppressed. I am well paid as such jobs go and have a lot of free time. She does not really need me but just likes to have a young person around. . . .'

I told Elizabeth about Mariabronn, and school, and also a little about the war, and about the university and what had brought me to Interlaken and eventually about my plans for the future. She was a good listener. I had never talked so openly about myself to anyone. By midnight I was deeply in love: she was admittedly a very pretty girl – of medium height, very slim, with shiny blue eyes and a wonderful smile. At three she said she was tired. We went back to the hotel; a sleepy doorman handed us the keys and wished us a good night. Much to my surprise I gathered courage to kiss her goodnight; Elizabeth did not protest but made it a short kiss.

The next morning Bornemann, who had had a bad night, interrogated me about the dance. I said I had met no one of interest, the dance had not been well attended and in any case I had not stayed long. 'For a short evening you look a little tired,' he said. At that moment the Countess entered the breakfast room, and in her wake Elizabeth. I greeted her, which was not easy with an eggspoon in my right hand and the salt in my left. There was a warm smile in my direction. 'Well done my boy,' Bornemann said. 'You are a lousy liar.' After breakfast I ran to Schuh, the leading *Konditorei* in town, and bought two pounds of their own pralines, and a great bunch of roses at the nearest florist, and had it all sent to Elizabeth's room.

At lunch I found a short note from her to the effect that she could not very well send back the chocolate and the flowers without creating a minor scandal, but she wanted me to know that she did not eat chocolate, and that it was out if place, indeed perfectly stupid, to send flowers (and above all roses) to someone who was virtually a stranger. She would be happy to send me a copy of Knigge (the German Emily Post), but inquiries at the local booksellers had shown that there was no copy in stock. Meanwhile she would be grateful if I would spare her such embarrassing attentions.

The letter was in firm handwriting; one would never have guessed that it had been written by a young girl. Her last sentence was a little ambiguous; she had not entirely closed the door, but left some room for hope: 'Such attentions', she had written. Did it mean 'all attentions'? I was resolved to find out. And so I wrote a little note in reply saying that not only my dancing was deficient; I was deeply sorry that I had committed a *faux pas*, but I had never had a chance to master the social graces thoroughly, and in any case I was always given to acting rashly in my enthusiasm. I had meant well, would she forgive me? And if she did, could we have another walk tonight? I did not wish to entrust this to a page-boy and so I crept through the long corridor and pushed the letter under her door, terrified all the time that someone would see me.

I stayed in the hotel, impatiently pacing my room, waiting for an answer. From time to time I would go out to the lawn for a minute or two where Bornemann was embedded among his newspapers, only to be told by him to relax. I asked at the reception at four whether there was a message for me, and again at five. When I came at six, the concierge said even before I had asked: 'There is no letter.' I could have killed him. I went out, very sad, determined to forget my young lady. It was quite hopeless; I was in love with her and she, quite obviously, was not interested in me – a young man, gauche, not particularly good-looking, not wealthy, perhaps even boring, someone not belonging to her own circle. Then I returned, quickly dressed for dinner, went to the Bornemanns and together we descended the great staircase.

Passing reception on our way to the dining room, a page-boy approached me and handed me a letter which I put in my pocket. 'Don't you want to read it?' Mrs Bornemann said. I assured her that it could be nothing of any importance. But I opened the letter as soon as I decently could during dinner; it was a very short message – 'Yes, at 9.30 outside the main entrance.' Having been utterly dejected I now passed within a few minutes into a state of exhilaration, talking without interruption, laughing without reason. Bornemann said, 'Either you have been drinking, or you are in love.'

He was utterly bored after two days in the resort, and the idea of several more weeks ahead depressed him. He was the kind of man who could not live without a twelve-hour working day. But the physicians had insisted *expressis verbis* that he was not to be bothered daily with files and dispatches and memoranda. Once a week some high official from his ministry would turn up and give him a half-hour summary of events. This, of course, was not remotely enough as far as Bornemann was concerned, who was deeply afraid of missing some important developments. But nothing much happened during July and August, for the other European foreign ministers were also on holiday: crises in this civilized age were postponed to September.

I was outside the great revolving door ten minutes early, Elizabeth came a few minutes late. She apologized; the Countess had mislaid a book and asked her to find it. She said that our meeting the previous night had been accidental, that the fact that we were the only two young people in a hotel mainly frequented by retired people meant that we were bound to see each other frequently during the next few weeks. She had no wish to quarrel with me or to ignore me, but she would be grateful if I would remember that this was a brief encounter in our lives and refrain in future from presumptuous gestures. I promised; I would have promised anything at that moment.

We then resumed our walk on the Hoehe Weg from the central post office to the Hotel du Nord, past jewellers, hotels and pharmacies. We went up and down ten times, perhaps twenty times, sometimes slowly, sometimes a little quicker. And again I took her arm and eventually kissed her, and not just a goodnight kiss. Next day we went to watch the birds in a nearby sanctuary, and the day after, the ibex in the Alpenwald park; on the third day we went to the Schynige Platte to look at some rare alpine plants. We saw three old castles, and when we had run out of ruins we went to the Harder Promenade which led to a pavilion dedicated to Weber and Mendelssohn, who was said to have composed there a song which everyone knew, 'Wer hat dich du schoener Wald . . .'.

On warm evenings we lay in the grass, on the Hoehe Matte, the meadow opposite the hotel; one day we went to see the waterfalls at Lauterbrunnen. But I am not going to write about the cascades – Byron and others have done it much better than I could – nor even about two young people in love; it has been done a million times and in all languages. All I remember is that I did not care about rare birds, or ibex or ruins or alpine plants, only about the girl next to me, who a week earlier I had not even known, and who was now for me the dearest and the most important person in the world. I had gone out with girls before, and I had slept with a few. I had lived with one for several months. There had been infatuations of shorter or longer duration before, but this was the first time I had been deeply in love. During the day we spent every free minute together, and after two weeks we were also together most of the nights.

Bornemann and his wife followed these developments with some amusement and teased me about my sudden attacks of forgetfulness and confusion. The Countess looked sterner than ever before, taking no notice of anyone she met. Once I thought she examined me through her lorgnon for a few seconds, but perhaps I was mistaken. Elizabeth and I still greeted each other in the dining room quite formally, as if we were strangers. It was a wonderful summer, with a few showers but not one rainy day; the hotel owners were happy because all rooms were taken, the guests were happy and Elizabeth and I were the happiest people of all. And I dreaded the day when this happiness would end.

The day of departure approached: the Countess was to leave next Monday, the Bornemanns on Tuesday. There was one excursion we had postponed, the one to Lake Thun. This meant absenting ourselves from the hotel for a little longer than usual; but eventually we got our employers' blessing and on the last day we could spend together we went to the old city at the other end of the lake. It was a Sunday, the church bells were ringing, but all I remember about Thun is that there was yet another castle to be visited, and that there was a curious old street in which the shops were below street level and pedestrians actually walked on the roofs. I also remember that we kissed and embraced a great many times, whenever we believed we could not be seen, that I was swearing undying love, and that Elizabeth promised to write every day.

The return journey was made by boat, which slowly progressed along the northern shore, past vineyards, chestnut trees, magnolias, bathing resorts, red-roofed villages, chalets and more little castles. Further on, as we approached the Beatenberg, the shore became more forbidding with high rocks. There were sailing boats and rowing boats on Lake Thun, and people swimming. A light breeze from the shore kept us cool and we drank countless bottles of lemonade. This was perfect peace; could one imagine a scene more remote from Ypres or the troubled years of the postwar period? And yet I was miserable, for by tomorrow morning the idyll would be over. Elizabeth had also fallen silent.

We were sitting on a bench close to each other, hand in hand, and as the steamer entered the canal which led from the sea to the landing station in Interlaken I told Elizabeth that it was quite impossible to go

83

our separate ways as if nothing had happened. What did I mean? Well, that I did not want to lose her. And what did that mean? That I wanted to marry her, even if I could offer her nothing at the moment, and very little in the near future. Elizabeth gave me a kiss and said that she had hoped for and dreaded this moment. She liked me more than anyone she had ever met, she probably loved me, but how could she be certain? She suggested that we should wait for a year, after which both of us would be much surer whether our decision was the right one. I said that a year was far too long; given our ages and the general situation it was almost an eternity. And so we agreed on six months, as the steamer anchored in Interlaken.

We were, I remember, the last to leave the ship. Elizabeth said that she wanted some time to break the news to her parents: 'It won't be easy and I don't want to hurt them.' 'Why would it hurt them?' I asked. 'They are old-fashioned, they live in a world which no longer exists – and you are not part of that world. But I will manage.' I had no rings, I was altogether unprepared, and there was no time to buy them, since Elizabeth was to leave very early on Monday. Being of a practical turn of mind, she observed that there was always the post office, which accepted registered packets of small valuables. So we kissed for a long time in front of the railway station, and this time we could not care less whether anyone was looking, and then we had a cup of coffee in a little place opposite.

It was the happiest day in my life, but it was by no means over. The funny and embarrassing part was yet to come. We had come back fairly early, for Elizabeth had to pack Countess Donner's things and her own, and I did not want to leave Bornemann alone for too long. I went to my room, rested for a while, took a shower, changed and went down to the hotel garden. I heard my name and looked up; it was the Countess, sitting in a corner with a book in her hands. I had greeted her in the dining room several times, but there had never been a chance to talk. 'Come nearer, young man,' she said. 'Nearer still, I do not mind shouting, but it may embarrass you. Let me look at you.' She looked at me through her lorgnon, and then asked me to sit down at her feet. 'Yes,' she said. 'You will do. Elizabeth could have done worse. I knew it the first evening. Curious thing this – female intuition, there is no accounting for it. I knew it before she did – or you. Tell me about yourself.' I talked to her, somewhat abashed at first, more coherently later, about my background, present work, future expectations and so on.

When I had finished she said: 'Well, she could do much worse. Poor girls always have a problem after a war. When I married in 1871, the going wasn't easy at all, and how many young men had died in that war?' I told the Countess that this wasn't really very complimentary to me. 'I am not accustomed to making compliments,' she said, and then, as if I was not present, 'She could marry a rich man, much older, or some aristocratic fool . . . wouldn't make her very happy.' I said that much as I wanted to marry Elizabeth nothing had been decided yet; her parents would probably oppose the match because I did not belong to their circle. The Countess said contemptuously: 'If you are put off by the parents you do not deserve the girl. You are Jewish – well, I am not blind. Would have been difficult in the olden days – no,' she said, 'come to think of it, half of my neighbours in Silesia married Jewish girls. They tried to keep it secret which was rather funny. Yes,' she said, again looking at me with her fixed stare, 'you are not stupid, you do not look like a criminal. This is about all one can reasonably expect these days. You will do.' Then, 'Take good care of Elizabeth. She is a fine girl, the best I ever had. I hate to lose her. Don't expect me at the wedding, I don't believe in these gatherings. One never knows whom one may meet. Give me a kiss. You may go now.'

I was quite dazed, but there was worse to come. At dinner Borne-mann was irritated because the schnitzel had not been done the way he wanted, nor had they given him enough lemon. Then he quietened down, and looking at me said: 'Well, you for one look happy enough, like the cat who swallowed the canary.' I thought this was the right moment, and using diplomatic language said that Elizabeth, meaning the young lady at the table opposite, and myself had reached a certain decision provided that certain difficulties could be overcome, and that neither of the contracting parties changed their minds in the near future. Bornemann got very excited; I tried in vain to point out that nothing, unfortunately, was certain as yet. To my great embarrassment he shouted: 'Don't be a fool. . . . You are afraid of the parents? I thought you had been in the war. I shall talk to them myself if you are a coward.' Then he congratulated me, hit me on the back so that it hurt, and ordered champagne; the orchestra was asked to play Mendelssohn's Wedding March, which was, of course, quite out of place.

The commotion at our table had not passed unnoticed. I got very red in the face and did not know where to look, but I had to look into many faces that evening. Elizabeth was invited to our table, and Mrs Bornemann kissed her and said how wonderful it was, and Bornemann went over with difficulty and kissed the hand of Countess Donner, and a great many people were suddenly drinking the health of the young couple. I had to shake many hands and Elizabeth, who was much less embarrassed, got many kisses. Then the manager of the hotel heard the good news and came to our table to offer respectful congratulations. He had a proposition to make: while a great many events, mostly of a happy nature, had taken place in the Grand Hotel, there had never been, to the best of his knowledge, an engagement, certainly not in his lifetime. This was a strange lapse and he was very happy that the record had now been set straight. Might he invite the young couple to spend their honeymoon at the Grand Hotel as the hotel's guests? Provided, he added as an afterthought, that it was not during the high season, when all rooms were unfortunately already booked. I told him that we were very grateful indeed, and that we were quite likely to make use of his generous offer, but certainly not during the high season. And then in the corridor I kissed Elizabeth goodbye; we had agreed that we would meet the next weekend, that I would come to see her parents, and she would meet mine.

But the long day was not yet over. I accompanied Bornemann to his suite, and he announced that her parents should be tackled here and now, and that he would teach me how to do it. He asked the telephone operator to connect him with Elizabeth's parents in Munich. Those were the early days of long-distance calls; it took an hour, and the line was atrocious. But Bornemann, who took a gloating pleasure in the whole affair, was not to be deterred; perhaps it reminded him of the days when he had to fight the social snobbery of the old ruling class.

The following conversation ensued: 'This is Dr Bornemann. Yes, the Reich Foreign Minister. On behalf of a young friend of mine, I would like to ask for the hand of your daughter Elizabeth in marriage. . . . No, this is not a joke, I have seldom been more serious in my life. Why have you not heard from her? Well, you will hear no doubt. . . . How long have they known each other? A long, long time, by today's standards. His name?' He spelled it. 'Yes, a good family. Father, old friend of mine,' he lied shamelessly. 'He is a physician. Future prospects? What a question – did you ever hear of a doctor who died of starvation? I didn't. No, he is not a practising Protestant. No, he is not Catholic – you don't want a bishop as a son-in-law. He is Jewish.' There was a short pause. 'Yes' – he raised his voice – 'I said Jewish. He was a lieutenant in the army and he has the Iron Cross, first class.' I wanted to leave the room, but Bornemann clasped my arm tightly and did not let me. 'He is a fine young man. Countess Donner? She thinks the world of him. Yes, you will hear from her. You have to think it over? By all means. Too sudden? Well, things do happen suddenly today, even engagements. You want to look him over next week? This is all I wanted to hear. And a very good night to you.' He slammed down the receiver.

Never had I spent a more uncomfortable five minutes. And even this was not the end of the embarrassment, for the journalists who had had so little to report about Bornemann's stay in Interlaken now descended on us, and the story of our engagement ('romantic' was the least of the epithets used) was published in a dozen countries, with and without our pictures. I was teased unmercifully by colleagues and friends, and for weeks I did not dare to open any illustrated weekly. The only one who did not mind the publicity was mother; I suspect she even enjoyed it.

The wedding took place the following January. There had been some resistance to overcome, both with Elizabeth's parents, who remained cool and reserved to the end, and unexpectedly with mine as well. My father mumbled things about being too young and unaware of responsibilities and unable for the time being to provide for a family. He also said that when he was a young man he had to get his father's blessing well before he put the question. (*Tempora mutantur*, when my two boys got married – no one seems to get engaged any more – I got postcards well after the event just to keep me informed.) But Elizabeth came to Mariabronn, and paraphrasing Caesar, she could say after her visit: I came, I was looked over and I conquered.

The Countess was as good as her word; she did not come to the wedding, but sent a short note, and a very valuable antique brooch. Bornemann said that he would be my best man, but a week before the wedding he had another attack. He promised he would be the godfather of our first child, but he died before Peter was born. Some of the historians of modern Europe have not dealt kindly with him; they have called him devious and unreliable. They may be right, but there was another side to his personality and I think of him with gratitude and fondness.

For our honeymoon we went to the Grand Hotel at Interlaken and were given the red carpet treatment. An enormous bouquet of red roses was waiting for Elizabeth and this time she did not protest. We were told, much to our amusement, that envious guests inquired whether we were perhaps royalty travelling incognito. The Bernese Oberland is as attractive in winter as it is in summer. Neither of us was a great skier or skater, but we went to all the obvious places, and some that were not so obvious; we ate a lot, had our lovers' quarrels and were very happy.

Eheu fugaces – almost fifty years have passed since these days, and it is almost twenty-five since I lost Elizabeth. Great was the joy and greater was the sorrow, the long night of doubt and loneliness. Gradually I buried my sorrow, but it is not buried very deep. It is only now, decades later, that I can think about the years of joy without feeling acute pain. I am standing at the window of the hotel's writing-room, and as I look out into the night I see the young men and women strolling along the Hoehe Weg. They smile, gesticulate, and some are quite obviously in love. One generation passes away, and another generation comes, and I wish them good luck. Considering the dangers and uncertainties of the years ahead, I do not even envy them. I shall take a little stroll outside before retiring to my room.

5. 1932: An Interim Balance

A man is walking through the streets of a Berlin suburb on a fine, sunny January afternoon. It is bitterly cold. He has a fur coat on and warm gloves; it is Sunday, and he is deeply immersed in thought. He has just left the house in Dahlem where he has lived with his wife and his two children these past few years. It was a memorable meal; they had goose and potato dumplings, his favourite dish, expertly prepared by Elizabeth with the help of a competent housemaid. He has to attend a meeting in town, but not until four, which means that for almost two hours he will be a free man. This is a rare luxury; he has been leading a hectic life of late. And so he decides to walk rather than take his car or the underground or a bus. He thinks best while walking, or in the bathtub.

It is the beginning of a new year, a good time for drawing an interim balance. What has he achieved of late, and where is he going? The question has bothered him for some time now – not acutely or oppressively, but somewhere in the back of his mind there has been a feeling of unease, a warning sign, telling him to be on his guard. He has learnt to listen to this voice; he was guided by it on more than one occasion during the war. He has been trained to look at things in a spirit of clinical detachment, and his own life, quite obviously, should not be an exception. But it is very difficult to observe oneself in a spirit of detachment; too many emotions are involved, and there is, too, a basic resistance against knowing too much about oneself.

The death of his father last year was a reminder that he will not be on this earth for ever. He is now thirty-four, which is to say that he has a good chance of being around for that number of years again, and some of the best years are perhaps still ahead. At his age one usually knows how far one will go – barring unforeseen circumstances. About the ultimate questions of life he has not thought since he was a boy. He is not religious, nor is he against religion; he simply lacks the religious sense. Its certainties and comforts are out of his reach. But why should he be preoccupied with these problems? Is it not unnatural for a man still young in years to raise questions to which there are no answers? Does it mean perhaps that in spite of all his achievements there is a feeling of uncertainty about the future?

It is now seven years almost to the day since he was married, and it has been a happy marriage, as marriages go. The blinding overwhelming passion has vanished; he has been attracted by other women and there have been passing fancies. He is enough of a student of human nature not to be shocked or suffer from guilt feelings. But a deep bond has grown between him and Elizabeth and he cannot imagine life without her. Relations have not always been easy; both are headstrong, impatient, easily offended, both are reluctant to admit that they might have been at fault. He is the more neurotic partner, she is the more obstinate. But there has been no lasting bitterness, and however often they quarrelled, they never let their quarrels spill over into a new day. All things considered he has domestic peace, which is more than can be said about many of his friends. Elizabeth seems to be happy, there are no regrets on her part.

Two sons have been born; one is now in his second year at school, the other in his first. He has not taken a very active part in their education, partly because he has been so busy, partly out of a feeling of incompetence. He knows from his psychological studies that the role of a distant father figure is the one in which he will cause least damage. He loves the children, but they will get from their mother most of the intimacy, the warmth and the love they need. Perhaps he is just rationalizing his fear of excessive emotional involvement, perhaps he has instinctively chosen the right way: he knows he would spoil the children and get angry with them, and then he would blame himself. Even as it is he buys them too many toys, and then he shouts at them. It is far better to leave their education to their more even-tempered mother. Education is always by example, and he doubts whether his example is what the children need just now. They seem to be perfectly normal, as loud, naughty and charming as most other little boys. He regrets that they are growing up in a big city, even though Dahlem is really a garden suburb. When he went to the forest as a child there still were wild flowers and animals; watching a squirrel in the Grunewald these days is not quite the same experience.

The boys have friends in their neighbourhood, they play football in the streets; in a few years they will start reading books, and then it will begin to be seen if they may have any special gifts and talents. Frequently they disturb him when he tries to work at home, but he cannot be angry for long; it is a good feeling to come home and to hear the noise from the children's room, to see their excitement, to listen to their complaints and see Elizabeth radiantly embracing them.

On a fine Sunday they drive out to the Spreewald, or to the Wannsee, where he taught them to swim last summer.

The man has made up his mind. He will walk through the Grunewald; it will take him a little longer, but the snow-covered pine trees are much more attractive than uniform rows of houses. And so he enters the forest, turning towards the old hunting castle and the Grunewald lake; the road will lead him straight to the north, to another little lake, and into the Grunewald quarter. Walking unhurriedly it will take him an hour, and there should be no trouble finding a taxi afterwards. Despite the cold there are quite a few walkers at this time of the day – fathers with their sons, some drawing toboggans, a few shouldering skis.

The man keeps thinking: We ought to do something for mother. She still lives in Mariabronn, but she cannot stay there indefinitely. She refuses to move in with us, not because she does not like us, but because she fears she would be a burden to us. I must persuade her to get a little apartment near us. She loves the grandchildren, and she doesn't have many friends left in Mariabronn. Relations with Elizabeth's parents are correct and cool. They visit us for a few days once a year. We have never quarrelled, but I have never established real contact. They do not want close links. They still resent the fact that I have taken away their youngest daughter, for whom they had higher hopes. Perhaps they will relent in time, but somehow I doubt it. They are certainly much nicer to the grandchildren.

He has many acquaintances but no close friends. If he were killed by a falling tree here and now there would be a considerable gathering at his funeral, but would anyone mourn him except his mother and Elizabeth? The children would soon forget, and in his circle of acquaintances he would be forgotten too, after a few months. But this is true for most people and should not depress him unduly. Some of his friends are professional colleagues, but he has gone out of his way not to limit his social life to his profession. There is nothing more boring than talking shop in the evening. His circle includes some writers and journalists, some men from the world of industry and banking, and there are a couple of younger members of the Reichstag. Elizabeth and he are quite often invited to dinners and small parties and receptions. He has friends on the far left, and some who are right of centre; some are poor and some are very rich, some are conventional, others highly eccentric. It is quite a mixture.

He does not regret settling in Berlin. He could have been the head of a hospital in a smaller town, and there was an offer from Munich.

But he does not like Munich, and it would have been too close to Elizabeth's parents. No one could possibly claim that Berlin is a beautiful city, but it is certainly the most lively place in Germany now, perhaps in the whole of Europe. Everything is concentrated in the capital: politics, literature, the arts, the press, the theatre and cinema; and in the field of science too, Berlin is now one of the world's great centres. A stone's throw from his house in Dahlem is the Kaiser Wilhelm Institute, which has collected more Nobel prizes than any other such place in the world.

Berlin is now one of the centres of the civilized world. It has not always been that way; fifty years ago it was no more than an overgrown village. It is still a young city and has developed too fast. It was the city of the Hohenzollern, but it is also the capital of German freedom, of the barricades of 1848 and of the Red Wedding, the working-class quarter. The Berliners are irreverent and snooty, but he likes their sense of humour. There is less *Gemütlichkeit* here than in his native South Germany, everyone is always in a great hurry.

The man who now makes his way through the pines of the Grunewald has also been in a hurry, and he has come a long way during the past seven years. He has never been devoid of ambition, and his marriage and the need to provide for a family acted as an additional spur. He knows his own limitations; he is not a genius but he has talent, and he has made the most of it. He is now widely known as the author of a weekly column on medical subjects in a leading daily newspaper, and twice a month he does a radio broadcast. But even his enemies, and he has some, do not dismiss him as a mere popularizer. He has published a book on recent advances in internal medicine which was well received, and several articles in the professional periodicals. He is talked about as one of the coming men. He could have chosen an academic career, but this would have involved waiting, perhaps for years; not many professorships are available these days. And so he has opted for concentrating on a private medical practice while keeping a foothold in the university.

From the beginning he was lucky, and now he has to turn patients away. Early on in his career he realized that one can usually tell in less than a minute what is wrong with a patient. But the knowledge is of little help to the patient and will not make him feel better. The patient came to get encouragement and reassurance and guidance on how to behave. Success, in short, is not chiefly a matter of diagnosis, but of approach.

He takes great care with his patients; he is never too busy to answer their questions, he has all the time in the world for them, he compels himself to be patient, precisely because he knows that he tends to be very impatient. Word has spread that he is not only a very good diagnostician but also a man of the world, wise beyond his years, and that he has, on occasion, worked miracles, which of course is utter nonsense. But he has a great influence on his patients, a power which many of his senior and more brilliant colleagues lack. He has been summoned to Paris and Amsterdam for consultations, to Rome and even to Moscow. It is still remembered that he once was Bornemann's doctor, and this has given him an entrée into the world of politics and high officialdom. He is frequently consulted by people from these circles and they recommend him to their friends. Some of them do not like Jews, but they have a weakness for Jewish physicians; perhaps they attribute to them magical qualities. He is frequently asked by senior and more famous colleagues to take part in consultations, and since he shows them due deference and gratitude, he is consulted more and more often. He must be careful not to become a fashionable doctor, resting on his laurels.

And yet, towards the end of a long working day he sometimes feels unhappy, and not just from sheer exhaustion. Occasionally he even feels a fraud, for he knows that those of his patients who eventually recover would have recovered in any case. There has not been substantial progress in internal medicine for many decades, and he is not at all sure whether there will be in his lifetime. He can alleviate symptoms, but has he ever effected a real cure? The field in which he is most interested is the interaction between internal medicine and psychiatry: everyone knows that there is some connection between the psyche on one hand and cardiac disease, tuberculosis, asthma and stomach disorders on the other. But how important is it? That remains to be studied. To be of real help to the patient, he would have to see them more than once a week and at some length, to study their psychological problems and, the most difficult thing in the world, to make them change their basic attitudes and responses. He could perhaps see thirty or forty patients this way; what would become of the others?

The one direction in which he feels real progress could be made is in preventive medicine, physical and mental, but this not a subject in which he is greatly interested or particularly competent. But even if he feels sometimes a little dejected, he will not give up his profession. He is no longer a student who can easily turn from one subject to another; he has a family to keep, he has other obligations and a certain standing in his field. He is now well paid; not remotely as well as one of the leading surgeons or gynaecologists, but he certainly earns more than he would have dreamed of even five years ago.

With all his uncertainties, he feels that he helps many patients by listening to them and giving them support. At university the virtues of science were extolled – it was after all science which made the difference between a European doctor and an African medicine man. But he has realized since that his function is quite often that of a spiritual adviser or father confessor rather than a man of science. If he has doubts about medicine as a scientific discipline, they have strengthened his resolve to keep abreast with developments in related fields. Perhaps a fresh impetus will come from philosophy, or from one of the natural sciences? It is not easy to read and to make notes after a long working day, but unlike some doctors who do not touch a book after graduation he feels that he has yet to learn a great deal. He is not altogether content, but then he has never been. But he also knows he should not complain, for he is one of the few people who find satisfaction and, of late, recognition in their work – and this at a time of major economic crisis and mass unemployment.

There is one cloud on the horizon. It is a major one, and there is nothing he can do about it. What will become of Germany? The rise of the Hitler movement seems irresistible; it is frightening how many decent people are jumping on to the band-wagon. The man is a dangerous demagogue; he may be raving mad, for all one knows. Yet they follow him; he has an hypnotic influence on the masses and his appeals fall on fertile ground. Even here in the Grunewald on a Sunday afternoon he has seen groups of the Hitler Youth in military formation, with their flags and drums – young boys full of faith and enthusiasm following the Pied Piper, the one man who will lead them into a better future, who promised to break the chains of the Versailles treaty, to restore Germany's erstwhile glory, to purge it of the Jews.

The Jews: the issue has become more topical than ever before. It has not affected him personally so far, but everyone talks about it, one cannot escape it. What will happen to the Jews if Hitler comes to power? It seems unthinkable, but he has been trained to face the unthinkable.

There are various possibilities. It is quite likely that the French and the British will simply not permit a Nazi victory. If nevertheless Hitler does come to power, it could only be with the help of others, and consequently he will be hemmed in by the old conservatives and nationalists: they will exploit him as a drummer for the national revolution. But once in power, they will no longer have any use for him. They will outmanoeuvre him. After all, the man is a mere demagogue, he has no experience of practical politics. Things may be unpleasant for a while, but not disastrous.

But there is also the possibility, however remote, that once in power he will get rid of his partners. This could be very serious indeed; but experience teaches that the responsibility of power always has a restraining influence. Anyone can utter extravagant promises and dire threats, but once in a position of responsibility a political leader will surely have to behave very differently. Perhaps it is even desirable that Hitler should be exposed to the realities of government; it will be an education for him. Either he will show that he is incompetent and ruin his movement, or he will have to stop playing the wild man.

And so, analysed rationally, things are not as bad as they seem. There may be difficult days ahead, but there is no reason for despair.

He leaves the forest where the Rot Weiss Tennis Club has its grounds, but there is no one playing today. As expected he picks up a taxi outside Grunewald railway station. He drives along the Kurfürstendamm, which is today empty of people; the big theatres are closed, one of the many consequences of the economic crisis. The new cinemas, real palaces, look more impressive than the theatres, he thinks, as he passes the Gloria Palast and the Marmorhaus. Then, quite suddenly, he sees a crowd, perhaps a demonstration; several hundred men in brown uniforms and swastika armbands are gathered in front of two cafés. Some shop windows have been broken, and leaflets are being distributed. A little man, a Jew, is chased and beaten up. Someone shouts '*Juda verrecke*'. The police make some arrests. The street is now cordoned off and the driver has to make his way through back alleys. 'What a nuisance,' he says. 'They do this now every weekend. I wish they would move to Pankow or Oberschöneweide. They only make life difficult for us. How can the traffic possibly get through?'

But perhaps the stormtroopers are not really interested in the free flow of traffic. The man has become pensive again. After a long detour the taxi draws up in a street behind the Kaiser Wilhelm Memorial Church where in a private apartment his colleagues are waiting. There are half a dozen of them, all but one of them Jews. He apologizes for being late and explains the reason. 'We shall have to live with this for some time to come,' a senior colleague tells him. 'I always avoid the

Kurfürstendamm on Saturdays and Sundays. You should do the same. . . .' The man says that it may not always be possible to do this, for all the detours may be blocked. This was a stupid remark, uncalled for and out of place, for surely there will always be a way out. The remark is received with the disapproval it deserves and they then sit down to deal with the business in hand.

6. To Leave or not to Leave

One day in the late summer of 1937 we went to see off Egon and his wife. Our ways had crossed first in Heidelberg, where he studied economics; I had not known him then at all well, but our acquaintance was renewed in Berlin in the late twenties; I became his doctor and the two families had met fairly regularly ever since. Egon lived in the centre of Zehlendorf, not far from us; he had worked first as economic adviser to various major banks and subsequently as a journalist, specializing in economic affairs. At the age of thirty he was deputy editor of the most influential economic journal in the German language. Then the Nazis came to power and his career, like that of so many others, had been cut short. Egon was better off than most of us; he had international connections, and after he lost his job he still wrote articles for economic journals abroad and prepared long briefs for British and American banks with commercial interests in continental Europe. He earned enough to keep his comfortable home in a fashionable suburb, but he was of course aware that this was no more than a hand-to-mouth existence and so he prepared for his emigration – unhurriedly, methodically, weighing various possibilities, writing many applications.

He had eventually opted for New York. He was in one way a lucky man, for unlike the rest of us he could pick and choose. And since the financial fraternity apparently took care of him, he did not have to worry unduly about visas, affidavits and other bureaucratic formalities which for ordinary mortals were from the beginning major stumbling blocks, and subsequently became a matter of life and death.

Why New York? Egon had explained to me one evening that ten years from now, quite irrespective of whether there would be peace or war, or another world economic crisis, American dominance of the world economy would be absolute. America would be the place where the action was most likely to be, and in America, furthermore, it was traditionally easiest for newcomers to grow roots; he would face less hostility than elsewhere, because this was, after all, a country of immigrants. A newcomer still had a chance to make his way, if he was any good; and this was no longer true for most other countries. Egon had married three years earlier and they had no children at the time.

They were our closest friends, and this was going to be our last visit to the house which had become so familiar to us, almost a home from home.

Zehlendorf had once been a rural village, just like Dahlem; but as Berlin expanded, as the subway and the buses extended even further from the city centre, it had become another suburb, just before the First World War. It was a nice suburb, clean, with large gardens, many trees and considerable distances between the comfortable houses. It was about half an hour's walk from our home to theirs.

With some unease we left the boys at home playing football in the garden. We had decided not to take the car. 'Our circle of friends gets smaller,' Elizabeth said. There was no denying it: during the previous two years about half our friends had gone, and of those who remained most were talking about their preparations for leaving. We had many more letters than before, from America and England, from Palestine and Brazil – interesting letters, letters of hope and disappointment, of complaint and sometimes of despair. But letters hardly compensated for direct contact, and we were beginning to feel lonely.

At first only those who had been politically active had left Germany, and some others who had a variety of reasons for fearing Nazi persecution, or had close contacts abroad and could easily establish themselves in another country. The overwhelming majority decided to stay for the time being, despite arrests, small-scale pogroms, legal discrimination, boycotts and their gradual elimination from economic life. In fact several thousands who had emigrated actually returned to Germany in 1934.

In later years I have frequently been asked by younger people to explain this suicidal paradox: why did the Jews not leave Germany immediately after the Nazis came to power? Were they struck by blindness? Had they no self-esteem, no pride? Had they lost their instinct for self-preservation? I cannot suppress a smile – a bitter smile – when I hear these questions and arguments, well-meant no doubt and emanating from a genuine wish to understand, yet hopelessly naive.

Individuals leave their homeland for a great number of reasons, but a community, tied by a thousand threads to its country, does so only when it faces a mortal danger. Few Jews believed in 1933 that there was such a danger: there had been many shortlived governments in the preceding years, and perhaps this one would not last long either. Or perhaps it would gradually mellow, like so many other radical movements. This was, of course, a fatal mistake but it is always easy to be wise after the event: Nazism was something totally new, and past experience was of no help in understanding its character or divining its future intentions. The elimination of Jews from German life was gradual, not immediate or total: some Jews were arrested, some were killed, some committed suicide, everyone was humiliated, the livelihood of most was gradually taken away. But even in 1937 the great majority of German Jews were not in concentration camps; they were impoverished but they did not starve. Persecution in Germany was a long-drawn-out agony; it would have been better perhaps, if as in Austria in 1938, persecution had been compressed into a few weeks, for this would have acted as a spur to emigration.

But even if German Jews in 1933 had all been young, highly mobile and farsighted, and had all accepted the urgent necessity of emigrating, they would still have had to face the question of where to go. It was difficult from the beginning and gradually it became next to impossible, for no country wanted Jews; there were barriers and they became higher all the time.

There was one exception – Palestine. But 'certificates' to Palestine (as the immigration permits were then called) were given only to young workers, to students and to 'capitalists', i.e., those able to raise a certain amount of money. A majority of German Jews did not belong to any of these categories, and after 1936 the gates of Palestine too were almost closed. It is easy to forget all this; hence the searching questions about the missed opportunities. And yet when all is said and done, German Jews, irrespective of obstacles and difficulties should, of course, have tried the impossible. As it was many stayed, not because they were resigned to their fate, but because they did not know what their fate would be.

I have strayed from my narrative. We are still in the summer of 1937 on the way to say goodbye to Egon, and I was depressed. 'I have not done enough,' I said, 'I should have written more letters, I should have answered the advertisements about openings for physicians in all those exotic countries.' I told Elizabeth that a colleague had just received a permit to practice in some Latin American country, and another had been invited to New Zealand. Elizabeth sensibly suggested that we should postpone the discussion, for we were already in Zehlendorf, approaching Egon's house, and the problems that were facing us would hardly be solved in a few minutes.

We rang the bell. Ilse, Egon's wife, opened the door, and apologized for not being properly dressed up for the occasion; they were in the middle of packing the books. Ilse, a tall girl in her late twenties, had been something of a celebrity a few years earlier: an accomplished skier, she had come first in the world students' games in both the slalom and the downhill. This had been in 1932 and had made the Nazis very unhappy, because much as they liked German victories in world championships they could not possibly have Jewish sportsmen representing the Third Reich. Ilse fortunately solved the problem for them by withdrawing from competitions even before her marriage and devoting all her time to her studies. She had been a student of medicine in her last semester but one when Hitler came to power, and like other Jewish students she was not permitted to sit for her final examinations. On my recommendation she went to the German University in Prague, got her diploma, returned to Germany, but was not allowed to practice.

Egon and she, so unlike each other, were a devoted couple, and Egon, who had earlier been a bit of a womanizer, became almost overnight a fanatical believer in the institution of monogamous marriage – a truly remarkable conversion. Whether Ilse would have been an outstanding physician I do not know, but she certainly was a warm, sincere, lovable and very pretty young woman. She had been born and grew up in a small town in the Black Forest area very much like Mariabronn, and I sometimes thought that my mother as a young woman must have looked and behaved like her. She was, needless to say, mother's favourite among all our friends.

For the past two years Ilse had spent sixty or seventy hours a week at intensive English and Spanish courses; she had also taken evening classes in nursing, for it was far more likely that she would get a labour permit abroad as a nurse than a doctor. She had also been continually nagging Egon to hurry up with his plans for emigration, for quite obviously there was no future for either of them in Germany. Egon did not really need much prodding, but he was a great believer in the scientific approach, always trying to calculate chances and risks. On many a long winter evening we had talked, and I had frequently been amused by his utter confidence in his own judgment. In 1936 he had argued that there was no immediate danger because the Nazis would be on their best behaviour for the Olympic Games. Now it was 1937 and he predicted that we should be prepared for things to get worse. But since German rearmament was as yet far from complete, there was no imminent threat of war. The next year, on the other hand, and the one after, would be critical: anything could happen after 1938. Hence his conclusion that he and his wife should be out of the country while the going was good; within the next few months, if possible.

I had occasionally pointed out to him that he was on shaky ground with his calculations simply because they were based on the assumption that people reacted rationally. But many of them did not, and further-more there was always the possibility of accident. He had always the same standard answer: he could not agree more, there was in human affairs always an element of accident, totally unpredictable. Further-more, what was statistically true, was not necessarily correct with regard to the individual. Chances of employment in Beluchistan could be bad, virtually non-existent. But through sheer good luck a single man or woman could still get a wonderful job there, and vice versa. But there was also a realm of probability, and this is where our trained minds should be applied. This was why he had decided to go to the United States.

Ilse looked happy for the first time in many a month. She showed us the half-empty room; most of the furniture had already been sold. Some of their more valuable and less bulky belongings were already in a big container in Hamburg harbour. 'Good riddance,' she said, 'it would have only been in the way. We won't have a house over there in any case, we shall probably start life in a single room.' But she was happy, because the agony of waiting was over and she could see light at the end of the tunnel. From now on it would depend on them whether they would make their life a success.

Egon was less sanguine: 'My dear wife is an incurable optimist, she always belittles the difficulties ahead. There will be no reception com-mittee waiting for us. . . . I have the promise of a job, but no more, and I know how much one can build on promises of this kind. I'll probably end up washing dishes in a cafeteria and Ilse with all her diplomas will have to night-nurse objectionable and cantankerous old people. We have a working knowledge of English, but what do we really know about America? Shall we ever be able to feel at home there? I have no illusions: everything will be strange and unfamiliar for a long time.'

He went on to inquire whether we had made any progress with our own preparations. 'Very little,' I said, pointing out that they were more mobile than we were, that two adults could live in one room, whereas a whole family could not, that physicians were the least wel-come of all professional people abroad; British and French doctors had thought of all possible barriers to keep out 'unfair competition'. German medicine, hitherto thought the best, or at least as good as any in the world, had suddenly become inferior, and those practising it, including some Nobel prize winners, were now people not to be trusted with human lives.

Until recently students had streamed to German medical schools from all corners of the globe, sitting at the feet of the professors, listening with great attention even if these masters were quite obviously talking nonsense. But now the training of yesterday's idols was no longer good enough, and those desiring to practice medicine abroad had to pass new examinations, like fourth-year students. And many of the foreign physicians were not even admitted to the examinations. For doctors had powerful lobbies, and they were pressing their governments very hard not to let in potential rivals.

Egon asked whether the situation was really as black; I admitted with a little hesitation that I could probably have gone to Turkey in 1933 as Nissen and others had done, but that I had missed this particular boat, and while there had been a few opportunities since there had been no certainties. Egon then engaged in a short disquisition upon certainty in life in general, and in the present world situation in particular. I listened with some irritation: Egon was of course right, but I was in no mood for reflections of this kind, and I would have answered sharply but for the arrival of new guests, one of Egon's colleagues and his wife, and a lawyer. Both couples were known to us, though not very well.

A curious mood prevails at gatherings of this kind: a mixture of fear and expectancy on the part of those about to leave, a combination of envy and compassion on the part of those staying behind. As these occasions became more frequent the envy certainly became stronger than the pity. But Egon was anything but exuberant. He, the least sentimental of my friends, was for once not only looking into the future. 'Damn it,' he said, 'you know how much I looked forward to this day, and now that it has come I am just beginning to realize what we are going to lose and miss.' Would he be able to forget the rivers, the forests and the mountains of his native country, or the foggy and wet city in north Germany in which he had grown up? One of the recent arrivals remarked that while he understood and sympathized with emotions of this kind, this was obviously not the moment for sentimental considerations; and he hardly needed to remind Egon that there were forests, rivers and mountains in many parts of the world. 'Yes,' Egon said, 'and some are no doubt more beautiful or impressive, but what do they mean to me? They are other peoples' forests and rivers.

We all had roots in this country, we are all about to be uprooted; some are more affected by this than others, but it is always a painful process.' And he quoted a line from a Nietzsche poem, familiar to everyone of my generation: 'Woe to him who has no native land.'

Our friend the lawyer dryly noted that there were moments in life when emotionalism of his kind became a luxury one could ill afford. We – all of Europe – were about to enter a period of unrest and tribulation, at the end of which one should be able to say 'We have survived' even if one has not saved much of one's baggage, material or spiritual. For all one knew, he said, many people might lose their homes and perhaps also their lives. Such periods had not been infrequent in the annals of mankind and the Jews were in some ways perhaps better equipped than others to cope with such situations; the past three generations had been able to live a quiet life, and the Jews had managed to forget that for centuries their ancestors had been on the move, and not because they suffered from restlessness. The image of the wandering Jew, once a symbol, had conveniently been forgotten. And in times like these, he concluded, one had to put first things first and forget about one's cherished belongings.

Rosenberg, the economist, who had once collaborated with Egon on the journal, said that he could not agree more. But where did the road to survival lead? He was usually a man who slept well (strong assent from his wife), but of late he had suffered from nightmares on successive nights: he was about to be caught in a giant mousetrap from which there was no escape. What did it all mean? Obviously a primitive dramatization of the fears from which we all suffered while awake. Would there be war, or would the Nazis go from strength to strength without ever having to face determined resistance? Mr Chamberlain and the French leaders would certainly never stand up to them. If so, would the Nazis in time become more moderate or, on the contrary, would their appetite grow? And how would it affect us? What should one do? 'Get out,' Egon said, 'fast.'

He had been to Paris the month before, and one evening in the home of a friend he had met some emigré politicians. They live in a dream world, Egon said, they could not accept that the Nazis were genuinely popular, that they would easily win free elections. The emigrés had persuaded themselves that the Nazi leaders were about to liquidate each other, that the church and the generals were in opposition, that the workers would strike, that the people was seething with discontent. Poor misguided people – they probably needed these delusions to keep going. He had never underrated the Nazis; if they were clever they could seize half of Europe without firing a shot, and their rule might last for a hundred years. But they were not clever, he said after hesitating for a moment, or to be precise they did not know where to stop – the old German weakness. And so sooner or later everyone would join the fracas, and then it would be 1918 all over again, only on a larger scale. It could be the ruin of Germany, but a great many other people would be hurt in the process. 'And this is why I say: "Get out." *Dixi et salvavi animam meam.*'

Outside it was still light, but clouds covered the skies and there was rain in the air. Egon's big German shepherd dog came slowly into the room, wagging his tail. Egon softly scratched the dog's head: 'He too will have to look for a new master,' he said. The question whether to dine out together was discussed and rejected; there were no places in the neighbourhood anymore where one could eat without feeling uncomfortable. Furthermore, we had left the boys alone and wanted to get home. Egon and Ilse said that they would write as soon as they arrived and that they would be on the lookout for opportunities for us.

As we were about to leave Ilse said that she wanted my advice on a personal matter, and could she see me alone for a moment. So we went into the ajoining room, where Ilse told me with some embarrassment that she had been very fond of me and that this was as good a moment as any to tell me. I gave her a kiss that was not entirely fatherly. Then she asked whether I would take it amiss if for once she volunteered some advice. 'Of course not.' Whereupon she said that I was acting irresponsibly by staying behind. It was not up to her to remind me of my duties to my family; perhaps there were reasons for my inactivity she did not know. But whatever the reasons, her instinct told her that I was doing the wrong thing, and while she was not the most obvious person to tell me, no one seemed to be doing so. Was I very cross with her for having spoken her mind so openly? 'Dear child,' I said, 'no one can possibly be cross with you.' She said that while she was very fond of me, she was not my child and couldn't I for once give a serious answer. I was very moved, because I had been altogether unprepared for this encounter. I promised that I would think about what she had told me, that I appreciated her concern, that we needed friends more than ever before and I hoped that we would meet again soon.

Elizabeth and I did not talk much on our way home. The boys were not overjoyed to see us back so early; they had eaten the sausage and potato salad which Elizabeth had left and had even made some preparations for washing and going to bed, but these preparations were not apparently far advanced. They were listening to the evening sports broadcast, and since Erich supported one local soccer team, namely Hertha B S C, whereas Peter was rooting for Tennis Borussia, they had become involved in a heated discussion, and might have come to blows but for our arrival.

'Why can't I join the Jungvolk?' Erich asked turning to Elizabeth; the Jungvolk was the younger section of the Hitler Youth, for children aged between ten and fourteen. 'Fool,' Peter said. 'But I have explained,' I said. 'You can't for a great many reasons, and in any case I am Jewish and they will not accept you in the first place, because they believe that the Jews do not belong here.' Erich, who was both bright and a quarrelsome boy, told me that my explanation was not convincing. Everyone in his class at school, including all his friends, belonged to the Jungvolk. All they did was to go to a summer camp; sometimes they would march through the streets of Dahlem, and they had nice uniforms. What had this to do with being a Jew? Anyway, he was fed up staying at home and playing with his brother. . . . I tried to explain that there were situations in life in which arguing was hopeless; there were forces stronger than him and me, and he had to accept this. He could not join the Jungvolk, just as he could not drive a car or a plane or jump from the roof of the house. 'But one day I will be able to drive a car and a plane,' Erich observed. Again my example had not been persuasive.

We had sandwiches and tea. Afterwards Elizabeth went to say good-night to the boys, a procedure which at weekends was likely to take half an hour or longer. I stayed in the living-room smoking a cigar, feeling more depressed than I had for a long time. The conversation at Egon's had been upsetting, and the last few minutes positively embarrassing. Ilse's criticism had stung, all the more because it had come from a close friend, from someone who genuinely cared. She knew as well as I did that I was suffering from depression. And since there was no time for more scientific treatment she had tried the old-fashioned approach, asking me to pull myself together. Dear girl, she was probably right, but what good was such advice? I knew myself what was wrong with me, and I had tried to overcome my dark mood without any palpable success. For unfortunately, as I had just told my younger son, there were forces stronger than me, forces with which there was no arguing, and it was owing to these forces that my professional career had been cut short in midstream.

Nevertheless, unlike most of my friends I could continue to work in my profession, and while my income had certainly very much shrunk, it was still sufficient. In any case, this was not the main issue. Again I had been more fortunate than some of my professional colleagues who had lost their university appointments and their sick fond patients; I had only an honorary university appointment and not many sick fond patients, and was therefore much less affected: I had become a consultant in a Jewish hospital and I was, in fact, almost as busy as before 1933. I could still see non-Jewish patients, though they were officially discouraged from consulting Jewish doctors: many of my old patients stayed with me and I even saw some new ones sent to me by non-Jewish colleagues.

Scientific work had, of course, become impossible. I had been asked to contribute to medical journals abroad, and in this respect too I was perhaps luckier than most of my colleagues. But there was no peace of mind, and though I tried on a few occasions to put some ideas on paper, I invariably found it impossible to finish the work. Someone with stronger nerves and greater self-discipline might have succeeded. I went on functioning, treating the sick and those who thought they were sick, but I was no longer capable of much beyond this.

Professionally I was a failure, and the fact that this was not through any fault of my own was small comfort. I would have borne this with more stoicism, I suppose, but for the general uncertainties and the worry about the fate of my family. Our situation was more complicated than that of either our Jewish or 'Aryan' friends. Their position had been made abundantly clear both in Nazi law and practice; our position was hopelessly confused because the Nazi lawyers were not able to agree. I was Jewish, my wife Aryan, and our children were mongrels, half-castes, *Mischlinge*, according to official terminology. There were various categories of *Mischlinge* according to whether they had one, two, or three Aryan or non-Aryan grandparents, according to their upbringing, according to their appearance; they had become a punch-ball between various factions in the Nazi hierarchy.

The radicals wanted to treat all *Mischlinge* as Jews, whereas the more moderate circles wanted to save as many of them – as they put it – for the German nation, not so much because they loved the Jews but because there had been a great deal of inter-marriage for the last few generations. They argued that many innocent people were bound to suffer for the lapse of some remote ancestor if the new laws were applied without discrimination. For if it became a matter of principle from which one could not deviate, why stop at punishing the one-quarter Jews, why not include those who were only one-sixteenth Jewish too? Perhaps then there might be some unpleasant surprises and quite a few loyal citizens of the Third Reich might turn into bitter adversaries.

A non-Jewish lawyer friend of mine who specialized in cases affecting *Mischlinge* and who had good contacts with the Nazi jurists told me that the whole issue had become something of a legal nightmare. Hitler and Himmler knew, of course, what they wanted to do with the Jews, but the lawyers had always pointed to legal difficulties, only confirming Hitler in his old belief that lawyers were hopeless cretins who should never be consulted on important decisions. In 1935, at the time of the discussions on the law for the protection of German blood, a true story about the absurdities of this law had made the rounds. If the Nazi leadership had its way a German father married to a Jewish wife would lose his citizenship. If the wife gave birth to a child, and both mother and baby died, but the child died a few seconds before the mother, the father would regain his 'Aryan' status. If, on the other hand, the baby died a few seconds after the mother, the father would have remained a Jew-in-law. This was clearly an utter absurdity even by Nazi standards, and the law had to be amended. But a great many other absurdities, and even more uncertainties, remained.

Erich's question as to whether he could join the Jungvolk was typical of the confusion in young heads; but this confusion was not just legal, it went much deeper. My generation could face the situation intellectually, and it had mental resources and powers of resistance; but how could one bring up one's children in these circumstances? They certainly were not Germans, but were not quite pariahs either; they were something in between, something for which there was no precedent, something well beyond the understanding of a child. A child needed firm ground to stand on, a child could not possibly accept uncertainties with regard to his or her identity, and it did not want to be different from the others.

The teachers in school behaved decently on the whole, but there was still a great deal of talk about the superiority of the Nordic race and the inferiority and the misdeeds of the Jews. Pictures of Jewish criminals were shown, horrible *Stuermer* types, and on one occasion Erich had come home weeping and declared that he would never go to school again; there had been no physical violence, nor had he been threatened, but the whole atmosphere was such that even a not very sensitive child was bound to reach breaking-point sooner or later. Elizabeth did her very best; she went to the school and talked with the teacher. Her reception was not unfriendly, but she was treated with the exaggerated consideration shown to someone beset by a serious affliction through no fault of his own.

I felt guilty towards Elizabeth and the children for having placed them in a situation which was increasingly less tenable and from which I could not extract them. There was never a hint of complaint on Elizabeth's part; if I regarded the Nazi regime (quite irrespective of its anti-Jewish policy) as thoroughly evil, her rejection was even more uncompromising. She hated the Nazis with a burning, absolute hatred; not for her the concessions ('But they did away with unemployment'); there were no excuses for the Nazis, as there were no mitigating circumstances for the devil.

She had no interest in political philosophy, but she felt instinctively what cleverer people failed to understand at the time – that what the Nazis did was not right, that it violated all norms of justice and humanity, and they did this deliberately, not out of ignorance. Her awareness was no doubt sharpened because of the suffering of her family. It is curious that I came across such absolute rejection of Nazism in those years more than once among unsophisticated people, among men and women whose sense of good and evil had not been impaired; intellectuals, on the other hand, were quite often subject to the infection of moral relativism. But perhaps this was only natural.

During all those years Elizabeth was far more optimistic than I was. As I saw it, the powers of evil had come to stay for a long time, probably for the duration of our lives. It was easy to think of reasons justifying such pessimism, for who was there to stop the Nazi juggernaut? The opposition at home had been effectively destroyed, the overwhelming majority of the German people actively supported Hitler, or had been cowed into submission. If I stayed sane at all, it was most of all owing to Elizabeth's primitive, obsessive belief that the ways of the wicked do not prosper. I knew it was not true, it was quite illogical, but her moral strength was more powerful than my doubts and general scepticism. And this kept me going, if not very well.

There had been growing tension in our marriage and it was, of course, entirely my fault. During the first years I had been exceedingly busy trying to make my way to the top of a profession which gave me both rewards and fulfilment. Professional success is not a necessary condition for success in marriage, but in my own case it undoubtedly helped. And equally when the descent began after 1933 it had a markedly negative effect on my personal behaviour. I became dissatisfied, moody, and difficult in a general way. I found a great deal to criticize about Elizabeth, and few words of praise for her, and there were recurring attacks of violent rage. I would of course feel sorry soon after and apologize, but this did not prevent it happening again.

In short, I felt sorry for myself, the feeling of impotence led to frustration and I became difficult to live with. All this was quite elementary stuff, but it is one thing to diagnose one's condition, and another, far more difficult, to overcome it. Elizabeth too would on occasion lose her temper, but on the whole she behaved with admirable patience, a patience that also did not come naturally to her. She understood me better than I did during that period, and her attitude towards me was that of a mother towards a child who was going through a difficult period; shouting and punishment would not help to reform the child, and one could only hope that in due course reason and maturity would assert themselves. I needed her in those years more than ever before, but dependence did not make me grateful; in fact it was a constant cause of resentment. I did very little to make myself likeable.

To resume the thread of my story: I was sitting in our dining room in semi-darkness, listening to a concert on the radio. I was not at all looking ahead to the coming week, and thought how different it had been even a few years ago. By nature a somewhat lazy child, I had become a hard worker in my student years, and when I was a young doctor, work took precedence over everything else. I would leave even the most interesting and congenial party at ten or at the latest at half past, so as to be fresh the following morning. And I would feel almost guilty if I had not done at least ten hours' work. I looked forward to the beginning of each new week with its new challenges and opportunities. In recent years my attitude had changed: I did my work perfunctorily out of a sense of duty, I was only too glad to get out of my consulting room and hospital, I hesitated to open my mail, for more likely than not it would contain bad news. In short, I acted like an old man and I had not even reached my fortieth year.

On that evening, admittedly, there was no reason to feel great joy. It was not that Egon and I had always shared our innermost thoughts and emotions; it has been said that few people have close friends after adolescence and I was no exception. But even if weeks would sometimes pass without a meeting between us, it was a reassuring feeling that he was a friend, one of a small circle, someone to whom I could talk about whatever pre-occupied me, and to whom I could turn in an hour of need. And now he too was about to leave, and I would be left with colleagues, mostly considerably older than myself, who felt they were too old to emigrate. For some of them I had respect, towards others I felt indifference; there was not one among them in whom I could confide.

Elizabeth came into the dining room announcing that though she had settled the children, and even extracted a promise that they would not bother us that evening, she would be very surprised if they kept their promise. For they had slept in the afternoon, and were full of energy. She had brought in her wool and knitting-needles; the pullover she was making had made only slow progress of late. Why had Ilse wanted to see me alone? I said that she had a medical question, but that it was nothing of consequence. Elizabeth looked at me as if to test me; every doctor had to be at least a moderately accomplished liar, but I had seldom been able to keep secrets from her. 'She also said that she wished we would not stay.' 'Amen,' Elizabeth said. And so I went over the old familiar ground again. She knew as well as I did that as a doctor I was welcome nowhere, and that in any other capacity I was even less wanted. All this was true, Elizabeth said, but wasn't it also true that a great many people had left Germany, invited by non-existent relations to accept fictitious jobs? What had become of so many of my colleagues, including men older or less well-known than myself? They had been helped by relations or friends abroad, and I unfortunately had neither. But what about my father's cousin in the United States, the one who had helped me during the inflation? He was dead. Did he have children? Yes, he had a son and a daughter, with whom I had no contact whatsoever. Had I tried to get in touch with them? No, I had not.

'I cannot understand you,' Elizabeth said, shaking her head. 'I once knew a young man, not that many years ago, who had various shortcomings, but he would not easily give in, even in the face of obstacles and difficulties and dangers. He would fight for the life of a patient and for his own career. We are older now, I know, and I too have my hours of fear and despair, and I am not at all sure that our story will have a happy ending. But to give up even without trying. . . .' She resumed her knitting.

'I wonder whether you wouldn't be better off without me,' I said softly. 'What precisely do you mean?' She put her needles aside. I said that it was a statement of fact; that I loved her, but the situation had become very difficult and it might become altogether intolerable. A non-Jewish woman with children from a mixed marriage would somehow be able to survive, come what may, even in the Third Reich. But I had been a burden for a long time, and the day was perhaps not far off when I would no longer be able to provide for them. I said that I would not have her go to work again as a companion to wealthy elderly ladies, and for all I knew this was not even the worst calamity facing us. I said we had to think of the children. . . . 'And what would you do?' I said that my zest for life was not what it had been. Doctors were fortunate, for they knew of various relatively painless ways to depart from this world. There were other possibilities; perhaps she should divorce me. When I married her I had wanted her to be reasonably happy. Now, older and wiser people, we knew that one felt real happiness only on rare occasions, and that it was not an inherent part of the human condition. Our hopes, I said, had become far more modest. But however modest, there was a limit below which the value of life and survival became questionable. And I for one was deeply unhappy, and worse still, I had almost lost hope to see one day the light at the end of the tunnel. 'In short, you'll be better without me.'

Elizabeth said that she hoped that I was joking. She got up, went to the window and looked out; she did not want me to see the tears in her eyes. After a few minutes' silence she turned to me and said: 'I never intended to tell you, but perhaps it is better that you should know. You asked me why I have seen so little of my family during the last two years. I have broken off relations precisely because they suggested, in a roundabout way, that we should separate. Everything would be so much easier. . . . Whereupon I asked them never to talk to me again nor to write to me. It was not easy for me to say this to my parents. What can I say? That I married you for better or worse, in sickness and in health, that even if I happened no longer to love you, it would be my duty to share your fate? But I do love you, and your children are my children. And I know in my innermost heart that this blight will not last for ever. If you mean what you say you are not the man I thought I had married. If you wanted to put me to a test, I don't think I deserved this after all these years. What kind of woman do you think I am?'

I felt more miserable than ever. I went up to her, drew her to me and kissed her. She dried her tears and said: 'Can you say with a clear conscience that you have done everything, I mean everything, for our future? Why don't we just pack a few suitcases and leave, never to come back?' 'My dear girl,' I said. 'How totally unrealistic and impractical, our money would run out after a few weeks.' 'And so what?' Elizabeth said; she never quite understood the importance of money. She had the arrogant attitude of the aristocracy: if one needed it, it would somehow turn up. For a moment it occurred to me that she might be right, but only for a moment; for outside there was a major uproar and the two boys stormed in. They looked at Elizabeth and myself and Erich said: 'Why have you made Mummy sad again? You should be ashamed of yourself.' 'I am,' I said. Elizabeth said, 'There are things you don't understand. Don't interfere in the affairs of your parents, otherwise I'll interfere in yours. You know, you should be in bed, I'll never be able to wake you in the morning.' 'But we can't sleep,' Peter said. Elizabeth promised to come to their room just once more, for two minutes.

She returned after half an hour, told me to turn down the radio and said that all things considered, we had wonderful children and that this was all that mattered. I could not fall asleep that night either; eventually I gave up and went to my study. How fortunate I was; I had married a woman of greater fortitude than myself. But perhaps she was wrong and her stubbornness would only prolong the agony? In the circle of our acquaintances, not a few mixed marriages had ended in divorce over the past few years, usually by common consent: in one case the Jewish wife had committed suicide.

I looked at my books. Schopenhauer – he wouldn't be of much help just now. Not long before I had finished reading the novel of a writer who was a great favourite of mine, and not only because he was born and grew up a few miles from Mariabronn. The hero, Harry Haller, was contemplating suicide; being a 'genius of suffering' he was firmly resolved to commit suicide on his fiftieth birthday. But for once I had not been able to follow my favourite writer; in fact I became increasingly impatient with the poor Steppenwolf. The type was not unfamiliar; I had seen people like him professionally in quieter days, people who like Faust suffered from the 'two souls in the breast', from solitude, or boredom, or who simply thought the world no longer attractive enough to make the effort to go on living. My impatience with them could be reduced to a single question: Had the Harry Hallers ever experienced real misery or danger? It was a primitive and stupid question; for the pain, the hopelessness, the despair generated from within, without any reference to the outside world, can be every bit as acute as physical pain, and imaginary fears as debilitating as those caused by realities. In a way I reacted to the Steppenwolf as Ilse had reacted to me. There was a time for everything, and this was clearly not the time for a man who had responsibilities to withdraw.

I scanned my book-cases, took out a book, read a few pages, and put it back again. Unthinkingly I took out my Bible, a gift from my father when I was a boy. I had not held it in my hand for many a day; what I had read of it in school had not whetted my appetite. One had to have a Bible, of course, it was part of one's general education. A few years earlier I had quickly read through the New Testament and found it even less interesting than the Old. Mechanically I had taken the book out, mechanically I opened it, mechanically I started reading a story I had never read before, the story of Ruth, the Moabite. After the death of her husband she is admonished by her mother-in-law to go back 'to her people and unto her gods'. But Ruth answers: 'Entreat me not to leave thee, to return from following after thee. For whither thou goest, I will go; and where thou lodgest, I will lodge, thy people shall be my people. Where thou diest, I will die, and there I will be buried; the Lord do so to me and more also, if ought but death part thee and me. . . .'

I broke down and I wept for the first time since I was a child; I had not known that I was still capable of weeping. Then I regained my composure and began pacing my study. I heard a noise from the boys' bedroom, went up and softly opened the door. But all was calm again; perhaps one of them had talked in his sleep. I looked at them for a few moments and then walked down the steps. I went to the window, pulled back the curtain and looked into the garden. Outside a new day was dawning.

Part Two

A View from the Ivory Tower

Last night we had the heaviest air raid so far. It lasted two hours, and when the all clear was given around midnight, I climbed from our little shelter to the roof. Burning and smoke was in the air, huge flames could be seen in the direction of the centre, and also in Charlottenburg and even Zehlendorf. What a spectacle it was: the red, yellow and orange flames blazing, fire engines racing along the street, the sirens of the ambulances, the searchlights in the sky and the noise of the night fighters returning from their mission. From time to time there was an explosion, delayed action bombs perhaps, or the bomb disposal squads at work.

Air raids are now becoming a frequent occurrence, and since the alarm is usually given ten to twenty minutes in advance, there is time to get to the big shelter in the nearby underground station. But I am not at all persuaded that these shelters provide much protection: in the West End there were some direct hits with great loss of life. Furthermore, in the communal shelter we are bound to meet some very undesirable people. And so it has become our habit to go to our own little cellar which had been reinforced according to the instructions sent to every household. Elizabeth has made it almost cosy; there is an old couch, several chairs, two kerosene lamps, some food and drink. I even keep a few books there, though I suspect I shall not do much reading. We have some games and a pack of cards. One could stay there for a long time; the only major drawback is that the cellar is anything but soundproof. In fact, sometimes I get the impression that we hear not only every explosion in Greater Berlin, but every heavy bomber as it approaches our city, and since the number of bombers and explosions is growing all the time the noise is really deafening.

A certain routine has developed: first there is an early alarm announcing the approach of enemy aircraft in the general direction of central Germany. They might be heading for Magdeburg or Stettin; their ultimate destination has not yet been discovered. A few minutes later, as it becomes more certain that their aim is Berlin, the real alarm is sounded. This used to be a long wailing of the siren – one of them is unfortunately located very near our house. Recently a change has been introduced because too many people mistook the early warning sound for the real alarm. From now on there will be in the first instance three short warning sounds instead of one long one. Some fifteen minutes later we hear the droning of a few planes; the pathfinders bring in their wake the big four-engine bombers, wave after wave.

The logic of the bombing is not always obvious: Teltow was one of the targets last night; and everyone in Berlin, and no doubt the chief operations officers in London as well, know that the big Telefunken plant is located there. But at other times the bombs have fallen in the suburbs without any apparent reason, and sometimes beyond the suburbs in open spaces. I remember from my own limited experience that many things go wrong in war; the weather is often far from ideal, and the British bombers frequently encounter stiff resistance – anti-aircraft artillery fire, searchlights and German night fighters. They are deep in enemy territory, and it will take them many hours to return to their base, to safety. Some of them are in a hurry to drop their loads, while others, more conscientiously, circle the city repeatedly and do not drop the bombs until they are reasonably certain that they are approaching their target.

From time to time a British aircraft is hit, and sometimes a German fighter; one spots a little flame which grows, and then after a few seconds, sometimes as much as a minute, the plane goes out of control and either explodes in mid-air or takes a nose-dive, plunging towards the ground. It disappears, and then there is a muffled sound; one is always surprised that the explosion was not much louder.

I have been watching the air raids from outside the shelter, much to Elizabeth's dismay. I have also on some occasions been admonished by our air raid warden. But Otto Jaenicke, I am sure, will not report me, and he also happens to be an amateur plane-spotter. It is not just boredom; I find the hours in the shelter difficult to bear. Nor is it really dangerous outside in the street. There have been no hits in our immediate neighbourhood and only few flying splinters and a little glass. The noise is unpleasant, but the artillery duels in 1917 were much worse. I do not believe that I will be killed in an air raid, but in other respects my insurance prospects would not just now be rated very highly.

The all clear was given at midnight, and shortly after we went to bed. Since I am a light and fitful sleeper these days I heard someone knocking softly on our garden door in the early morning. It was well before seven; in the semi-darkness outside I spied my old friend Otto. After some token resistance he agreed to join me in having a cup of what now passes for coffee. 'And to what do I owe this honour?' 'Well,' he said, 'we had an air raid last night, and I just wanted to know whether all my protégés have survived. . . . Anyway, blackout tonight is from 18.42 to 6.10.' 'Otto,' I said, 'I am not deaf. And I do read the newspapers. . . .'

He lowered his voice: 'This was the biggest so far. We got first reports from our district headquarters: the Church of St Hedwig has gone, and several other churches, old people's homes and hospitals, and the technical university in the Tiergarten.' 'Only churches and hospitals?' 'Of course not,' Jaenicke said, 'but that's all that will be reported in the papers. Anyway, they claim to have shot down seventeen enemy bombers. But the damage is enormous: emergency hospitals have been established all over town. There won't be much transport today. Tonight we may have a repeat performance. You know what they say in town? That this is retaliation for the deportation of the Jews.'

'I wish I could believe you,' I said, 'but generals do not care about losses, least of all about civilian losses.' 'How long will this last?' Otto said. 'Stalingrad, North Africa and now our cities destroyed one by one. What will be left?' I said that this did not unduly worry me since I was not at all sure that I would live to see the end. 'You will,' Otto said, 'and I think I may too, and don't forget: 18.42 tonight, and if you need me, just leave a note with the old lady. . . .'

My experience in recent years has not strengthened my belief in human nature. Otto Jaenicke has been one of the few exceptions. I first met him in 1932, when he appeared in my office, awkward and timid, accompanied by a small boy. In his strong Berlin dialect he said that we lived in the same street, that he had seen the sign in front of my house and had heard about me as a leading doctor. He was not a wealthy man, but he wanted to consult me on a matter of urgency. I first saw him alone, then for a long time I examined the boy, then the father again. The boy had been seen by half a dozen colleagues, and they had all reached the same verdict. He was pleasant, lively, intelligent and confiding, the kind of youngster one cannot help liking. I talked to him, hiding my concern, and tried to make him laugh. But I have seldom felt more miserable; is there anything sadder than to know there is no hope for someone who by all accounts should have his whole life before him?

When I saw the father later on I held out no false hope; only God could help him, mortals could not. But I said that one could keep him comfortable, for a year, maybe two. One should be very nice to him.

The son was called in again and I told him that although he would not be quite well for a long time he must not worry; he could do almost everything he wanted to, as long as he did not get too tired. Was there anything he in particular wanted? The boy hesitated for a moment, and then said that he would like to see Hertha BSC play, and that he would be thrilled if he could get Hanne Sobeck's autograph. Sobeck was the great forward player of the time, the idol of the many thousands who flocked to soccer matches every weekend.

I pulled a few strings; the medical adviser of the Hertha team was a distant acquaintance. He talked to some of the players, and they behaved very handsomely indeed. The next Sunday all of us, including my sons, were invited to the match and were given seats in the front row of the grandstand. It was a wonderful day, and when the match was over and Sobeck had scored twice, the boy was escorted to the dressing room. The players chatted to him and fed him with chocolate, and gave him a football signed by all of them. What a gift! He radiated happiness. We went home in high spirits.

The boy died the year after, but Otto became a friend and reappeared from time to time. He was a native of Berlin, and a printer like his father and grandfather. He had been a staunch Social Democrat, full of contempt and distrust for the Nazis; before 1933 he had been quite active in his party and for all I knew (these things were no longer discussed even among friends) he still saw his old comrades fairly regularly. Like many others he had been in a concentration camp for a week or two in the early days of Nazi rule, but he was not considered dangerous and they soon released him. We talked about anything under the sun, and when it emerged that we had served in the same division on the Western Front in 1917 he took me under his wings for good. 'You may be a clever man,' he said more than once, 'but I doubt whether that will help you now.' He did not have much formal education, but had read a great deal quite indiscriminately in his spare time; above all he was a man of character, of great tact, and he had the sense of humour for which his native city is rightly famous.

Otto was perfectly right: he was of great help to me in many ways. He usually knew a day or two in advance when the police would call on us, and on a few occasions he warned us against informers. I have no idea how he obtained this information; I suspect that some of his old comrades passed it on to him. The Berlin police had been heavily Social Democratic before 1933, and many of them stayed on after

Hitler came to power. The Nazis had moved into the key positions but they did not want to serve as policemen on the beat.

Soon after Otto left, Elizabeth got up; we had breakfast and I told her that I would try to get to work. 'No one will be at the hospital,' she said. 'Perhaps not,' I said, 'but I want to go out for a bit anyway.' 'Be careful,' she said, as I picked up my little leather bag which had seen better days. Elizabeth had known all along that I would not stay at home and had prepared a sandwich: she knew me too well. I kissed her and stepped out into the cold.

The first part of the journey was uneventful; the suburban trains were running, and so were the trams. The difficulties began as we came into Wilmersdorf. We had to leave the train, and I made my way on foot and then on a truck towards the centre of the town. Wilmersdorf had been a middle-class neighbourhood; many of my friends, colleagues and acquaintances had lived there, on both sides of the Kaiserallee. Much of it was now in ruins – the Wilmersdorf Rathaus, large parts of the Kaiseralle, Prager Platz, Motzstrasse. There was an enormous crater in the middle of Nuremberg Square and the underground station had disappeared. I wanted to make a little detour to see the house in Rankestrasse where I had once lived as a young doctor, but the street was cordoned off, which was not a good sign.

It is not easy to describe faithfully the specific atmosphere of a morning in early March 1943 after an air raid – an atmosphere to which we have gradually become accustomed: the hustle and bustle in the street, the smoke clouds, the acid smell, the houses and factories still burning, the streets littered with glass. Everyone knows what to do – the demolition squads, the stretcher-bearers, the workmen repairing burst gas and water pipes. They have become an almost permanent feature of our life, as in more peaceful days were the milkmen, postmen and newspaper boys making their early morning rounds. The only ones not acting with clockwork efficiency are the poor people whose houses have been hit, who are now searching for their belongings in the hope of salvaging something. From time to time one sees people weeping; but on the whole calm prevails and everything proceeds in a very orderly fashion.

Once upon a time the Reichsmarschall had announced that his name would not be Goering but Meier if even a single enemy aircraft succeeded in penetrating German air space and dropping a bomb on a German city. Many thousand bombs later, the population has got used to accepting air raids as part of their way of life: great are the powers of human adjustment. There is much spontaneous mutual help, and some of the damage is quickly repaired. If London could take it, the Nazis say, we can take it too. In any case there is no alternative; for there is no surrender to enemy aircraft. For the time being the air raids, as far as one can ascertain, are a major nuisance, but no more than that. But what if they should become even more frequent and extensive? How much would remain of Berlin and other German cities after a year of air raids? The question has begun to preoccupy a great many people.

The people hurry through the streets; there are long queues at the bus and train stations, even though there is no certainty that normal services will soon be resumed. Men and women are more than usually talkative after a night like this. Everyone has to contribute a little piece of information, and there is, of course, a feeling of elation because nothing has happened to oneself. The Gestapo would take a dim view of these conversations, but quite obviously there have been instructions not to interfere, and in any case people tend to be less afraid after a night like this. It also occurs to me that fewer civilians are wearing a swastika than even a year ago. Nor are there many children around; normally this is the time when one would have seen them in their hundreds hurrying to school. The authorities have quietly begun to evacuate the children from Berlin.

I buy a morning newspaper at a street corner and read while I walk. For once the air raid is prominently featured: cowardly terrorists have penetrated German air space and caused considerable losses and damage among the civilian population. But Great Germany will soon teach them a lesson they will never forget. There is an appeal by Dr Goebbels, who is minister for progaganda and leader of the party in Berlin, and another by the mayor of the city. The behaviour of the population, he said, has been exemplary – sharing the sacri.ice and suffering means that the burden will be easier to bear. The editorial says that the welfare of the community transcends the interests of the individuum – whatever that may mean. The words 'sorrow' and 'suffering' recur frequently; this is a new departure. There are several dozen obituaries of officers and soldiers who have given their lives for their country and their Fuehrer. One of them is well known, Eicke, a general of the Waffen SS and the first commander of the concentration camps. The fighting on the Eastern Front apparently is not going too well. German troops have evacuated Rzhev according to plan and a hard battle for Orel is in process.

There is a lot of useful advice: how should one deal with phospherous bombs? Do not be afraid, the article says, but do not take foolish risks either. Women are advised to cover their hair with scarves so as not to expose themselves to needless risks in the vicinity of a fire. Restaurants are admonished to give their clients a bowl of soup without insisting on food stamps. An edition of *Mein Kampf* has appeared in Braille in twelve volumes.

One sees more blind people than usual these days, many of them soldiers who have been injured in the fighting. If the war continues much longer there will be an increased demand for Braille literature; but will they want to read *Mein Kampf*? The papers also say that one should be careful driving a car in the dark. But not that many people still have a car, and even fewer have petrol coupons. Two thieves who have stolen property from an air raid shelter have been executed. There is a toy collection; the toys are to be kept in the waiting rooms of railway stations. The Berlin theatre season is at its height, and tragedies do not seem to be in fashion. The State Opera is putting on *The Marriage of Figaro*, the German Theatre *Amphytrion*, the Staatstheater, *The Taming of the Shrew*, and the Theatre of the People that old popular farce, *The Beloved Augustin*. The great cinematic sensation, to be viewed in the UFA Palace Zoo, is the story of the fabulous Baron Munchhausen, starring Hans Albers. I have seen it; it is certainly technically superior to any film shown before – one of the first movies in colour. There are fewer and fewer advertisements in the newspapers because there are fewer consumer goods. Someone wants to exchange a wrist watch for a doll's pram; someone else a pair of ladies' boots for two quilts. Such exchanges in kind were customary in the First World War and its aftermath: history is repeating itself. The most notable item in today's radio programme is a drama called *Kunersdorf*. But Kunersdorf was the most disastrous defeat suffered by the great Frederic of Prussia: following this battle, his fortunes sunk to a low ebb. It seems a curious choice to boost morale on the home front.

To read as one walks is not a practice to be recommended. Once I stumbled, and then I collided with an elderly lady who, quite rightly, was very indignant. I muttered my apologies and walked on quickly. But I noticed that many other people did as I did; there was a greater interest than usual in the newspapers that morning.

I reached the Pariser Platz shortly after nine. Everyone who has ever visited Berlin must have been to the Pariser Platz, unless miraculously he managed also not to see the great Doric columns of the Brandenburg Gate. The gate was built by the great architect, Langhans, at the end of the eighteenth century, in imitation of the gate which leads to the Acropolis. Eventually it became a Prussian Arc de Triomphe, and the Pariser Platz served as a reception room to the city.

It is located at the eastern end of the Tiergarten, an island of old shady trees and green meadows. With ministries on both sides, and the embassies – the French to the left, the British and Russian to the right – the Hotels Adlon and Bristol, the finest in Berlin, this has always been one of the busiest spots in town. One of the houses in the square belonged to the famous Jewish painter Max Liebermann, and we had been there on a few occasions. Liebermann died in 1935; his widow, a lady in her eighties, was deported with one of the last transports. The world was ablaze, thousands of people were dying a violent death every day; millions would die before it would be over, but on this morning, outwardly at least, Berlin seemed quite peaceful.

For someone not born there, Berlin always remains an alien place; it is a rough and tough city, not one of soft lines or colours, certainly not a city for dreaming. But it is a very lively and refreshing place even in its ugliness. There had been a hit song just before the First World War to the effect that even Berlin's air was different, bracing and invigorating, and I think there is much truth in this: one could work longer hours in Berlin than anywhere else without getting tired. When I first arrived there in the 1920s I could not envisage living for any length of time in this enormous and formless ocean of buildings. Yet gradually something in the spirit of the city captivated me like so many others, and over the years I had grown almost fond of it. I also had a certain fondness for its natives, and not only because of their sense of humour: of all the big cities in Germany, this was the one which had been and remained most sceptical of the Nazis.

I continued along Unter den Linden, that majestic street, the Via Triumphalis, the Champs Elysées of Berlin. Surrounded by elegant and expensive shops, showrooms, big banks, major travel agencies, and state buildings, this was an imposing street even on a morning when the city was not at its best, with some of the shops closed and a few windows smashed. I was stopped by a young lieutenant who had just arrived and wanted to find Café Kranzler. We walked together for a few minutes; he had arrived from the east and thought that we in the rear were very fortunate indeed; we had no idea of conditions at the front. He corrected himself. Out there, he had not been aware that

German cities were being bombed. Did I have close relations in the army? 'No,' I said, 'I have not, I am Jewish.' I added that I was not altogether unfamiliar with the horrors of war. My companion stiffened and looked at me with visible embarrassment: 'I am sorry. I should not have asked.' He then said that war was indeed quite different from what he had imagined; a lot of things happened which should not, and he strongly doubted whether the Fuehrer knew about them.

We had reached the corner of Friedrichstrasse and at Café Kranzler it was business as usual; the two coffee houses opposite, König and Unter den Linden, had also opened. The lieutenant took his leave; a nice, sympathetic well-behaved young man. He would now have a drink at the place that had been frequented by generations of lieutenants of the old imperial army. He would return to his company in a week or two. Would he still be alive in a month, or a year? Probably not, but then perhaps neither would I.

His chances of survival, I thought, were probably slightly better than mine. A column of army trucks was speeding along the street. Unter den Linden seemed to be undamaged: the university, the state library, the Zeughaus, the great army museum. Then I saw from afar my favourite park, the Lustgarten, adjoining the Cathedral and the castle. The Cathedral is of recent date and pseudo-baroque, but most other buildings around here were built much earlier, in a multitude of styles. Some are classic in their simplicity, others quite pompous and over-burdened with ornaments. There is much less uniformity in Berlin than most visitors suspect.

But then I looked to the right, and there were unmistakable signs of recent bombing. Further on, the right side of the street was cordoned off; policemen were asking the passers-by to move on, not to impede the traffic; giant cranes were moving in. The Opera House had been hit, how badly I could not judge from this distance, and the Catholic Hedwig Church had more or less disappeared. I obeyed the police; this was not a time to show unhealthy curiosity.

As one crosed the Spree, just behind the Opera, one entered old Berlin, the real Berlin, the site of the two little villages first mentioned in the thirteenth century from which the capital later expanded to the north, the south, and above all to the west. In this part of town there were no embassies and few expensive shops. This was where working-class Berlin began: the markets, post offices, railway stations, narrow streets, inexpensive department stores. A bit further on is the Alexander-platz, the square which thanks to Doeblin has a place in literature.

This was the Berlin of the Great Elector, of Fontane and Raabe, who wrote of it with so much love; the Berlin of the fish market, the Christmas market and many other markets – and there is even one remaining wooden bridge. I had often been in this part of Berlin, I had shown it to visiting friends, and even become something of an expert on it; but all that seemed ages ago. I had no more friends and my services as a guide were no longer needed. In fact, I should no longer have been there.

What little work I had left was concentrated in this general neighbourhood. Most of the Jewish institutions in the west had been closed down; the synagogues had been burned or taken over by the authorities. But here in the Rosenstrasse and the Grosse Hamburgerstrasse there still were some offices, and a hospital and a synagogue. The return of the Jews from west Berlin to the east was perhaps symbolic: it was here that they first congregated in the Middle Ages. In 1348 they were accused of spreading the great plague and the consequences were, as usual, unfortunate. For the next four hundred years there were no Jews in Berlin. A few were permitted to return by royal edict in the eighteenth century and they again settled here. Their number grew, and in the next century the better off among them moved west. Once there had been a quarter of a million; soon no one would be left.

There was a little Jewish cemetery in the Grosse Hamburgerstrasse, a secluded place, an island in the big city, with trees, shrubs and hedges; on fine summer days I used to spend my lunch-breaks there. This little cemetery was famous mainly because Moses Mendelssohn is buried there: a key figure in modern Jewish history, the little hunchback from Dessau, the first Jewish intellectual, the father of the Jewish enlightenment who, we were taught in school, had led the Jews out of the ghetto. And now, a few steps from here, the gates of the ghetto had again closed behind them. Within less than two hundred years German Jewish history had come full circle.

Grosse Hamburgerstrasse was the major concentration point for those about to be deported. It was from there that the great trek started. Its direction was unknown; all we knew was that no one had come back. Walking on, I suddenly witnessed a scene the like of which has not been seen in Germany for many years: a spontaneous demonstration.

The background, briefly, was as follows: Jews had been rounded up all over Berlin on 27 February for deportation to the east, and to the best of my knowledge it was still going on; the air raid would hardly have upset the time-table. A truck would suddenly appear at the factories where Jews worked or in front of their apartments, and they were taken without any forewarning to one of the concentration points. But somehow word got out, and quite a few did not appear at work that day; I shall have more to say about their fate later on. In this operation, about a hundred Jews in mixed marriages were also arrested. They were separated from the rest and taken to Rosenstrasse. It was apparently intended to deport them too, which would have been a complete break with established practice.

Something very strange happened now – a small-scale rebellion in Germany in the middle of the war. The non-Jewish wives and children of those arrested quickly found out their whereabouts, and began to assemble in front of the prison camp in Rosenstrasse. On the first morning there were only a dozen of them; they asked to see their husbands. Their request was turned down, but they did not leave. By the evening a few hundred were encamped opposite the gate, shouting 'We want our husbands' and 'Release our parents'. The next day their number had swelled to about a thousand and they had become quite obviously a major nuisance, sending delegations to nearby police stations and even to Gestapo headquarters.

The authorities were surprisingly forthcoming, even polite. There was no reason for excitement, it was said, nothing had been decided yet; the whole affair was being examined. But the wives were not pacified by non-committal talk: what was there to be examined? The husbands should be set free at once. After all, they claimed, the Fuehrer himself had decided that those living in mixed marriages should come to no harm. (Hitler had decided nothing of the sort, but on the other hand there was no order to deport their husbands either, and the wives knew that a bureaucracy, however powerful, which has no clear orders is a blind, headless monster which can be challenged with impunity.)

When the authorities said that the men could not yet be released, the women suggested that they should be reunited with their husbands in prison. They were told that this could not possibly be allowed, for the men were still under arrest. But Rosenstrasse was no prison, the women argued, and they were entitled to enter the building. Surely the Fuehrer would never sanction such lawless actions. . . . The officials had no ready answer, and asked their superiors for urgent instructions. Rumours were flying all over Berlin: demonstrations were taking place in the very centre of the capital, people were openly defying the authorities! Already some foreign correspondents, Swedes and Swiss, had been seen in the neighbourhood; quite inconspicuous, of course, they just happened to be passing. . . .

As I approached the old grey and white Garrison Church, I saw from a distance a crowd of several thousands; the relatives had been joined by friends and acquaintances. I knew that among those arrested were the husbands of various well-known actresses. Actors are a breed of men not normally known for solidarity and common action; there are too many primadonnas among them. But on that morning they were out in force; there had even been a delegation sent to Mrs Goering, who under the name Emmi Sonnemann had once been a well-known actress. No one knew whether she would be sympathetic, nor whether she could influence her husband who, in any case, was said to be no longer as powerful as before.

I took up a position near the church, or to be precise, I kept slowly circling it; this was clearly not a good time to attract attention. On my explorations I had often visited this church, which does not look like one because it has no spire. Opposite in the Heidereuter Gasse there was until recently the Old Synagogue, frequented by a type of Jew very different from those one saw in the fashionable west: recent arrivals from Poland, Orthodox Jews, and, above all, poor Jews. According to the official propaganda all Jews were rich, parasites and blood-suckers. But in fact for every wealthy Jewish merchant there had been five poor tailors or pedlars. Their names did not figure in the news-papers, nor did they appear at fashionable receptions. But they were the majority, the little men and women from the dark streets of east Berlin.

In the house opposite there had been once a pharmacy, and one of the apprentices was named Theodor Fontane. He was the last great German novelist, a troubadour of the old Prussian virtues. According to all the rules he should have been a favourite of the new masters invoking incessantly the spirit of Potsdam, but he has in fact become suspect. He was too decent and too tolerant a man to be quite acceptable to the Third Reich. His heroes were imbued with a sense of duty to humanity; towards the end of his days he became increasingly critical of contemporary society and its laws – he almost became a radical democrat. He has been dead for forty-five years, but he clearly had had presentiments.

In every great city there are a lot of curious people; in Berlin folklore there has existed for centuries the character called the *Eckensteher* – the corner-boy – with his hands in his pockets, watching the traffic, looking bored, attentive, scornful in turn, greeting friends, giving free advice, criticizing and joking. On that day all the male and female *Eckensteher* and a great many others seemed to be having a get-together in the Rosenstrasse. There were also a few policemen, but they tried not to be too conspicuous. From time to time a limousine with drawn blinds would make its way to the concentration point; some high official had come for consultations or to give new instructions. Part of the crowd moved on to another little street, Burgstrasse; it came to a halt in front of one of the first houses, an undistinguished office building, with no name-board or brass plate in front and no illuminated sign – the district headquarters of the Gestapo. The tension mounted, and I felt strongly inclined to leave the scene of these dramatic developments; for quite obviously a crisis was at hand, and there could be little doubt about its outcome. A police unit or S S unit would be called in, there would be mass arrests and quite likely people would get hurt – or worse. In short, the neighbourhood was rapidly becoming dangerous ground.

The sky was leaden and a few snowflakes descended. But curiosity proved stronger than fear and I continued my seemingly purposeless walk around the Garrison Church. I had watched many a crowd in my time and knew that every one is different. There is the crowd at a football game, full of tension and expectation; the crowd at a political meeting, swayed by a demagogue; there are accidental crowds, dangerous crowds and good-humoured crowds. The crowd that morning was well-disciplined but quite obviously defiant, a crowd mainly of women and children, and it knew what it wanted. It shouted in unison: 'Give us back our husbands'; there had been no rehearsals; it was an amazing scene. Poor women, I thought, how long would they last once the police or the S S appeared? The women were desperate, they had nothing to lose, what if there was a massacre of German women in the centre of Berlin in the middle of the war? It could not be kept secret for long, and what impression would it make among the soldiers fighting in the icy fields of Russia? Perhaps they had a chance after all. . . . But I could not stay, I was expected at Hamburgerstrasse.

The concentration point in the Gross Hamburgerstrasse was in the hands of the S S; there were uniformed guards in front of the gate. I produced my permit, they let me in, and I went on to the room of the chief Jewish administrator of the camp. The S S and the Gestapo do not want to be bothered with small details; the administrators are given a figure, and this was their target for the next day; there was no questioning it. Recently this had ranged between 1,500 and 1,600 people to be deported. Would the Gestapo be satisfied with less in view of the air raid and the dislocation of the traffic in the capital? I addressed the little man whose name I always forgot. He sadly shook his head: '1740.' I had again underrated the voracity and the efficiency of this horrible machine, relentlessly pursuing its aim: deporting Jews had been given the highest priority, it was even more important than sending trains with provisions and ammunition to the front.

The sad little man told me that my presence was required in the sick-room. There were, as usual, a few who had tried to commit suicide during the night. The SS commander regarded this as a personal insult; he was responsible for orderly transports, suicide is lawless behaviour and must not be tolerated; it should be severely punished. I proceeded to the sick-room; three of the culprits could no longer fear any punishment, a fourth was still alive but would not last long either. My services were not needed that day.

That night, after a dinner which consisted of soup and some vegetables, I told Elizabeth that I had asked a non-Jewish colleague of mine to examine her the following week. Elizabeth had been more than usually pale since the beginning of winter and she had lost weight; once or twice she had fainted. She did not complain – she never would – but quite obviously she was not well. I got evasive answers from her: No, she did not feel acutely ill, she was a little weak but this was of course due to the general tension. There was nothing to worry about. But I did worry.

She had a startling piece of news: the siege of Rosenstrasse had ended. The Jewish husbands had been released. The incredible news had quickly spread all over town. I told her about my experiences in the Hamburgerstrasse: little did I think when I became a physician that one day my main occupation would be patching up veins and pumping out stomachs. According to the Hippocratic Oath a doctor should spend his life in purity and holiness; and while, of course, there was no reason to assume that doctors could possibly be purer and holier than their fellow human beings, they should not use their knowledge and skill helping with the destruction of life. I had been deeply worried for months, and had decided to stop working in the camp. But how could I do this without exposing myself to immediate retaliation? I would have to think of a plausible excuse; perhaps I might volunteer for work at the one remaining old people's home in the Auguststrasse?

Elizabeth had seen a few friends in the neighbourhood, and she had stood in the queue at the local grocery. Her observations confirmed my own impressions: the summer before there had been great confidence and the firm conviction that Germany would win the war. Now there was growing scepticism, and the belief in the omnipotence of the Fuehrer was vanishing. Of course Hitler was not openly criticized, people were much too afraid. But there was universal grumbling and suggestions that there were many villains going about their nefarious business: if the Fuehrer only knew what happened behind his back! But he was busy, devoting all his time to the conduct of the war. Only a few still referred to the Jews; one woman in the queue had said that it was a shame that the Jews got food stamps at all, since there was not enough for the German children. This upset Elizabeth very much. But most of the women had been indifferent: 'There are not many of them left,' one of them said. So they did know. . . . Young people apparently still retained their belief in Nazism; they were indoctrinated in school, they did not have to queue and, generally speaking, were much less exposed to the suffering and the deprivations of wartime.

After dinner I retired as usual to my study. We had been lucky, having been able to keep our house at a time when so many people had lost theirs. But Dahlem is not very much in demand, since it is not considered safe. More and more people had left Berlin with official encouragement and the pressure on accommodation was not as great as might have been expected. I had hardly any correspondence, but somehow I never found the time to put in order my various notes and newspaper-clippings. Several months earlier, walking in the city one winter day, it had suddenly occurred to me that I might well be one of the last witnesses of a historical era which would be quite inexplicable to future generations, and that I perhaps had an obligation to collect material that had any bearing on this period. I began cutting articles out of the papers; I made a few notes from time to time and even appropriated some old files from the office.

Initially, I did this without much enthusiasm, out of a sense of duty. Events during these past months seemed to bear out my pessimism; Roman citizens living through evil days or a medieval monk expecting the world to end in the near future may have had similar feelings. Later this new preoccupation of mine became almost a passion: the feeling that I was one of the last witnesses gave a new purpose to my life. I did not wish to depart from the scene before I had finished my work.

This is not an uncommon phenomenon; I once had a patient who according to all the evidence should have been dead long ago. But he had set his mind on finishing a book that was dear to him. And so he hung on for six months, a year, two years, until the day he had finished correcting page proofs.

So I started my collection, but I knew that a miracle would be needed to save it from the general disaster towards which we were slowly heading. And assuming it would be saved, of what use was it likely to be? Future historians would be reluctant to touch the subject, and how could one blame them? For this was the story of a gigantic funeral, and most people do not like funerals. After all these years I still had to force myself to attend a funeral; it is a duty for which one feels a natural disinclination. Much of Jewish history had been a story of woe, of persecutions, expulsion, and suffering and murder; and it was probably for that reason that it had not attracted many great historians, and not very many readers. It was depressing; was it ever likely to change? I certainly did not have the confidence of the ancient chroniclers, of a Thucydides, who thought that his story would be a 'possession of all time'. Torn between a feeling of duty and a feeling of despair, I went on collecting my documents.

How difficult it is to recapture the mood of 1943! More than half the war had passed, but no one, of course, knew this at the time. I was living in a country which had once been my own but to which I no longer belonged. My very survival depended on its military defeat on the one hand, and on not attracting any attention on the other. I had succeeded so far, but my luck – if indeed one could consider it luck – was running out. Against heavy odds I had survived the First World War, but it seemed to be against all laws of probability that I would also survive the second. But there was still a remote chance, and I felt I had to try; I owed it to my family. The end of the war was still far off, and the Nazis intended to imitate the Nibelungen, bringing down everything (and everyone) with them in the general disaster.

In the hours of enforced idleness I reflected on past sins of omission: I could have left the country before the gates were closed. Why did I not emigrate? Up to 1938 our situation deteriorated only slowly and there were, of course, enormous difficulties in finding suitable work abroad. I was half-offered a job in a Latin American country but the job was vague and the conditions unsatisfactory. I had letters from friends in the United States trying to persuade me to come: No one, they said, would employ me sight unseen. But my name was still remembered in the profession, and while there would be certain obstacles to overcome it was almost certain that I would find suitable work once I appeared in person. But I still hoped for some more definite offer, and I found it almost intolerable to wait in queues in consulates and offices; it made me tense and apprehensive. It was much easier to do nothing.

And as I procrastinated the obstacles grew, and getting any foreign visa or permit became more and more complicated. Not so many years have passed since, but it is already half-forgotten that it was next to impossible to move legally from one country to another in the late 1930s, if one happened to be a Jew from Central Europe. There were always a few possibilities, but they were not above board and a man of my upbringing and my position would not consider them. Only much later did I begin to realize that my upbringing and position were quite likely to prove fatal, since they had not in the least prepared me for survival in the jungles of the Third Reich.

My generation had been educated as law-abiding citizens. The idea of not obeying the law, of being less than truthful even with regard to paying taxes, appeared outlandish and altogether repugnant. We knew of course that there were countries in Eastern Europe and other parts of the world in which the authorities could be bribed, and where, in fact, one had to cheat to survive. But Germany was a civilized country, and though 1933 had been a deep shock, the great majority of us still believed that there were limits which no legal authority could possibly overstep. We had been educated, in short, to behave according to certain rules, and I realized only belatedly that the rules were no longer in force.

In November 1938, following the famous Crystal Night, our situation deteriorated rapidly; but again I escaped more lightly than others. During the first half of November I was on a visit to Mariabronn, trying to unravel on the spot some complications that had arisen in connection with the estate of my parents. When they came to my home to fetch me I was not to be found, and the information provided by Elizabeth – that I was travelling in southern Germany – was not very helpful. The S S went away saying that it did not really matter, since they would get me in the end, and that she, Elizabeth, should be ashamed of herself for associating with a Jew. (They used considerably fouler language.) Elizabeth phoned me in Mariabronn, and suggested in veiled language that I postponed my return until it was safe to do so.

I stayed with friends in Munich for a few days, and after a week I returned to Berlin. The worst was over, the first people were released from the concentration camps; some, admittedly, did not return and others died soon after. Between November and the outbreak of the war less than a year later, there were a great many changes, all for the worse. Most Jewish associations were dissolved and the Jewish newspapers ceased to appear except for an official gazette to keep the Jews informed about new measures taken against them. They were no longer permitted to drive a car or go to concerts or the opera; many places were out of bounds to them; a 'J' was affixed to their identity cards. Every male got a new compulsory first name (Israel) and so did every girl or woman (Sarah). Some Jewish property was seized, but there were no deportations as yet. I again inquired about work abroad but by then the queues in the consulates of the few countries willing even to consider applications had grown tenfold, and there were even more obstacles of every possible kind.

We could have sent the boys on a children's transport to England, and I cannot forgive myself to this day that we did not. Again, it was mainly my fault. Elizabeth was quite willing, even though the decision to part with her children was terribly painful for her. But again I procrastinated, weighing the pros and cons, and by the time I had made up my mind the war had broken out: 1939 was not a good year for irresolution.

Once the German troops had marched into Poland, further anti-Jewish measures followed in rapid succession. Jews were permitted to leave their homes only in the daytime; their telephones were seized and they were not permitted to use public phones. They had to hand in their phonographs and typewriters. They were not allowed to keep dogs, cats or even singing birds; cameras and bicycles had to be surrendered. Electrical blankets and irons had to be handed in. Jewish schools were closed and private tuition was banned. Jews received no clothing coupons; after the outbreak of war they could no longer even buy a pair of socks. In the beginning they received food coupons, though considerably less than non-Jews, but later on meat, eggs, milk and other foodstuffs were deleted from the list. Most of them had to leave their homes, and they were concentrated in small places in certain ghetto-like parts of town. Those able to work were employed only in factories contributing to the war effort. As in the Middle Ages, the wearing of the Jewish star was made compulsory. Violation of any of these orders was severely punished.

And yet, even at the beginning of the war there were still a few opportunities to leave the country. A couple who lived in our neighbourhood left for Palestine in the late spring of 1940, just a few weeks before Italy became a belligerent; lucky people – we had a letter from them via Switzerland the year after. A few others left for the United States in January 1941, and a colleague of mine went to Shanghai the following April. But in June of that year the gates were closed finally, irrevocably, and there were not even emergency exits any more.

Then came the time of great despair: the whole of mainland Europe from Lapland in the north to the Peloponnesus in the south was in Nazi hands. Only Britain had not been defeated, but her surrender seemed only a question of time. On 21 July 1941 the Wehrmacht invaded the Soviet Union and over the next few months made amazing progress; every day there were special communiqués over the radio announcing great new victories. I never quite trusted the official figures about the dozens of divisions, the hundreds and thousands of Russian tanks and aircraft destroyed; I knew from my own experience that in war there was always a tendency to exaggerate. A single aircraft or tank destroyed would be claimed by several units, and so in the end the figure would be swelled three or four or even five-fold in the official communiqués. But many cities and whole provinces had, after all, been occupied; the Ukraine was in German hands and so were the Baltic countries and indeed much of European Russia. The United States had not yet entered the war. It was not certain that Stalin would admit defeat; perhaps Soviet resistance would continue from behind the river Ural.

But Hitler was triumphant, and seemed invincible; no one could resist him. All his predictions had come true, and those who opposed him had fallen, never to rise again. There was great jubilation and a general feeling that the war was virtually over; I well remember the reaction of many of my German acquaintances (I was still seeing quite a few of them at the time), men who had opposed Hitler all their lives, who had never accepted his evil philosophy. But even some of his staunchest opponents were now wavering, asking themselves whether they had perhaps not been wrong after all. For success is a very strong argument. All the forces resisting Hitler had collapsed, and a new order in Europe had come into being. Some were now reasoning that the very fact that his opponents had been defeated was proof that they had been wrong.

135

It was during this summer of 1941 that my depression lifted and that I came out from my lethargy. I cannot provide a satisfactory explanation, except perhaps that I was exposed to massive shock therapy. I even became cautiously optimistic – a highly paradoxical reaction at the time of the great Nazi victories. By December 1941 there were some first faint rays of hope: America had come into the war, and in the east the German military machine had fought to a standstill; there were even some setbacks. The winter, it was said, had been more severe than usual, German units had to be withdrawn from exposed positions, the front was shortened 'according to plan': this kind of language I knew from another war. Friends told me later that the Russian winter had been no more severe than any other, but Hitler and his generals had simply not thought that far ahead: they had been convinced that by November it would be all over. Now it suddenly appeared that the Russians had more reserves in men and material than anyone had anticipated. But this was a temporary reversal; the winter would soon be over, and then a great offensive would force a rapid decision.

For a month or two it indeed seemed that victory was just around the corner. There was more rapid progress and the German flag was hoisted on the Elbrus, the highest peak in the Caucasus. But the fighting was heavy, the German offensive was no longer kept up along the whole front, but only on two sections: Moscow and Leningrad did not fall. Instead, in July the army became involved in the battle of Stalingrad; and the rest of the story is well known. The general mood became far more sombre; more and more often one met people whose sons or brothers or husbands had been killed on the Eastern Front. The stories told by those who came on leave by no means tallied with the optimistic accounts in the newspapers. Victory, in short, was no longer in sight. But as far as I was concerned, and my family, the danger was growing every day.

I was wide awake now: acute danger can lead to prostration and collapse, but it can also bring about miraculous cures of the body and mind. Folk wisdom on this point is quite correct: people literally forget their illnesses, the lame are suddenly able to run and even weak people may summon up the strength of a lion in extreme situations. The last years before the war had been bad, but there had been no immediate danger to our existence. Only now, as the infection spread, threatening the whole organism, the antibodies went into action and I found myself suddenly full of energy, just as I had been ten years earlier. But there was no outlet for this newly found energy: the last trains to safety had departed and I was condemned to total inactivity. Even my old ambitions re-emerged, and it would have been only too easy for me to play a leading role among what was left of German Jewry. A voice told me that I had a responsibility, a sacred duty to help my people, for those who could have led it had disappeared. But there was another, even more insistent voice, telling me that these were delusions, that I could not help, that I would merely become a tool in the hands of those who wanted to destroy the Jews.

According to the then prevailing laws I was a 'privileged Jew', being married to an 'Aryan' who had not converted to the Jewish faith, and whose children had not been brought up in the Jewish religion either. This was a curious and illogical provision in Nazi legislation, for if according to Nazi philosophy 'blood' and 'racial' origin mattered, and not religious affiliation, why was this made the decisive criterion? Illogical or not, this was a matter of greatest importance; in fact it soon became a question of life and death. Those in non-privileged mixed marriages were treated as Jews, whereas the others were temporarily safe.

Our children had not been brought up in the Jewish faith because Elizabeth and I had agreed soon after our marriage to register them as 'dissidents', thus leaving to them the decision to opt for one religion or another, or for none, once they reached maturity. I shall soon come to the grave difficulties that faced them during the next few years, which were similar to those confronting me, but in some important respects peculiar to their own situation.

I had no ties with the Jewish religion; if after 1933 I went to the synagogue once or twice a year it was mainly as an act of solidarity, since I found it morally reprehensible to dissociate myself from a persecuted minority. Being a 'privileged Jew' meant that certain special restrictions did not apply to me. I was not, for instance, required to wear the Star of David. Sometimes the situation was altogether nebulous: according to the regulation of May 1942 I was not allowed to keep goldfish, but Elizabeth could; according to a law passed in February 1942 I was strictly forbidden to buy a daily newspaper, but it was left open whether I was permitted to buy one for Elizabeth, acting, so to speak, as her agent. These were difficult questions; the jurists issued guidelines from time to time, but the Gestapo hardly took any notice.

All this time our life was hanging by a thread. For there were powerful forces insisting that both the 'half-Jews' and those living in mixed marriages should be treated like Jews, and by late 1942 this meant deportation. I heard about these discussions in high places from an old friend, Ernst Bergen, head of a department in the Ministry of Justice. He also lived in Dahlem, and our families still met from time to time up to the outbreak of war. Later on Ernst had indicated, albeit with great tact, that there were some fanatical Nazis among his neighbours and that one of them in particular would not hesitate to denounce him to the Gestapo if there was an opportunity to do so. I said I fully understood, and we no longer went to their house. But Ernst still came to visit us, at rare intervals to be sure, alone and always after dark. On one occasion he even crossed the street to talk to me: a chance meeting, after all, could perhaps be justified to the Gestapo.

Ernst was a state official and utterly correct, and normally it would have been quite unthinkable that he would talk to me about any official business. But when I had last seen him he was quite obviously troubled by certain new developments in his ministry – things he had not been told and was not supposed even to know, but which had come out indirectly and implicitly. He was consulted from time to time about the legal status of half-Jews and Jewish partners in mixed marriages; the prevailing vagueness was anathema to his superiors, not because they loved the Jews or the half or quarter-Jews, but because every bureaucracy feels uncomfortable without clear instructions. The party radicals, Himmler and the SS, wanted a 'radical solution' to the Jewish question; but Hitler for once was undecided, or perhaps did not want to be bothered by such marginal isues while the war was not yet won.

Thus the status quo was not to be changed – Jews were to be deported, and the fate of the marginal cases would be decided after the war. But meanwhile the radicals demanded that at the very least all half-Jews and all quarter-Jews who looked like Jews should undergo voluntary sterilization: those who refused to be sterilized would be deported to the east. But the bureaucracy claimed that there were not enough doctors available during the war.

These and other problems were discussed at a conference which took place in a Berlin suburb in January 1942. The minutes of this meeting were top secret and Ernst had not seen them, but he had received some working papers concerning mixed marriages which recommended that they should be forcibly dissolved. The proposal had come from one Dr Stuckart, who was one of the top officials in the Ministry of the Interior. The 'Aryan' partner was to be given a certain period, between three and six months, to apply for the annulment of the marriage. If he or she failed to do so, the State Attorney was to ask for an annulment, and in this case both were to be deported. But the Ministry of Justice resented the administrative intrusion of another ministry, and their lawyers announced (with due respect . . .) that while they ardently wished to purge the Reich of parasites and criminal elements, the job ought to be done efficiently and professionally. In other words, there should be clear norms according to which they could act, and unless there was a clear definition as to who was a Jew, the Jewish question could not be solved.

The radicals spluttered with rage at this juridical hair-splitting, and knowing of Hitler's contempt for lawyers they appealed to the Fuehrer. But Hitler did not want to discuss the subject for the moment, and the jurists feared furthermore that dissolution of marriages involving 'Aryan' partners and their deportation would cause difficulties with the Vatican and make a bad impression both inside Germany and abroad. So the tug of war continued and no one could be sure what the outcome would be; for the radicals were, in principle, far more powerful than the lawyers; the Gestapo in any case did what it wanted.

What emerged from the hints Ernst gave me in instalments was first, that the category to which I belonged was in grave danger, and secondly, that there was a chance, but not more than a chance, that the closed season for us would continue for the duration of the war. But there was no doubt about the decision Hitler would take once the war was over. Ernst tried to be helpful in small ways, advising us what to do and what to refrain from doing. But he always stressed that he was quite powerless; in lawless times, he used to say, jurists were no longer in demand and the cleverer among them kept silent.

These bans and restrictions imposed on the Jews aimed at their return to ghetto life, as in the Middle Ages. But these measures were based on the assumption that the Jews continued to exist, and the ultimate aim was, of course, to get them out of Germany. Hence the deportations, which started on 18 October 1941. The responsibility for arranging the transports was put on the Jewish community in the Oranienburgerstrasse and the General Association of Jews in Germany in the Kantstrasse, the two remaining Jewish institutions. They prepared lists of those to be deported and gave them exact instructions, such as taking warm clothes for the road because the weather in the east was said to be inclement.

But the candidates for deportation were also told that they should not take more than they could carry, for there would be no porters at their destination. Those on the lists had to appear within forty-eight hours at a given concentration point; they were then driven in trucks to a railway station, usually by night. From October 1941 to the end of 1942 some twenty-five such transports left Berlin, each with approximately a thousand people. There were also several smaller transports, almost weekly, to a place in Czechoslovakia called Theresienstadt, for people who were either too old to too sick to undergo the hardship of a journey to the east.

On one occasion I was asked to provide medical assistance at the departure of a transport. I had to appear at Putlitzstrasse, a station I had never heard of before; it turned out to be a goods train depot not far from the Spree Harbour. I had some difficulty finding it in the blackout, and ended up in a building that had been very familiar to me at one time – the big Rudolf Virchow Hospital in which I had trained after graduation from medical school. At the entrance I asked for directions; the first person I spotted was the old janitor who had been there almost twenty years before. When I called him by name he was delighted and pretended to recognize me, though thousands of young doctors must have passed through this entrance since my time. He had come back from retirement because all the young janitors and orderlies had been drafted. When I mentioned the Putlitzstrasse Station, he gave me directions, adding that it had never been a salubrious place and was even less so today.

The station was cordoned off. At the gate big furniture vans were drawing up, unloading people, most of them elderly; there were also a few young children and some stretcher cases. Jewish orderlies were in charge and only a few SS men were to be seen; people were standing around in small groups, a few were sobbing, but they were comforted by others who reassured them that it would be, after all, only a short separation. Conditions out there would no doubt be harsh at first, but one would get used to it. Those about to depart promised to write immediately after their arrival, sending their new addresses. Despite explicit instructions a few had appeared in shoes and clothes that were quite obviously unsuitable to climatic conditions out in the east, and they were upbraided by others. Some appeared to be well-informed; they knew all about their place of destination which they said was Litzmannstadt, formerly Lodz. The men would work in construction, it was rumoured, the women in textile plants. At the beginning there would be overcrowding as several families were to be housed together in one apartment, but gradually there would be more room for all. Could parcels be sent on, someone inquired? Of course, they said. Would there be medical supervision? Yes, the usual procedures. Some had taken reading material for the journey. Several families and individuals had actually volunteered for the trip; they were unemployed, or had felt lonely in Berlin. And since they would all eventually have to leave Germany in any case, why not take an earlier train? They were perturbed by the fact that they were to be transported in a cattle train. But they thought that once the journey ended, the worst would no doubt be over.

I talked to a railway worker, who said he did not know the final destination of the train; he had been told that the cargo would be unloaded on to another train. He was unhappy about the whole affair for it meant extra hours for him and his mates, and night-shifts after that. But he did not blame the Jews; after all, they had not chosen this hour of departure.

The furniture vans kept arriving. An elderly lady fainted, and this was the only time my services were required. The mood, as far as I could discern it, was subdued, a mixture of resignation and faint hope. Some young people started to sing, but they were told by the SS in no uncertain terms that such behaviour was unseemly and in any case showed lack of consideration for the people living in the neighbourhood. Among the workers in the station there were some French prisoners of war. They were constantly driven on by their overseer, but quite manifestly were not out to exert themselves greatly. I talked to one of them who had absented himself from his group, which was not difficult in the darkness. 'How's it going?' 'Badly,' he said, 'the food we get wouldn't be given to pigs back home.' But, he said, they were still better off than the poor beggars assembled in the station. 'Why?' I asked. 'Don't you know?' he said. When I said I did not, he crossed himself, shook his head, looked up at the sky and quickly returned to his gang.

This had been in June or July of 1942. Since then the transports had continued, but people no longer vounteered and there were many rumours. Letters, it is true, were received in a few instances from some of those who had been deported but they were very short and after a few weeks they ceased altogether. According to some reports those who had arrived from the Reich were given Polish districts for resettlement from which the original inhabitants had been evacuated; something akin to a little Jewish state was to emerge, under German supervision, of course, in which they would enjoy limited autonomy. Others claimed that the passengers had simply been dumped in the big ghettos in Poland; yet others maintained that most of those deported were no longer alive – some had died from starvation, others from epidemics and the rest had been shot. But no one knew for sure.

Then, in November 1942, I heard a BBC broadcast which said the Nazis had started the systematic extermination of the Jews in Poland and Russia, and that a million or more had already been killed. But there was still no certainty; we knew from past experience that there is always a great deal of atrocity propaganda in wartime; the thousands of Belgian babies allegedly bayonetted by German soldiers in the First World War were still remembered. The BBC broadcast, which was heard by many, invoked the authority of the Allied governments for the truth of the report. But how could they possibly know all the details? Poland, after all, was a long way from London. Somehow it seemed illogical simply to kill millions of civilians, and even though the Nazis were barbarians, would they not have more urgent preoccupations in wartime? In the last resort there was only one indisputable fact: many had disappeared, and we had not heard of them again.

One morning in December 1942 I went to Kantstrasse 152, which was still the headquarters of the Association of Jews in Germany. Founded after the Nazis had come to power, this body was responsible for all matters concerning immigration and community life, for culture and sports and social welfare, and it represented all Jews as far as the German authorities were concerned. Negotiations between the two sides, needless to say, were not exactly as between equals; but the Association still had some leverage and even autonomy, and it was only after the burning of synagogues in November 1938 that it became a sort of transmission-belt for conveying Nazi orders to the community.

After the outbreak of the war cultural work and other non-essentials were discontinued, and now it dealt only with social welfare; the number of employees working in the Kantstrasse offices was reduced every month. I had been asked to attend a committee meeting in this melancholy place which, however shabby and rundown, was still kept spotlessly clean. One had the feeling of a bankrupt firm about to be closed for good, or a summer resort at the end of the season: there were still a few guests around, but everyone knew that soon they too would be gone. People with sad faces whispered and walked slowly through the building.

As I passed through a corridor I almost collided with Dr Leo Baeck, who asked whether I could spare him a few minutes. I was early for my meeting and gladly went to his book-lined room; there was a couch and an easy chair, a few pictures on the wall, and that was all. Baeck was in his late sixties at the time, a tall man, looking even taller than he was, with a fine face, rimless glasses and white hair. He had represented German Jewry on countless occasions as the president of the Association. He had no real power, but his authority was still great and most people deferred to him, though his past experience had not been in the affairs of this world.

Baeck was not a man exuding great warmth; he was not approachable or easy to know, and his critics, of whom there were not a few, said that his sermons were like a private conversation with God. I met him occasionally in the late 1930s in the home of a friend who hosted a small group which met infrequently to discuss philosophical questions. His erudition was legendary, and even at his advanced age he would get up at four or five in the morning and devote a few hours to the study of the Bible and the Talmud, to Greek and Latin authors, to philosophy and theology. My impression at the time had been that behind his great, perhaps excessive, politeness there was a man who did not encourage any intrusion into the private sphere. He was a shy person who had become even more withdrawn following the death of his wife. Nor was he a born leader, even though fate had put him in a position in which many people looked to him for guidance.

Baeck's position became increasingly difficult: thousands were looking for advice and words of comfort, yet what advice could he offer at a time when Jews had no longer any freedom of action and when words of comfort were bound to ring false? He was a man of steadfastness and character, not perhaps well loved but widely respected. It would have been only too easy for him to leave the country before the outbreak of war, for he had many invitations to foreign countries. But he had decided that his place was with his community; as long as there was one Jew in Germany he would stay. When he took this decision he probably did not know how little help he would be able to extend. But his decision, I suspect, would have been the same in any case; he was a modern rabbi in every respect, yet like his predecessors in the Middle Ages his feeling of duty was absolute.

Baeck told me that he had very few visitors of late and was virtually cut off from the world. 'Not a great loss,' I interjected. 'I do not complain,' he said. He inquired about my family and I reported to him in brief about our life in a twilight zone; forgotten people for the moment, but for how long? Baeck said: 'You live on borrowed time, but you go on hoping and so do I; as Luther said, everything that is done in the world is done by hope.' And this, he went on, was especially true for the Jews. How could one explain otherwise their tremendous will to survive against all odds, in the most wretched conditions, over so many centuries? How to explain that Job in Jewish theology had remained an outsider, that Jews on the whole have not cursed the day they were born, and have but seldom complained that God has forsaken them?

We had never discussed religion before. Baeck knew that I was not a believer even by the lenient standards of liberal Judaism to which he belonged. While my parents were alive I went to synagogue at New Year and the Day of Atonement out of a feeling of filial piety, and if I resumed the habit after 1933 it was not because of renewed belief. I told Baeck that my 'privileged' position constituted, in some respects, a moral dilemma. Instinct told me to make use of every little concession and exemption like a drowning man grasping a life-buoy. But was it right not to wear the Jewish star, was it not cowardice?

'If we were Catholics,' Baeck said with a half smile, 'I could (or could not) give you a dispensation. Our faith does not bestow such power on me, and in any case, I don't know the answer myself. If you were a leader, if people looked up to you, if you were expected to set an example, your duty would be clear. But there is not a categorical imperative binding every individual in an emergency: Kant lived in a more civilized age. And, in any case, most of the decisions will be made for you. . . . This has been a perennial debate in our history; there is a time to live and a time to die.' There were the Zealots with their uncompromising rejection of Roman rule, and there was the great Yohanan Ben Zakai who accepted that his people had fallen among low men and evildoers and saw his main task as the establishment of Javne, a great centre of spiritual learning to hand on the torch to later generations. For the Zealots, willing to die, Rabbi Yohanan was a coward if not a traitor. What does history teach us? Very little, and in any case the Romans only wanted submission; it was not their policy to destroy the Jews. Perhaps there was a duty to stay alive and convey a message to subsequent generations. 'It will be an uphill struggle,' Baeck said. 'Some will not want to hear the story of the dark years because their conscience is not clear, and mankind will be preoccupied with new dangers and challenges and problems.'

I asked Baeck in strictest confidence whether he knew about the fate of those deported to the east. He said that he had no special source of information: there was every reason to believe that those in Theresienstadt were alive and reasonably well. No one knew for certain what had become of the others. I told him that there were rumours that many of them were no longer alive. I could not mention, even to a man like Baeck, that I had listened to foreign radio stations, for this was a crime punishable by death according to wartime laws, especially if it involved the 'dissemination of atrocity stories'. But I did say that if these rumours were even partly true, was it not our duty to refrain from helping with the transports? Should one not encourage people to try to save themselves one way or another, however faint the chances of success?

His face grew dark. He said that his authority, for all practical purposes, was non-existent, and his advice no longer asked: 'But it would be cowardly to evade your question.... From time to time young people come to see me with all kind of schemes for hiding and escaping. I always cut them short; I prefer not to know the details. I tell them that I have no experience and no wisdom to offer, that these are decisions to be taken by everyone for himself, and that I am an old man burdened with various obligations.... I hope that they take the hint, but I fear they may be disappointed because they do not get a clear answer. But what do they expect?'

He said that the great majority of those remaining behind were neither young nor strong, but elderly people who had been educated to be law-abiding citizens. They could no more change their ways and settle into hostile surroundings than he could. Would it be of any help to try and save people who could not save themselves in any case? At the moment no one knew for certain what happened out there in the east. Perhaps the war would draw to an end faster than one thought, perhaps the deportations would be stopped, perhaps many of those already deported would survive.

'I told you,' he smiled bitterly, 'we are the people of hope par excellence. My Christian colleagues have always given far more thought to despair and much can be said for such preoccupations from a theological point of view. But they tend to forget that they are pastors first, not philosophers. Of what benefit will a theology of despair be for their flock? I have been rereading Kierkegaard of late' – he took a volume from the desk and read to me: 'When death is the greatest danger, one hopes for life, but when one becomes acquainted with an even more dreadful danger, one hopes for death.'

'Very profound,' Baeck said, 'but the author lived in Copenhagen and has been dead for almost a hundred years. I have been making the case for hope to you. Future events may bear me out. But what if our worst fears come true? Should I still give comfort to my people when there is no comfort? Should I be silent? Or should I spread the word that German Jewry has been under a sentence of death for a long time, and that the sentence is now being carried out? Is there an obligation to speak the whole truth in all circumstances, even if it causes nothing but anguish and torment, even if it does not help to save the life of a single human being? Perhaps there is no answer. When we were young they taught us at the Rabbinical Seminar to face hundreds of recondite, far-fetched problems, most of which, it was clear even then, would never confront us. But facing the most important decision of my life, I am no more prepared than anyone else in the community. . . .'

He looked out of the window, and added as an afterthought: 'I would be grateful if you would keep this for yourself at least for the moment. I don't expect to be around here much longer.' 'What makes you think that?' 'Nothing definite, as usual, but the Gestapo have been dropping hints and been making threats. I would like to see my daughter in America once again, but perhaps it is not to be. I am ready. . . .' 'To whom do they talk?' 'Poor Eppstein,' he said with a sad smile. 'We should include him in our prayers.' I left his room having expressed the usual wishes concerning his well-being, words that belong to a bygone era and were now singularly out of place.

Further down the corridor, people were constantly entering and leaving Eppstein's office. I had to wait for a little while, but when the door again opened he recognized me and called me in. 'You have talked to the old gentleman, I hear. He is a little dejected these days, we all are.' Paul offered me a cigar – a rare luxury in those days, heaven knows how he had obtained it. He did not look well and was even more nervous than usual. A man in his early forties, of medium height, with thick black hair, he spoke with the soft accent of his native south-west Germany which reminded me so much of home. I no longer remember when I first met him; perhaps when he was a lecturer in sociology at some provincial university, perhaps shortly after his arrival in Berlin. I faintly recall a political discussion on the eve of the Nazi takeover when he told a little group of us that despite all the setbacks it was far too early to write off the Social Democrats. They still had the support of the majority of the working class, and what could the Nazis with all their stormtroopers do if Social Democrats were to declare a general strike which, for once, would be fully supported by the Communists?

It was a heated discussion, and someone pointed out to him that a general strike was almost certainly bound to fail at a time when so many workers were unemployed and the rest afraid to lose their jobs. And how could one be certain that the Communists, who firmly believed that the Social Democrats were a greater menace than the Nazis, would now make common cause with them? But Eppstein, a man of the left at that time, was certain that we were wrong and out of touch with the masses.

After 1933 I met him again from time to time. He began his career as a youth leader; not a charismatic leader, but an efficient organizer. He gradually became part of the community bureaucracy and worked his way up to the top. A man of considerable organizational talent, with charm, genuine musical and literary interests, great drive and also much ambition, he was made head of the social welfare department and participated in most of the negotiations with the German authorities in charge of Jewish affairs. These in the early years were the Ministries of Foreign Affairs, Economics and the Interior, but later on contact with them ceased, and the Gestapo came to act as the only German liaison office with the Jews.

No one thought any worse of Eppstein at first: someone had to represent the Association in these vital dealings, and few envied him the job, which caused him a great deal of heartache and gained him no power. A year earlier I had seen him by chance just as he returned from a meeting with an SS leader named Eichmann who was head of the Jewish department of the Gestapo. He was sweating profusely, his hands trembled, he was incapable of talking coherently for a while; this was clearly a man near collapse. Some time in 1941 he had been arrested for a few days for some alleged act of disobedience, and when he returned to his desk – for Eichmann, a man of settled habits, still liked to deal with him – he was a broken man. But he continued his work and became, in fact, the central figure in the Association. According to rumour, a direct telephone line had been installed in his room connecting him with Gestapo headquarters.

Eppstein apologized for having made me wait, but said the pressure of work was greater than ever. He had been wanting to consult me professionally for a long time; he was not feeling at all well. But this was not why he had called for me on this occasion. He had received instructions to reorganize what remained of the health services of the community. The Nazis were dissatisfied with the present arrangements; he could think only of two candidates for the job – one was Dr Lustig, the other myself. He had no reason to doubt Lustig's professional competence, but for reasons which he did not want to discuss he would greatly prefer it if I accepted the job. It would mean that I would become one of the members of the executive council of the Association. But this aspect of my work need not be too arduous and time-wasting; the other members would fully understand if I chose to attend only those meetings in which affairs relating to my own department were discussed.

This came as a great surprise. I was firmly resolved not to accept the offer, but I could not think of any convincing reasons for declining it on the spur of the moment; so I asked for a few days to think about it. This he accepted quite willingly. Our conversation was constantly interrupted by incoming phone-calls, and there were a dozen people waiting for him outside. We arranged that one evening the next week he would come to my house for a consultation, and by that time I would have made up my mind about his offer.

I told Elizabeth about it, and her misgivings were even stronger than mine. I also mentioned it to Otto, who was equally emphatic: I would be able to help no one, but at the same time I would be accepting responsibility for an untenable situation. 'It is a trap,' he said. 'Do you believe for a moment that the Nazis want to keep your co-religionists in a state of good health?' It was one thing to extend help to a dying; anyone qualified had the moral duty to do so. But I was under no obligation to become a public official at a time when elementary prudence dictated extreme caution. Otto sighed – why were intellectuals so utterly naive when ever they had to face the real world? If I tried to do the job thoroughly and conscientiously I would soon come into conflict with the Gestapo. Alternatively I would simply be their tool. Either way I would fail, quite apart from the great personal danger I was likely to run into.

One evening, six days later, Eppstein arrived at our house un-announced. I took him to my study; he groaned and let himself fall into the chair, saying that he felt worse than ever. I gave him a thorough examination; there was nothing essentially wrong with him, and I told him so. And the quick pulse, the missing heart-beats, the insomnia, the occasional faintings? He was overworked and, above all, he was under great stress. In normal times one would have prescribed a month's rest and a tonic. He could still have the tonic. . . . He broke down and began sobbing. I gave him some bromide, and later a little glass of brandy (German, needless to say). I sat silently in my chair watching him. After a few minutes he regained his composure and we began to talk.

I told him that having given much thought to his offer, I had reached the conclusion that for a position in which organizational ability was essential, Lustig, an older and more experienced man, was the more suitable candidate by far. (I hardly knew Lustig, but I had found out meanwhile that he was indeed an older man, that his wife, like mine, was not Jewish, and that he had organizational experience, having been adviser of the Greater Berlin municipal health department before 1933.)

'I don't blame you,' Eppstein said, 'and I do not believe your arguments for a single moment. I distrust Lustig; he may do harm.' And then, quite abruptly: 'What do they say about me in the community?' I told him that I had never been closely involved in community affairs, and in any case hardly saw anyone these days. He insisted: 'And what do you think?' This was of course most embarrassing, and all I could do was to tell him, quite untruthfully, that I did not really know too many details about his activities, but that I certainly did not envy him.

'The details? A story of sordidness and constant humiliation.' He became agitated again. 'Once upon a time I was working for the benefit of the community. I was a youth leader, organizing summer camps and excursions. Then I tried to organize help for those who needed it most, and there were more of them than anyone knew. I took care that the homes for the aged and hospitals and the schools got their allocations in time, and I appointed qualified people to run these places. The Nazis always had the last word, but one still could argue with them, one could suggest alternatives, one could try to show that some specific orders could not possibly be carried out.'

He went on to relate in some detail how since the outbreak of the war all this had changed. He was now reduced to receiving direct orders, several times daily, and he was personally responsible to the Gestapo for these orders being carried out. 'When I began work in Berlin,' he said bitterly, 'I did some good. I knew what they were saying about me behind my back – a pusher, a careerist of boundless ambition. Well, I was ambitious, but I knew that I could do some things better than other people could. Was this a crime?' 'No,' I said. He knew that it was no crime to be ambitious, why should he blame himself? 'I blame myself, because I did not know what I let myself in for . . . ,' he said.

He told me about the meetings of the executive; no one ever openly criticized him these days, they were all most understanding. They even expressed sympathy. But deep down he felt that they held him in contempt and suspected him of cooperating too closely with the Gestapo; they thought every new message of doom was as much his fault as the Nazis'. I said that if his conscience was clear, it would be foolish to worry about what others thought of him.

He said his conscience was clear; but why did no one understand the horrible dilemma facing him daily. He had to make frequent visits to Gestapo headquarters, where he was kept standing, sometimes for hours, as Eichmann and his underlings shouted at him, insulted and threatened him; he had to keep cool and be polite and comply with intolerable demands. How much longer would he be able to continue? It was all too easy for the others to blame him, but how would they behave in similar circumstances? Would they be heroes, facing the power of the Third Reich from a position of utter weakness, reduced to saying 'Yes, of course', and 'That will be done immediately'. He did not expect gratitude, but at least some occasional sympathy.

I said that if he felt so miserable about his work – and I had no reason to doubt his words – why did he not find some plausible excuse for withdrawing from his exposed position? He was, after all, under great strain, and if he wanted a certificate to this effect, I would be only too willing to provide it.

'I appreciate your offer,' he said, 'but I know that Obersturmbann-fuehrer Eichmann will not be impressed by your certificate. Their reactions, unfortunately, are only too predictable. They will never let me go, I know too much about them. You give them one little finger, and from that moment on you are in their hands.' I said that we were all in their hands, but he waved my argument away.

'Partly I have myself to blame. . . . Perhaps I was too eager to represent the Association, perhaps I should have let others speak on its behalf, perhaps I was wrong to think that I am a better negotiator. . . . How did I fail to realize that they were not looking for a negotiator but a liquidator? Once I thought I could be of help steering the community through these storms.'

Even two years ago, he said, there still had been some hope – the war would not last for ever and perhaps in the end normal conditions would again prevail. Even now there was a flicker of hope from time to time, a chance to save something from the ruins of German Jewry. But probably it was a mere *fata morgana*, a delusion.

He talked about the transports to the East which his office had to organize. Of course they always tried to temper, to allay, to relieve, to prevent excessive hardship. But if the Gestapo said they wanted a thousand Jews, they would not budge, and if twenty on the list had suddenly disappeared, or if some had died or committed suicide, others had to be found as replacements, the quota had to be filled. He had often tried to persuade the Gestapo to slow down the transports, but they had brushed his arguments aside: 'If we can find the trains you can find the Jews. And if you can't, perhaps you and your family would like to join the next transport?' He had often fought at a great personal risk for some individual who was of particular value to the community. Sometimes he had even succeeded, but it always meant that someone else had to take his or her place.

What about the ultimate destination of the transports? He did not know. How could someone in his position fail to know? Well, this was wartime, and there were certain things one could not even ask. He tried to get as many transports as possible sent to Theresienstadt, but the Gestapo had already told him that this show-place, their *Musterghetto*, was virtually full and that only special cases could be considered in the future. How often had he tried to explain to the Gestapo that most of the Jews still remaining were doing work that was of importance to the war effort? He had even tried, despite the grave dangers involved, to enlist the help of the War Ministry. The Gestapo was singularly unimpressed: 'We'll win the war without your Jews; you do your job, we'll do ours.'

He paused for a moment. And then again: 'I am doing what I can. I'm only human. If the transports are stopped tomorrow, if the war is over soon, I shall be celebrated as a hero, a saviour. If not, my name will be cursed, I shall be the archtraitor.'

Why indeed did it have to be him? A man who in normal times would have been an efficient administrator, not a saint, not a great leader, but certainly not a villain. A man who had wanted to serve the community, not to harm it. I asked whether the leading members of the Association, or he himself, had ever received promises that they and their families would be spared. 'Never,' he said. And even if there had been such promises, everyone knew only too well what they were worth.

'How will they judge us afterwards?' Eppstein asked again. 'They will remember that we handed over to the Gestapo the list of all the Jews in Berlin, because we were threatened that unless we cooperated the SS would take over and Germany would be emptied of Jews in a much more brutal way. Our judgment may have been faulty, but we did it in good faith, we thought we were acting in the best interests of our people, and for this we shall be condemned. They will not remember that Leo Baeck could easily have emigrated before 1939, that I could have left, and most others. Some, like Seligsohn, had actually returned from America, because they felt they were needed. Why did they remain at their posts? Why did they return from safety – to be killed like Seligsohn in a concentration camp for having disobeyed some Gestapo order? Because they were careerists – or because they acted out of a sense of duty?'

We went on talking a little longer; he thanked me for having examined him and said that if he could be of any help to me, he would gladly oblige. He added quickly: 'The little I can do. . . . And probably not for much longer at that.' He disappeared into the darkness.

Elizabeth had been sitting up, waiting for me. I told her about my guest, and the reason for his visit: 'Poor man,' I said, 'he meant well, no doubt he still does. There but for the grace of God. . . .' 'A weak man,' said Elizabeth, 'he does far more harm than good. Who asked him to be liquidator-in-chief? There is always a way out.' I told her she was too harsh; could she be certain that she, or I, would have behaved any differently? She said that this was no argument; if we could not find the strength to resist evil, we too would become guilty. Eppstein was a tragic case, but tragedy did not expiate guilt.

Elizabeth had always been inclined towards intolerance whenever matters of principle were concerned, whereas my weakness, reinforced by professional experience, was to be generally too indulgent about other people's motives. One could always think of mitigating circumstances, but how heavy did these weigh in the scales? Did it mean that one should refrain from passing judgment? What were the limits of compassion? As I lay awake during the night it occurred to me that more could be said in favour of Elizabeth's harsh judgment than I had been willing to concede.

Eppstein had come to my house in early December 1942. Christmas that year was a sad affair in Germany; this was the winter of Stalingrad and the final defeat in North Africa. When I went to the Kantstrasse in late January there was greater dejection than usual. Leo Baeck and Eppstein had been arrested that very morning. No reason had been given – it was part of the scheme to evacuate all Jews from Germany. The presence of the leaders was no longer needed, and the removal of those remaining was now only a question of time. Baeck's secretary told me that as a special favour he had been given an hour to pack up, but he was already prepared; the few things he needed were ready in a little suitcase, the same one he had used as army chaplain in the First World War; and so he used the minutes that were left to write a farewell letter to his daughter abroad.

The secretary also said that she had a little parcel for me. When I unwrapped it at home I found an early edition of one of Josephus Flavius's books – *Against Apion*, a refutation of the antisemitic pamphlet of an Egyptian writer. There was an inscription from the Psalms, a well-known passage: the one which says that one should not be afraid of the terror by night, nor of the arrow that flieth by day.

On my way back home that day I had some urgent business in the centre of town and I decided to walk through the Tiergarten. On that January day the Tiergarten was white: a fine blanket of snow had covered the whole city. Ever since I was a little boy, I have always associated a snow-covered landscape with a feeling of elation, and I believe most people in our part of the world feel the same way. On that morning, however, I felt no particular pleasure walking in the snow, and neither apparently did anyone else: no toboggans or skis were to be seen and the few children around were almost as subdued as the adults. No one was throwing snowballs or building snowmen. There were no leisurely strollers and the only cars and trucks I saw belonged to the army.

The arrest of Baeck and Eppstein, though not unexpected, had still come as a shock. As long as they had been there, a semblance of continuity was preserved; with their departure, the end was now in sight. There was reason to believe that my own 'privileged' status would not last much longer either.

People in my profession witness death more often than others, and in order to continue functioning they have to develop a certain callousness: a doctor cannot possibly die with every patient. But this does not make him braver or more composed; he clings to life like other mortals. I have seen hundreds of people die in the war and later in hospitals and private homes, I have seen happy and miserable deaths, painless and horrible ones, and I have often wondered what makes some people face the inevitable with such dignity in their last hours, and others cling to life so desperately. The night before, leafing through my copy of Montaigne, I had read Socrates' words: 'What does it matter when it comes, since it is inevitable?' To the man who told him 'The thirty tyrants have condemned you to death,' Socrates replied: 'And nature them.' Such stoicism is rare in our age. Death may be

153

inevitable, but most of us still hope – frequently against hope – for a postponement. I for one would certainly have given a great deal to see the thirty tyrants go before I did. . . .

By any rational reckoning my prospects for survival seemed dim on that morning; yet our moods, as is well-known, are not determined by cool analysis of our situation and prospects. We know so much about human beings and yet so little; objective circumstances do not change, yet our moods do. As I walked through the snow in the Tiergarten I was telling myself that with so many of my friends gone life would hardly be worth living. Survival, in any case, hardly depended any longer on what I did or did not do, since I was no more than a minute particle in a world which had gone raving mad. But then it occurred to me that even in the world of physics accident has a role to play, and the fate of minute particles cannot be predicted. Perhaps I did have a chance after all, and if I had been spared so far, perhaps this was not the time to surrender; perhaps one should hold out a little longer, even if only to defy those who wanted my destruction. 'My destruction' – why should I be so preoccupied with my own fate in the face of this enormous tragedy? But why not, I told myself; do people react differently when their ship is about to sink? They may eventually decide that life is no longer worth living with so many of those close to them gone. But this is hardly ever their first reaction.

I must have been walking for a long time, oblivious of my surroundings. As I crossed the street a car screeched to a halt, and the driver shouted at me. I had had a lucky escape – a good omen perhaps? I was now in the Victory Alley, that broad north-south axis lined by the monstrous sculptures of the Prussian and Brandenburgian rulers of several centuries. This led to a built-up area, where most of the ministries were concentrated. In front of nearly every building policemen or soldiers were on guard, freezing in the cold. There was Hermann Goering Strasse, leading to one of the most important and best-known streets in the city, the Wilhelmstrasse. The huge department stores such as Wertheim and Tietz, now renamed, were in this neighbourhood. Students of architecture still came to see the Wertheim building which, completed in the 1890s, was a landmark in modern architecture because of the liberal use made of iron, glass and limestone. In the distance the great hotel, the Kaiserhof, could be seen; Hitler, Goebbels and their assistants had their headquarters there before they took over in 1933. Once the place had been swarming with foreign visitors; who, I wondered, was staying there now?

The Wilhelmstrasse is Berlin's most heavily guarded street; one does not linger there unless one wishes to attract attention. One walks, neither too slowly nor too fast. It had taken me quite a while to relearn to move normally and inconspicuously in this city. I had become self-conscious, which was dangerous in dark times like these. It was vitally important to look straight at other people, not inquisitively of course, but normally, as if one had nothing to hide, as if one were in no way different from the rest of the crowd. I had been told that the security forces took a special interest in people looking down as they walked along the street. . . .

I passed the Chancellery, the office of the President. Hitler no longer resided there; he was running the war from his headquarters some-where in the East, in the Ukraine according to rumour. Next to it was the Ministry of Foreign Affairs, once as busy as a beehive but now a desolate place, for Germany had no longer many foreign affairs – there were only enemies or satellites. But there was still some coming and going, and big limousines were parked outside. Suddenly I heard my name being called. I turned round and saw a man just about to get into one of the chauffeur-driven cars. The face was vaguely familiar. 'How nice to see you again. I would never have thought . . .' he stopped in mid-sentence.

It took me a few seconds to recognize him, but his voice gave him away. It was Dr Abegg, who had worked with me at Riemwalds clinic some twenty years ago. We had shared many a difficult night at work, and we had explored Berlin together; both of us were then newcomers to the capital. He was a profoundly decent man, always good-humoured, a good comrade, a man to be trusted. I had always regretted that we lost contact after he returned to his native Zürich, though I had met him once or twice at medical conventions and had seen his name men-tioned in a professional journal. But then for years I heard nothing of him; someone had mentioned that he was no longer practising medicine and had become a diplomat of sorts.

Abegg asked whether I was in a great hurry; he had to deliver an urgent letter to the Swiss Embassy but would be free after that. I got into the limousine and he began to ask me questions about myself. I said, 'It's a long story, I don't really know where to begin,' nodding my head in the direction of the driver. He said, 'Yes, we shall have plenty of time later on. . . .' The Swiss Embassy was in the Bismarck-strasse in those days, a mere stone's throw from the Victory Column which I had passed earlier that morning. He delivered his letter while

I waited, and then we walked round and round the column, up and down to the Spree, and when we got too cold we went to a nearby coffee house.

Abegg told me he had joined the International Red Cross some five years ago; he was now one of the leading figures in the organization, and was in Berlin on official business. He had been to the Foreign Ministry in connection with some problems that had arisen over the care of German prisoners of war in British hands. Abegg wanted to know what had become of several of our contemporaries with whom we had worked in the 1920s. I could give him some news of them, but it was not up to date since many of them were presumably now in the army. By mere chance I had seen an obituary of Generalarzt Kraus in the *Voelkische Beobachter* a few weeks earlier. 'Poor Kraus,' Abegg said. 'A good doctor and a great busybody who wanted to get to the top quickly. He had his hour of glory....' He then asked about my own doings in recent years: 'I heard you were not doing badly at one time.'

I told him briefly about my work and my family up to the outbreak of the war. 'The rest you can imagine.' 'Why didn't you leave while you could?' I explained, but my explanation did not satisfy him: 'You know, you could have been helped. Like Roland at Roncevalles you refused to blow the horn while you would be heard. And now....' I wanted to explain to him that I had not refused out of pride; but would he have understood? We walked on for a few minutes in silence. He then began to tell me about his work.

I found him exceedingly well informed about conditions inside Germany. He told me that in his view Germany had lost the war, but that my people and his were still in mortal danger. I am summarizing now a fairly long conversation; Abegg moreover chose his words carefully as befitted a diplomat – obviously this had become second nature with him. Switzerland, he said, was bitterly criticized for not having done more to provide asylum for refugees, and perhaps a little more could have been done. But it was a small country, an island in a continent dominated by the Germans. Until recently, there had been at least one partly open border – that with Vichy France. But Vichy too had now been occupied, and the Swiss authorities had to be very careful not to offend the Germans, who were constantly lodging complaints and protests. Almost the whole male population of the country was kept under arms.

He again fell silent; something seemed to be bothering him, as if an idea had occurred to him and he was hesitating whether to take me in his confidence. I asked whether he knew anything about the transports of Jews from Germany and their ultimate destination. 'Nothing definite,' he said, except what he had read in newspapers outside Germany. The Red Cross was not dealing with civilians – only with prisoners of war, and only with those from countries which were signatories to the Geneva Convention. And what had he heard unofficially? Again he was silent for a minute or two. And then: 'Only rumours, but the rumours are disquieting. Our emissaries are not usually permitted to travel in Eastern Europe, even under escort. But others have. Does the name Rudolf Hauber mean anything to you?' I had never heard of him. 'It doesn't matter,' Abegg said, 'he is a colleague, a well-known doctor in Zürich whom I have known for years.'

Hauber, it transpired, was a member of a Swiss medical delegation which was permitted to visit the Eastern Front. And he saw things which quite obviously he should not have seen; even German controls are not infallible. He saw executions and he heard from German doctors that mass gassing had begun. On his return he reported his findings to his superiors in the army, and also gave lectures to invited audiences. He was threatened with expulsion from the army, having acted in contravention of Article 16 of the army code which refers to the oath of silence. But by that time thousands had heard his account, and the newspapers, sometimes in defiance of the censorship, had begun to publish stories about the transports last September. But Hauber was not the only one. Sergeant Blaetter, who was the driver of a second medical delegation to the East, had even more horrible stories to tell. He had written a book, but it was doubtful whether it would appear.

There had been news from other sources: a few prisoners of war had escaped, and they had been interrogated. Some seriously injured prisoners of war had been exchanged in Constance, and they too had stories to tell. 'Then there was the affair of the Red Cross letters in which we were directly involved.' I professed ignorance. He again paused and then said: 'I should not tell you, it may endanger the success of other operations. Like Hauber, I too am breaking my oath.'

He then explained that from the beginning of the war the Red Cross, with the permission of the belligerents, had provided a postal service by means of special forms in which short messages of up to twenty-five words could be exchanged between citizens of countries at war. These messages took weeks, sometimes months, to reach their destination. This service had worked well until last autumn, when thousands of messages had referred to the resettlement of Jews not only from Germany, but also from France, Holland and other countries in Western Europe. Since then the messages had virtually dried up. The Red Cross had frequently been asked to investigate, but it could not of course do so. They had, with great caution and strictly unofficially, tried to make inquiries but there had been a blank wall of silence. There were implausible explanations: 'Postal services in Eastern Europe do not function well.' Either the officials in the German Foreign Ministry knew nothing or, more likely, they had orders to keep their mouths shut. And since the Swiss ambassador in Berlin was against asking the Germans embarrassing questions, there had been no further explorations.

What had emerged from the interrogation of those who escaped or been repatriated? 'Something is certainly happening,' he said, 'and on a vast scale at that. The evidence is not conclusive, of course; we know that ten of thousands are living in Theresienstadt, and we may in fact be invited to go there.' But it had also been reported that most Jews from Central and Western Europe had been taken to huge concentration camps. He had read the conflicting evidence provided by two Jehovah's Witnesses from Holland who had recently been released from one of the biggest of these camps, Auschwitz, near the Polish-German border. One of them had given specific details about the gassing and burning of thousands of Jews; the chimneys in the camps were working day and night, and could be seen at a distance of many miles. But the other had declared equally categorically that he had seen nothing of the sort; this was a labour camp; leading German factories had established branches in the camps, and the chimneys were apparently serving industrial plants. And what about the horrible stench of burnt human flesh which the other had noticed? There was a stench, he said, but it was more like burnt rubber. . . . What was one to believe?

We had talked for a long time, and had meanwhile reached Unter den Linden again. Before we parted he said that our meeting had confronted him with something of a dilemma. He fully understood my plight and the dangers ahead, and he deeply sympathized; but in his official capacity he could do nothing, and as a private citizen next to nothing. I had to understand. I understood. He then asked me to memorize the name and address of a close friend of his in Basel, who was perhaps in a better position. . . . A better position to do what? He did not answer my question, but said that we had been followed for the past half-hour. 'Don't turn around, there is a man in a brown over-coat and a folded newspaper under his arm. They won't arrest me, and in any case this will be my last mission to Germany; I am about to be transferred to another post. And they will not arrest you either while we are together. They probably don't know who you are, and we should be able to shake him off.'

I was not too worried; darkness came early on those winter days, and the blackout would make pursuit next to impossible. We went into a department store, mingling with a big throng of people; as we stepped into the elevator, I saw the man in the brown coat trying to push his way through the crowd. He made himself rather unpopular, and in any case he did not get to us; the elevator was full. We parted on the third floor. I made my way down the stairs, and regained the street through the emergency exit. It was by now quite dark; the blackout certainly had its advantages.

I arrived home late. Elizabeth was agitated; she had been worrying again. I told her over dinner about the events in the Kantstrasse and what Abegg had told me. She said she was saddened but not surprised. How could people like Baeck, or Eppstein or indeed her husband, so much cleverer than herself, have nursed any illusions? I casually mentioned that Abegg had given me the name and address of an acquaintance in Basel. 'An acquaintance in Switzerland?' She thought for a moment, and then said that this could only mean that the friend was either a courier or a *passeur*, or he at least knew one. 'What is a *passeur*?' I asked in astonishment. 'Someone smuggling human beings, though he may on occasion also take alcohol or coffee.' 'How did you come to hear of these things?' 'I just know,' she said impatiently. 'A man in Abegg's position does nothing without a purpose. He has to be careful of course. . . . But we ought to pursue the lead.'

I told her that she was carried away by false hopes; there was no smuggling these days, certainly not across a border so well guarded as the one between Germany and Switzerland. 'We have nothing to lose,' she said. 'How do you know the border is so well guarded? I shall write a letter right away.' And that very night she wrote to a perfect stranger saying that she was very glad to have heard from him again through a mutual friend who had passed through Berlin, that she was very well, but that a relation in Freiburg was dangerously ill and she would soon have to visit him; perhaps a meeting could be arranged on that occasion. She would be most grateful to hear from him soon. To me it made no sense.

A few weeks later, in mid-February, we were invited to dinner by one of Elizabeth's cousins, Joachim von Trostenburg. This came as a surprise for a variety of reasons; people were no longer entertaining – we had not been asked out by anyone for almost a year. Trostenburg was a professional army officer who had been pensioned off the year before. It was most unusual for an officer of his rank who had not reached retirement age to leave active service in time of war. There was quite obviously a reason, but no one had told us what it was – which was not surprising since I hardly knew him. He had been to our wedding all those years ago, but since then we had not seen him more than three or four times, and since the outbreak of war, needless to say, there had been no contact at all. Elizabeth had been to their house once, to express her condolences when their younger son, a parachutist, had been killed during the fighting in Crete in 1941.

I was incredulous, and interrogated Elizabeth; had she understood rightly? Trostenburg had never shown particular friendliness towards us. Yes, they expected us on Thursday night. He had also said that we must not have exaggerated hopes as far as the dinner was concerned. Those had been his very words, as far as she could recall. Would there be anyone else there – after all, this could be quite embarrassing. . . . 'Leave it to Joachim,' she said, 'he is no fool.' It would be even more embarrassing not to go.

So we went to his little villa in the Grunewald, a neighbourhood I had once known only too well. Trostenburg opened the door, greeted us and helped us out of our coats. He explained that they had no domestic help; a woman came twice a week to help clean the house. His wife Elsa loved cooking, and he hated having unfamiliar faces snooping round the house. One never knew who one was dealing with these days.

Elsa joined us, a friendly, grey-haired, motherly woman in her early fifties. We had drinks and we had dinner and we talked. Elizabeth and Joachim chatted about family matters; later on the effects of war on our daily lives were discussed. I tried to broach the question of his retirement from the army, but the general was in no mood to discuss the subject: there had been legitimate differences of opinion, a quite natural thing to happen when people worked together under stress. Their elder son, already a major, had recently been on leave from the Eastern Front. The general was working on a study of military history, or more precisely, on a long essay trying to prove that the study of military history was still of relevance to contemporary strategy – a proposition denied, he said, by some of his younger colleagues.

It was all very civilized, but also somewhat unreal. They seemed not to be particularly interested in our affairs. Why had they asked us to dinner? As we finished the dessert, he said he would make the coffee himself, and asked the ladies to excuse their husbands – we would retire to his study for a little while.

Fom the kitchen I followed him down a corridor. It was a typical officer's home, hung with war relics such as sabres and pistols, some dating back two or three generations, medals and decorations, a few pictures, enormous antlers – Joachim was a passionate hunter. He drew his chair closer to the fireplace and after a short pause, looking into the fire, said that he owed me an explanation. He would be blunt: he had not been educated to talk diplomatically. I would have to forgive him for his outspokenness as well as for the fact that his story would be neither short nor coherent.

He began by telling me that he had never particularly liked me, and that he had been less than enthusiastic about our marriage at the time. There was nothing personal in this, it was simply the fact that I was a Jew, and therefore a stranger to the circles to which his family belonged. He had no particular aversion to Jews, except that at one time there had been too many of them in positions of influence. He had known perfectly decent men of Jewish origin, as well as others of less admirable character, but this was neither here nor there. What mattered to him, a German patriot of the old school, was that the country could not absorb too many foreigners. The British and the French were in a different position; they could assimilate their Jews, but Germany had not been a nation for long and was still unsure of itself. The Jews were clever and ambitious, they aspired to positions of leadership, and this was bound to create problems. He agreed on the whole with the suggestions that had been made by many of his friends to restrict the influence of the Jews.

I became more and more bewildered and did not interrupt him. But this, he said, was now past history. He had certainly never envisaged such a tragic end to the relationship between the two peoples. Germany was now ruled by a gang of criminals. It had taken him years to accept this fact, but it was becoming clearer every day. At first he had welcomed the Nazis, though he had always disliked the plebeian streak in Hitler and his cohorts, the coarseness, the appeal to base instincts, the mendacity in his speeches. But this seemed a small price to pay

161

for the great achievements of the Nazis, such as the restoration of full sovereignty – meaning the rebuilding of a powerful army – in defiance of her enemies. He agreed with the Nazis that a great injustice had been done to Germany by the Treaty of Versailles and this had to be rectified – diplomatically, if possible, by force of arms, if necessary. But this too was now past history. Hitler and his lieutenants were out to conquer and to subjugate all of Europe, and for all one knew, even countries beyond.

But a people of seventy millions could not possibly rule four times as many other Europeans. A new order in which there were only masters and slaves was against human and divine law. He had seen atrocities committed for which he could find no possible justification, atrocities not committed in the heat of the battle as happens in every war, but deliberate cruelty and murder in cold blood as systematic policy. And so he had decided to retire from active service, giving bad health as a reason. 'Not a very heroic act,' he said, 'but the only possible one in the circumstances.' In the olden days a general would have sought death by exposing himself to danger in the front line, but he was not at all convinced that he had to commit suicide to atone for crimes committed on Hitler's orders. The Nazis would not last for ever, and for all he knew he might be needed after the war.

He had written a personal letter to the field marshal commanding the Eastern Front in which he had mentioned some of the real reasons. He had expected understanding, for another commander in the East, Blaskowitz, had warned against the 'extreme brutalization and the moral degeneration' which would spread like pestilence among the army and the whole German people as the result of actions not befitting decent men, let alone soldiers. But this had been before the invasion of the Soviet Union; the field marshal had had a short talk with him and told him that Germany was involved in a life-and-death struggle, and while the crimes committed by the SS and the *Einsatzgruppen* were regrettable, everything had to be subordinated now to winning the war. All other accounts would have to be settled after victory.

But the war could not be won, Joachim said; the most one can hope for is some sort of stalemate, and even this was becoming less and less likely every day. Meanwhile the good name of Germany had been besmirched for generations to come. He was bitter not only about the 'gangsters' to whom initially he had given credit, but also about so many of his fellow officers who dared not speak up. 'No one can accuse our people of cowardice,' he said, 'but there has never been a surfeit of *Zivilcourage* in our midst, not enough resistance to illegal and evil acts committed by those in authority. Was it shortsightedness or moral indifference? Why did people fail to understand that those who did not register any protest in the face of injustice became guilty themselves? 'Good Germans, good Christians – and yet they refuse to stand up and be counted.' Visibly agitated, he was pacing the room.

I was both intrigued and embarrassed by his confession and thanked him for being so frank with me. 'There is worse to come,' he said. It was of course known that mass arrests had been made, that hostages had been shot all over Europe and particularly in the East, that people were worked and starved to death. There had been rumours that horrible things were planned – the systematic killing of the mentally ill, of gypsies, of Jews and others. But these had been mere rumours, he had never seen anything in writing, and he had only recently received irrefutable evidence.

What was the evidence? He spoke haltingly. His son, a major, who had been on leave the month before, had told him about it in this very room. During one of the long Russian nights, he had taken refuge from a sudden heavy snowstorm in a little railway junction; he had to wait for hours for the lines to be cleared. There was a little group of officers there, and among them two SS *Sturmfuehrer* who had recently been in charge of a camp called Belzec, near Lublin. They had all been drinking; the SS people drank more than the rest, and they talked out of turn. According to their account the camp was not just another concentration camp, but an extermination factory for many hundreds of thousands. At present they could 'absorb' two thousand a day. There were other camps like it, and they were working at full speed. It was not a pleasant duty, the SS officers said, but it had to be done, and now they were trying to forget about it.

Later in Minsk the major had seen enormous warehouses full of personal belongings – the spectacles, toothbrushes, combs, shoes, of people who had been murdered. He had never seen anything like it, and he had been sworn to secrecy. In short, there could be no doubt. . . . And his son had asked, 'What can I do?'

'You will wonder why I am telling you all this,' the general said. First, it should no longer be a secret. The more people who knew about it, the better: 'I doubt whether even these madmen will dare to confront the German people and the world with an open admission of mass murder.' But there were also practical considerations. He had heard about the transports from Berlin, and he had no doubts about their ultimate destination. He was an officer in retirement and as such without influential connections. But he could at the very least utter a word of warning; what did I intend to do in the face of danger? I said that we had given much thought to it all, but saw no way out at the moment. Hadn't he heard about the suicide of Jochen Klepper, the famous author, two months earlier, because his Jewish step-daughter had been refused an exit visa to Sweden? Klepper had been a man with excellent contacts in the very highest circles, but this had not made the slightest difference. 'Yes,' Joachim said, 'I heard about Klepper. He was a highly strung man. May his soul rest in peace.' But there might be ways other than the legal ones; he, for one, did not believe in suicide.

I said that my experience in such matters was limited; I had never crossed a border illegally. 'Nor have I,' said Joachim, 'but there must be ways and means.' He said that among the congregation at his local church there were people who had connections with church circles in neutral countries. They had been able to extend help in a few cases. I said I would be very grateful if he could put out feelers. 'More than feelers will be needed,' he said grimly, 'I shall have to stick my neck out and others will have to do the same.' But there was no other way. And again, after a short pause: 'I have an old-fashioned belief in divine retribution. As a boy I was told that God's mills grind slowly but exceedingly small, and by and large my experience has confirmed it. Heaven help Germany. . . .'

We rejoined our wives and after a little while Elizabeth and I departed. Joachim said he would be in touch with me in a few weeks, earlier if possible. We went out into the cold and the darkness, just in time to catch the last suburban train back to Dahlem. I told Elizabeth about our conversation. She said she had always known that Joachim could be trusted. God had been willing to save Sodom if ten just men could be found. There were no doubt others like Joachim – but then the sins committed nowadays were so much greater.

I now have to write about the most painful days of my life, and I shall be brief. I have mentioned that for a long time Elizabeth had been in indifferent health, and while there were no specific symptoms, and while she did not complain, she was visibly growing weaker. She went to see the specialist, there were tests, and then I was called in to see him. I was in and out of his office within ten minutes. He greeted me politely, but there was not much to discuss. When I had seen his impassive face I knew all; I had been through similar situations too often myself. There was nothing that could be done, and the only question to be decided was whether to tell her. We agreed not to do so for the time being.

At home I tried to behave as usual, which was, of course, impossible. One cannot feign unconcern towards a human being one loves, who knows one intimately, and with whom one spends most hours of the day and night. I tried to be a little more cheerful than usual, but Elizabeth was not fooled; I suspect she had known for a long time. We always tend to take the existence of those dear to us for granted, and when disaster strikes and our happiness ends we are always unprepared. How could it be otherwise? To be happy – Pascal remarked – man would have to make himself immortal. But not being able to do so, he has learnt to prevent himself from thinking of death. It is one of the oldest stories; everyone dies alone, grief cannot be shared and there is no comfort.

During these long months we discussed her illness only twice. The first time was in April 1943, a few weeks after I had seen her doctor. One evening she put her knitting aside and said that all things considered we had had many happy years together. She had dreamed the other night about our first meeting at Interlaken, and it had been a pleasant dream; she was a very young woman again and I had pursued her with my (not unwelcome) attentions; the old Countess and the Foreign Minister had also come into the dream. In some ways, she said, ours had been a fairy-tale romance, and though we knew that nothing lasted for ever we should be grateful for so much happiness.

I was glad to see her in such good spirits and said that it was too soon to talk about it as if the best were over: for all one knew there might be still happier days in front of us. No, she said, she knew that her days were numbered, and while she had every intention of living as long as possible, she knew that the drugs she was getting served no useful purpose and had no effect. I respected her too much to contradict her, but simply reminded her that perfectly healthy people could die from one moment to the next, while others given up as beyond human help went on living for years. She changed the subject of conversation.

The other talk was much longer and more painful. It was in late June of the same year. By a strange coincidence we had received two important messages in the same week. One came from Abegg's friend in Basel; he would be glad to meet Elizabeth and her husband in Freiburg and it was quite likely that he would be able to repay the kindness she had shown him on past occasions. Following some more of this apparent gibberish he suggested a date for a meeting in the coming month, and this, of course, was the one important point in the letter.At the same time I had a message from Joachim asking me to go the next day to a house in Charlottenburg. The name of the person whom I was going to meet meant nothing to me.

A lady in her fifties opened the door and ushered me into her dining room. She was in mourning; her only son had recently been killed. She cut short my condolences and said, 'I have known about you and Elizabeth for a long time.' She was a niece of Countess Donner, who had talked about us to her years ago. Her husband had died, and now her only son. She was a deeply religious woman, active in church work, and she heard about our plight. Then she came to the point: she had inherited some land between Lake Constance and Singen, a nearby industrial town. Her neighbours were Swiss farmers who had land on both sides of the border which was only a few miles away. Since they crossed the border almost daily, they knew every tree, every hedge, every little path in the neighbourhood. They had been of help in the past, and they might help again, though they would probably want some money. She said that it could be arranged at a few days' notice. In some ways it would be easier to cross the border in winter, as it would not be so well patrolled, but on the other hand this involved a considerable physical effort.

She seemed very well informed. She said that the main difficulty would be to reach the border area itself, which was under special control, and stay there for a few days if necessary without attracting attention. But perhaps this too could be arranged, since so many people were bombed out now and looking for shelter elsewhere. I thanked her profusely, and said I would be in touch with her in a few days. I told her I would have to discuss the plan with my wife who, unfortunately, was not in good health.

I was deeply moved that so many people took an interest in our fate, but the scheme was simply not practical. Elizabeth could no longer walk unaided for more than a few minutes; it was quite unthinkable that she could face up to the strains of an escape, involving walking possibly for hours, through forests and over mountains. I decided not even to mention the plan to Elizabeth.

But she knew about the appointment; she pressed for information and I had to tell her in the end. She thought for a few moments and then said: 'You have to go. Next week, immediately.' I said she knew perfectly well that I would not leave her. She argued that it was absolutely necessary. If I stayed with her, it was certain that I would be deported, for after her death I would no longer be protected. She said she would die in peace if she knew I was in safety, whereas with a sentence of death on my head, she would live out her remaining days in fear. I had a duty to stay alive, the boys still needed me. I replied that the boys would soon be grown up, it was doubtful whether they needed me even now. I also said that eventually we would all be gone, but that it was much too early to talk as if everything was finished; there was a good chance that both of us would live to see the end of Hitler's Thousand Years.

I battled with her for hours. I reminded her of the story of Ruth. 'But that was different,' she protested, 'it was not a matter of life and death for Ruth.' I said that no one could be sure these days where life was, or where death; I might be shot while crossing the border, or worse still, captured. She was already very weak and in the end she had to give in. The subject never came up again. I do not think that she ever accepted my arguments, but she knew that I had made up my mind and would not be deflected.

During the next months we lived in greater harmony than ever before. We would not exchange more than a few sentences throughout the evening. I would take her hand for a moment, she would stroke my hair as I was reading, there was complete understanding, no words were needed, and the fact that we knew that our time together was limited gave our relations a serenity which had not been there before. It helped her in her suffering, and I am sure it made it easier for me to carry my grief. Together, as it were, we slowly entered the gardens of Persephone:

> From too much love of living
> From hope and fear set free.

But sometimes we looked back, for we had not given up hope altogether. Our case was no more clear-cut than that of Persephone, who can never quite make up her mind whether she belongs to Olympus or to the realm of the dead. In the end some compromise is reached; she keeps shuttling between the two places.

The story of Persephone is part of the Eleusian mysteries, and our twilight existence in those months was also shrouded in mystery. Sometimes, when I was in low spirits, another of these mysteries came to mind, the story of Pyrrha and Deucalion, the only two human beings left after Zeus in his wrath had devastated the earth. According to the myth Deucalion looked around and saw the land ravaged and silent as the tomb. Tears were running down his cheeks as he said to his wife: 'My only and beloved companion, in all directions as far as eye can reach, I see no living thing. We two are the only humans left on earth; all the rest have been drowned in the flood. And even if all danger were past, what would two lonely people do on the abandoned earth?'

But this story has a happier ending for, with the help of the gods, life on earth was again created. While we live we are prisoners of hope.

And so the days went by, the weeks and months. At any time there could have been a sudden and final deterioration in Elizabeth's condition; and at any time they could have come to take me away from home, never to return. But summer came and went and turned into autumn and there was no change in Elizabeth's condition. Nor were there any ominous knocks on our door.

How did I spend these long days and nights which dragged on with no end in sight? I no longer left the house every morning as I had done all my life, but spent most of the day at home. Such a change in my routine was not at all easy at first, but I became adjusted more quickly than I would have thought possible. Twice a week I would go to town on various errands and to buy food; sometimes my way would take me on a round of second-hand bookshops where business was flourishing. As one of the owners told me, the consumption of alcohol and of books rises sharply whenever things are not going well. I would take a walk in the Grunewald for an hour or two, or I would go in another direction and come back by train or bus or tram.

Most of the time I spent with Elizabeth, reading, listening to music and the radio. I had acquired a substantial library over the years, but there were a great many books I had never read. I was, broadly speaking, familiar with the great writers in my native language, but I was much less at home in the literature of other nations. And so I began to read, more or less systematically, the major Greek and Roman authors, some of which I had been made to study at school without, of course, always appreciating them. I had been fascinated even as a small boy by the stories about the Argonauts and Heracles, about Troy and wily Ulysses, but it was only now that I realized how much wisdom there was in these stories, how much shrewd observation of human character and also, incidentally, how much symbolism. I was greatly intrigued by a letter written by Aristotle to an intimate friend: 'The lonelier I am, the more of a recluse I become, the greater is my love for myths.'

And so once more I went out fighting with Achilles and Hector and Diomedes, and I wept, reading the last part of the Odyssey – Ulysses' home-coming – where Penelope tells her long-lost husband that the deathless gods sent them suffering because it would have been too much bliss for mortals to spend their youth in joy and travel a smooth path to old age.

> So they came
> into that bed so steadfast, loved of old
> opening glad arms to one another.

I then proceeded to Cervantes and Shakespeare; I read some of the great French and English writers of the past century and discovered the world of the Russian classics. During the winter of 1943–4 I taught myself Russian; I had a grammar and a good dictionary, and I also got lessons from an old lady in Wilmersdorf. She was an emigrée who, like so many of them, had seen better days; but she showed a remarkable lack of self-pity, had a sense of humour as well as genuine teaching ability, and her enthusiasm for the great classics was infectious. She would come to our house once a week, or I would visit her, and while being treated to her strong tea, and the kind of sweet marmalade Russians have with their tea, I would be moved by Tatyana's letter to Onegin, and would resent his indifference; with Lermontov I would travel to the Caucasus, and while the world around us was on fire I would marvel at the great artist who had written such idyllic poems as the one about the lonely white sailing-boat in the blue sea (*Beleet parus odinoki...*). Best of all, I would read Tolstoy, the greatest of all novelists, and I totally forgot the world around me as a I saw Prince Andrei lying mortally wounded in the Rostovs' home in Yaroslavl, and read how Natasha nursed him, the 'unsettled question of life and death hanging over Bolkonski and over all Russia'; with Pierre Bezukhov I walked, as in a trance, through the battle of Borodino.

There is a moving poem by Alexander Blok describing how when escaping the storms and the violence outside he found shelter in the Pushkin pavilion of the Russian Academy of Science. In the solitude of my library I too was distracted from the miseries of the outside world, and found comfort to a degree I would never have expected. The great books diverted me from my own pain; they opened my eyes again to the richness and poetry of life and also to the essentially tragic quality of human existence. Normally, I would have been a very busy man, with no time left for reflection except on those problems which faced me in my profesional life. As it was, reading became an almost religious experience; it gave me some of the comfort traditional religion offers. The total faith of the true believer was beyond my reach in any case.

Then, of course, there was music. I had grown up in a musical family; I greatly regretted that I could not play an instrument well and that I had missed so many opportunities of going to concerts in the years between. There was an incredible wealth of talent in Berlin in the 1920s and 1930s, but for me there had always been other, more urgent preoccupations. I could have gone even now to the opera and the Philharmonic concerts, for musical life was considered part of the war effort. But it would have meant queuing up and staying long hours away from home, and this I did not want. The quality of sound reproduction for gramophones was not very developed at the time, and long-playing records had not yet been invented. This ruled out most of the longer works, but I had a good collection of operatic arias. Lastly there was the radio: the standard of performance was high, with the very best orchestras conducted by Furtwaengler and Knappertsbusch, Karl Boehm and Clement Kraus. Bach, Mozart and Haydn were played and listened to avidly; the most moving, the most intimate and humane music was played, while the greatest horrors were being perpetrated. 'O embrace now all you millions with one kiss for all the world' – they were fervently signing the 'Ode to Joy' as the millions were held in a deadly embrace.

There was also an abundance of catchy tunes which appeared over-night. The age of the great composers of light music was long over, but from morning to night one heard these new tunes about 'Bel Ami' (who was so lucky with the ladies), about Lili Marlene (waiting underneath the lamp post) about the mariner who was not shocked by any disaster ('Das kann doch einen Seemann nicht erschuettern'). These songs were as catchy as any I had heard in my time, or as any that my father hummed. They were no more Nazi in inspiration than the films shown in the cinemas; the openly antisemitic and chauvinistic films were on the whole an exception; most of them simply sought to enter-tain. It goes without saying that soldiers in constant danger of being killed resent indoctrination. But this applied equally to those at home who had no first-hand knowledge of the horrors of the war. Could the Ninth Symphony still have been performed against the background of the guns of Stalingrad and the cries of Auschwitz? Human beings have an infinite capacity for forgetting what happened even a few hours ago and to compartmentalize their actions and feelings. On one of my rare forays to the cinema I saw a newsreel showing a large group of SS men somewhere in Eastern Europe listening with great devotion to the St Matthew passion. There was no reason to doubt the genuineness of pictures and comment.

Time did not stand still even in my ramshackle ivory tower, nor had I ever tried to shut out the concerns of the outside world. I was still passionately interested in the unfolding drama with the radio serving as the main link for me, as for millions of others. We had bought a big radio set in 1936, a Telefunken, one of the most advanced available at the time. It received long, medium and even short waves; some sixty stations were listed on its dial and I listened countless times every day to the BBC news bulletins in English and German, to Radio Beromuenster from Switzerland, to Moscow and even the United States; some of the east coast stations such as WRUW and WRUL came through loud and clear. I learnt all about the best hours for reception, about sunspots and the ionosphere, and their influence on reception.

Only those who have lived under a murderous and highly effective modern dictatorship can possibly appreciate the vital importance of the radio, the only lifeline with the outside world. In peacetime, in a democratic regime, the radio is no more than a cheap source of entertainment. But in the giant prison that was Germany it made the difference between hope and utter despair; it was a supply of fresh air without which one would have suffocated. The heart beat faster when one heard the bleeps – three short, one long, the morse code sign for the letter 'V' preceding the British news broadcast, or 'The Star-spangled Banner', which was played by the American stations at the end of the day.

The German newspapers and radio stations were mouthpieces of mendacious but cleverly orchestrated propaganda. A careful reader or listener would soon realize that all was not going well, but such admissions were always rather imprecise, and buried under mountains of reassuring promises that all would soon change for the better. The 'enemy stations' also engaged in propaganda but they did not hide defeats and setbacks. If they said that the battleship *Scharnhorst* had been sunk or Foggia had been taken by the Allies, one could rely on them. The German radio, on the other hand, specialized in news items about heavy fighting in the 'general direction of . . .'. Gone were the days of the solemn announcements with which in the early years of the war the programmes had been interrupted so often: 'Belgium has surrendered', 'The French have abandoned Paris'. Instead there was the sonorous bass voice of Yuri Levitan announcing over Moscow radio on 2 February that the last German forces had surrendered at Stalingrad, and later, in early August, that the mammoth battle of Kursk had ended with a German defeat.

Then in November 1943, the German forces in the Crimea were cut off and Kiev was retaken by the Russians. Meanwhile, on 12 July, the Allies had landed in Sicily, and Mussolini had been deposed and arrested. German submarines suffered such heavy losses during the summer that the offensive against Allied shipping on the Atlantic had to be discontinued. The air attacks against German cities became more systematic and heavier; Hamburg was all but destroyed in a series of attacks in late July.

Listening to enemy stations was a crime against the state and punished most severely. Mussolini's fall, for instance, was not announced by the German press and radio for a long time, yet the news spread in Berlin within a few hours. We were fortunate in that in the privacy of our house we could not be overheard by neighbours. Others, less fortunate, had to bury their radio sets under layers of blankets, quilts and cushions, and press their ears against the loudspeaker. I spent long hours in front of the set, much to the annoyance of Elizabeth, who would remark that I had already listened several times to the same news bulletin. She was quite right, but there was some news one could not hear often enough. The tide of the war had turned, the end was in sight. But it was still a long way away, and however often one measured distances on the map, and made calculations, we were still in grave danger.

During the day I read and I observed. It came as a great surprise to me how much one could see even from an unpromising observation post such as the window of a suburban house, how much one heard simply walking the streets of a big city. My powers of observation had been stunted, but now they became acute. The rations, I realized, had become smaller and the official propaganda shriller. How did people react to the deprivations and the ebbing fortunes of their country? The men and women I watched in the streets, in the buses and trains, were subdued; one hardly ever heard them talking in loud voices. Their daily routine had not changed; they still left for work in the morning and came back in the late afternoon. But their clothes had become a bit shabbier, they seemed more tired and the expression on their faces surly.

Many thousands had left Berlin; the newspapers now announced that those who had no cogent reason to stay should depart, and they were promised that half the cost of moving would be borne by the state. On the other hand there was a large-scale invasion of foreigners; one heard much French and Dutch in the streets and buses, and even Polish and Russian – forced labour mobilized for work in local factories. Official slogans were still repeated, and I heard some antisemitic remarks ('What – some of them are still around? ... and I had thought they had gone for good').

But most people were obviously preoccupied with their own affairs, and above all with the desire to get home before the air raid sirens sounded, which happened very often indeed, usually in the early evening. The prospect of spending hours in a shelter was not inviting, but at least they would be with their friends and families. People lost their homes and their belongings, but there was no spirit of rebellion in the air, only apathy: it was fate, it had to be accepted. People were dulling their senses: an old doctor told me that the requests for sedatives and sleeping tablets had quadrupled. Berlin was no longer sleeping well. The well-to-do younger crowd went to hectic parties, which again was quite understandable, for time was running out.

In our little street I was, of course, quite well known. Some regarded me with open hostility, some with indifference, others looked away when they saw me leaving the house, entering a shop in the neighbourhood or waiting at the local station. A few greeted me – not with 'Heil Hitler', of course, but 'Good morning' or 'Gruess Gott'. On occasion someone would try to involve me in a political conversation. I had become exceedingly cautious, and moreover Otto had warned me against a lady named Krause further down the street, the wife of a minor party official, and a middle-aged man called Bueckling who had recently moved into our neighbourhood, and whose precise occupation was unknown. Whenever they enquired after Elizabeth and the children or asked whether they could be of any help, I would thank them very politely and point out that in these difficult times one must on no account impose on others. I would then look at my watch and say that I was a bit late for work, and much as I enjoyed our conversation and wanted to prolong it, duty clearly came first. Eventually these two stopped pestering me.

But one day in July, after dark, we had a visit from a policeman from the local station, whom I had known, though not by name, for years. He said that it been reported that strangers were staying in our house; this caused something of a panic, for the previous week the boys had indeed brought home two of their friends who were quite obviously on the run. These friends had stayed in the house for several days and had left us only that very morning. I told our policeman that we had indeed had visitors, but this was no more than doing our duty, for had not Dr Goebbels himself appealed for solidarity in helping those who had been bombed out? 'I thought as much,' he said, 'but one has to be very careful these days. Do you know their names?' I truthfully said that I did not, adding that the Good Samaritan had not asked for identity papers either. The policeman smiled and said: 'Tell that to the Gestapo. . . .'

On the way out he looked at our radio set, expressed admiration, and then fiddled with one of the knobs. In the doorway he said in a low voice that one should never leave the indicator pointed to a station which, quite obviously, did not belong to the Grossdeutsche Rundfunk. In my absent-mindedness I had left the set tuned into the BBC.

A few days later Otto reported that he had heard through his police contacts that Mrs Krause had indeed turned up at the local station and asked for immediate and drastic action: suspicious people had been seen entering and leaving our house. We were under observation and we had to be even more careful.

Most of the Jews still remaining in Berlin had been deported in the 'factory actions' of early March 1943. The trucks and vans appeared at their places of work; the Gestapo no longer trusted the good sense and discipline of the Jews to come voluntarily to the concentration point on receipt of a 'call up' notice. As a result, those about to be deported had to leave in their working clothes, losing their previous privileges, namely permission to take with them two suits, three shirts, two pairs of shoes, two pairs of pyjamas, six pairs of socks and six handkerchiefs. By the end of March 18,515 Jews were left in Berlin, of which 9,330 did not have to wear the star and were exempt, for the moment, from deportation.

The 9,185 who were not exempt were deported in the months that followed, mostly in small transports: on 19 April there was a big transport 'to the East' with 983 persons, and on the same day a hundred left for Theresienstadt. On 17 May, 395 were sent to the East and a hundred to Theresienstadt, and on 18 and 19 May another hundred left.

The transport which left on 29 May was different from the preceding ones: for the three hundred that left on that day did not walk but were carried. These were the inmates of the nursing home in the Auguststrasse, and they were bedridden almost without exception. It was a scene such as I had never witnessed: very old people, incurably ill men and women, some very quiet, others agitated and shouting as if delirious, they were carried in a long and orderly procession from the vans and ambulances to the platform of the railway station. They had to wait several hours for their train, and there was a great deal of moaning and crying; some were asking for water or for their medicines.

These old people were not intimidated by the shouts of the SS guards. Old people are obstinate, used to getting their own way, and they are no longer particularly afraid of anything. And so the SS guards were quite helpless; they did not know how to silence these incurables, short of strangling or shooting them, which clearly would not have done at all in a Berlin railway station. How relieved they were when at last the train came in! The head of the home, Mrs Oberlaender, accompanied the transport, and so did some thirty or forty doctors, nurses and orderlies. They raised one important point: who would carry the stretchers on their arrival? But the question was waved aside by the SS officer in command: minor technical problems would be solved on the spot, surely they trusted the competence of the German authorities?

Twelve days later the Gestapo appeared in the offices of the Association in the Kantstrasse, and in the Jewish community in the Oranienburgerstrasse, and announced that since the Jewish community had ceased to exist, the administrative work had come to an end and the offices were to be closed. Those who were not 'privileged' were arrested and taken to Grosse Hamburgerstrasse. A few Gestapo officials remained behind and affixed seals on various filing cabinets and doors. One of them was overheard saying that the vermin destroyers would have to put in some intensive work before these places would be fit for human use again. His solicitude was unnecessary, for nine months later the building was destroyed in an air raid. But on the whole the Gestapo did not seem triumphant; for them, after all, this was only another job done. Perhaps they were even a little sad, because they had got used to dealing with the Jews, who never gave them much trouble. Perhaps they were afraid they would be reassigned to more demanding work.

The former employees of the Jewish organizations were kept six days at Grosse Hamburgerstrasse; at noon on 16 June they were transferred to the railway station, and in the evening they left, together with some five hundred patients from the Jewish hospitals. This was the last major transport to leave Berlin, and on the very same day Dr Goebbels, in his capacity as Minister of Propaganda and *Gauleiter* of the German capital announced that Berlin was now *judenrein* – empty of Jews.

Strictly speaking this was not quite true. For apart from those who had gone underground, perhaps several thousands, there were those 9,000 in a 'privileged' position, and there was even one Jewish institution still functioning – the Jewish hospital at the corner of Iranische Strasse and Schulstrasse, in the grey desert of Berlin's north-eastern working-class quarter. This was headed by Dr Lustig, who was now the sole remaining member of the Association and acted as its chief representative in all dealings with the Gestapo. In his medical work he was assisted by Doctors Cohen, Helischkowski, Hirschfeld and a few others; only one or two were personally known to me.

Dr Lustig's little empire consisted of nothing more than a small hospital; most of the inmates were Gestapo prisoners. There was a little administrative section, which took care of the transfer of Jewish property to the Reich treasury, and also administered those Jewish cemeteries which had not yet been destroyed. There was apparently a dispute among the bureaucracy about the fate of the cemeteries. Then there was the pathology building, which served as the concentration point for the small transports; the camp at Grosse Hamburgerstrasse was no longer needed and had been closed down. Lastly, there were a few Jewish artisans, messengers, and shady characters best avoided hanging around in Iranische Strasse; no one knew why they had been spared, but sometimes even the ways of a methodical organization such as the Gestapo are quite inscrutable.

There was a Gestapo office in the compound, and they of course were the real masters to whom Dr Lustig was responsible. Everything was now very much reduced in scale; if Lustig had become 'head of the Jews', the job of dealing with them on behalf of the Gestapo was left to one Dobberke, a mere *Oberscharfuehrer* – something in between a sergeant and a lieutenant. Seen in broader perspective, Dr Goebbels's announcement about Berlin's Jews was not so wrong after all.

September passed, and October, all too slowly, and we were still sitting at home waiting. The Red Army was approaching the old Polish border, the Allies had taken Naples and slowly made their way up north. Salerno featured prominently in the news; we remembered a beautiful holiday we had spent there in 1930. Peter had been five then, and still vividly remembered the trip on the funicular railway outside Naples.

The days became shorter, the trees lost their foliage. Elizabeth left home only on rare occasions. She was husbanding her strength. The illness was proceeding much more slowly than we had feared. I do not know even after all these years whether one can actually 'fight' a disease of this kind. But the opposite is certainly true: some people simply give in, whereas Elizabeth, a strong-willed woman, had decided to live as long as possible.

There was not much to eat, and even less variety. But Elizabeth had not much appetite anyway, and I found, somewhat to my surprise, that the human organism can function with much less food than is commonly supposed, especially if one is not engaged in heavy physical work. I prospered on a diet of cabbage and turnips and inferior spinach. I had no serious illness; I was never, in fact, in better health.

But if my body functioned well, I nevertheless found the waiting quite intolerable. It has been said that genius is nothing but patience; unfortunately, nature has endowed me less in this respect than most other human beings. I have always found it almost impossible to wait in a queue for more than ten minutes, and rather than wait I have willingly done without all kinds of benefits. Wrong decisions which I have made in my life were more often than not the result of my inability to wait a little longer. As a student of human nature I have not found it too difficult to explain my lack of patience, but intellectual under- standing has been of little help in effecting any change. Now for the first time in my life I was forced to wait, and these long months were an iron taskmaster; quite frequently I felt an overpowering desire to force a decision. But this would have been suicidal, and the remnants of what good sense I had, reinforced by Elizabeth's insistence, kept me from doing anything very foolish. Grinding my teeth, *la mort dans l'âme*, I went on waiting.

One day in mid-October I had a strange encounter which left me more confused than ever. In the morning I went to the Prussian State Library in Unter den Linden, to consult some books I needed for my work. It is an impressive building with a majestic entry hall and a reading room with a cupola forty metres high. It houses a collection which is in many respects unique; its holdings on the history of music, for instance, are unrivalled. It is also a most agreeable place to work; the librarians are efficient and polite, and since during the war there were hardly ever more than two dozen visitors (there is room for 400) they had been treating me very well indeed.

Earlier in the war I used to spend many a morning there; it is extraordinary that in this haven, in the busiest street of the German capital, one could forget the outside world for a few hours. Recently I had been there less often, but the elderly librarian to whom I handed my requests greeted me as an old acquaintance. After a little while he came to my table and said that to their great regret they had not been able to locate the books. He would insist on a special search; could I perhaps come back in an hour or two? He hoped I would understand, they had had to employ new assistants who lacked experience. This was inconvenient, but since I had come all the way from the suburbs, and since it was a fine day, ideal for walking, I said that I would come back around lunchtime.

I crossed the river, walked twice round Monbijou castle, which, I believe, one of the Prussian kings had built for his mistress, and then sat on a bench. But for an old lady feeding the birds, I was all alone in the little park. It was chilly even though the sun was shining, and so after a little while I got up and began to make my way back to the library. I left the garden by the north exit which leads to the English church and then to Oranienburgerstrasse. Just past the main telegraph office, I stopped for a moment and looked at the house in which the offices of the Jewish community had once been. What had become of the people who had worked there? How many of them were still alive?

As I was about to continue my stroll, I saw to my surprise two men leaving the building, and almost at once I recognized the smaller of the two, Dr Krebs. He had been the managing director and legal counsel of the Hilfsverein (the relief organization), one of the leading institutions of German Jewry which, founded at the turn of the century, had assisted many thousands of those who had emigrated to countries other than Palestine. Dr Krebs was also a leading official of the Association, and he had been deported with the others in January – yet somehow he had returned to Berlin. I crossed the street, walked a little quicker, caught up with them and greeted Krebs. He nodded and slowed down as if he wanted to talk to me, but his companion brusquely pulled him aside, and curtly told me to disappear if I knew what was good for me.

There was no doubt about it, Krebs had returned to Berlin, but what did it mean? Had he returned alone and for good? That evening I phoned one of the few doctors still employed in the Iranische Strasse. When I mentioned the name Krebs he pretended not to have heard me and changed the subject of conversation, which of course made it even more mysterious. But I met him the next day and the following extraordinary story emerged.

Krebs had indeed returned from Theresienstadt, and with him Fabian, another leading official of the Association. They were kept incommunicado by the Gestapo, but they had rooms in the Iranische Strasse compound. They had been brought back on the insistence of the Berlin treasury which complained that in view of the abrupt deportation of the Jews, the German state stood to lose millions of Marks. There was no clear picture; not all the assets of the Jewish communities could be traced, and there was the question of the life insurance policies of those deported which should now of course revert to the state since the former policy-holders no longer needed coverage. Unless there was an orderly handover, it was more likely that unauthorized persons or institutions would profit. This was an argument which even the Gestapo could not refute; perhaps they too expected to pick up a few millions.

Krebs and Fabian were brought back, and for ten hours a day they worked their way through the files. But more importantly, they had news of those who had been deported with them. Baeck and Eppstein were alive; conditions were bad, but not much worse than they had been in Berlin towards the end. More worrying was the fact that for many of those deported Theresienstadt was no more than a transit station. After a few weeks or months they were again deported to places further east. No one knew what had become of them.

In mid-November our friendly neighbourhood policeman again paid us a visit. This time he came during the day, and he wanted to have a word with my wife alone. I ushered him into her bedroom. He was visibly ill at ease and said that there had been a query from the treasury with regard to the ownership of the house, a purely legal investigation of not much consequence. The problem could surely wait until Madam was feeling better. It was one of Elizabeth's good days; she was at her most gracious and started to look for the papers. But he was not really in the least interested and seemed only too glad to accept a cup of tea.

The three of us went to the kitchen. He put his helmet on a chair and told us he had been in the force for a quarter of a century, first in East Berlin and now in Dahlem where, of course, it was much nicer; he had dealt with hardened professional criminals and petty thieves, he had seen service during the turbulent last years of the Weimar Republic, he had lived through good times and bad, and he had only one more year to go now until he retired. He liked Dahlem, it was a quiet place and there was very little crime, especially now during the war; if it wasn't for the occasional traffic accident and the air raids they would be underemployed. Unfortunately there was this new plague of informers. Some people seemed to have too much time on their hands; perhaps they should be sent to a factory to do some useful work. 'We have instructions to check every report, however stupid, which of course is quite impossible.'

He told us that some of these dangerous busybodies did not feel happy unless they visited the station at least once a day, notifying the police about some crime against the state committed or about to be committed by their neighbours. They were not even paid for their efforts. 'How would you react,' he said in a low voice, 'if someone had reported to us that Madam had died months ago and that the doctor was living alone in the house?' Elizabeth smiled. 'I would say that someone is certainly very interested in our well-being, and if we knew him or her we ought to express our gratitude.' 'Madam takes a philosophical view,' the policeman said, 'but it is no fun for us.' He thanked us for our hospitality and took his leave.

The next evening Otto came in and we heard the full story. He had been playing billiards with the policeman (an old party comrade). The two informers down the street had told the police that something very strange was going on in our house; the wife had not been seen for a long time, perhaps she was dead? They were surprisingly well informed; they knew that I would be arrested and deported if Elizabeth died, and maybe they also wanted to stake a claim to our house. They were in a hurry. 'Stupid people,' Otto said, 'greedy and hateful people. They forget that our bureaucracy opens files and keeps them for ever. One of these days they will have to answer for their crimes....'

The week after, on 22 November to be precise, Berlin sustained the heaviest air raid ever. A big bomb landed some three hundred yards down the street and several houses were flattened. I do not know what became of our informers, but they did not bother us again.

Everything that happened before November 1943 had been no more than a prelude. It was only during this month that we got a real taste of the air war, and then the raids did not cease for many weeks. They became the central events in our life. Every war produces its crop of armchair strategists; during the past years we had gradually become experts in air warfare. I had seen my first plane when I was ten years old; the younger generation knows about these contraptions from history books or museums. They had tyres not much stronger than those on bicycles, flimsy frames of wire and plywood (steel tube fuselages were not introduced for some years), and primitive rudders, throttles and ailerons. The pilots were exposed to the elements, and if they had the misfortune to be overtaken by a storm, there was no certainty that their planes would withstand the sudden strain. In the First World War planes were used mainly for reconnaissance, and it was only towards its end that they began to engage in more or less effective bombing. Then, in the 1920s, aircraft design developed by leaps and bounds and it became evident that in a future war air-power would not just be an adjunct of land forces but a decisive weapon. Preparations were made for long-range bombing of enemy industries and centres of population; dress rehearsals took place in Ethiopia and in Spain.

The Battle of Britain did not break the spirit of the population, but this was not necessarily a refutation of the new doctrine; I heard it said even in the early years of the war that Germany with all its experts and its developed industries had not yet succeeded in producing an effective long-range heavy bomber. The Ju-88 had the necessary range, but its defensive armament was insufficient and there was little it could do without massive fighter support; and the maximum range of the standard fighters such as the Messerschmidt 110 was less than 600 miles. They could stay over Britain for only a few minutes, and they were less manoeuvrable than the Spitfire and Hurricane facing them.

There was not much bombing of Germany in 1940, for the British were preoccupied with the defence of their own country, and in 1941 they had to secure their sea lanes. The Russians, on the other hand, did not believe in strategic bombing in the first place. But in 1942 the situation changed: in late May of that year more than a thousand bombers of Britain's Bomber Command attacked Cologne and caused heavy damage. Then in 1943 the United States Air Force joined in and a division of labour evolved: the British, using radar to locate targets, would engage in what was called night-time saturation bombing, whereas the Americans concentrated on daylight precision bombing. Gigantic new planes made their appearance, such as the Lancaster and the Boeing B-17 (the Flying Fortresses), which had a wing-span of more than a hundred feet and a range of 1,500 miles.

Frequently they suffered heavy losses, as when they attacked Schweinfurt in October 1943; and from time to time there would be a pause in the Allied air offensive. But then after a few weeks or months spent perfecting some new technique the attacks would be renewed with a vengeance. Bombs became both bigger and smaller; there were general purpose bombs and delayed action bombs, high capacity bombs and deep penetration bombs, small magnesium bombs and large incendiary bombs with liquid fillings.

There was a major air raid against Berlin in early March 1943 which coincided with the last great wave of deportations. Then there was an interval, apart for one major attack in late March, two in late August (the British announced that 1,647 planes had participated on this occasion), and another in early September. On 23 August 1,700 tons of bombs were dropped over Berlin, and 1,800 on 31 August. The Allies were clearly out to establish new records.

At one stage, the German air command believed it had discovered a new and effective way to cope with the intruders. When the Allied bombers appeared in the skies above Berlin on 31 August, giant magnesium torches were dropped by German fighters from a very great height, brilliantly illuminating the whole scene. It was certainly a most remarkable sight, but the military effect was virtually nil, for these torches also showed up only too clearly the German night fighters, and the Allies actually suffered fewer losses on this than on other occasions.

With each attack the Luftwaffe was less and less in evidence; was it lack of planning, or of pilots, or of petrol? Once upon a time, not so long ago, Germany's air force had been hailed as the strongest in the world, and now all of a sudden it had disappeared, which had a bad effect on morale on the German home front. Where are our planes? people asked. But there was no answer.

At first other parts of Germany suffered much more than Berlin: in March 1943 it was the turn of Munich and Nuremberg as well as the cities of the Ruhr such as Essen and Duisburg; in May Wuppertal, in June Cologne and Muenster again, Luebeck and Rostock – and many other cities besides.

All previous attacks were dwarfed by what happened in Hamburg during the last week of July. The raid began on 26 July; the fires caused were so extensive that the local fire brigades were quite powerless and the engines brought in from other cities could not cope either. There were incessant attacks for four days; fire swept through streets and squares like a tornado and consumed everything. Goebbels admonished the British: they should not think that their nerves were stronger than those of the German people, and he denounced their attacks as bar-

barous crimes against humanity. He also said that the terror would be answered by counter-terror a hundred times more horrible, for the Fuehrer was working day and night to prepare a blow which the Pluto-crats would never forget.

During the summer the Allied offensive was mainly directed against military and industrial targets such as the submarine construction works in Wilhelmshafen, the installations in Peenemuende, and centres of the aircraft industry elsewhere. But other targets in west Germany were also under almost constant attack; no German city was safe any more, and even the area around Vienna became a target. Bombers coming from Britain now engaged in shuttle missions landing in southern Italy, or vice versa.

The Nazi leaders feared that these raids would become even more extensive; in a speech in July Goebbels said that those who had returned to Berlin in view of the lull in the bombing had acted rashly; anyone who had no urgent business in Berlin should leave, taking with him clothes, bedding and other essentials. Whole schools were evacuated.

The exodus from Berlin quickened after the air raid of 23 August, when in less than an hour the whole area between the zoo and the Potsdam Square railway station was severely damaged; around the Wilhelmstrasse and the Friedrichstrasse few houses were left standing. The Kaiser Wilhelm memorial church was destroyed, and not much was left of the Tauentzien and Joachimsthaler streets, once among the most elegant in town.

But this was only the beginning; these sporadic attacks were followed by the great series of sixteen raids which took place between the end of November 1943 and March 1944. I shall describe what I witnessed after one of them – the fifth, I believe, on 3 December. We had just finished our dinner, and I had been reading to Elizabeth a newspaper article written by a professor of hygiene on how to keep healthy despite air raid alarms in winter – strange how these small details stick in one's mind. I went on to read another article on how to keep children happy on the long railway trips that evacuation entailed. (Mothers should not get nervous and shout at their children; fresh air in the compartments was essential, children should not be too warmly dressed. There should be a plentiful supply of picture books and games for the journey, and so on.)

I had not finished reading when the first bombs fell. I went out; the skies were heavily overcast. There were more searchlights than ever, but they did not penetrate the clouds: one could hear the droning of the bombers, but nothing could be seen. Yet despite the poor visibility the bombs continued to fall and I heard later that on this raid the British had used new guidance instruments which made their aim far more accurate, quite irrespective of weather conditions.

It was cold that evening, and after a few minutes I stepped inside the house again and we went down to the cellar. This was fortunate, for soon after there was a heavy thud very close by; everything shook, the light flickered and then went out altogether. When I later inspected the house I found the glass in the front windows broken.

Next morning we discovered metal splinters in our front room and a good deal of debris in our little garden. The roof had not been damaged, but the glass could not, of course, be replaced. I had to shore up the windows with thick cardboard and wooden boards, which could not possibly keep the cold out: we would freeze this winter.

I had tried to go into town the morning after the first very heavy attack on 22 November, but this proved to be impossible, for public transport had come to a standstill and there were no private cars on the road. It took several days to restore the electricity supply in our part of town. The radio gave very few details: some historical monuments had been destroyed, some churches and hospitals, and the population had suffered losses. From neighbours we got some more information: it had been particularly bad in the Tiergarten area and the vicinity of the Potsdamer Platz – the big department stores had been hit, and also some of the suburbs in the east. The BBC provided some additional details: more than 2,000 tons had been dropped in one single raid.

The British also announced that the total of bombs dropped on Berlin now exceeded the 11,000 tons which Hamburg had absorbed, another new record. When the last planes to participate in the raid arrived they had needed no one to lead them to the target; the sea of flames could be seen from more than a hundred miles away.

On the following evening there was another air raid, almost as heavy, and then another and yet another. We listened to the usual concerto of bombs, anti-aircraft shelling, heavy thuds, sirens. An air raid is a theme without variations; it may last ten minutes or two hours, it was always the same, and always a little different – unless, of course, one happened to be hit.

After the fifth air raid I managed at last to make my way into the centre of town. It was a long, weary and not particularly interesting trip. One could smell the destruction even out in the suburbs; a

184

cloud of soot, smoke and dust had settled which made breathing difficult, and the nearer to town I got the worse it was. The electricity supply had been restored, but it was so dark that the lights had to be turned on even during the day.

One of the newspapers, the *Lokalanzeiger*, had managed to print an early edition. I glanced at the headlines which announced, quite truthfully, that Berlin had changed its face – a reminder of Hitler's promise soon after he had come to power: 'Berliners, in ten years you will not be able to recognize your city....' The heart of Berlin had gone; the whole area north and south of Unter den Linden, including the Zeughaus, one of Berlin's great baroque buildings; the State Library, my favourite retreat, and the big hotels, such as the Bristol, were all in ruins. House Vaterland at the Potsdamer Platz, Berlin's greatest restaurant, no longer existed. There had been a dozen eating-places in this big building, a Turkish and an Italian restaurant, a Viennese and a Bavarian, an American (until recently) and a Rhine Terrace restaurant. The decor and the food reflected the *genius loci* as did the waiters in their regional costume. What with food rationing and so many of its clients gone, its splendour had diminished in recent years and now it had disappeared altogether.

Most underground stations in the centre were out of action, many ministries and embassies and most big stores were partly or entirely destroyed. Large sections of the centre were still cordoned off; as for the effects of the raids in the outlying districts, one still had to rely on rumours. In places the smoke was so dense and corrosive that the fire brigades and the police had to wear gasmasks. The last time I had seen this was twenty-five years earlier: it was a quarter of a century since the First World War ended, and I had not been alone in believing that never in our lifetime would we see such sights again.

Berlin was like an ant-hill into which giants had dropped heavy stones. Huge damage had been done, but the ants continued to crawl along, making their way around the obstacles which had suddenly appeared in the midst of their colonies. Ants do not reflect, there are no councils of war for mapping out new strategies; they instinctively start rebuilding new streets from and between their nests. They go on weaving, hunting and carrying loads. Berlin reacted like an ant-heap, unthinkingly and vigorously. But the ants have no history, whereas Berlin had one: it was incongruous to think about the past in the middle of this destruction, and yet time and again, walking through the ruins, one was reminded of the former splendour and vigour of this city.

Berlin had seen good times and bad. At the end of the Thirty Years War it was no more than a neglected village with perhaps a few thousand inhabitants. There were many greater, richer and more important towns in Germany and it could not, of course, compare with centres such as Paris and London. But in the following centuries Berlin overtook all its rivals and began to catch up with other capitals. It became a centre of industry, of trade, of banking, and the capital of a united Germany. It even became gradually a centre of culture and learning: Hegel taught and Marx studied here, and for the past seventy years it had attracted the great and famous like a magnet, as well as those who still had their names to make.

After the war of 1870–71, its population exceeded the one million mark; in the 1920s there were more than four million. No other big city had grown this fast. Berlin had an exemplary underground railway system and an equally efficient surface railway, the Schnellbahn. It had one of the most modern airports in the world, Tempelhof, with facilities for a hundred planes. A stranger with ample means who came to Berlin had the choice between a dozen hotels of world renown – the Esplanade with its wonderful garden, the Eden with its famous roof garden, the Bristol and Continental with their exquisite restaurants. If he wanted to see how the natives amused themselves he could spend an evening in one of the garden restaurants which still displayed the old announcements: 'Families are permitted to prepare their own coffee here.' Or he could visit Circus Busch with its infinitely varied repertory, or take a steamer ride on the Havel or the Spree. He had the choice between three major opera houses, and a dozen world-famous theatres directed by Reinhardt, Jessner and others.

Even cursory visits to the major museums would take more than a week. How could he possibly miss the Pergamon altar and other impressive examples of Greek and Roman architecture? He was morally bound to look for at least a few minutes at the Ishtar Gate and the Babylonian procession street dedicated to the god Marduk in the Museum of Near Eastern Art. He had to see the Duerers, Holbeins, and Cranachs in the German Museum and the countless examples of the work of Rubens, Boticelli, Michelangelo, Rafael, Correggio, Titian, Velasquez and others in the Kaiser Friedrich Museum. There were more important pictures by Frans Hals in Berlin than anywhere else except perhaps Haarlem, where he died; there were more Rembrandts here than in any other museum outside Holland. They included two self-portraits, the 'Man with the Golden Helm', 'The Good Samaritan', a picture of Saskia, 'Jacob wrestling with the Angel', 'Susanna and the Elders', 'Joseph's Dream', the portrait of a rabbi and others.

But this seemed to belong to the past; not many well-to-do strangers came to the German captital nowadays, and a visit to the museums was not uppermost in their minds. The Pergamon treasures had been stored in the cellar of the big flak-tower next to the bird sanctuary in the zoo, and few people knew the whereabouts of the Rembrandts and Duerers. The garden restaurants were desolate and the brass bands no longer played: Berlin had gone underground.

The age of massive bombing had dawned, and the city was now systematically reduced to rubble and ashes. It could have been foreseen: soon after the Wright brothers had gone up in their biplane in November 1903, it occurred to a few men of imagination that modern airships would have a tremendous military potential. On 1 November, 1911, at the time of the war in Libya, an Italian lieutenant named Garotti dropped four bombs, weighing four pounds each, on Turkish targets. This was the first recorded case of bombardment from the air, and it is not known whether any damage was caused.

But the planes got bigger and so did the bombs: in summer 1918, I was invited by a fellow officer, strictly against regulations, to join him and a few others as an observer in a training flight. It was my first flight and I was, of course, nervous; I remember very little about the technical details, except that it was difficult to climb into the monster plane belonging to the new R series. It had six or eight engines, and its wingspan was enormous – more than 130 feet, more than even the biggest bombers of the Second World War. We were told that it could carry a bomb-load of 4,000 pounds. The flight was an exhilarating experience, mainly perhaps because it was so slow: the maximum speed was about eighty miles per hour. We were gliding noisily but effortlessly over north Germany and Belgium. Meanwhile the British had constructed a long-range bomber of their own, the four-engine Handley Page which could carry a 2,000-pound bomb-load.

The planes were slow and therefore vulnerable, but they could carry enormous bomb-loads, and this led some strategists to believe that destruction from the air alone would win the coming war. The main protagonist of this school of thought was an Italian general, Giulio Douhet, and his famous book was published in 1921; a German translation came out in the late thirties. Systematic bombing (Douhet claimed) could paralyse all the main enemy centres in a few days. A thousand bombers would suffice to achieve this aim. A one-ton bomb, Douhet figured, would destroy everything within a radius of 180 feet, and on the basis of this calculation he reached the conclusion that there would be unparalleled death and destruction; people would pour out of the big cities in panic and within a few days the country affected would have to surrender.

But Douhet did not take into account the fact that as these planes became faster and bigger, they also became much more expensive. He belittled the impact of anti-aircraft fire from the ground. He ignored the fact that the bombers would be attacked by fighters, which would make aiming difficult. Above all he overrated the extent of damage inflicted on the ground in cities where the buildings were solid concrete structures with steel frames. He assumed that many thousands would be killed in each air raid. But it soon became apparent that about a ton of high explosives was needed to kill a single human being. Thus in a raid in which a thousand tons of bombs were dropped on a city, a thousand people were likely to be killed. Sometimes, as in Hamburg, there were many more victims because the fires got out of control, but quite often the number of casualties would be much less. As the sirens were sounded those living in the cities would make their way into their cellars and shelters. They would stay there for hours, and after the all clear was given they would emerge, dazed, stunned but still very much alive.

Aerial bombing was not then the most effective way to kill human beings. But it had a great many other effects: for every one that was killed three or four were injured; factories and homes were destroyed, communications interrupted; people arrived late at work and there was absenteeism. The damage to industry was quite often temporary; what was easily destroyed could sometimes be quickly repaired. But morale was certainly affected. In the long evenings people in the shelters whispered to each other, and some even spoke out loud: they made jokes about the official communiqués, which were so quite obviously mendacious; and there were jokes about the Nazi leaders who were responsible for Germany's misfortunes. Above all there were wild rumours – the whole of Germany had become one giant rumour-factory. There was no active opposition against the regime, but faith in the leaders and in victory was undermined.

In Berlin faith had virtually disappeared by December 1943. People began to be afraid that the attacks would go on, night after night. Large parts of the city were without water, electricity and gas for long periods. Tens of thousands of people were stranded in emergency camps waiting for trains to take them out of the capital.

I saw a few cars and trucks slowly making their way through the streets between the debris and the craters. Supplies were still getting through: on the walls I saw special announcements that there would be an additional distribution of food – two hundred grams of meat, and ten cigarettes or five cigars. The population was to be kept in a good mood at any price. There were strange rumours: parachutists had landed in the suburbs, forged banknotes and ration books had been dropped, German scientists had invented a death-ray and the Fuehrer was about to announce its application, the war would be over next week, the Allies had demanded German surrender, or all German cities would be bombed simultaneously. Hitler had gone to Moscow; Stalin had arrived in Berlin; the Allied invasion had started.

From a distance I saw the clock of the Kaiser Wilhelm memorial church; the hands were at half past seven, as they had been ever since the church had been hit in a previous raid. As I turned into the Budapester Strasse I heard some shots. I did not pay any attention; but then there was a burst of machine-gun fire nearby and I took cover in the entrance to a coffee house a few steps away. Some to my right shouted, 'Enemy parachutists.' Then there was silence, suddenly inter- rupted by a heart-rending noise, piercing, inhuman. I looked up; in the middle of the road a little pack of dogs was speeding into the direc- tion of the church. One was bloodstained and had fallen behind. Further away a couple of zebras were galloping along, and behind them an enormous giraffe, apparently quite bewildered. Another burst, and the giraffe fell on its knees and collapsed. Those who had taken cover around me were now on their feet again. 'Wolves!' shouted one, 'Hyenas!' another. They were mowed down by the SS men who had taken up positions at the street corner.

During the last air raid bombs had fallen on the zoological gardens a few hundred yards away. Some animals had escaped through doors that had been forced open; others who were kept in the open without cages had panicked and somehow managed to jump over the broad ditch which divided them from the public. A few devoted keepers had tried in vain to head the animals off, but they had escaped into the nearest street. It took the machine-gunners only a few seconds to shoot them, but a solitary orang-outang escaped. Moving with great caution like an experienced street-fighter he jumped from cover to cover close to the walls of the houses, evading the snipers, and eventually disappeared in the ruins of the church. I watched the scene with fascination; my sympathies were with the ape, and I breathed a sigh of relief as he disappeared. The crowd began to disperse despite the rumours that the area was still unsafe, with tigers and poisonous snakes allegedly hiding in the neighbourhood.

The carnival of the animals had turned into a slaughter, a grotesque sideshow soon to be forgotten in the general inferno. Once upon a time on fine summer evenings we had sat at tables in front of this very coffee house. It was here that the cultural avant-garde had met – poets who had never written a line and painters who had never produced a single picture, but who had the reputation of being men of genius. The great theatre critics used to repair to these tables after first nights to write their reviews. There were always a great many pretty girls around with heavy make-up. Once we had shared a table with George Grosz, who had been in one of his most charming moods – until he got drunk, when he became morose and quarrelsome. We had made the acquaintance of some surrealist poets, but even they, in their wildest imagination, could not have conjured up a scene such as that I had just witnessed, only a few steps from where we once had our coffee and cake.

Often on Sundays we had taken the boys to the zoological garden and watched the ostriches in their Egyptian-style houses, the antelopes surrounded by Moorish sculptures, the artificial swamp in which wild boars had made their home. Whenever we lost the boys, we could be sure to find them either in front of the enormous new monkey cages near the artificial lake, called the Vierwaldstaetter See, or at the elephant house further on. On summer evenings there had been open-air concerts and dancing behind the enormous restaurant which boasted that it could cater for some 20,000 visitors.

What happened to the animals outside the Romanische Café in the semi-darkness might have intrigued a Hieronymus Bosch, who would have drawn the humans with animal faces and vice versa; perhaps in his madness he knew something which his sane contemporaries could not grasp.

The workmen in the streets were cutting off dangling wires and repairing burst water-pipes and sewers; an emergency electricity supply was already functioning. The remaining street lamps came on, and a raucous voice could be heard from the loudspeakers which had been installed some years ago all over the city centre. Someone was reading out today's editorial from the *Voelkische Beobachter*: 'Berlin has not lost its nerve. There is no panic: to this brutal cruelty the German people respond with hate. We have shown that we are stronger than fate.' Then the voice of Dr Goebbels: 'Once we were a sentimental people, but the British have taught us to hate. The day of retribution is near!' But there was no hate, and men and women no longer listened to speeches.

At the entrance to a gutted building in the Tauentzienstrasse a woman was weeping bitterly, crying 'Save my son! Cowards, will no one help me....' She was surrounded by a group of neighbours and air wardens with smoke-stained faces. They said that this house had been one of the few left standing before the last raid. The family had gone back to salvage some of the furniture despite the warnings. They had managed to carry out a few chairs, a sewing machine, some coats and a little bird cage. Then the son had gone back once again and been caught by a beam which collapsed. Furthermore, there was a bomb somewhere under the roof which had not exploded. They had tried to call an ambulance, but the medical personnel said that they had strict orders not to enter buildings about to collapse and in any case were not equipped to do so. 'Save my son,' the woman sobbed. There was a moment's silence, and through the silence one could hear a monotonous wail: 'Help, help. Get me out of here.'

Once upon a time I had been trained to respond to calls for help without reflecting on the odds. But for years now my services had not been wanted. If there had been time to think, I might well have reached the conclusion that I did not owe a moral duty to the mother in her despair. For moral obligations had been dispensed with, and for all I knew the woman and her son would not have lifted a finger to save my family. It would have been prudent not to get involved, not to take risks on behalf of people for whom I was an enemy, subhuman, lower than vermin. Perhaps the boy was beyond help in any case; why not leave the rescue to his compatriots, who had been told by their leaders to live heroically and make sacrifices?

The poor people of Berlin were to be pitied; many had been killed, many more had lost all their possessions. If there were many more air raids like the last one their city would no longer exist. But most of them would survive; one day there would be peace again, and a new city would be built on the ruins. But those who had been deported would not come back to life, their departure was final. There was, in short, no good reason that I should come to their help. But one does not reason in such moments and so I gave my coat to one of the bystanders and went in.

Recalling the scene many years later in the solitude of my study I still cannot find a satisfactory explanation for my behaviour. I was not braver than other people, nor did I want to impress anyone, for this was hardly an auspicious time for heroic gestures; if I had been killed that day, no one would have even known about it. Was it an act of despair, was I acting as I did because I felt that there was no way out for me in any case? Hardly, for if I had reached this decision, I would have carried it out at a time and place of my choice.

Another explanation has occurred to me: the night before I had had a strange dream; the war was over, and I was resting somewhere on an island in the sun, looking at sailing-boats and palms. Ridiculous, I told myself in the dream, those days will never come again. No, another voice said, a thousand will die, but you are fated to survive. . . . Ever since boyhood I had been fascinated by an incident in the song of the Nibelungs: Hagen of Tronje has just been told by the mermaids that if they crossed the Danube on their way to the Huns, no one would survive with exception of the king's own chaplain. To test the prediction, Hagen pushed the cleric who could not swim into the torrent, but 'by God's own hand, he still came out, unhurt, back again to land'. For he was fated to live and all the others were to die: as Hagen says at the end, 'all has turned out as I thought'. Perhaps I too wanted to test fate. It is a far-fetched explanation; perhaps one should not analyse too closely actions taken on the spur of the moment.

I went with another man who volunteered to accompany me into this gutted house in the wasteland. Half of it had already collapsed, and the debris barred the way. We advanced slowly, but however cautiously we moved, from time to time some more debris would come down. There were ominous creaks, and a piece of metal hit me on the shoulder. I went down a long corridor in what had once been a first-floor apartment; a door-frame had collapsed and with great care we pushed some of the masonry aside, squeezing our way through. All the time the boy kept on moaning; I called to him that help was on the way, but he probably did not hear me.

My companion, a younger man who had lost an arm in the war, pointed to the roof. The upper part of the house had been neatly cut in half; in the part which was still standing and which we were now about to enter there was a large hole in the roof, and through it the lower section of a bomb could be seen, swinging gently. It was not a very big one, as bombs go, but big enough to bring down the remnants of the house and to bury everything beneath it. Was it a time-bomb likely to go off at any moment, or would it only explode once it hit the ground? We continued on our way.

This had once been a perfectly ordinary building in a high-class neighbourhood. On the ground floor there had been a furniture shop; most of the chairs, tables and desks were smashed; the neighbours would soon make use of this welcome supply of firewood. The first floor had been divided between two families; the apartments now looked as if a giant, not aware of his strength, had turned upside down all that had come to hand, just as a naughty child might destroy his toys in a fit of rage. Some pots and pans had rolled into the corridor, most of the plaster had fallen from the ceiling and so had the lamps; a picture, quite incongruously, still hung crookedly on the wall; there was a doll, a football, some illustrated magazines, a half-burnt carpet and, every-where, glass splinters.

It seemed a very long time since I had entered the building, but in fact no more than a few minutes had passed by the time we reached the boy. He was aged about fifteen, seemingly a perfectly ordinary specimen, white in the face, obviously in considerable pain. He was lying face downward on the floor; a heavy beam had smashed his left leg. I cut off his trousers, and felt but could not see the fracture. It was a nasty injury, but while his leg was pressed to the ground there was nothing I could do. I tried to extricate him very slowly, but realized that I was about to set in motion a further avalanche of debris from the upper floor. I talked to the boy, gave him a drink and told him that he would be got out very soon and that he need only hold out a little longer. He looked at me with great eyes, not fully taking in what I was saying. But he implored me not to leave him again. He was in a state of shock and needed an injection.

I slowly made my way back to the street, reassured the mother, and by good luck found a pharmacy a few steps away. It was closed, but my companion kicked the door open without ceremony. I found mor-phine and also syringe. As I was about to re-enter the building, men in the crowd told me that more big pieces of debris had come down, and when I went in I saw that the bomb had moved downwards a bit and was now swinging more menacingly.

Now I knew the way I reached the boy more quickly than before; he was half-delirious, and his moaning had become weaker. As I prepared the injection I asked him whether he liked sports, and what job he would like to do; he said he wanted to be a pilot. Within a few seconds he fell asleep. Not more than twenty minutes had passed since I had first entered the building, and as I was debating with myself whether I should go or stay, I heard shouts from above.

A rescue squad had arrived at last, and from the roof of the neighbouring house, which miraculously was still standing, a bomb disposal expert had been lowered. With great care, he was tackling the bomb. He had to decide whether it would have to be blown up on the spot or if it could be dismantled: I watched him with fascination listening through a sort of stethoscope. After a minute or two he shouted that there was no immediate danger; I should leave, and in a few minutes his colleagues would come into the house from the front and carry the boy out.

I made my way back, slightly dazed, and to my horror realized that the crowd had swollen to a few hundred. The mother embraced and kissed me and said she did not know how to thank me; my coat was returned to me, one man shook my hand, another said he was a reporter and could he have an interview? But he was pushed aside by two men in uniform who said that they had been passing by and had heard the story. They were the advance party for Dr Goebbels, who was due to arrive here on a tour of inspection in about ten minutes. They had decided that I should be introduced to him, and the whole scene was to be filmed.

I had faced the peril inside the house with some stoicism but now I was in cold sweat. When I stammered some excuses about patients waiting for me, one of them said rather brusquely: 'No nonsense, please. The patients can wait. What you just did was an act of great heroism, worthy of the highest praise. Herr Reichsminister himself will want to congratulate you. Your action should become an inspiration to millions in this hour of trial. We should have more people like you.' He told me to have a drink if I felt faint, and took out a bottle of brandy from under his tunic.

They kept me under guard, and the next half-hour was one of the most unpleasant of my life. I could, of course, brazen it out; I could give a false name and in the general confusion I would be forgotten in a day or two. But my picture would be all over the newspapers and the cinemas; sooner or later I would be located and they would, of course, never forgive me having fooled them, however unwittingly. The only correct course of action would be to tell my companions that I was a

Jew, in which case they would either release me, or alternatively I would be arrested for having extended medical treatment to an 'Aryan', which was strictly prohibited.

But my courage had left me; I could not make up my mind to tell them that I was not made for the role of national hero, and as I agonized more members of the Goebbels party arrived in cars and on foot. I overheard parts of their conversation: one man, apparently a representative of the Foreign Ministry, was saying that the Swedish Embassy had burned down, and the Finnish was destroyed, and the Hungarian and the Danish and the Dutch too. 'We don't even have a full list as yet.' The man next to him remarked that this was the least of his worries, and that the Danes and Dutch, in any case, did not need embassies. 'We take good care of them. . . .' The Foreign Ministry man said: 'But we still need the buildings. Speer's ministry has collapsed except for the first floor. He now wants what used to be the French Embassy, which is only half-destroyed.'

A big car arrived, and a small man in a dark leather coat alighted. Goebbels, surrounded by a dozen aides, was gesticulating: a sudden crisis had developed. Again I heard parts of the conversation: 'Send all the fire brigades to the Alkett factory,' Goebbels shouted, 'top priority, the self-propelling gun, one of our most effective weapons. . . .' Alkett was the big factory out in Reinickendorf or Ruhleben, I forget which. His advisors tried to explain that there were not enough fire engines, they were all out doing urgent work of equal importance; it would take hours to redirect them because so many streets were closed, and if they were diverted now the overall damage would be even greater. 'You got your priorities all wrong,' Goebbels shouted. 'I shall not be overruled by the experts, they have misled me time and again.' The controversy was likely to go on for a long time; messengers arrived on motorcycles and handed dispatches to Goebbels. My two companions had joined the circle of advisers around him, leaving me alone at the entrance.

I walked away. Once or twice I looked furtively back, but no one paid any attention. I turned the corner into Budapester Strasse; no one had missed me. The hero had already been forgotten.

When I reached home in the late afternoon Elizabeth wanted a full account. I said that a great many familiar sights had disappeared and that it would take a long time to clear away the rubble. After I had had a drink I related my own adventures, though not in full detail; she laughed and became apprehensive in turn, and said that even at my mature age I could not be trusted to walk alone through the streets of Berlin without getting involved in dangerous adventures. 'What was the boy like?' 'A perfectly normal boy with brown hair, grey eyes and of medium height, he reminded me of our Peter.' She turned aside and fell silent. I should not have mentioned our son.

Next day there was a short feature in the local Berlin newspaper entitled 'The Story of a Brave Man', an allusion to the title of a well-known nineteenth-century German ballad. Grossly exaggerating the dangers, it described in vivid and colourful detail the story of a boy who had been trapped in a house, threatened both by its collapse and a time-bomb about to explode. It then related how an elderly citizen (I liked that!) who turned out to be a doctor had passed by, and with utter disregard of his own safety had volunteered to make his way into the house, facing almost certain death, and had saved the boy. Instead of waiting for official recognition for this act of heroism, he had quietly disappeared into the crowd. The unsung, unknown hero in civilian clothes symbolized the people's spirit in this hour of supreme trial: their heroism, their willingness to make sacrifices and their utter modesty. Such a people could not possibly be defeated.

I was neither annoyed nor amused, my thoughts were far away: I was thinking of my own sons of whom we had not heard for many months. I did not want to admit it to myself, but I was no longer certain that they were still alive.

Part Three

The
Happy Wanderers

Peter and Erich left school in early 1943. Yet another regulation had just been published concerning children of mixed marriages. It was vague, like most of the regulations concerning mixed marriages: children who were already attending school were permitted to stay provided classes were not too full. Since the evacuation of children and young people from Berlin was well under way they could have continued at school, but they had no wish to do so. Peter was seventeen at the time, and Erich a year younger, and they found the atmosphere at school difficult to bear even though school was less politicized than most outsiders thought. But young people are usually more sensitive to dishonesty than grown-ups and less capable of engaging in constant duplicity. Since they solemnly promised me that they would continue their studies at home, I did not insist. I had time to spare and coached them; the son of friends, a student, who had been invalided out of the army, helped them with mathematics, physics and chemistry.

The boys were quite conscientious; they spent a great deal of time reading, though frequently they disappeared mysteriously, and on occasion did not come back all night. When questioned by their anxious mother next day, they would say that they had been staying with friends in a remote part of town, and that by the time they wanted to come home the last suburban train had gone. Surely we did not want them to walk home?

It sounded very plausible, but I had my doubts. They were tall, strong boys and while there was no opportunity for engaging in organized sport, they certainly liked physical exercise; they ran in the Grunewald almost every day, and they could have got back from even the most remote corner of Berlin in less than two hours if they had wanted. Nor were they timid young men; if anything, they tended to be reckless. But I preferred not to inquire. I knew they would not have told me the truth in any case.

One evening after dinner they asked me about my years in Heidelberg; they knew, of course, the old song 'Old Heidelberg...'. Was it an old folk song? Not really, it was of comparatively recent date; it came in Scheffel's *Trumpeter of Saeckingen*. They wanted to know more about the Trumpeter. I told them what I remembered of the story of Werner Kirchhof, who came to a little town in southern Germany and fell in love with the beautiful Margarita, the daughter of a retired army colonel of Thirty Years War vintage. Young Werner had much to recommend him; he was good looking, played the trumpet exceedingly well, and distinguished himself defending the colonel's castle against attacks. But when he asked for Margarita's hand he was turned down flat for he was not of aristocratic background; and so he plays 'Preserve thee God! My joy seemed then undying', and very sadly departs, never to forget Margarita, who does not forget him either. A few years later, the two meet again in Rome, where Werner has been directing the Pope's orchestra and choir. Innocent the Eleventh hears the story, makes Werner a nobleman – the Marchese Camposanto – and thus seals the happiness of the young couple.

The boys were listening with fascination; I found a copy of the book in my library and read them the scenes describing how young Werner, rowing on the Rhine, serenaded his beloved in her castle. Then I read to them Werner's excursion to the gnome's cave, which ends with the gnome advising his visitor that 'if the world above does vex thee, here thou e'er wilt find a refuge'.

They took the book, and a few evenings later wanted to hear about Ekkehart, the Latin teacher who had been appointed by his abbot to improve the education of the Duchess Hadwig. The young monk fails to realize that the Duchess is far more interested in his physical presence than in the study of Virgil. When at long last he falls in love with her, he has missed his chance; he is incarcerated in the Duchess's castle on the Hohentwiel, but succeeds in escaping with the help of Praxedis, the Duchess's Greek maid. He hides in the Saentis mountains in nearby Switzerland where he writes the Walthari song, one of the landmarks of early medieval literature.

Scheffel had been one of my mother's favourite authors; he was widely read and admired all over Europe at the time, but his fame did not last and after a few decades he was forgotten, unjustly perhaps, because the 'Trumpeter' is still a charming poem. *Habent sua fata libelli* – overpraised authors quite often fare badly as far as posterity is concerned. But my two youngsters certainly liked Scheffel; and I did not realize till months later that their enthusiasm had not only to do with the literary merits of the books. Parents tend to be rather naive about their own children.

All this happened while they were still attending school in late autumn of 1942. It was a few weeks later that they asked me if I would be willing to talk to some of their friends who wanted to consult me on a matter of some urgency and importance. I knew that lately they had been seeing a lot of a group of Jewish boys and girls of their own age. From time to time some of them would come to our house, but I never talked to them at any length, nor were my sons over-eager for me to know too much about their friends.

Though I hardly knew them, and was aware of the dangers involved, I was glad of what was obviously a conscious decision, an act of identification. Children from mixed marriages were so often confused; they simply did not know where they belonged. The 'Aryan' side rejected them, and for the other side some of them had nothing but contempt and even hate. For it was difficult for young people not to be influenced by a propaganda which told them day in, day out that Jews were not only physically repulsive, but criminals, the scum of the earth.

Most Jews I knew were not only more handsome than fat Julius Streicher (who edited the *Stuermer*) or Dr Goebbels, but also morally superior, which admittedly is not saying much. But the younger generation had no experience from which to draw comparisons; many of them had hardly ever seen a Jew, for the Jews had disappeared. Children of mixed marriages quite frequently blamed their Jewish father or mother for their plight: why should they be mistreated and isolated in school? Why should they be discriminated against in every way, why should they not be permitted to attend university? Why could they not be like everyone else? I knew quite a few cases where the Jewish partner in a mixed marriage had committed suicide not because of Nazi persecution, but because of the attitude of his own children. But I also knew of many cases in which children reacted quite differently. Young people have a strong sense of fairness; they tend to be conformists, but they also react violently against injustice, especially if they happen to be the victims. If they are punished and are unaware of having committed any offence they feel a deep grievance, and this shapes their whole attitude towards authority.

I had never tried to indoctrinate my children, but they knew my attitude instinctively even though not a single word was spoken. In short, they became ardent little anti-Nazis, so much so that I had to caution them from time to time; I was afraid that they would be unable to restrain themselves in public; that one day they would get carried away, with disastrous consequences. But they reassured me: they knew exactly how to behave outside the house; they had to appear as loyal young citizens of the Third Reich, believers in Adolf Hitler and final victory, who precisely because of their unfortunate racial origins would be exemplary in their behaviour.

I found such cynicism prudent but also very frightening. Would not this kind of controlled schizophrenia gradually become second nature? Would not lasting damage be caused? Could young people, having been exposed to such expedients, still believe in any moral values?

But this was a time in which almost everything had to be subordinated to survival. So they went on leading their double existence; outwardly they were slightly blemished young Germans, affected by some of the anti-Jewish laws but not immediately threatened by deportation and death. At the same time they were active members of a Jewish youth group to which they could be of great service, because not having to wear the Jewish star they could move more freely than the others. I was glad that irrespective of the risks (for by associating with Jews they forfeited in the eyes of the authorities their special status) they had now become active, and could even be of some use to the group; and the least I could do was to see their friends.

The encounter took place in our house one evening in October 1942. There were three of them, two young men and one woman all in their early twenties, and they did not arrive together; for any 'organized' assemblies were, of course, strictly forbidden. The one who came first, a tall man with black hair and a moustache, introduced himself as Michael Wolf; he added apologetically that this was not his real name, but that it would be better for all concerned if I did not know his identity. By the time the others had come my sons had left the room; we retired to my study, and Elizabeth brought us tea.

They went straight to the point: what did I know about their organization? Very little, I said, but my son's friends were my friends. . . . 'But we know you,' they said, and as they refreshed my memory, the details came back.

Shortly before the outbreak of the war, I had been invited to give a talk to some two hundred youth leaders at an agricultural training centre not far from Berlin. I had been impressed by the audience; there was not much sophistication, for these earnest young people had never been to a university. But there was genuine intellectual curiosity; the questions were very much to the point, and sometimes I was hard pressed for an answer. Our discussion continued until well after midnight and covered a great deal of ground.

They were members of a world-wide youth organization, founded some thirty years earlier. Influenced by the youth movements which had proliferated in Europe during and after the First World War, they were organized in groups of ten or twenty, headed by self-chosen leaders only a few years older. Their aim was to educate their members (who were aged between twelve and twenty) for life in the collective settlements in Palestine, to give them a grounding in agricultural work, to prepare them for life in a community, and to impart some general and some Jewish education.

Once there had been a few thousand of them in Germany; most had been able to leave in time, legally or illegally, with their parents or alone; many had reached the shores of their promised land, others had landed in America or elsewhere. Four hundred of them were caught when war broke out; a hundred or so had still been able to emigrate in 1939–40, another hundred had been deported. By now about two hundred were left, half here in Berlin, the rest in Neuendorf, an agricultural training farm not far away.

Alfred, the second young man, told me that those in Berlin were still meeting once or twice a week, though any organized activity was, of course, strictly forbidden. On Sundays they went hiking in nearby forests, and during the week they would meet at night in the homes of their members' parents – which again was strictly illegal, for Jews were not permitted to leave their homes in the evening. They would sing their Hebrew songs, but not too loudly for fear that they would be overheard by neighbours who might go to the police. They listened to lectures on Jewish history, Palestine and the kibbutz and their life after the war. These meetings were the only moral support the young people had; what they heard at home, in the streets and at work induced only despair.

I did not interrupt his account, though I had many questions: I had had no idea that their organization was still in existence. It seemed altogether unreal; boys and girls singing songs in the middle of this tragedy, learning Hebrew, walking in the forest, discussing problems that might face them after the war – if they lived that long, which was not too likely. It seemed touching but altogether futile. But then I thought, perhaps they were right. They had not given in, they still had hope, and for this very reason they probably had a better chance.

What could I possibly do for them? Michael first implored me never, under any circumstances, to reveal the contents of our discussion, for the fate of many young people might depend on it. I promised. He continued: 'We knew you as the father of two of our members, and some of us know you by reputation. We came to you not as a medical man but because we need advice on a very different matter.'

Their problem, to cut a long story short, was whether to go underground with all their remaining members. Was it the right thing to do, and would it be physically possible? The young woman, who had given her name as Esther – she was hardly more than a girl and wore no yellow star (another *Mischling*?) – said with some passion that there was every reason to assume that the deportations would continue and that soon not a single Jew would be left in Germany. They had not heard from their own comrades who had been deported; she for one had never shared the optimism of some of their friends who thought that those who had been deported were now doing agricultural work somewhere in eastern Poland or White Russia. Quite frankly, she doubted whether they would see any of them again. They had a duty to save as many as possible of those remaining, for if they went on as before, they would be picked up one by one and deported. Going underground was dangerous; it would not be easy to get lost in the big city. But at least there was a chance: they would remove the yellow star, somehow get new identity papers, and some of them at least would live to greet the day when the nightmare would be over.

Alfred listened to her without once interrupting, but when she had finished he said: 'We cannot agree, and this is why we wanted to consult an outsider. I have misgivings too about the fate of our comrades who were deported – and I fear for the fate of those who remain. But we cannot be sure that a disaster has happened; perhaps they are still alive. Yet even if the worst has happened, do we have the right to save ourselves, not to share the fate of the Jewish people in their hour of trial?' In the Middle Ages whole Jewish communities went to their deaths; only traitors tried to escape. Furthermore, he said, one did not know for certain whether the deportations would continue: perhaps the war would be over sooner than we thought. Perhaps the Nazis for whatever reason would show greater restraint. Granted, these were faint hopes, but could one dismiss them altogether? And lastly, on a purely practical level, how could boys and girls, most of them mere children, possibly survive illegally in hostile surroundings? They had read the accounts of professional revolutionaries of the past, men and women with great experience of living outside the law. But in spite of knowing all the tricks, most of them had been caught in the end.

'It may be a little easier for women than for men,' Alfred said, looking at Esther, 'for the military police will not be after them. But where will we get papers, shelter, food and above all money? How can we train thirteen or fourteen-year-old boys and girls to keep the rules of conspiracy day and night – and not betray the others if they are caught? A few communists may succeed in outsmarting the Gestapo – they have contacts, money, powerful help from abroad. What do we have?' He shook his head sadly. 'I am afraid it is only a chimera....'

They looked at me. I said unlike Alfred I did not see any moral problem. The Jewish people was not facing a trial but a catastrophe, and there was no moral duty to go to one's death just to share the fate of the other victims. One had the duty to risk one's life if one could help others, but if one could not, it was just a heroic gesture. Nor could I see any parallel with the Middle Ages when many Jewish communities, too upright and too proud to dissimilate their beliefs and lead an undercover existence, had let themselves be slaughtered rather than undergo conversion. In those dark centuries this was the only way to show their courage: death and torture were preferable if they could not openly live as Jews, and there was always the hope that their martyrdom would eventually make their prosecutors relent. But the Nazis would never relent; they did not aim at religious conversion.

But did Esther fully understand the practical difficulties of an underground existence? She interjected: 'We may get some money from abroad.' 'That might solve some problems, but not others,' I said. 'Have you talked to the people at Kantstrasse?' They had, and they had been advised not to engage in any foolhardy illegal action. 'I don't trust them any more, Eppstein and Co,' Michael said. 'I don't blame them; they and their families would be taken away if they did not comply with the Gestapo's orders. But we shall no longer get disinterested advice from them.'

I told Michael that the questions they had raised were practical rather than philosophical in nature, and for this reason they might not have come to the right address. In the abstract, the case for going underground was overwhelming. But could it be done? I wanted time to think about it; perhaps we could meet again soon. They thanked me, but Esther said as she left: 'There may be less time than we think.'

The next day Otto dropped in on one of his rounds as sub-district air warden, and I asked him a number of hypothetical questions. I probably should not have done, but I had learnt long ago that there were situations in which one had to take risks. What if there was a group of boys and girls facing grave danger? Otto immediately said that anything was preferable to deportation; he had always assumed the worst as far as the Nazis were concerned, and he had almost always been right. But he, too, needed time to consider various aspects of the question.

A week later he came back smiling, saying that his instinct had not betrayed him. He had discussed with his old comrades in the police force – on a purely abstract level of course – the chances of survival with false papers in Berlin. They had told him that the chances were good, unless the persons wishing to hide behaved with unpardonable stupidity.

By now everyone in Germany was supposed to have about a dozen different identity cards: birth certificate, military pass or some letter from one's place of work, an *Ahnennachweis* (something like a family tree), ration book, post office card and so on. Since no one could possibly have all these papers – let alone carry them around all the time – the police were usually satisfied with one of them. Some were difficult to obtain, others very easy – the post office card, for example, which merely entitled one to collect registered letters. Ration books could be bought on the black market, a document of employment could easily be forged if one had the right stationery. Once one had one or two of these documents it was not too difficult to get the rest. The golden rule was never to appear flustered or nervous; if there was a check-up in the street not to evade the police or SS, but to approach them and appear confident and sure of oneself.

Given these elementary precautions, one stood a very good chance of never being caught. Control had become almost impossible as the bombing made thousands of people homeless. Many people had lost their papers, many had to move to new quarters; the bureaucracy could no longer cope with these constant changes. But was there not a danger that the authorities would check on someone who applied for new identity papers? Yes, but they would make spot checks only. The police had simply not enough manpower to cope with a situation that was becoming more and more chaotic, what with the constant stream of foreign labourers in and out of Germany and the migration of Germans from place to place trying to evade the air raids. Top priority would still be given to the search for spies and foreign agents, but the security authorities had virtually accepted that lesser villains would escape their dragnet. They would be caught only by accident. Nor could they any longer investigate every report about suspicious movements.

There were endless possibilities for hiding in a big city like Berlin; some people would provide shelter for money, others because they hated the Nazis. There were thousands of houses destroyed or half-destroyed; there were boathouses on the river and little huts on the garden allotments which no one used in winter. There were whole sections of the city which were hardly ever patrolled by the police. Anyone could find a part-time job these days without too many questions asked. In short, while the police still had the reputation of being omniscient and omnipotent, there were very narrow limits to both its knowledge and its efficiency.

I met Michael and Esther again in November; they were agitated, for Alfred had been arrested a few days earlier. (They did not yet know that he had been shot.) I told them what I had heard. The dangers of waiting were greater than I had thought, and the risks of an illegal existence were less formidable. But in any case they had already made up their minds; Alfred's arrest was the last straw.

Thus, in the middle of winter, in the last week of 1942, they went underground, defying those who wanted to destroy them. They were totally inexperienced, virtually without any outside help. It was easy to remove the Jewish star, which made them so conspicuous, but they had to find new papers straight away and they needed money for their new existence. Their training as boy and girl scouts had not prepared them for a life in which courage, an iron nerve, inventiveness, infinite patience and sometimes utter ruthlessness was needed.

I often thought about this in later years, and I still cannot understand where they found the mental resources, and what kept them going through those long months of adversity and constant danger. I later heard similar stories about street-gangs of ten-year-old boys in Warsaw who had lost their families and survived the war selling matches in a central square, hiding their true identity. But it still remains a riddle; for what were they looking forward to?

It is possible to face even the greatest dangers if one sees the light at the end of the tunnel, if one knows that in a year, or even two, the tribulations will be over. But in late 1942 there was no such prospect; this was even before the German defeat at Stalingrad and the change in the tide of war in North Africa. At that time a German victory still seemed very likely indeed, and for all one knew Nazi rule would go on for ever, and no escape seemed possible. Without the benefit of hindsight, the decision to go underground was foolhardy to the point of madness. But then there are periods in the affairs of men when salvation lies only in madness, and when a sober, rational calculation of the chances of survival can only lead to perdition.

Suddenly, in 1942, I realized that my sons were no longer children but had become young men. Physically they were fine specimens, a little taller than me; the lack of food during the war had no obvious detrimental influence on them; they were clearly prospering on various kinds of spinach and cabbage. They were beginning to show a spirit of responsibility and maturity which I certainly had not possessed at their age, which was wonderful and also somewhat frightening. For they were precisely at the age when they were expected to behave irresponsibly, to sow their wild oats.

Erich, the younger, was the more introverted: a boy of few words, very deliberate in what he said, the more intellectual and also the more obstinate of the two. From an early age there was no stopping or deflecting him once he had made up his mind, and his mother and I had given up trying to long ago, since his resolutions were usually quite sensible. Peter was less reserved and secretive, and more friendly; but he too had learnt at an early age to behave like a little diplomat. The boys always had to be on the alert; they could never afford to relax, let alone let themselves go; there were no unguarded moments for them.

This frightened me, for while grown-ups may behave like this for months and years, without lasting harm, an adolescence of this kind, I suspected, would leave terrible scars. I clearly underrated the almost infinite capacity of human beings to stay relatively normal even under conditions of great strain. Their fate, like mine, was forever hanging on a thin thread; there were constant rumours of enforced divorce for mixed marriages, of sterilization, and of deportation. These were by no means unfounded rumours, for all these possibilities were indeed discussed by the authorities.

We lived in a twilight zone, and this was more difficult to bear than any certainty – even the certainty of disaster; there is an old German saying about an end with horror being preferable to horror without end. I had always regarded this a stupid, irrational sentiment until I found myself in a similar situation.

Some of my 'Aryan' friends suggested that we should find a third Aryan grandfather or grandmother for our boys, for this would have solved most of their difficulties: if a 'quarter Aryan' was treated like a Jew, those with only one Jewish grandparent were usually considered 'Aryans'. As a result a frantic search began in some families for adulterous mothers and grandmothers; it may sound funny now, but then it was quite often a matter of life or death. I would not have agreed to go through such a procedure; the boys in any case had already chosen – and theirs was not to be the line of least resistance.

So they left school, and it was not a great misfortune; many of the better teachers had been called up, and education in the Third Reich had very much deteriorated. Their future was now quite unclear; until recently young men of mixed origins had been called up into the army – but they could not be promoted, they had to remain privates for ever. This regulation was changed in the middle of the war, and they were now enlisted at eighteen to serve in labour battalions, frequently outside Germany, always in execrable conditions; they had to work long hours, housing was bad, food altogether insufficient and they were systematically harrassed and humiliated by their superiors.

Peter and Erich had decided to evade service in these battalions and fortune, for once, seemed to smile on them. For by some mysterious circumstance their files in the local labour exchange had disappeared in the general confusion, or had been mislaid by an unknown well-wisher. Normally, on leaving school they would have received an order to work in a factory until they were old enough to join the labour battalions. But these call-up notices never came; the boys had apparently been forgotten. But for how long? They knew that there was no lack of informers around, and so they left home in working clothes in the morning and returned in the evening: to all appearances they were part of the giant war effort working for the final victory.

In actual fact they acted as couriers for their comrades who had gone underground. They did not have to wear the yellow star, they were permitted to use public transport and, above all, their identity papers were in order. They volunteered to carry messages or sums of money that had been received from abroad, and sometimes they forged documents. On any given day they would meet a visitor from Switzerland who had been sent by one of the rescue committees abroad or negotiate with some underworld character selling ration books or offering shelter. They moved carefully, always checking whether they were being followed. But they still had to take great risks; their contacts could be Gestapo agents, and if they were apprehended together with one of their 'illegal' comrades, they would of course have shared their fate.

I did not know all the details, but not much imagination was needed to understand that they were in constant danger; if they were not home in time for dinner I could not settle down to work. I admired their courage. True, they were still very young, and for them the element of adventure was an additional attraction. They courted danger and did not think much about the possible consequences. Most of the beautiful things which I had experienced at their age were not for them, nor could they possibly have high expectations for the future. And yet they were usually in high spirits; they seldom quarrelled with one another, and on rare occasions they were even willing to help a bit around the house.

During the winter of 1942–3 they had to take us into their confidence, for at that period one of their main assignments was to find safe quarters for some of their comrades. The number of illegals was still small at the time, but during the spring and summer of 1943 it grew to hundreds, perhaps even thousands. Most of them were acting quite independently of each other; Peter and Erich were responsible only for the twenty members of their own group. But the fact that there were now so many in hiding alerted the Gestapo to the problem, and underground life became daily more dangerous.

From time to time we would provide temporary shelter for one of the illegals who had had to give up his old quarters and was now desperately looking for a new place to hide. The dangers involved were obvious; if we were caught it would have meant, at best, instant arrest and deportation. Whenever we had one of these guests we got little sleep, afraid of every noise in the street, waiting for the morning to come, and his departure.

It was equally obvious that we could not have refused, however great the risk. On one occasion during the height of the winter we had a sweet girl staying with us, Miryam, who had contracted pneumonia. For a day or two it was not certain whether she would live, but we nursed her back to health. The neighbours were told that she was Elizabeth's niece from Munich, who had come to help her aunt but had instead fallen ill herself. I shall have to say more about her later on.

One evening in March 1943 Michael called on me again. He now had new papers according to which he was a Dutch-born engineer employed by a Dortmund firm producing electrical equipment for the army. These papers would not have stood up to any thorough examination, but for routine checks in the street or at railway stations they were quite good enough.

Life underground, he said, was even more difficult than they had imagined: they were constantly on the run. In view of the enormous risks involved there were few people who would put them up, and they had hardly any connections among non-Jews. During the last month he had stayed first with a half-Jewish couple, then with an elderly lady, a devout Christian who helped Jews in every possible way. She kept a little shop in the north and he had slept in the store-room. He had then stayed for a few nights with a down-and-out tramp in one of the darkest slums in east Berlin; this was the safest place he had found so far, but it was full of rats and bugs and lice. It had also been an educational experience, for the tramp was a man with wide cultural interests and they had discussed eighteenth-century literature for hours.

For two or three nights he had been without shelter; together with a friend he developed a certain routine. They would spend the first part of the night in the opera, and after midnight travelled on all-night trams and buses just to keep warm. One could always get a little sleep during the day in a cheap coffee house or a movie. There were no searches in places of public entertainment, and only infrequent ones in the trams and the buses; the disruption to urban traffic would have been too great. The places that had to be avoided at all costs were railway stations.

It was a horrible way of life, and more than once, in a moment of weakness, he asked himself whether he would have the strength to go on – tired, hungry, freezing, moving through the streets of the city like a hunted animal. But then he would think about the younger members of the group – some were only in their early teens – who had to endure the same hardships: only one of them had given up, and this had been a special case. None had been caught, whereas of those who had not gone underground most had been apprehended in the 'factory action' of late February 1943.

For the Gestapo no longer relied on the willingness of Berlin Jews – there were virtually no others left in Germany – to appear voluntarily at the concentration points to be deported. To prevent any attempts to escape, no advance notice was given in late February, except to the managers of the factories concerned. To their credit some of them had warned the Jews, and as a result a great many had not shown up at work on 27 February, or on the days after. Some of these were arrested later in their homes, but most were no longer to be found at their old addresses; they were walking the streets of Berlin in desperate search of shelter. Among them were a dozen members of the youth group who earlier on had refused to join Michael and the other illegals.

Those of us who watched the deportations were desperately un-happy about what was happening. Every case hurt, but there were some which hurt even more than others. One of these concerned Miryam, the girl who was taken ill at our house. One could not help liking her; she was one of these fortunate human beings whom nature has endowed with the gift of inspiring trust and friendship. While she was staying with us she was constantly afraid that her presence would be a cause of concern and embarrassment. She had all the freshness and the charm (and the remarkable poise) of a girl who was just blossoming into young womanhood.

Elizabeth was captivated by her, and I looked forward every day to talking to my patient. She was the child of poor parents in the east of Berlin; her father had died when she was still very young, and her mother was in bad health. For her, as for so many others, belonging to the group provided more than an agreeable pastime and an opportunity to meet like-minded people of her own age. It gave her the strength to cope with an otherwise hopeless situation. Her great dream was to become a children's nurse in a kibbutz in Palestine once the war was over, perhaps a paediatrician, and she questioned me more than once about the difficulties of the profession and whether she would be up to it. The moment she felt a little better she wanted to help around the house, and had to be almost forcibly restrained. She was a lovely girl in every respect, one of the most unselfish beings I ever met, and I came to like her very much indeed.

But there was one member of our household who took an even closer interest in her, and this was Peter. He fell in love with her, and the two of them, breaking all rules of conspiracy, met almost daily during the spring of 1943. They went to the Spree forest or to the Grunewald; they sat on benches in the Tiergarten or some other park, quite oblivious of the weather; and they were, of course, quite safe, for who would pay any attention to a very young couple so obviously in love? It was Peter's first great love, and it was to remain, I believe, his only one for a long time to come.

Once a week, always at night, Miryam would go home to see her mother, again in contravention of the rules of underground life. When she returned she was always very sad: her mother was very ill, she was too weak to cope, she needed her at home. And then a few weeks later there came the dreaded day when Miryam came back weeping: her mother had been informed that she would have to join the next transport as one of a group of invalids. There was no danger that they would escape, so they had been given due notice to prepare themselves.

Miryam did not hesitate; she would accompany her mother. Peter talked to her for a whole night but without avail: for seventeen years her mother had taken care of Miryam, the least she could do was to be with her now when she was most needed. Peter said that there were others who needed her, her friends, the country to which she would go once the war was over, the kibbutz, the children she was to take care of, and also her own children, as yet unborn. Why did she not think of the future?

But Miryam just became even sadder, and said that if Peter really loved her he would not make it more difficult for her. She was aware of all the arguments for and against; of course she wanted to live, and work, and have children of her own. But her first duty was still to her mother, who at this moment needed her more than anyone else. How could she go on living knowing that her mother was somewhere in a ghetto in eastern Poland, ill and desperately miserable? But what could she do for her mother, Peter wanted to know. She too had heard the rumours that the transports might never reach their destination. But Miryam was not shaken: she could not leave her mother alone. In the group she was expendable, but no one else could now help her mother.

Two days later she left Berlin; the S S was only too happy to have an additional member of the transport, and no questions were asked about her whereabouts in recent months.

That day Peter came home white in the face, went to his room, and for a long time spoke to no one. I left him alone in his grief. Three days later he went out again on his job, taking even more foolish risks than usual. I had a long talk with him and tried to impress on him that however great his loss, he had no right to endanger himself and others.

I was feeling the grief almost as acutely as he did that day, and for many days after. I carry her picture with me to this day, and whenever I look at it I am overwhelmed by sadness. Sweet little Miryam, with your great eyes, life had not been very good to you in your seventeen years; you had known nothing but suffering and danger. Yet this is not how you saw it; you were one of the happiest creatures I ever knew, and a joy to all who knew you. May your soul rest in peace.

Miryam was deported in early April, and then on the eighteenth, a few days before Passover, there was another shock. It was the last time I did night duty at the Grosse Hamburger concentration point. I have mentioned before that about half the members of the youth organization to which Peter and Erich belonged had been working on farms, some in Neuendorf, not far from Berlin, others in Lower Saxony. They felt reasonably safe, for their work was certainly essential for the war effort, manpower in agriculture being in short supply. But they had not taken into account the relentless working of the bureaucratic machine:

they thought they had been forgotten, but one day someone at Gestapo headquarters came across their file and their fate was sealed. In mid-April all fifty of them were brought to Berlin to join the next transport, which was to leave on the nineteenth.

They occupied four large rooms in the building. Having arrived on a Friday afternoon, they immediately started preparing for the celebration of Sabbath. Few of them came from religious homes, and strictly speaking few would have been considered believers even now. But a service of this kind assumed in those days a significance far beyond its traditional character.

Never before had there been a group like this in the camp, only individuals who had little in common except their tragic fate. Now for the first time there was a group which felt that doing things together gave it strength. They were sitting on the floor in the corridor, singing about the great future of the Jewish people returning to its ancient land, about Galilee and the Yesreel Valley, about work in the fields and the chain of generations which had not broken and would never be broken. Late at night they danced the horra.

On the next evening they celebrated the Passover service as best they could; they had no wine, nor any of the ingredients of the festive meal, such as parsley or horse-radish. But they were elated by the spirit of the feast of liberty which commemorates the exodus from Egypt – and from slavery. One of them had prepared a topical Haggadah – the ritual recital. They repeated after him, with fervent intensity, 'This year we are here, next year may we be in the Land of Israel. This year we are slaves, next year may we be free men.' And again towards the end, 'Pour out thy wrath' – calling for vengeance on those who were oppressing Israel.

The Haggadah is a story of miracles, of captives set free from the house of suffering and iniquity; never have I heard it read in stranger circumstances. The S S guards looked on impassively and incredulously: why were these young Jews so happy? Later in the night I talked to some of the group. They were more optimistic than anyone else I had met in recent years, perhaps because they had led a sheltered life on their farms: history had bypassed them. What awaited them out in the east? No one really knew, but they felt they had a chance if they stuck together, whatever happened. Their solidarity was their strength; in the group they felt protected, alone they would be lost.

A few weeks earlier I had been reading about the fate of the Jews in medieval Germany and one episode had stuck in my memory, the fate of the community of Nordhausen. This was in 1349, when the Black Death took its toll in Europe and the Jews were made responsible for the epidemic. According to the chroniclers whole communities were put to death; in Nordhausen, a little town in central Germany, the local community asked the magistrate for a little time to prepare themselves for martyrdom. Permission being granted, they hired musicians to play dance tunes 'so that they should enter the presence of God with singing'.

As I witnessed the dancing and singing I was reminded of Nordhausen. But the young men and women I was watching had not the faintest intention of dying; they thought that there was a future for them, if only they had the strength to survive the trials; they were confident that they would live and be led out of captivity. Had they ever considered going underground? They were reluctant even to discuss the subject; was it not cowardice to save one's own life when there was no chance for the rest of the community? Was it not treason? Above all, it would have meant splitting up. And so they had persuaded themselves that together they might survive, whereas alone they had not a chance. On 19 April their train left Berlin.

May passed, and June, and in early July we found a letter in our mailbox addressed to Elizabeth. It was a short note from Miryam, and it came from a place called Auschwitz of which none of us had heard until a few months ago, but which of late was mentioned more and more often. We had no idea how the letter had been smuggled out; most probably one of the guards going on home leave had taken pity – there were a few such cases.

The letter had, of course, to be couched in vague terms. Miryam wrote that she was as well as could be expected; her mother suffered no longer, and she had been very glad to meet the members of the agricultural group who had arrived in April. She added two words in Hebrew: *Zikhronam lebrakha*, of blessed memory, the traditional formula used about people no longer among the living. She was thinking of us and the group, and above all of Peter. She was sure we understood that she had only done her duty. If this turned out to be her last message, we were to think of her from time to time when we saw the dawn of a new day. I passed the letter to Peter, and left the room.

In July some twenty-eight members of the youth group were living illegally in Berlin. About half were girls; one of them was only eleven years old. The young men in their late teens and early twenties were of course in greater danger than the others, because by right they should have been in the army; they would be an object of interest not only to the police but also to the military police in their search for deserters. Some of them wore bandages or walked with a stick, but this was not an ideal solution since it drew attention to them, and the golden rule of illegal existence was to be inconspicuous.

Those underground needed three things above all – new identity papers, shelter and money. Forged identity papers could be bought, but they were not cheap, and Jewish boy and girl scouts had no contacts with the milieu in which the professional forgers operated. But necessity is the mother of invention, and little by little connections were established; there was one man who supplied army passes, a graphic artist forged ration books, and eventually every one of the illegals had some sort of identity card. Whenever he encountered a police patrol he would shout 'Heil Hitler' – this became almost mechanical – produce his papers and hope for the best.

To find shelter was even more difficult. After each air raid, emergency offices were established in public institutions to help those who had lost their homes, and it was, of course, possible to apply there, and ask for both new papers and quarters. But this was considered too risky and only a few of the illegals dared try it.

A few left Berlin for other parts of the country. The girls worked as domestics, the young men on farms, in factories or workshops. Millions of people were drifting from place to place at the time; whole factories were transferred, families split up, and in Berlin alone there were about 100,000 foreign workers; the arrival of newcomers did not arouse as much curiosity as it would have done under normal circumstances.

But the great majority of the illegals remained in Berlin. Some found a little attic or a cellar or a blockhouse which they would leave only in an emergency. For food and drink they had to depend on others; when they were ill they could not see a doctor. Adults could perhaps survive an existence of this kind, but for very young people a life of total inactivity, of sitting and waiting, was almost impossible to bear. On a rare occasion my sons took me into their confidence: a fifteen-year-old boy had been in a little attic for six months; he began to behave strangely, and I advised Peter to get him out as quickly as possible. The boy had relations in occupied Denmark and I suggested that he should try to make his way to Copenhagen. He did so, alone, without papers and money, without even a map. It was a desperate case, but a good angel must have guided his steps; we later heard that he had arrived safely and ended up in Sweden.

Sometimes the illegals were put up as relations or acquaintances of the host family. But there was always the danger that some inquisitive busybody in the neighbourhood would take an interest, and then the illegals would have to leave immediately. It was of cardinal importance to be on good terms with the concierge, who of course knew about all comings and goings and who was also the first to hear of any impending danger. The elementary rule of conspiracy was that people should know as little as possible about each other's whereabouts and movements. Michael, who still acted as head of the group, dealt only with Peter, Erich and Rita, another *Mischling*. Each of these was entrusted to keep in touch with seven or eight youngsters, so that in the case of an arrest only part of the group would be endangered.

Yet despite the danger they still managed to get together in small groups; once a week during the summer they made excursions to the Spreewald, meeting somewhere in the forest at a point agreed on beforehand. Small groups would visit a museum, the opera or the theatre, passing each other in the passages as if they were strangers. Meetings of this kind, the confirmation that their friends were still alive, gave them fresh courage.

They constantly needed money. Before the chief organization of German Jews had been closed down by the Gestapo, Michael had obtained a certain sum; but this had been spent within a few weeks. Some of the illegals had found work, but this was usually badly paid; they preferred to get food rather than money, and were overjoyed to be invited for a meal. Money, while still the legal tender, was no longer that much in demand; Germany was gradually reverting to barter trade. But the illegals had nothing to barter.

Small sums of money arrived occasionally from abroad. News about the mass exterminations reached the Jewish rescue organization in New York, London and Jerusalem in August and September 1942. At first there was disbelief, but as more and more details came in from different sources the general picture became clearer, even though the magnitude of the disaster was not yet fully realized. The rescue organization then renewed its efforts to help through its representatives in Constantinople, Geneva and Lisbon. They tried desperately to find agents to visit Nazi-occupied Europe under some plausible cover and transmit letters and money. But among the agents there were few philantropists and a great many dishonest characters; they usually demanded exorbitant compensation for their services, and even then some would disappear without trace – together with the money. But a trickle did reach the illegals, and so they continued their precarious existence, still hungry, with no money to buy clothes and shoes, or to pay their hosts.

Officially, I knew nothing about all this. But from time to time they had to take me into their confidence in some emergency. Once when they desperately needed money they came to me; I had no cash, but sold some rare books and old medical instruments from my collection and this helped them for a little while. Then there was the case of the girl who became pregnant and for whom I had to arrange an abortion. They came to regard me as an ally, even though this entailed an additional risk, and Michael too would turn up from time to time and discuss the general situation with me.

My admiration for the illegals was increasing; only yesterday they had been mere children, and I would not have dreamed of dealing with them as equals. They were not particularly clever: there was little of the traditional Jewish intellectual genius in these boys and girls, and this included my own sons. In fact, they were rather uneducated – and how could it have been otherwise under the circumstances? But their characters were steeled in adversity; they showed astonishing maturity and unselfishness. They reminded me a little of my own generation which had grown up in the deadly thunder and hail of the First World War. But we had been led and commanded, whereas with them everything depended on their own initiative. We had been trained, whereas they were totally unprepared, and quite a few years younger at that. The other day my Russian teacher gave me a Gorky poem to read which ended: 'I sing this song to the madness of the brave', and I immediately thought of these unlikely young heroes.

In early August there was a sudden crisis. Peter did not come home for several nights, and when he eventually returned he was visibly upset. But he was unwilling to talk, and I came to know the full story only weeks later. Several of the illegals had reported that they felt apprehensive, as if someone was closing in on them. They could not put their finger on any specific incidents, but living underground they had developed a sixth sense, an instinctive warning system. Then, suddenly, disaster struck.

Ilse, one of the illegals, had met Rosa Sterner, a young woman in her early twenties, who had been vaguely known several years earlier on the sidelines of Jewish youth groups. Rosa accosted Ilse in the street and said that she had also gone underground and she was eager to establish contact with others. She had many contacts with non-Jews and said she could be of great help to the other illegals. Ilse said she knew no other illegals, and subsequently reported the incident to her friends. But she had already agreed to meet Rosa again at the entrance to one of the underground stations in the centre of town. She had misgivings, and so had her comrades; but what if Rosa really had those contacts? It was a risk that had to be taken, like so many others.

Ilse went to the meeting place accompanied by Peter, who followed her at a distance of some twenty yards. Rosa welcomed Ilse with great exuberance; but then they were suddenly joined by two young men who took the resisting Ilse in a firm grip and led her towards the train. She had been arrested, but did not dare to cause a commotion. The last Peter saw was Rosa lighting a cigarette, her face expressing obvious satisfaction over a job well done.

This was a major disaster; for even though Ilse had known the whereabouts of only two or three of the others (including Peter), there was now a real danger that the Gestapo would gradually unravel the whole network, and it seemed only a question of time until everyone would be taken. Peter went to Michael, and they decided on a plan of action: the two illegals known to Ilse had to leave their present shelter at once. Then they must find out whether contact could be established with Ilse in prison. Though she did not know Peter's address she was aware of his identity, and he was therefore in immediate danger. And lastly, there was the question of what counter-measures were to be taken against the informers.

To find new quarters was always easier in summer than in winter; one of the two girls affected found shelter as a domestic help in the house of a clergyman in the Rhineland, and the other obtained employment in Potsdam, where there was little chance that she would be detected by Rosa and her helpers. As for Peter, it was decided that he should stay where he was; if arrested he would tell them he had an affair with Ilse, that he had not the faintest idea that she was Jewish and living illegally, but had always assumed that she was another *Mischling* who had left home because she did not get along with her parents. It sounded superficially plausible, but it was doubtful whether this story would have held up under the interrogation of experienced and ruthless professionals. Peter said that we should be prepared for our house to be searched.

After a few days it emerged that Ilse was being held in the hospital at 3 Iranische Strasse. While being escorted to Gestapo headquarters she had thrown herself from the moving train and had been injured.

For several days she was not in a state to be interrogated, and by the time the Gestapo talked to her she had prepared her story. The Gestapo did not pay great attention to her; for them she was just another young Jewess living illegally in Berlin, and they were not particularly interested in her story. Ilse furthermore behaved admirably; she got frequent hysterics, claiming that Rosa had informed on her in revenge because of some young men on whom she had designs but who preferred Ilse. The Gestapo interrogator got very impatient: but why had she not registered as a Jewess? Ilse said that she had been told she was only half Jewish, but that the procedure of changing her status would be protracted. The story was more than threadbare; the Gestapo rightly suspected she was lying, but assumed that the true facts would prove to be banal and of no great interest.

They assigned the file to a young official only recently recruited who was very thorough, took a long time, and eventually sent the papers for corroboration to Cologne where Ilse had been born. At about that time there was another air raid on Cologne and the local Gestapo headquarters were destroyed, and with it Ilse's file. Ilse was still in prison, but no one remembered the circumstances of the case any more, for those who had originally interrogated her had long been transferred. She could have been put on the next transport, but this would have been against the rules of the bureaucratic machinery. She had quite obviously committed a crime and the case had to be reopened. A new investigation was begun, but her case officer was again transferred, and when his successor finally concluded his work it was January 1945, and the transports to the east had ceased as the result of the Russian offensive.

On the day war ended Ilse was still in her cell at 3 Iranische Strasse. There were several dozen similar cases: for a Jew, the chances of survival were greater if he or she had committed a crime against the state – such was the logic of this extraordinary period.

The most important assignment for her friends was to find out more about those who had spied on Ilse and arrested her. Michael and Peter were greatly alarmed; they knew that these agents were now the most dangerous of their enemies; left to its own resources the Gestapo apparatus was not very effective in dealing with illegals, but their Jewish helpers constituted a major threat. Unlike the Gestapo they knew quite a few of the illegals by sight; they were familiar with their habits and some of their connections and they could guess where one was likely to find them. Who were these assistants of the Gestapo? This is a sordid chapter, but it is as much part of our story as the many acts of courage and decency. The illegals set up their own little court of investigation, and with the help of outsiders they soon knew all there was to know about the informers and their motives.

For years the Gestapo had been trying to find agents inside the Jewish community, but up to the outbreak of war it had not been successful. There were a few doubtful characters, to be sure, from whom they occasionally got some information, but everyone in the community knew that these people were not to be trusted and consequently the Gestapo did not learn anything of major importance. When the deportations started the Gestapo made a new effort to enlist Jewish agents, partly because it was understaffed. It also assumed, quite rightly, that Jews would be more effective in hunting out fellow Jews than the ordinary Gestapo official. For contrary to official race-doctrine a great many Jews looked like Germans, and quite a few Germans looked like Jews, and the racial stereotypes taught in schools were of no practical help.

The Gestapo was now able to offer a much higher premium than before: they promised their agents that they and their families would be exempted from the anti-Jewish measures. The Gestapo was keen to enlist men to do guard duty on the Grosse Hamburgerstrasse and other concentration points, and thus relieve the SS from watching over those about to be deported. They enlisted some ten or twenty miserable creatures, some Jewish, others of mixed origin. A few behaved quite decently, while others tried to emulate the SS. I have often asked myself what made people act so despicably, but the answer is, of course, quite obvious: among a hundred thousand people one always finds a certain number of asocial elements, just as there is always a certain percentage of sick or mentally deficient. If the community is big enough one invariably finds a handful of traitors, acting from a variety of motives – greed, frustrated ambitions, feelings of grievance against society.

Among the Jewish helpers of the Gestapo there were a few criminals in the strict sense of the term, but most of them were quite ordinary, law-abiding people. I was told moreover that most real criminals were outraged by the traitorous behaviour of the agents: the underworld, too, has its code of honour, and it puts a great deal of importance on solidarity. Seen in this light the offence of the Gestapo helpers was quite unpardonable.

The assistants of the Gestapo were usually people of weak character, easily swayed and rather stupid. For with a minimum of intelligence they should have realized that in the case of a Nazi defeat they would be called to account for their misdeeds, whereas if the Nazis succeeded in liquidating all Berlin Jews the services of the Jewish helpers would no longer be needed, and they too would eventually share the fate of those they had betrayed. But all these wretched persons saw was that the others were being deported, and they would do anything to gain a stay of execution for themselves.

One of them was Rosa Sterner (née Rosa Kugler), and it did not take long to piece her story together. She came from a middle-class family. Her father, a musician and composer, was closely involved in Jewish affairs; he wrote liturgical music and was a conductor of synagogue choirs. He was a pompous man, a bit of a windbag, but apparently quite harmless – which was more than could be said for his shrewish wife, a small woman, incessantly talking, always deriding or finding fault with her fellow human beings. She had what Italians call the evil eye; in the Middle Ages she would have been burned as a witch.

Rosa was their only child – a tall girl with light brown hair in her early twenties, quite good looking, who was proud of passing as an Aryan. Those who had known her at school said that she was in no way outstanding except perhaps in her desire to have a good time; she was an empty-headed girl.

Easily swayed, she became an informer more or less by accident. At the age of eighteen she fell in love with a young man a few years older named Leo Sterner who was in many ways her counterpart – not a 'born criminal' but weak, vain and unstable. The two did not steal, blackmail or engage in any other such activities; they simply wanted to enjoy life as much as possible; their great dream was to spend a week in a luxury hotel somewhere in a fashionable resort on the North Sea, and to attend once in a while an afternoon dance in one of the leading hotels. These were not unreasonable aspirations, but unfortunately they were quite unattainable in the circumstances. Yet they persisted in their dreams – why should they be denied a little happiness? If it could be achieved without harming others, well and good, but they would not think twice if their only way out was betrayal. They had the full support of Rosa's mother, who for unknown reasons took a positive delight in the suffering of others, excepting her immediate family. Her father, I suppose, did not know, or did not want to know, to what he owed his permission to stay in Berlin when everyone else was deported.

222

Rosa became a Gestapo agent, or rather, a decoy duck, in late February of 1943. One night the Gestapo came to the room she shared with Leo, and something was found to be amiss with their papers; it appeared that they had failed to inform the police that they had changed their address three days earlier. This was, of course, a minor technical infringement; nevertheless, the couple assumed that they faced immediate deportation. But the Gestapo, who had been interested in them for some time, had other plans for them. They were given five minutes to choose between deportation and what was delicately put as 'occasional assistance'. If they would provide this to the satisfaction of their masters, and, of course, keep absolutely silent, they and their families would be spared. Even the slightest attempt to disobey would immediately have the gravest consequences.

Rosa and Leo did not need five minutes to make up their minds. But they had one request. They had never had a proper honeymoon: would it perhaps be possible to get permission to spend a week in the mountains – they would, of course, pay. The official said that this could be arranged, but that he expected them to show proper gratitude through loyal service.

So the couple went to Garmisch-Partenkirchen, looked at the snow-covered mountains from the Hotel Schoenblick, sipped lemonade on the veranda of the Kurhaus restaurant, went to Riesser See and to Kreuzeck by cable-car. Since there were not many guests at the time other than a few young officers – some of them convalescing, others with their young women – the service was excellent and they thoroughly enjoyed themselves.

After their return they were given their first assignments. Their duties were not too strenuous; twice a week they were called to the Prince Albrecht or Burgstrasse headquarters, shown photos and asked to identify people. But they could not be of much help, and in early April they were given a new task.

It was known that several thousand Jews were hiding in Berlin. Eventually, of course, said the Gestapo official who briefed them, all of them would be apprehended, and the sooner the better. Rosa and Leo were to walk the streets and to keep their eyes open: they would surely know where to find them. Once they had located someone they were to follow their victim home and to inform the Gestapo. They were expected to deliver to the Gestapo at least ten illegals a week. If they exceeded this schedule they would get a bonus. But if they brought in less, their case would have to be reconsidered, and it was doubtful whether the Gestapo would have any further use for them.

Rosa told him they lacked experience; they did not even know where to begin. The Gestapo official replied that they had to use their wits. Perhaps they should start by just travelling around for a few days on the trams or subways, sooner or later they would meet some suspect characters. But this was entirely up to them. He had more urgent business to attend to. When Leo asked if he could enlist an old friend who was absolutely trustworthy, the official agreed, stressing that they would bear full responsibility for the friend and if anything went wrong. . . . He did not finish the sentence but passed his index finger across his throat. His gesture was understood.

And so Rosa and Leo and their friend began to prowl the streets of Berlin. Sometimes she went out first by herself, followed by Leo and Salo, their friend; sometimes she took Leo's arm and talked to him, oblivious as it were to the rest of the world, but keeping, in fact, a close watch on the passers-by. They spotted a few illegals the first week, and a few more the second and third. But the system was as yet far from perfect for they could not, of course, arrest anyone; once they stopped an elderly couple and had them seized in their presence by a policeman who happened to be in the neighbourhood. But they preferred not to be seen too often, assuming that if it became known that they were working for the Gestapo, word would quickly spread and their task would become much more difficult.

Rosa developed a new technique: when she saw someone who looked like an illegal she tried to befriend him: she was on the run herself, could he possibly help her? In a few cases help was extended – with fatal consequences; in others people agreed to meet her later but did not show up for the rendezvous. Once or twice she had blundered badly: for instance, she had accosted people whom she had taken for Jews on the run but who were actually Nazi party members, who furiously handed her over to the police. The Gestapo had got her out of jail quickly, but she had been taught a lesson.

In July Rosa had spotted Ilse somewhere in the centre of town. She was desperate; for two weeks they had not caught a single 'submarine', as the illegals were called, and the Gestapo were about to lose patience. Rosa had not known her well at all, and Ilse had first maintained that it was all a mistake. But Rosa was not a bad actress and her story seemed quite plausible; Ilse met her a week later and was promptly arrested. For Rosa and her friends were by now so desperate to fulfil their schedule for the Gestapo that they seized her in public despite the risks involved.

Her arrest presented the youth group with a major crisis: what if she cracked under Gestapo investigation? Michael, Peter and a third young man met in an unlikely place – the Wannsee beach. It was the hottest day of the year; they swam out towards Schwanenwerder with its water-tower and villas, and while they swam they discussed what further measures were to be taken.

Michael said that all of them would have to find new quarters within the next few days. He assumed that within a week at the most the Gestapo would have extracted from Ilse all she knew; he did not know that she was still unconscious and could not even be interrogated. 'But we could not find twenty new places even if we had a whole month,' Peter said in despair. The third young man suggested that if the worst came to the worst some of them would have to move out of Berlin into the Spreewald. The nights were quite tolerable now, one could sleep out in the forest. But this, Michael thought, was no solution, for once in the woods they would be cut off from the world, and their chances of finding shelter in town would be virtually non-existent.

Peter said that only those whose lodgings were known to Ilse would have to be moved. Once this was accomplished the most urgent job in hand was to kill Rosa and Leo. He said it casually, and the other two were shocked. Neither of them had ever been involved even in a fight, and but for the fact that Peter was not given to hyperbole or exaggeration they would have dismissed his proposal as a juvenile fantasy.

But Peter had never been more serious in his life. He explained that he was not motivated by feelings of vengeance. The decisive factor in his eyes was that with Rosa and Leo around the danger to every one of them would be immeasurably greater. Michael said that the Gestapo would not take it kindly if two of their agents were killed; a massive hunt would be set in motion, which, however indiscriminate, might result in more arrests. 'I doubt it,' Peter said. 'They would not know where to go.' But if there were other Jewish spies? Again Peter had an answer: the news of their removal – he shunned the word murder – would spread, and act as a deterrent.

The other two reluctantly agreed with him. Their education had not prepared them for decisions of this kind; the worst punishment meted out in their movement was ostracism and exclusion from the group. Did they have the right to kill anyone? Had they not been educated to believe in the sanctity of human life? Did their religion not forbid murder in all and any circumstances? No, Peter said; it was lawful to kill an informer anywhere, in fact it was a duty. Maimonides said so, for unless the informer was eliminated in time, the disaster caused by him could not be prevented. And he referred to a famous case in which an informer had been executed on the Day of Atonement. Michael, who had grown up in an Orthodox family, was taken aback: 'And what do you know about our religion?' 'Next to nothing,' Peter said quite truthfully, 'but during the last few days I have considered this carefully and I have also been reading. . . .' And who would kill them? 'I will,' said Peter. Michael revealed that he had an army revolver and a few rounds of ammunition which he had bought from some underworld character a few months earlier. He did not carry it around with him nor, never having tried, did he know whether it was in working order.

They swam back, collected their clothes from the locker-room, and no one seeing them would have assumed that a decision had been taken affecting the lives of at least two human beings. In the evening Peter collected the revolver, and in the early hours of the morning went to a remote part of the Grunewald to try it out. He fired it twice, and it seemed to work; but there was not enough ammunition for him to have any more practice. Later in the morning Peter took Erich aside, told him about his plan, and asked his brother to accompany him, since he might need help. Erich, generally so reluctant to take a decision on the spur of the moment, simply said: 'When do we start?'

On the afternoon of 8 August Peter and Erich departed, having bidden us farewell more ceremoniously than usual, which is to say that they announced they would be back a little later than usual. Their plan was straightforward: they knew that Rosa and Leo shared a little apartment in Nettelbeck Strasse and usually went out together, returning home just before or just after dinner. Peter and Erich would try to intercept them in the hall or on the staircase and shoot them on the spot, if they were unaccompanied. To attack them in the hall was not without risk; the shots would echo throughout the building, and within a minute the hunt would be on. But by that time they would have made their getaway, and if, as they hoped, darkness had set in, they would be far away by the time the search started. If on the other hand they could not face their victims alone in the entrance hall, they would try to gain entrance to their apartment a little later and shoot them there. In this case it would probably take longer for curious neighbours to arrive on the scene; but on the other hand the escape down the stairs from the third-floor apartment would not be without risk.

They arrived in front of the building around six, went briefly up the stairs to familiarize themselves with the surroundings, and then left again. The entrance hall was similar to that of a thousand other houses in the West End; it was rather dark, and there was a board with the names of the inhabitants – but the Sterners did not appear on it. There was a big wooden outer door, and a second glass door inside, which had been damaged in an air raid. The stairs presented no particular obstacle; with two or three big strides they could jump down a whole flight. The porter's lodge was in the back part of the building, near the exit to the courtyard. The danger of being intercepted on their way out was less than they had feared.

They would have to hang around for a long time without attracting attention, as there was nowhere to hide in the hall. Every few minutes someone went in or out; a doctor had his office on the first floor and the patients were still coming and going. Reluctantly they dismissed their first plan as impracticable, and decided to split up: Peter was to lounge near the entrance, and wait for the couple to arrive. They did not have to wait long; shortly after seven the pair entered the building. Peter went to tell his brother and they decided to wait a little longer, since it was unlikely that they would go out again that evening. They would wait until darkness set in and then pay their visit.

To kill time they went for a short walk through the neighbouring streets – Luetzow Strasse, Schill Strasse up to Luetzow Square with its sculptures showing Hercules fighting centaurs, lions and other enemies; they went up to the nearby Landwehr Canal and back again. This was Berlin's old West, a well-to-do neighbourhood, but many houses had already been damaged in the air raids.

It was still warm with hardly a breeze. Peter was carrying the revolver wrapped in a newspaper. There was little traffic and only an occasional pedestrian. Night was about to fall. As they slowly walked around the block they talked about a great many things but not about the deed they were about to commit, nor about its likely consequences. Peter was not particularly excited, nor did he have any pangs of conscience. In normal times the very idea of killing a human being would have seemed inconceivable. But these were not normal times: they had seen so many of their comrades arrested, and deported to at best unknown destinations. Some had been tortured and killed in Berlin.

For many months now they had been risking their lives daily, helping the illegals. Hundreds of innocent people were killed in the air raids. In short, the value of human life had sharply decreased. There was no moral problem as they saw it: Rosa and Leo had forfeited their right to live by betraying fellow Jews to the Gestapo, and by threatening to bring about the arrest and very likely the death of others. They felt themselves neither criminals nor heroes; they wished that there had been someone else to carry out this assignment. But there was no one else. And so they continued their walk, little suspecting that it would be their last evening in Berlin.

It was nearly nine when they went up to the Sterners' apartment, meeting no one on the stairs. They rang the bell; a young woman hesitantly opened the door, her face expressing surprise. Peter politely said 'Good evening,' and explained that they had come at the suggestion of a common friend because they had some news which could be of interest. Could he and his friend talk to them for a moment? Rosa was bewildered and called her fiancé; Leo appeared, Peter again began his story, and while he was speaking he unwrapped his little parcel. Erich stood to one side and now broke in with something quite irrelevant, about how difficult it had been to find their place. 'But who gave you our name and address?' Leo asked impatiently. At this moment Peter fired; Leo fell. Then he fired twice more and Rosa also collapsed. Almost simultaneously the air raid sirens sounded; in a few seconds the stairs would be swarming with people. Peter snatched up a notebook he had seen on the table, and slammed the door to the apartment. As he and Erich ran down the stairs some of the other doors were already open, and in the entrance they collided with an elderly couple. They began to run; no one paid any attention, for they were not the only runners. Within a few minutes they had reached a big public shelter in Wilmersdorf.

After the all clear had been given they made their way through the desolate streets of Berlin to the place in nearby Schmargendorf where Michael was hiding at the time. Michael was not very pleased: late-night visitors were not welcome because they always attracted attention. But this was clearly an emergency. Peter handed the revolver back and reported that Leo had apparently been killed and perhaps Rosa as well. But they could not be certain, there had been no time to find out. The Sterners had seen their attackers, and if they lived long enough their description would be circulated to all police stations in the morning. There was even the faint danger that someone had seen them in the entrance. Peter remembered the notebook and handed it to Michael.

228

It contained a number of names and addresses, some underlined, others with question marks. It appeared that Rosa had been even more efficient than they had feared, and one could only hope that the addresses had not yet reached the Gestapo.

Michael suggested that Peter and Erich should stay at home for a few days until they heard whether they had succeeded and whether the police had any leads. But Erich had reached a sudden decision: 'We should try to reach Switzerland.' 'Don't be a fool,' Michael said. 'You don't stand a chance, and anyway your very disappearance will create suspicion.' But Erich, as usual, was obstinate.

His point was that the position of the illegals was becoming untenable in any caes. Even if they found new shelters in summer, most of those places would be uninhabitable in winter. The Gestapo were getting closer and the war would not be over quickly. So instead of remaining in Berlin they ought to try to escape. Sweden was too difficult, but Switzerland was a possibility. Peter and Erich stood a better chance than the others simply because they had legal identity papers. They would act as scouts; if they found a way to cross the border, they would immediately get in touch with Michael and then others could follow, using a similar escape route. A great many explanations could be given for their disappearance from Berlin.

Peter was gradually convinced, and Michael reluctantly also gave his assent. He gave them a hundred Marks – about a third of the group's money – embraced them and wished them the best of luck.

They returned home in the early hours of the morning and started packing the knapsacks which had accompanied them on so many excursions. Each took a warm pullover, a spare pair of trousers, a raincoat, some shirts and socks. Then they woke their parents. They said that something unforeseen had happened, but that this was not the time to go into details. They would make their way to Switzerland and would somehow let us know once they had arrived. We were instructed not to worry if we didn't hear from them for some time. There was a slight danger that the police would call, in which case we should tell them that they had left a few days ago; as far as we knew, they were hitchhiking to Kolberg, a little town on the Baltic where they had once been in a children's camp.

Elizabeth was much more composed than I was; as she saw it the boys had obviously made up their minds, and it seemed pointless to try and dissuade them. Needless to say, I was deeply perturbed, because I saw the dangers only too clearly: it was a suicidal adventure. They were completely inexperienced; their chances of reaching the border, let alone crossing it, were small, and if they were arrested they were likely to be executed. I began to say all this but the boys were not listening and Elizabeth interrupted me: 'Don't make it more difficult for them. . . .' So I gave them all the cash I had with me, some two hundred Marks. I then remembered that the Countesses niece had told me about the Swiss farmers near Singen. When I mentioned this I had their undivided attention, and they made a note; as an afterthought I gave them my copy of Scheffel; they would at least have something to read on the train.

They kissed their mother, saying that they hoped she would forgive them; it was very difficult for them to leave her while she was not well, but there was no alternative. They even kissed me, which they had not done since they were small children, saying they hoped we would all meet again in the near future.

They left home at five in the morning on 9 August 1943. Soon after, Elizabeth broke down. I put her to bed and held her hand for a long time. She fell into an uneasy sleep as the first rays of the sun appeared in our bedroom. I did not think I would ever see my sons again.

Only a long time after was I to learn the reason for their sudden departure. The police did not call; after a few weeks, when neighbours inquired about the boys, I told them that they were helping with the harvest somewhere in Pomerania. After a while even the inquiries ceased; by the autumn of 1943 everyone had become accustomed to minding his own business. Otto, as he later told me, guessed that they had left for good, but he never asked.

Rosa and Leo had not been killed; Leo's shoulder had been grazed by a bullet, Rosa was unhurt. But they decided (as it emerged in their trial after the war) not to tell their bosses that the attempt had been made. For they assumed, correctly no doubt, that the Gestapo would conclude that the identity of their helpers was now known among the illegals and that they could be of no further use. This they dreaded more than another attempt on their lives. But all this belongs to a much later period; Peter and Erich certainly did not know this until well after the war.

They reached the Anhalter Bahnhof early, but there were already long queues in front of the ticket counters. This was one of the biggest railway stations on the Continent, and masses of passengers thronged there, even though hardly a single train was leaving on time. Peter and

Erich got a cup of coffee and a sandwich in the railway buffet. There had been no time to plan ahead, and now they had to improvise quickly. After studying the railway maps and timetables on the wall, they decided that they would try to get to Stuttgart, change trains and proceed to Singen.

They joined the queue and after an hour their turn came. The man behind the counter wanted to see their travel permit. They mumbled something about visiting their parents who had been evacuated; the official hesitated, and the people in the queue behind them became restless: 'What's the problem – hurry up, be quick!' The railway official sold them two tickets, remarking that there would be controls on the train and that they would not get far without the right papers.

They went to the platform and bought a morning newspaper. There was nothing about the air raid, let alone about the assassination of two small-time Gestapo agents: they had not really expected it. On the platform there were a few policemen passively looking on; they could not have carried out a systematic check, what with the masses of people swarming in every direction; almost every inch of ground was covered by suitcases, bags and rolled up mattresses.

Their train was not due for a long time; no one, in fact, could tell them when it would arrive or depart. As they stood on the platform among this great mass of people, impatient and apathetic, good-humoured and irritated, it dawned on them that they had taken the first step on an adventure that would have been exceedingly dangerous even if minutely planned. They were totally unprepared, and as the excitement wore off they grew depressed. But their pride, if not their sense of duty, made it impossible to go back. They began to discuss their next moves; the story about visiting their parents would probably see them through to Stuttgart. But where could they stay there? Or should they immediately move on to Singen? And how would they find the Swiss farmers when they did not even have a name or address?

At noon they left Berlin on an overcrowded train; in the late afternoon they reached Leipzig. At first there was standing-room only. They looked out of the window, but the sights were not particularly interesting. After Leipzig the train stopped frequently, and in Nuremberg they had to change trains contrary to what the timetable said. There was a field kitchen in the station catering for evacuees and children; they queued up and got a bowl of hot soup. The compartment was half-empty now, and no one tried to draw them into conversation. When they left the train at Stuttgart an elderly lady said: 'Have a nice holiday, boys. . . .'

There was no control on the platform but they saw SS guards at the station exit, so they decided to buy tickets to Singen and continue the journey as soon as feasible. They had a cup of coffee, and bought a few biscuits for breakfast and sandwiches for the road. Then they realized that they needed a good map of the German-Swiss border; but there were none in the station book-shop – perhaps they had been withdrawn for the duration of the war. They found a pre-war guide book about skiing in the Black Forest and hiking in the Lake Constance region. It had no maps, but provided some useful information, and having studied it they modified their plan. Singen was not a big town, nor a tourist centre; the presence of strangers was bound to attract attention. What if they went instead to the Lake Constance region, full of famous tourist resorts? They had never been there, and so picked a place at random. Peter had a friend who had been to the well-known school at Salem, north of the lake. So they decided on Salem, calculating that it would not be inside the border area, for which (as they had just read on an official poster) according to wartime regulations special permits were needed, obtainable in certain police stations.

They boarded the train shortly before noon and began what would have been in other circumstances a most enjoyable journey. Unhurriedly the train ascended the pleasant valley of the Neckar river; in the distance the Swabian Alps could be seen. They passed old cities, churches and monasteries, castles and ruins, walls, Gothic towers, and factories, farms and gardens. Their fellow passengers were more relaxed and talkative than the evacuees from Berlin. Having found out that the boys came from Berlin they provided a running commentary on the attractions of Boeblingen, Rottweil, Tuttlingen and the other places they passed.

At Immendingen there was a control point; they produced their identity cards and were told that that was not enough. They repeated the story about going to see their parents who had been evacuated. No one had told them that special permits were needed. 'Where are your parents?' the SS man wanted to know. 'In Beuron,' said Peter quickly, thinking of the famous monastery and place of pilgrimages. 'I am from Beuron,' the guard said. 'We have no evacuees.' A passenger who had been listening to the conversation said 'There is Beuron and Beuren – near Singen. What do you expect of boys who do not know the region?' 'Yes, of course, I meant Beuren,' Peter said. The SS man still had some doubts, but returned their papers with a reprimand. When he had left, their new friend told them that if they wanted to continue beyond Singen they would have to get a special permit; they would not be let off that lightly nearer the border.

They thanked him for his advice, got out at Singen, and for a moment felt inclined to follow it. However, they knew the police here would not be satisfied with vague answers; they would want to see letters from their parents and other documents. They decided not to risk it, had another bowl of soup and a pair of frankfurters at the station restaurant, and bought tickets to Salem. Salem was not on the railway line; they would apparently have to get out at Memmenhausen and take a bus. They later found out that they had been given wrong information: there was a small local train connecting Salem with the main line. But perhaps it was a blessing, for the less they used the railway in the border area, the better.

The trains got smaller and smaller; when they left Berlin they had been inconspicuous in a big crowd, but now they felt awkward. Boys in shorts with knapsacks were a familiar sight in peacetime, but there were hardly any around now. Their route was through hilly forests, beside lakes and rivers, with more castles on the horizon; later the track continued right along the shore of Lake Constance – one one side the water, on the other steep, overhanging rocks. It was a clear day; they had a good view over the lake, and beyond it, for the first time, they saw the mountains of Switzerland.

They left the train at the small station; the bus was waiting and soon they were in Salem. They had now been on the road for two days and a night and were very tired indeed. Half of their money was gone, and Erich argued that they could not afford to spend any more on a room in a hotel. But Peter said that looking for anything else would only arouse suspicion at this late hour. Erich was tired, and gave in. They went to a guest house in the centre of the little town and asked for the cheapest room.

The woman who owned the place smiled and said that she had a son only a little older than Peter who was now in the army, and she knew quite well that young people seldom had much money to spend. An attic room was free, as it happened; they could have it for half-price. Would they want dinner? No, they said, they had eaten a big lunch. She looked at them incredulously and said in her sing-song dialect: 'Well, have some hot soup anyway, it will do you good.' It was their fifth bowl of soup since they left Berlin; they had not had that much in as many years. The guest house was one of those attractive old places with dark rooms, a squeaking floor, many staircases, smelling of beer, leather, tobacco-smoke and soap, with old drawings on the walls. It had probably not changed much for the last hundred years. A few regulars were sitting near the entrance and while seemingly immersed in their conversation went on observing what went on in the street. Erich could hardly keep awake during dinner, so they went to their room immediately after and fell asleep at once.

They were woken next morning by the owner who brought them breakfast – coffee, fresh rolls and even a little honey. They had not seen honey for a long time, the lady had quite obviously taken a fancy to them. Their mood had greatly improved; they packed, paid their bill and were given a couple of sandwiches free of charge with the compliments of the proprietor.

Salem lies in a valley, surrounded by fruit orchards, and as they left it they again saw the Swiss Alps quite clearly. But they wanted to have an even better look. They followed the signs to the peak of a nearby hill from which, as they had expected, the whole area could be viewed. Lake Constance, surrounded by fruit trees, reeds and even palms, was now at their feet only a very few miles away. There were a few vessels on the lake. To their left was Friedrichshafen where the Zeppelin had once been built and where, as every enthusiast knew, the Maybach engines were produced. Opposite, on the other shore of the lake, was Constance. The border, they gathered from their guide book, went through the middle of the city. To their right there was a long peninsula, behind it the little island of Reichenau. It was a most attractive sight, like one great garden, but their eyes turned time and again to the barren mountains beyond, to the chain of the Saentis.

For Lake Constance with all its beauty spelled danger, whereas in the mountains they sensed freedom. The lake region was densely populated, especially along the shore; it seemed one continuous built-up area. Part of the shore east of Constance was Swiss territory, but how would they get over the lake? To cross the border by land seemed equally unpromising; there were too many people around, and no cover. Nor did they know exactly where the border was, or how well it was guarded, and whether there would be barbed wire or other obstacles. They remembered that for wide stretches the Rhine served as a border, but in some places there were Swiss enclaves north of the river. They had heard that there were Swiss villages in the middle of German territory, and German villages in the middle of the Swiss area; but how would they find them? It was all very confusing.

Having rested for a while and discussed the situation they decided to return to Singen to find out more about the Swiss farmers, if this could be done inconspicuously. If not, they would reconnoitre the border area and somehow make their way unaided into Switzerland. They also decided not to use the railway any more, because controls were more likely there than on the roads. They walked down to Ueberlingen, another of those little medieval towns which in time of peace attracted thousands of visitors from abroad. But Peter and Erich's interest in crenellated walls, Baroque Madonnas, cathedrals and altars was limited at the best of times; they were fascinated by old castles, but had seen enough of these during the last few days.

For the first time since they had left Berlin they could now relax a little. On the railway they always had to be prepared for a police control, and even in the guest house they had felt under observation. Now they were alone as far as they could see; it was pleasantly warm, and they could take stock of the events of the last few days. They wondered whether the hunt was now on, what had become of their parents, and what had been the fate of their comrades, the illegals. They were very worried but one of the advantages of being young is that one seldom worries for very long. So far everything had gone well for them, even better than expected; but the difficult part of their journey was only now about to begin.

Ueberlingen, which they reached two hours later, is one of the most beautiful old towns in south Germany, built on a giant rock; the reflection of the houses could be seen in the deep blue water. Once it was a 'free city' and the substantial remains of the fortifications show that it was also a minor military power. But as the two entered the city there was nothing further from their minds than sightseeing; they had a rest and went to the lake baths, and then sat down on a bench in the Kurpark.

The need for a good map had become even more urgent; without it they were doomed to fail. At their second attempt they succeeded; in a nearby second-hand bookshop they found an old guidebook which contained what they wanted. They also bought mountain walking-sticks, not only because these would come in handy but because they would make them look more like real tourists. In a nearby shop they could have rented bicycles, but they no longer had the money to pay the deposit.

They went on walking; on the outskirts there was a petrol station, and after a few unsuccessful inquiries they found a truck-driver willing to take them to Radolfzell. This time they slightly changed their story: they had been visiting their parents but wanted to take the opportunity to do some sightseeing. The driver was a native of Radolfzell and a mine of information. He told them about Bishop Radolf who had built the place a thousand years ago, about the relics of the many saints in the town – what a pity that they would miss the famous annual procession. They ought to hire a boat and row out into the lake. There was nothing more romantic than watching the sunset over the Hegau mountains from the lake. When he had been courting many years ago, he had done it many a time. All the girls loved it, and most men too. Peter said that he had always wanted to make a boat trip down the Rhine valley, but it was of course quite impossible now because of the war. Yes, the driver said, it was quite dangerous.

But then they gathered a very important piece of intelligence: while lake and river were closely guarded, the rest of the border apparently was not. He said jokingly that if any local man wanted to cross the border and return the same day he could do so, and no one would be any wiser. The border was long and complicated; to watch every little footpath day and night tens of thousands of border police would be needed and they, of course, were now in short supply. 'I would not advise anyone, however, to risk it,' he added as an afterthought. The driver bought them cold drinks in a roadside inn; they arrived in Radolfzell in the late afternoon, and went to a private house he recommended which let out rooms.

They were the only guests; it was now the peak of the tourist season, but there were only a very few, even less than the year before. The room was simply furnished, the old lady friendly but a little too curious for their liking. In the evening they walked to the lake promenade and admired the panorama. The Swiss mountains seemed very near, even nearer than indicated by the map. For a moment they felt tempted to try their luck that very night. But they dismissed the idea almost immediately; it was too risky, the region still too populated, and while they knew the general direction, they would, if unlucky, walk straight into a trap.

They bought some bread and sausage and walked back to their quarters. The lady was waiting for them, and said how nice it was to see young people for a change, now that so many of them had to serve in the army. Would Peter have to join up soon? Yes, he said, but he had almost another year to go, and wanted to make the most of it after working so hard for his examinations at school. What a pleasure it was, he said, to get away from the air raids for a little while, and to sleep at night without being woken up. Yes, she understood that; but had their parents really permitted them to make this trip alone in the middle of the war? Friedrichshafen, after all, had recently been bombed, and no one knew which town would suffer next. Wasn't it a little unusual? She would have been terrified to let her own children go off on their own; what if something happened to them? 'Well,' said Peter, 'soon I shall be in the army. . . .' She had not thought of this, he was quite right, and he would surely take good care of his younger brother. . . . They were relieved when at long last she bade them good night.

Early next morning they went on to Singen. It was another fine day; the larks trilled in the fields, the trees glistened with morning dew. It was ideal for walking, and after a good two hours on the road the first houses of Singen could be seen. They passed the town centre, crossed a little river and found themselves at the foot of the Hohentwiel, the strange, forbidding mountain of which they had heard before. Further on they saw yet another volcanic mountain rising steeply from the plain – the Hohenkraehen. They climbed Hohentwiel and sat down in the shadow of the ruin of the lower castle: looking at their map, they realized that they were now two miles as the crow flies from the Swiss border. At their feet lay Singen, a bigger town than any of those they had passed in recent days. Railways crossed the landscape, straight lines transferred from the drawing-board without any concessions to the vagaries of nature. There were several big factories near the centre of the town.

Another ten minutes' walk on a narrow path took them to the ruins of the upper castle, but only the church tower was still intact. There was a steady trickle of visitors, who came up to enjoy the panorama from a round bastion named 'Augusta'. An elderly couple who had watched them for a little while drew them into conversation: how nice it was to see young people at this time. Had they come far? Yes, they had. And had they heard before about the Hohentwiel? Of course they had, they had a special interest in old fortresses. Then they couldn't have done better, because this was the biggest ruin in the whole of Germany. . . . The couple was genuinely touched to hear that the boys even knew about the poet and writer who had made their town world-famous. They said that in town there were streets and squares, schools

237

and hotels named after Ekkehart and the other characters, but no one seemed to take an interest any more. How nice to meet someone from outside who still cared.... Would the two young gentlemen join them for a drink on the lower-level restaurant?

The husband was a native of Singen; he told them all about the Hohentwiel, how at one time it had been the seat of the Dukes of Wurtemberg, and how it had been finally destroyed by Napoleon; how Singen had been a mere village when he was born seventy years earlier, with just one main street, and a little building which housed both the major's little office and the local school. And now there was big industry, three great factories. Had they ever heard of Maggi soup cubes? Of course, who did not know Maggi.... He had started there as an apprentice when the factory opened in the 1880s and had worked his way up to become a foreman. It had been very different in those early days – long hours and not many holidays. But there had been compensations. Maggi and the other two factories were owned by people over in Switzerland; for a time he had worked in the Swiss branch of the concern.

Peter said that he had heard that there used to be a great deal of traffic across the border in peacetime; some farmers, for instance, lived on one side, while their land was on the other. 'Very likely,' the man said. 'I wonder who drew the border; it is totally illogical.' He took the old telescope he was carrying and gave it to Peter: 'Do you see the road from Singen to that big village to the right? This is Gottmadingen. Look at the two single houses to the left of the road.' Peter saw the substantial buildings. 'One is a tavern called Zum Frohsinn, the other belongs to a farmer, the Spieshof. Those two houses are in Switzerland. In the olden days we often used to have a pint of beer in the tavern on a summer evening.'

Peter was still looking; he noticed that the forest extended from the outskirts of Singen almost to the border and even beyond, with only a few clearances in between. They were still talking about Singen and how rapidly the city had grown after it had become a centre of industry and a railway junction; how its inhabitants had lived in harmony, Catholics and Protestants. Had there been any Jews in Singen, Erich wanted to know. The old man hesitated, he did not remember. 'Of course,' his wife said, 'there had been the shops in the Hauptstrasse and the Hedwigstrasse, and there had been a doctor.' 'Yes,' her husband confirmed, 'there had been some.' Were they still in Singen? Oh, no, they had gone, who knows what had become of them. A great many people had come and gone, that was the way of the world. They were still talking as they descended together from the Hohentwiel, and then said goodbye.

In the evening Peter and Erich walked slowly through the city like genuine tourists, crossing the Aach river and discussing their plans. It seemed fruitless to continue the search for the Swiss farmers: they would not only attract attention and furthermore the farmers would probably ask for money. They had seen the two houses on Swiss soil, and knew the general direction. They still had to decide whether they should cross by day or night. In daytime they would not lose their way, but they were also more likely to be observed. They agreed that on balance it was best to cross when there was a little light, perhaps during the early hours of the morning or in late evening. They also agreed to stay for a few more days; they would gather some more information which could be of use. Perhaps there were even more promising places to get into Switzerland. They must try to find out whether the border was marked, and how, and whether there was barbed wire. In a hardware store they bought a pair of pliers which they said they needed to repair their bicycles. They went to bed early.

Nothing much happened on the following day. They overheard a conversation in a shop which taught them that a big SS garrison was stationed in Radolfzell, but they could not find out how the border was guarded. When they bought rolls in the bakery a woman complained that while everyone here in Singen had to preserve total blackout at night, the Swiss, over the border, were still merrily illuminating their houses. They were enjoying life while others suffered, which wasn't fair, and furthermore these lights would one day provide guidance for enemy aircraft; the enemy pilots would know where they were. Peter and Erich had been so accustomed to the blackout which had now been in force for four years that they had forgotten that these regulations were not in force, or less rigidly observed, in neutral countries. Thus they had almost missed an important clue: if they saw lights, they could be sure it was Switzerland.

When they returned to their guest house they had an unpleasant surprise. The owner, a squarely built man with a red face who looked like a butcher, and, as it emerged, had been one until recently, called them aside and said that it was none of his business, but that he strongly hoped that they had all the permits necessary for visiting the border area. From time to time guests in the hotels would be checked. And since this usually took place in the early hours of the morning he wanted to get it over as quickly and smoothly as possible – no banging of doors and loud discussions at night. Peter assured him that they had all the necessary papers. But did they come that often? The man smiled cunningly: he had not said that they would have visitors this very night. They came every few weeks, and there had been no visit now for a long time. So it stood to reason that they would pay a call one of these nights and furthermore, this was a small town, everyone knew everyone else and what he was doing.

They went to their room in a state of some perturbation. They had intended to cross late the next day, but would now have to change their plan. But their sudden disappearance would be equally suspicious; there would be undesirable inquiries. They wrote a note to the inn-keeper saying that they had just received a cable from their parents telling them to come home immediately. They enclosed some money and left the envelope on the table; the cleaning woman would find it in the morning. Having quickly packed they left their room shortly after midnight, tiptoeing to the front door. They listened for a few seconds: there was no noise at all. They left Singen by way of the main road to Gottmadingen.

It had been another hot day, and even now it was quite balmy. Peter walked slowly through the darkness, Erich following at a distance of a few yards. The two kept close to the walls of the houses. They passed a hospital, then crossed the railway lines and after that they found themselves out in the open. Should they continue on the high road or walk across country? That would mean a big detour, and so they kept to the road, going very carefully. They walked some fifty yards, then stopped and listened for a few seconds. According to the map (which they now knew by heart) they would have to walk for two miles and then turn to the left. They moved very slowly, met no one, and it was almost an hour before they came to the crossroads. There they heard voices in the distance and saw two men coming towards them on the road. Peter and Erich jumped to the left and hid behind an old tree; these were border policemen. They smoked and talked as they slowly walked towards Singen. Peter and Erich waited for a few more minutes and then went on; they knew they had only a few hundred yards more to go. Their excitement grew as they saw on their left a substantial building; was it the Frohsinn or the Spiesshof? But it was Swiss territory in any case. They turned in this direction.

A few moments later Peter suddenly stopped and cursed; his trousers had got tangled in barbed wire. This then was the border. The wire was laid in reels, little more than three feet high and about the same in width. In daytime they would have jumped over it, but now they would have to cut it, and quickly at that. It took them a few minutes which seemed like hours, and in their hurry they got some scratches. Peter was for pressing on, but Erich insisted that they should reconnect at least some of the wires they had cut. He was thinking of those who might come after them; they might be at a disadvantage if it were known that someone had crossed the border here illegally.

It was now past two in the morning of 14 August 1943, less than five days after they had left Berlin, and it had been almost incredibly easy going. They feared that they might inadvertently take a wrong turning and end up in Germany again. They knew that they must keep to the south and that they should reach a village, Ramsen, in about half an hour. Consulting their compass and the map from time to time, they went through the forest side by side. They began gradually to feel less tense after the feverish excitement of the previous week; at last they were on the road to safety. So far all their thinking had been about the moment they would cross the border. Where would they turn now? Their original aim had been to find out whether the border could be crossed, so that the other illegals could follow as soon as possible. They would now have to report to the rescue committees in Zürich or Geneva, and they would pass on the message that there was an escape route.

They did not meet anyone during the next half-hour, and the only sound they heard was the barking of dogs in the distance. Then they reached the first houses of Ramsen. They thought there was a railway station nearby, but they did not find it in the dark; since there would be no trains at night and since they had no Swiss money they discontinued the search. Should they go to the nearest police station in the morning? Erich had misgivings; they might be arrested for having crossed the border illegally, and this would make it impossible to communicate with the rescue committee in Zürich. Perhaps they should telephone first and ask for instructions. Peter said that this was not Germany; sooner or later they would have to report to the Swiss police in any case. But there was no reason to be afraid, for what they had done was no more, after all, than a technical infringement of the law, and the Swiss would understand.

They slept for an hour or two and as dawn broke they continued towards Stein, the town on the Rhine. In the market place they asked for the nearest police station. The policeman on duty was in no hurry to listen to their story; he wanted to know their full names, see their papers, where they had been born and when; there was clearly a certain routine that had to be observed. He then led them to a little room and said they would have to wait. They told him that they had not eaten for a long time. He would send someone out, but did they have any money? They produced some coins. He looked with some disdain at their German money.

They were brought breakfast, and ate their first meal in freedom ravenously. They had to wait a long time for a police officer to arrive. At last a man in officer's uniform came in, accompanied by a younger man also in uniform, his aide or secretary. He looked at them without great interest, and spoke slowly and coolly. They had to go over their evidence again. He took it that they were aware they had committed a serious crime by entering Switzerland illegally. They had no valid visa and should not have crossed the border. 'But we are escaping, we are looking for asylum,' Peter said; but the officer waved this aside as irrelevant, and said there were some points in their evidence which were not at all clear. They had said they were Jewish, but there was nothing in their papers to this effect. People were inventing all kinds of stories just to be allowed to stay in Switzerland. And even if they could prove it, it would not help them. Why not? The captain explained: 'Not everyone can come here illegally and claim that he was persecuted. He has to show that he personally was in danger. Probably you just quarrelled with your parents and ran away.' 'But why should we run away to Switzerland?' 'I don't know, but your story is most unconvincing.'

Erich suddenly said: 'But we are in danger of our lives, we have killed two Gestapo agents.' Peter looked at him disapprovingly. 'You have what?' asked the officer, showing surprise for the first time during their interview. Erich told him the story without going into all the details. 'Can you prove it,' asked the officer, 'was it reported in the newspapers?' 'We don't know,' Peter said. 'I have only your word for this most unlikely story. I am sure you just made it up.' He told them to wait.

He left the room, followed by his assistant who carried the files. They could hear him phoning from the next room. The walls were thin but he talked Swiss dialect which they found difficult to understand, and there were furthermore mysterious references to 'the decision of 13 August 1942', regulation number two', 'Territorialkommando'. Words were used which were obviously German, such as 'refoulieren', 'aus-schaffen', 'zurueckstellen', but they had never heard them before; what did they mean? But even if they did not understand this curious language they realized that their fate was to be decided in the next few minutes and that the officer was speaking to his superiors in Schaffhausen. He then placed a call to Berne to the chief of the police department, Dr Heinrich Rothmund; again they could hear only part of the conversation. The officer said that he would like to report a case somewhat out of the ordinary. Later: 'Not very likely, but could just be true, obviously a borderline case . . . No, the newspapers have not heard of it, the rescue organizations have not contacted me, thank God . . . Usual procedure? Should one talk to von Steiger? . . . No, the Bundesrat could not be bothered with every little case.'

They heard the officer say that there still was a problem. As Herr Dr Rothmund no doubt remembered he had a gentleman's agreement with the police chief in Singen not to let those who had crossed illegally return at will. They would have to be handed over to the German authorities. But on the other hand he felt inclined to turn a blind eye in this particular case even though it might endanger relations with the German authorities . . . What if the boys were seized upon their return? Well, he could tell his German colleague that he had not thought it necessary to report foolish pranks committed by minors. What did Dr Rothmund think? That the decision should be taken by the local commander? Unpleasant business, but one had to be firm.

The captain had replaced the receiver, and sat for a few minutes drumming the desk with a pencil. And the two young men in the next room realized that they had become entangled in the web of high politics, of paragraphs and regulations which were all-important as far as their future was concerned. And they had foolishly thought it would all be so easy.

Then the captain's assistant joined them. He told them that he was a theology student from Zürich university who was now serving in the army – as everyone had to. He was quite obviously ill at ease. Why, they asked, were they treated like criminals? The student said that too many refugees had tried to enter Switzerland. It was a long story, complicated and sad; but on that morning in the little city of Stein am Rhein, of which they had never heard before, it was a question of life and death for these two young people.

On 13 August 1942, the student told them, the Swiss government had passed a decree which redefined and restricted the right of asylum.

When the war had broken out there had been about nine thousand refugees in Switzerland, more than most Swiss thought acceptable. Then, as the war spread, hundreds more tried to make their way into neutral Switzerland – escaped prisoners of war, French workers who refused to work in Germany, anti-Fascists from Italy and France and, of course, Jews. They were received with much kindness by individual Swiss citizens and assisted by rescue organizations. But the Swiss government decided to stop the influx of these undesirable elements which, it believed, was getting out of hand.

They were undesirable for two reasons: their presence was a provocation to Nazi Germany, which was so much stronger than Switzerland; Holland, France and Denmark had been occupied, and it seemed not unlikely that it would be Switzerland's turn next. Also, the Swiss thought that their country was already overpopulated; the arrival of thousands of refugees made them very apprehensive about the economic, political and cultural future of their own people.

After the decree of August 1942, exceptions were made only with regard to deserters and other military personnel. Civilians were told to return at once at the place where the illegal entry had been made. If they resisted, they were handed over to the border guards on the other side. But even those who left quietly were warned that if they attempted to cross illegally again no mercy would be shown, and they would be handed over to the German or Italian authorities.

Discretionary exceptions were sometimes made for the very old, the very young, invalids, and political refugees. Those persecuted for racial reasons (meaning the Jews) were not considered political refugees, unless they happened to be military personnel, which was unlikely, or 'emergency cases'.

In July 1942 Swiss newspapers had published reports to the effect that more than a million Jews had already been killed in Eastern Europe, but as Von Steiger, the Swiss minister responsible for justice and police, put it in a speech, Switzerland was like a lifeboat which was full beyond capacity.

(Nevertheless, the lifeboat was not quite full, as became obvious after the tide turned in 1943. With Italy out of the war from September there was a new influx of refugees from the south, and this time many thousands were permitted to enter – 1,672 civilians in September 1943 alone. At the end of the war there were some 90,000 refugees, including 25,000 soldiers, in Switzerland. Rations in Switzerland did not have to be cut as a result; the lifeboat did not capsize.

But in August 1943 the practice of sending refugees back was still in force, and it appeared very likely that the two young men who, perhaps foolishly, had turned up at the police station in Stein am Rhein would be among those not permitted to stay; they would be returned to face what was called, somewhat euphemistically, an 'uncertain fate'. The student told them that if they tried again, they should plan their story beforehand very carefully; he was not, of course, making any suggestions, but he knew that people tried again and again, and some of them succeeded in the end. Others, admittedly, had been handed over to the Germans and were never heard of again.)

The student left and they were alone for several hours. More food was sent up. From the window they could see the market square surrounded by old houses, richly decorated and with little alcoves and balconies. In the middle of the square there was an imposing building, obviously the town hall, and next to it an old fountain. A child helped by his kneeling mother was feeding the birds. They were still in a state of shock: everything so far had gone so well. They had been prepared for all kinds of dangers, but the idea that once having reached this haven they would be told to return had never occurred to them.

Should they try to escape from the police station? They could perhaps make their way into the streets of Stein; the door to their room was not locked from the outside. But they would be apprehended almost immediately. With a little luck they would regain German territory unnoticed, but what then? They had not enough money to buy train tickets to Berlin, nor did they know that they would not be arrested on their return. Perhaps they could stay somewhere in Germany for a little while, and then try to cross the border elsewhere, having learnt from their mistakes. But it seemed now far more uncertain – what if they were returned a second time? The various possibilities did not look any more inviting as they went over them for the tenth time. In the end Peter said resignedly: 'There is no alternative. . . .'

Next an elderly gentleman came into their room, introduced himself as a doctor, took their pulse and blood pressure, listened to their breathing, asked them to bend their knees a few times and congratulated them dryly on their state of health. 'Perhaps they are worried that we shan't be strong enough to make it back to the border,' Peter said. But he was mistaken; the medical check-up was just part of the routine. Then the student soldier came in again, went over the protocol yet again in great detail – and in a whisper, before leaving the room, wished them good luck. They still hoped for a miracle, but it was not to be.

For in the end the captain came in and, impassive as ever, told them that they could return that very night by the place they had entered. He was willing to assume that they were not refugees at all, but had inadvertently strayed into Swiss territory. Or, if they preferred, they would be handed over to the German authorities.

They said they would make their own way back to Germany. In that case, the captain said, they would be accompanied up to a short distance from the border; they were to obey the instructions of their escort, and he had to warn them that if they tried to enter Switzerland illegally again, they would not be let off so lightly. Speaking personally, he would advise them to return to their parents' home. They were still very young; he could not believe that they had anything to fear, whatever they had done. He left the room having told them to be ready for their departure at ten in the evening – they would get something to eat and drink first. There were no questions, nor did he expect any.

After darkness had fallen they were driven beyond Ramsen. The van stopped at the entrance to the forest. A sergeant and a private took them close to the Spiesshof and then just said: 'Straight on.' They crossed the border shortly after midnight. They were neither seen nor heard. They walked north all night and when day broke they were some ten miles away in a forest where they lay down and slept. Towards noon they woke up hungry, depressed, and feeling as if they had been beaten black and blue. A few minutes later they saw a horse-driven carriage approaching on a nearby path. The farmer took them to a nearby village; he was a man of few words. They bought milk and bread with the little money that remained. They passed a vineyard and picked some grapes; they were sour, but seemed delicious. In the distance they saw the foothills of the Black Forest and continued in that direction.

The Black Forest is one of German's most attractive regions. To the Romans it had seemed a sinister and impenetrable forest, hence the name 'Silva Negra'. But since then, it had been penetrated not only by many thousands of settlers but by millions of tourists in summer and winter, seeking rest or solitude in a valley off the beaten track, or exploring some of the most beautiful and romantic countryside in the world. Wild hyacinths and foxgloves blossomed there; there were wild strawberries, cranberries, bilberries and raspberries.

To this earthly paradise the boys directed their steps, not to enjoy the marvels of nature, but in the prosaic hope of finding food, work and shelter without arousing too much curiosity. Something they had overheard while under arrest in Stein had given them a new idea: Alsatians who had been called up to join the German army were apparently crossing to Switzerland in growing numbers; they now wanted to find out about this, and if possible to join such a group. Gradually a new plan emerged: they would make their way slowly into Alsace. But they had hardly any money left, their shoes needed new soles and their clothes had grown threadbare. This was not only inconvenient but also dangerous, for if their appearance was not more or less presentable they would be suspect; questions would be asked and they might be arrested as vagrants. They would have to earn some money, and since new clothes and shoes were now available only on ration cards, they would somehow have to acquire second-hand ones.

During the following three weeks they worked for a day or two, or sometimes even three, and then walked for a day or two. It proved easier to find work than they had expected; they would arrive in a village, call at one of the houses, tell the farmer or his wife that they were on a hiking tour but short of money; did anyone in the neighbourhood need help? Usually they found work quickly, and there were not many questions asked. For the young men were all in the army, and a great many jobs on the farms had been postponed. They helped felling trees and carrying them to clearings in the forests. In one village they helped to pack cuckoo clocks for dispatch; elsewhere, they followed after the reapers in the fields and bundled the hay; they helped with repair jobs and with bringing in the harvest.

They were strong, but they had never worked for ten hours or more in the open air. During the first week they were exceedingly tired at the end of the day and their hands were covered with blisters. But they quickly got accustomed to the work and even liked it. They met friendly people, and one or two who worked them like slaves. But the Black Forest farmers and foresters were not wealthy, and all they could expect in payment was food, which was plentiful, and some pocket money. In one place they were given a pair of old shoes as a present, in another two pairs of old working trousers which did not quite fit even after the farmer's wife had altered them. In three weeks they did not see a single policeman or soldier. They were now sunburnt, and had discovered a new world; but they had not made much progress towards their destination.

One evening at the end of this period they found themselves in a village not far from Mariabronn. Since they could find no place to stay for the night in the village they moved on towards the little town in which their father had been born.

It was close to midnight when they arrived, and though they had saved a little money they did not want to spend it on lodgings. At the outskirts of the town they saw a little public park; they jumped over the wall, and made their sleeping quarters in a half-empty toolshed. But next morning Peter was in pain; he tried to get up but could not. He had not felt well the evening before but had tried to ignore the discomfort; now he was quite obviously running a high temperature. He asked his brother to find a pharmacy and buy aspirin or quinine; they would have to stay in the shed for the day. When Erich returned he found his brother much worse; he moaned, he was shivering, and he had difficulty in breathing. His pulse was rapid and he was talking incoherently.

Erich was more afraid than at any stage during the trip. He feared his brother was about to die and wanted to get a doctor, but Peter absolutely refused. What was he to do? Just then he saw through the little window two elderly men slowly approaching the shed: their presence was about to be discovered and this could be their journey's end.

The man who came in first was obviously a gardener, and he was holding a club in his hand. What they had taken for a public park was in fact a graveyard, and it belonged to the church nearby, which they had not seen in the darkness. The gardener had watched Erich leave the shed and had gone to alert the priest, who was pruning the rose bushes in front of the little parsonage. He was a thick-set old man, looking more like a Black Forest farmer than a member of the clergy. He moved with some difficulty in his black cassock. He now took over, while the gardener stood in the entrance blocking the exit. He shouted at Erich, but his eyes were kind. Erich said, 'Father' – somehow he remembered the correct address – 'We are in trouble, my brother is very ill.' 'If so, he should be seen by a doctor. . . .' 'No,' Erich said, 'my brother does not want a doctor.' 'Why not?' 'I cannot tell you.' The priest asked the gardener to fetch some water and sat down on an old chair. He then turned to the boy and said, 'You have to tell the truth if you want my help. Where are you from? Have you run away from home?' 'No,' Erich said, they had not run away from their parents, nor had they committed any crime. 'What is your name?' 'Lasson,' Erich said. The priest raised his eyebrows and looked at him searchingly: 'I know that name, and it is not a common one. Was your father by any chance born in Mariabronn?' Yes, he was. 'What is the name of your mother?' Erich told him. Where were they now? Still in Berlin.

The clergyman looked out of the window and fell silent for a few minutes. 'How do I know you are telling the truth? What was the name of your grandfather?' Erich remembered. 'Tell me more about your father; did he go to school in Mariabronn?' Erich did not know. Where had his family lived here? Erich did not remember. He felt he was failing the test and grew desperate. 'Try to remember,' the old man said, 'take your time, your father must have told you something about his childhood.' 'Well,' Erich stammered, 'he told us they had a house on the outskirts, he could see the mountains from the top window; as a boy he used to ride on his bicycle to a forest.' And then suddenly all kinds of stories came back to him, glimpses from his father's childhood, some altogether unimportant, some sheer fantasy. But he did remember that his grandfather had owned a factory and that they used to make music at home, and that his grandmother had come from a nearby village.

The man in the cassock relented and smiled: 'We shall help you as much as we can. But I had to be sure, it would not have been the first time....' He stopped in mid-sentence and looked out of the window as if to ascertain that they were alone. He then said: 'Your brother cannot stay here, he has to be taken to a hospital. Don't be afraid, I know a place where they take care of people in trouble.'

When the gardener came back they carried Peter to the parsonage; he seemed to assume that strange people would turn up from time to time. The clergyman then disappeared, and Erich, alone with his brother, was again in a state of apprehension. What if he returned with the police? When he did come back eventually he was accompanied by a woman who carried a little bag. She put her hand on Peter's forehead, took a stethoscope out of her bag, listened for a few seconds to his breathing, and then said that the young man was seriously ill and should be taken to hospital straight away. She put some medicine on the table and left the room with the clergyman.

Erich, alone again, looked at the old furniture, the heavy old curtains, the old books, the Black Forest clock; he felt a little relieved that their fate was now in the hands of strangers. When the clergyman returned, he sat down in a high-backed armchair, heaved a sigh of relief and told Erich that since there was nothing to be done he might as well sit down too. Soon he would fix a little meal. After dark his brother would be taken to a convent close by. The clergyman had spoken to the abbess, who was an old dragon but could be relied upon. She strongly disliked the idea of a young man, however sick, being housed in her place, but the priest had persuaded her, applying gentle moral pressure: 'I have done a few things for her over the years; they too have been in trouble more than once. You will be put in a little village not far from here; the local priest is a friend, we took holy orders at the same time.' He was sure that the farmers could use help at this time of year. He did not know how long the brother would have to stay in hospital. A week, maybe longer. Erich would be kept informed.

The boy was grateful and yet his old uneasiness returned. For the first time the brothers were to be separated. Could he trust those who were to care for Peter? The clergyman sensed his anxiety and said: 'I knew your grandfather, I even remember your father, though he is quite a bit younger than me. Even the lady doctor whom you just saw knew him, a long time ago. It's a small world. You and your brother have been very lucky....' He then said: 'I want to show you something.' They stepped outside the door and looked out into the bright sunlight. He pointed to one of the larger houses further down the road: 'This is where the Lassons once lived. I don't know who it belongs to now.' They went back to the room and the priest said: 'You must trust me; you are taking a risk, but so am I. I do not know why you left home, I do not really want to know, but I can imagine. Without trust and faith what future is there for mankind? Unfortunately there is very little faith just now....'

In the evening the gardener called and took Erich to the nearby village. For several days he did not hear from his brother, and when they were later reunited Peter could only give him a hazy and incomplete account of what had happened. He had been taken away late at night, the trip to the convent had been awful, he couldn't remember whether he had been driven in a car or a horse-cart. Then he had been washed and put to bed. He feebly protested when they gave him a nightshirt which he always thought effeminate rather than pyjamas, but he had been told to shut up.

The next thing he remembered was being in a big soft bed and enjoying the clean white linen. He was still running a high temperature and sweating a lot. He did not remember any faces distinctly; there had been several nuns, all experienced nurses; they had looked after him very well, some with anxious, careworn faces, others smiling. They had talked to him, but he had no idea whether he had answered, and what. The first night one of the nuns had kept watch by his bed.

He was delirious, and they feared he would roll out of bed. The room was a small one up in the attic, but it was light.

When his temperature dropped on the third or fourth day he felt very weak. He had woken up not knowing where he was; he thought for a few moments that he was a small boy again, and that his mother had just left the room for a minute. He looked at the ceiling and saw the reflections of passing cars; he had watched these reflections when he was a child and he had never asked for an explanation. He felt safe; the nuns never stayed very long with him, but they spoiled him. One day the mother superior came, a bad-tempered old lady, and said she was glad to see that he was so much better now, and that she hoped that he would soon be on his way, for his presence in the convent was, of course, greatly upsetting their routine. She left the room shrugging her shoulders, but not before putting in front of him a bowl of strawberries and whipped cream, something he had not tasted for many years.

The nuns were concerned about his spiritual welfare and had put a Bible on his night-table. It was the only book he had, and there was, of course, no radio. He began to read the Bible for the first time in his life and found parts of it of absorbing interest. They would ask him every morning whether he had made any progress, and he would say that he had read not just one chapter but a whole book: they thought he was joking, but it was quite true.

The lady doctor had visited him every day, sometimes in the morning, sometimes late at night, but only for a minute, and she never said more than a sentence or two. Then on the eighth or ninth day (he had lost count by then) she said that he would be able to leave the next morning. She sat down at the foot of the bed, looked at him for a moment and said: 'You are very like your father. We used to know each other; he was about your age, and I was a little younger. If you see him, give him my regards. My name is of no consequence, you will forget it anyway. But he will probably remember. One seldom forgets what happened in one's youth. . . .' She then said that he would be well advised to rest somewhere for another week, and that he was still too weak for major exertion. She kissed him on the forehead and left the room without further ado. Peter thought that adults were unfathomable and sentimental people. But he had come to like her very much, and anyway, she had saved his life.

He left the building very early on the morning of the following day, having told the nuns how much he owed them and that he would be grateful for ever. One of them said that they had only done their duty; didn't he know the story of the good Samaritan? Peter had to admit that he had not yet progressed beyond the Old Testament. 'A young heathen,' he heard her saying to another nun, 'but well-behaved; he probably comes from a good home.'

They had given him more food for the road than he could possibly eat in three days. They had even put into the parcel a bottle of their own herb wine, which had not much alcohol content, but contained some substance conducive to stimulating the appetite, though the nuns must have known that ever since his temperature went down Peter had no need of any encouragement in that respect.

He went to the old vicarage, where he was expected. The priest was an early riser; he was again cutting the hedges. Peter collected his rucksack and was given a short homily to the effect that he had had a narrow escape and that he should be more careful in future. Father Borromaeus – Peter had heard his name mentioned in the convent – admitted that, in the circumstances, this was easier said than done. He had told Peter's brother that men could not exist without trust; he wanted to tell him now that he should never give up hope. When the danger was greatest, God's help was nearest.

But Father Borromaeus was not only a pious but a practical man, and realized that even divine providence sometimes needed man's active help. He suggested that Peter should join his brother in Wildbrunn for a few days; he had heard the other day that Erich had made himself useful in the village and was well liked. After that, well, there was perhaps a way to earn a little money. The son of a good friend and parishioner of his (and a practising Catholic, he stressed) was manager of one of the hotels in Badenweiler, the well-known resort on the western slopes of the Black Forest. He would not give him a letter, but if Peter said Pater Borromaeus had sent him, it was quite likely that there would be jobs for both of them. As for the more distant future, he could only repeat that one must never lose hope. He was a poor man and could not give him money, but since his parishioners brought him clothes and shoes for the needy from time to time, Peter was welcome to help himself if he could find something to fit him in the large closet in the adjoining room.

Peter, not usually at a loss for words, was for once tongue-tied. He had not experienced much kindness outside his family and immediate friends in recent years, and he had come to believe that the outside world was not a friendly place. But during the past few days he had been the object of much kindness from perfect strangers, and at considerable risk. Most of them did not know who he was, and it had not made the slightest difference. Nor did he know their names, except that of Father Borromaeus, and he knew that in all probability he would never see any of them again. Peter, the tough boy who seldom showed emotion, was so moved that he fought back his tears only with considerable effort. In the end he managed to find a few words of thanks, shook the hand of old Father Borromaeus and went on his way.

He stayed four days with Erich. In the morning they worked in the garden of the local vicarage, in the afternoon they went on leisurely walks in the neighbourhood and discussed their future plans. Badenweiler seemed too good a chance to miss, for they badly needed money. Erich had some misgivings: in a hotel they would meet more people, and this was dangerous. Moreover, he had heard that the Badenweiler March was Hitler's favourite tune, next to the Horst Wessel song, which was not promising. But Peter now felt more confident; Badenweiler had existed, after all, long before Hitler was born or the march had been composed. Furthermore, he did not see any alternative at the moment.

One day in late August 1943 the postman delivered a picture postcard at our home in Dahlem. It was, I believe, the first picture postcard I had received for years. The picture was of something very familiar to me – Mariabronn cathedral. The postmark was 'Mariabronn'. There were four or five words written on the card: 'Don't worry' and 'Yours ever' – the handwriting was familiar. It was the first news we had had since they had left Berlin, and it was to be the only news for a long time to come. For a moment we were very much relieved, but almost immediately we began to worry again. It did not make sense, why had they gone to Mariabronn?

They reached Badenweiler in one day. This was a far more elegant place than any they had seen of late. Badenweiler was in the mountains, a tourist resort dominated by the Kurpark and the many hotels and sanatoria around it. There were also coffee houses and expensive-looking shops. To the west, beyond the Rhine, they saw yet another mountain range – the Vosges. They went straight to the Roemerwald Hotel and asked to see the manager. The doorman looked at them with some astonishment, and so did the manager; in their new attire they looked quite respectable, but not exactly like people who had any business in a grand hotel.

They told him that they were from north Germany, had been hitch-hiking in the Black Forest, were not expected back home before late October, and their good friend Father Borromaeus had said there might be an opening for two young people willing to do any kind of work. Herr Laemmel, the manager, said that he indeed needed help – but that unless they were experienced cooks or had been trained to serve in the dining room, he could not see in what way they could be of any assistance. Peter replied that they could do almost anything, provided that they were shown how. Laemmel smiled at his self-confidence and said that he was willing to give them a chance. They would get twenty Marks a week, board and lodging. The season ended in late October, but if they were not of use he would not keep them on, not even for the sake of Father Borromaeus, who had christened and confirmed him. He also said that something would have to be done about their attire, which, to put it mildly, was unsuitable for a hotel of this class.

One of Herr Laemmel's assistants took them to the hotel's tailoring room where they were given a uniform as well as various trousers, jackets, shirts and ties left or forgotten by guests. They looked in the mirror, they looked at each other; but for the necessity to behave with a gravity befitting their new status, they would have laughed aloud. In the afternoon they went to explore Badenweiler; they looked at the big Roman baths and even went halfway up to the Blauen, the mountain overlooking the resort. They had an excellent dinner in the kitchen, and when they went to bed Peter said that if one day they were to tell their story, no one would believe them. Ulysses had been thought to be a liar, and their adventures would sound equally unlikely.

Next day they began to find out for themselves that there is a great deal more to running a hotel than the doorman, the receptionist and the waiters: like an iceberg, or a theatre, the greater part is always submerged. The Roemerwald was a good-sized hotel with 200 beds, and it employed mechanics, electricians, gardeners, plumbers, carpenters, cleaners, laundrymen and women, secretaries, accountants and even a hotel detective – a retired local policeman. The hotel was almost full; Father Borromaeus could not have known that it had been taken over a few months earlier by the German Wehrmacht. The guests were, without exception, army, air-force and Waffen SS officers; the three groups kept very much to themselves. Before the war a cure in Badenweiler had been prescribed for complaints of the heart and lung, but few of the new guests suffered from afflictions of this kind. Most of them had been sent to the hotel to recuperate after a stay in hospital, having been wounded in the war. A few were there, quite obviously, to restore their shattered nerves. There were no women, and most found the place exceedingly boring. From time to time some drinking would go on, but on the whole the guests were quiet and their behaviour exemplary.

The first assignment given to Peter and Erich was to peel potatoes in the kitchen; later they were sent to fetch luggage to and from the station; on occasion they helped the cleaning women on their morning rounds. They moved furniture, and on Sunday evenings they even had to help serve in the dining room. Quite often they were called to act as bell-boys; they took morning coffee, drinks and snacks up to the rooms, and since most of the guests were not stingy with tips, they had earned at the end of their first week a sum much in excess of their wages. They felt like little millionaires. Laemmel once or twice expressed satisfaction, as he met them on his daily round; he said that the hotel uniform fitted them very well indeed. Perhaps they had found their vocation; this was a field in which clever and adaptable young people could go far.

The mood of the guests was subdued. From time to time Peter and Erich could not help overhearing conversations between the officers, and while they did not often talk politics it soon appeared that few felt optimistic about the outcome of the war. All had their Iron Crosses. On occasion a few displayed the Knight's Cross or the German Cross in gold, and these were the most reckless – they would not lower their voices or interrupt their conversations when strangers approached. Having gone through the horrors of war with little hope that they would emerge unscathed, these men were freely speaking their minds.

The Italian armistice and the Allied landings in early September caused another wave of dejection; when Mussolini was freed from internment on 12 September, toasts were drunk to Skorzeni and the other commandos who had carried out this spectacular coup. Anti-Italian jokes were heard. The war (it had been mistakenly thought) would take two years and two weeks – two years for the British and Americans and two weeks for the Italians. But the Italians had been overrated; it had taken only four days to finish them off. But these were tired jokes, and no jokes were made about the Russians; everyone who had been on the Eastern Front agreed that the Soviets were now superior to the Germans in every respect, and that the retreat would continue indefinitely. When Peter and Erich compared notes at the end of the day they were again and again astonished by the fatalism of these young officers. If they were convinced that the war could not be won, why did they go on fighting and dying?

On Sundays they went for walks to the Kurpark with its exotic cedars, pines and laurels; sometimes they climbed up to the ivy-clad walls of the castle from which, on a clear day, they had a magnificent view. Once upon a time, local residents told them, Badenweiler had been a cheerful place, what with the dances and the military bands playing in the Kurpark, but these days had passed long ago. In an ice-cream parlour Peter and Erich made friends with some local girls and soon they were in considerable demand, but they were only amusing themselves. Their aim was still to move on to Alsace, and they had only postponed their departure because they thought they would need more money.

One day this idyllic existence came to a sudden end.

They were on friendly terms with the others in the hotel while keeping very much to themselves in their spare time. Among the employees was a young man who had tried to befriend them from the beginning; according to some he had not been taken by the army because he was an epileptic, though no one had ever seen him having an attack, and he would not volunteer any information about his state of health. The two had not liked him, perhaps because he had been too eager to show them the few local attractions, too anxious to visit them in their room. He talked incessantly, and his curiosity was insatiable. They found various pretexts not to see him. He then appeared one evening with a handwritten satirical poem on Hitler; would it not be a good idea to copy this and to leave copies in various public places? Peter said it would be a very bad idea, and not only because the poem was childish; people who did such things would soon find themselves in grave trouble. Surely he had not been serious? Of course, the young man said, it had only been a joke, he had just wanted to test them.

But from now one he was no longer their friend; he resented their success, the fact that they were presentable, more adroit, better liked by the officers. Although they had joined the staff only recently, they received more substantial tips. One day one of the air force majors announced to the management that he was missing a valuable gold cigarette case. Almost immediately their erstwhile friend told the other employees that he had recently seen such a case in Peter's possession.

The rumour eventually reached Laemmel, who interrogated the young man who had been spreading it. Yes, it was true, even if he could not be absolutely certain. A search was made in Peter's room and nothing was found. Their enemy said that he had never assumed that Peter would be that stupid. . . .

The same evening the major let it be known (with many regrets about the inconvenience caused) that he had found the cigarette case in the inside pocket of another suit. Laemmel demanded an apology to Peter in front of the staff; the young man, who had become very quiet for once, complied without further ado.

One evening, the week after, Laemmel knocked on Peter and Erich's door and told them that the local office of the German Labour Front had suddenly taken an interest in their presence. He just had some inquiries over the telephone; they had wanted to call on him immediately, but he had used delaying tactics. One of their men would turn up early next morning and he wanted to warn them. He had taken it for granted that their papers were in order; he could well imagine who had informed on them. Peter said that while their papers were in perfect order, it was quite possible that they had not conformed with some minor regulation; there were so many of them these days and they were so confusing. They had not, for instance, made any insurance payments since their work was only temporary. Also they had not asked permission of the local labour exchange when they had started work at the hotel. If someone wanted to trap them he could always find some technical violation of the rules. In the circumstances it might be better if they left. Laemmel could tell his visitors quite truthfully that they had been employed on a temporary basis only.

Laemmel regretfully agreed that this was probably the best course of action; he paid them their wages up to the end of the week, and told them that he was truly sorry to see them go. Would they now return to Berlin? Perhaps, Peter said; they had originally wanted to visit Alsace and work there for a few days, before they went back. This could perhaps be arranged, Laemmel said; he had close contacts with some vine-growers at Reichenweiher; the grape harvest was now in progress, and he knew that they never had enough help during those hectic days. He gave them a letter to Herr Merckmann, and they departed very early in the morning; the doorman was still half-asleep and just nodded as the two left the Grand Hotel Roemerwald.

They went by a little local railway which took them to Muehlheim, through the Klemmbach valley, where they changed trains and crossed the Rhine on the way to Muehlhausen. Even before they reached Muehlhausen their suspicions grew that there was something amiss with their plan. The controls on the Rhine bridge had been more thorough than they had expected; the guards had not liked their papers, even though they had shouted 'Heil Hitler' very loudly, and despite the fact that they now had a letter which said that they had worked to everyone's satisfaction in the Roemerwald Hotel in Badenweiler. They were allowed to pass only after some hesitation, and they did not like this.

Muehlhausen with its many textile factories is not an inviting city, and there were too many police around for their liking. They decided to leave as soon as possible. They were as yet some thirty miles from their destination, and they had the choice between the high road to Colmar, which would take them to the vineyards in little more than an hour, or the much longer Route du Vin, through the vineyards, or finally the Route des Crêtes, high up in the mountains. They opted for the mountain road: they argued they would see enough vineyards in the days to come, and on the high road, they thought, there might be more controls. Why were police so much in evidence in the streets? They would soon have the answer.

The Route des Crêtes was built across the ridge of the hills by the French army in the First World War so as to assure quick communications between the various valleys on the western slopes of the Vosges. While this had not been one of the major theatres of war, it saw a great deal of intermittent fighting. When they reached the Hardmansweiler Kopf they saw the enormous cemeteries in which 60,000 German and French soldiers had been buried. The French military engineers had been guided by strategic and logistic considerations, but they could not have planned the road any better if they had been employed by the regional tourist association. The two young men made their way along the crest of the hills, through pine forests, with the passes and the 'Ballons' to right and left, alpine meadows, terraces and lakes at their feet, and a brilliant sun shining on the vine-growers' villages in the distance; they were very glad indeed to have left Muehlhausen. But the people they met were taciturn; they would provide the information requested, but no more than that. Quite often they would answer in a dialect which Peter and Erich found difficult to understand. On the second day they began to realize that there was no personal animosity in this coldness; but it was assumed that they were young Germans from the Reich, and these were not particularly welcome.

By bus and on foot they made their way to Muenster, which lies in the valley leading from the Route des Crêtes down to Colmar. This little town is mainly known for the local cheese; its name is German, the language spoken by the local people is a German dialect of sorts, and yet as they walked through its streets in the evening they were struck by how different it was in many ways from a German town. They were now on the boundary between two nations and cultures, and one did not have to be a specialist to detect the influence of both.

It was getting cooler in the evenings, which reminded them that time was pressing. They would have to establish local contacts quickly for in winter it would be very difficult to cross the border. But where would they find contacts?

The next morning they went to Colmar, and through Colmar to Reichweiher. On the way they stopped at Wintzenheim, an undistinguished village. They remembered that their grandfather had been born here, and that their father's family had lived here for generations before they had moved to Mariabronn. In front of the town hall there was a map, and as they studied it they found the location of the Jewish cemetery; someone had forgotten to erase it. It was in a side street only a few steps away, surrounded by a high wall, utterly neglected. They stopped as if in conversation near the closed iron gate, but spotted nothing of interest to them.

As they continued their journey they passed through a number of villages or little towns which followed each other in rapid succession – Türkheim, Ammerschwihr, Kayserberg – but these places seemed deserted; the whole population was out in the vineyards on both sides of the road. Some were picking grapes, others carried willow baskets, yet others pressed the grapes into wooden containers placed on long carts. On the roadside there were vats of all sizes. All this was new to the boys, and they stopped and watched the scene for a long time. They heard it said that it was a good year for the Riesling and the Gewuertztraminer, the Edelzwicker and the Sylvaner, and everyone shared the general enthusiasm. Then they made their way into the little town and had no difficulty in finding the office of Merckmann and Son; Herr Merckmann was glad to get a letter from his good customer in Badenweiler. They could start work whenever they wanted.

When they went down to the vineyards the next morning they were infected with the general excitement: this was the culmination of a whole year's work and waiting. But they again felt that the welcome was less than cordial. When they joined the other grape-gatherers at lunch the conversation suddenly ceased. Quite obviously they were considered intruders.

On the first day they ate more grapes than was good for them. In the evening they had a wonderful meal in a little restaurant, an Alsatian choucroute and a Kugelhof. When they expressed their appreciation to the proprietor he said, 'Oh, you should have been here before the war.' They then walked through the narrow streets of Reichenweiher, or as it had been called for a long time, Riquewihr. It was obvious that little had changed for centuries, neither the buildings nor the habits of the local people. Everything centred around vine-growing; the prosperity of the local people depended on it, and so they were all experts. Even the presence of storks, venerated in Alsace since time immemorial, was thought to be connected with the success of the vine.

On the third day Merckmann appeared in the vineyard, and asked them whether they liked their work. They said they did, but somehow they had the feeling that they had unwittingly offended the others: was there perhaps a local custom which they had not known and thus violated? Merckmann said that they were no doubt imagining things. There was always a certain reserve towards strangers, but this was true everywhere. Alsace, after all, was a region with its own specific character, and it usually took newcomers quite a while to understand this. His explanation seemed plausible enough, but it did not quite convince them.

At the end of their first week they began to understand. Proclamations that appeared on the walls announced that following the recent introduction of compulsory military service in Alsace those born between 1908 and 1913 were now called up. Alsatians would be happy to do their sacred duty to the country to which they belonged and with which they had been reunited for ever. They would serve their country with a feeling of joy at this hour of decision. But the Alsatians were not overjoyed. There were angry scenes in the shops, restaurants and other public places. Groups of people gathered in the streets. Some said that the Alsatians should have been consulted, others claimed that they had served in the French army, and had been released only upon their oath that they would not take up arms again for the duration of the war. To compel them to enlist was in contravention of all law. But the protests did not bother the German authorities: those who had been called up were to appear at the railway station next Sunday morning.

Peter and Erich joined the crowd which accompanied them. The enthusiasm of the Alsatians to defend Western civilization under Hitler's supreme command was less than ardent: some were singing the Marseillaise and other French songs, one even carried the French flag, to the consternation of the few *Reichsdeutsche* in the crowd. The orders of the officers were disobeyed, and whenever this happened there was enthusiastic cheering from the crowd. At last a small unit of armed SS arrived and tried to arrest those who had figured most prominently in the protests. But the SS found itself hemmed in by the crowd, and those they wanted to seize escaped. Then the train left.

Peter and Erich had watched these events from a distance, for they feared arrest themselves. They then went back to the vineyard, for during the harvesting Sunday was no rest day. As they rode on one of the carts throught the vineyard they saw some men hiding: these were the leaders of the demonstration. Then an SS patrol appeared out of nowhere, and their leader stopped next to Peter who was standing up on a cart. They described the men and asked him whether he had seen the deserters. Yes, Peter said, he had seen some men running towards the village in the general direction of the Obertor, the upper gate of Riquewihr. But he had not known, of course, that they were deserters. The patrol quickly drove on to Riquewihr on their motorcycles.

When work was about to end Peter and Erich were asked by one of their fellow workers whether they would join him that evening; there was a good film showing in Colmar, and a truck would leave in about an hour; there would also be transport back. They went to Colmar and saw a film starring Zarah Leander, the most popular actress of the day. They liked some of the catchy tunes, but found the story inane. It was quite early when it ended, and since their truck was not to leave for another hour they went for a walk through the streets of Colmar. They were walking beside a river in a district called 'Little Venice', a few steps behind the others, when an unknown man suddenly appeared out of the darkness. He introduced himself and invited them for a beer. They hesitated, but he took them by the arms and said that Alsatians when one got to know them were hospitable people, and that in any case he had no evil intentions.

They walked together through the old centre of the city, found an open restaurant and a free table. The unknown man, who was in his twenties and had introduced himself as 'Gustav', asked them point-blank why they had come to Alsace. Peter said that they had very good reasons for leaving Germany. 'We thought you were spies,' Gustav said. 'We have had too many of them.' But they had been watched, and the fact that they had misinformed the SS had established their *bona fide*....He then said that the deserters were probably now on their way to Switzerland; perhaps they had already crossed the border. But their families would still be arrested – the Germans had their names and it was their practice to take hostages. The families would be deported to East Germany. Peter said, 'We want to go to Switzerland. Can you help us?' Gustav replied that he could not help, and that they would be well advised not to try their luck at the former French border. This had been quite easy up until the previous winter, but it had now become very dangerous. It had been made a 'border region', and everyone above the age of twelve needed a special permit to enter it. The German border guards had been reinforced and they now used bloodhounds. It had become risky even for locals; strangers to the region would not stand a chance. But Peter was not so easily discouraged; he explained that it was not just a question of saving their own skins; they were looking for an escape route for others who were in mortal danger.

They were taking a risk by talking so openly to a perfect stranger, but it was the first such opportunity, and for all they knew they might not have another. Peter decided to tell him about their past misfortunes. Gustav said that he had received information that the Swiss authorities had become more generous in recent weeks about refugees. There was no certainty that this would last; perhaps the policy would change again. He told them that he came from an old Alsatian family and that he had served as a lieutenant in the French army in 1940. Now he had been called up together with other former French officers. Some of them had reluctantly joined the German army, others had escaped to the occupied zone. Those who had stayed on openly defying the authorities had been sent to a concentration camp near Hamburg. He had gone underground; in a few days he too would have gone. Gustav smilingly said that he did not risk much by talking to them quite openly; in a few minutes he would again disappear into the darkness. He was safe among his people. While there had not been much open resistance in Alsace, there was not much collaboration either, and even those who had initially welcomed the Germans wanted to get rid of them now. Above all, no one believed any longer in a German victory.

But the Alsatians were German-speaking after all, Peter said, their culture was German, did they not feel some solidarity with Germany? 'Our culture is Alsatian,' Gustav said. They had much in common with Germany, just as they had much in common with France.

Napoleon had said about Kleber, one of his best marshals, that he spoke German, but the language of his sword was French. For a long time they had tried to be a bridge between two great nations: 'We had forgotten that everyone steps on a bridge, and this can be very painful indeed. We had our quarrels with the French, but these were family quarrels. The Germans, despite the common language, have been more alien to us.' Furthermore, they had always sent people to administer Alsace who knew nothing about local customs and traditions. 'When they came back in 1940, the first thing they did was to rename not only our streets but even our own names, if they happened to be French. They destroyed our statues if they recalled the non-German past of Alsace. For generations our people had said 'Bonjour' and 'Adieu' and 'Merci' and worn berets, and this too became a crime, a 'manifestation of the French spirit'. They are surprised now that they are so much disliked, they have lost Alsace for ever.'

It was late when Peter and Erich regained Riquewihr. The next evening when they returned from the vineyards they had made up their minds: they would try once again to cross the border. Their fellow workers had become much more friendly during the day and even arranged a little party for them in the evening, since they would miss the great harvest festival to be held a few days hence. There were toasts, and everyone wished them good luck.

Afterwards, they took out their map again and studied it for a long time. East of Basel the Rhine formed the border between the two countries as far as Lake Constance. There were three Swiss enclaves north of the Rhine, but they all belonged to the Canton of Schaffhausen, and in view of their experience they thought that this was a bad omen. They could make their way to Bregenz and try to cross the Swiss border from Austrian territory. The border would probably not be very well guarded there, but the trip would take them into unknown and difficult territory: snow might have already fallen in the mountains. As they looked at the map and followed the course of the Rhine their eyes fell on Saeckingen again and again. There was a bridge there which was no doubt guarded; but east and west of the city there were forests which might give them cover almost right up to the river, and once they were on the other shore there was a main road to Zürich.

Next morning, 1 November, they took the train to Freiburg, crossing the Rhine back into Germany. They could have continued on another train to Loerrach, whence a third train would have taken them to

Saeckingen. But the train to Loerrach was the Basel express, on which there would be strict controls. They were feeling uncomfortable in any case in Freiburg station; there were too many idle people hanging around, too many eyes were observing them; or perhaps they were just no longer used to moving among so many people. The train from Loerrach onwards would run alongside the border; it was bound to be closely watched.

They decided to approach Saeckingen from the north, which meant travelling through the southern part of the Black Forest which they had come to know so well. The Freiburg bus station is just outside the railway building, and they caught the bus to Todtmoos. On winding roads they drove almost straight south, skirting the Feldberg, the highest mountain in the Black Forest. There were no tourists, but only locals in the bus; they had been shopping in Freiburg or perhaps been there on business. Two men behind them spoke about the local sleigh races; it was explained to them that these were special toboggans called 'Pulka', drawn by Siberian huskies, Samoyeds or even Greenland dogs.

Their impatience was growing: they had very much liked the Black Forest, but they hoped they would soon have seen the last of it. They had been very lucky so far; it had been almost a miracle. But miracles, they felt, would not last for ever, and they could not afford a single mistake. It became markedly cooler as they continued their trip, and the peaks of the mountains were fogbound. In Todtmoos they had a meal and continued on another bus leaving from the post office to Saeckingen. The road went uphill and downhill, through a forest and past waterfalls; every few miles there was a big saw-mill. This was the Hotzenwald – for centuries its inhabitants had been known as saltpeter-makers and backwoodsmen. They had also been known as fierce fighters for their independence, strange, peculiar people, jealously preserving their customs. Even the houses seemed different here; once this had been a free state, and it was less than a century since it lost its privileges. Nature seemed to have been harsher, more severe here than in the other parts of the Black Forest.

Again the bus was only half full; it stopped frequently, passengers alighted and new ones got in, mostly with bundles and various pieces of luggage. They passed Herrischwand and Herrischried, the Hetzen-muehle and the Wickartsmuehle, Willaringen and Rippolingen – strange names and strange people. Then, after Rippolingen, as they crossed a little river and the road took yet another sharp turning, they saw the river on their left and beyond it, Switzerland.

In Saeckingen they went to the Hotel Rheinblick which, as its name implied, overlooked the river; the veranda had been closed for the winter and there were only a few guests. The receptionist wanted to have their ration books; they said that they were on an excursion, would stay only for a day or two and would not be in for meals.

It was now almost dark, but as they did not want to spend the long evening inside, they sauntered through the streets. The shops were about to close, and there were not many people about. They passed the Cathedral of St Fridolinus, the Irish patron saint of Saeckingen who had come here as a missionary more than a thousand years ago. They had first heard of Saeckingen because of the 'Trumpeter', and at any other time they would have made a pilgrimage to the churchyard where the historical Werner Kirchhof and his beloved wife rested; they would have been fascinated by the memorials to Hidigeigei, the clever cat, and they would have wanted to see the old castle, so lovingly described in the poem.

But they had seen too many old houses in recent weeks, and they did not want to go too close to the river because it was obviously well guarded. From a little distance they saw the covered wooden bridge over the Rhine and the border police stations on both sides. They did not want to stay a minute longer than necessary. Switzerland was less than two hundred yards away; what if they slowly approached the German border station and then with a sudden spurt dashed to the other side? The border police would not have their fingers on their triggers, and by the time the police were ready to shoot they would be on Swiss territory. But they knew from bitter experience that their trouble might not be over once they were in Switzerland. They clearly needed a better plan, even though with every hour in the border region the danger was growing.

Early the next morning they were awakened by loud knocking on their door. They opened it and two policemen entered their room. They looked at their papers and did not like what they saw. What were they doing in Saeckingen, did they not know that a special permit was needed? They told again their old story – they had been visiting their parents who had been evacuated to a place near Singen and since they had heard so much about Saeckingen they had wanted to look at it before they returned. The policemen were unconvinced, and wanted to see their rucksacks. Peter and Erich unpacked their dirty clothes and then put a book on top of the pile. The older policeman, who seemed to be a local man, opened the book: 'Have you read this?' 'Of course,' Peter said, and began to recite:

> To the Schwarzwald my song . . .

and then

> From true love and trumpet blowing
> many useful things are springing. . . .

The policeman smiled: 'And I had thought no one outside Saeckingen read this any more. . . .' He told them to visit the Bergsee and the castle and then take the first bus out of town. With a loud 'Heil Hitler' the two departed.

Peter and Erich needed a little while to recover from the shock. This time the Trumpeter had saved them, but their luck was running out. They had a day, at most, to make their escape. Up they went to the Bergsee through a forest of dark pine and fir trees, and from a nearby peak they looked down into the valley. The border was not heavily watched; the main obstacle was the river. The bridge in Saeckingen and the nearest one in Laufenburg, a few miles upstream, were clearly unsuitable for a crossing. The river was not very broad, but there was a very strong current and now in November the water was icy: no one could survive in that temperature for more than a minute or two. And even if they made it to the other shore, they would arrive wet and exhausted. The Trumpeter had purloined a little boat as he went serenading his girl friend: 'In a quiet hidden inlet where lay boat and rudder ready.' But they would not have such luck, and if they were to go for a search along the shore, they would be bound to get caught.

They looked at the map again. The areas west and east of Saeckingen was wooded on both sides of the Rhine and there were trees right down to the river bank. One could approach the river unseen, by forest paths. They chose a spot just two miles east of Saeckingen near the village of Murg, and decided that they would walk more or less parallel to the river through the forest and then go down to it. It seemed easy enough, but would they find the way by night? When they played Red Indians in their younger days, it had been customary to send out scouts in front of the war party. This time they had to be their own scouts. They went back most of the way to Saeckingen and then for almost an hour walked through the forest until they had reached a place only a few hundred yards from the river. It was not too complicated; first they went on the road on which they had entered

Saeckingen by bus the day before, and then turned sharp right. From this point on, they realized, it would be a matter of luck; perhaps they would find find a raft, perhaps there was a ford across the river. The plan was clearly deficient – a miracle was needed to get them safely over the Rhine. But they could think of no other way.

The last few hours in Saeckingen were perhaps the most difficult they had experienced so far. Peter wanted to leave at seven, and then again at nine. Erich restrained him – it was no good, there still would be people around. They would be seen leaving the hotel and arouse suspicion. They left shortly after midnight. A fine rain was falling, and they shivered in their old coats: perhaps it was a good omen, border guards did not like getting wet. They walked slowly uphill, and turned into the forest at the right place. Making frequent stops, they still lost their way twice and after a short whispered consultation retraced their steps. But in the end they did find the spot from which the final descent had to be made: the Rhine could be heard from there all too clearly. They rested for a few moments. On this last stretch, they knew, they had first to cross the road from Saeckingen to Murg, then the railway line, and after a few more yards they would be on the river bank.

Everything went according to plan: they crossed the road and railway line and then began to walk slowly along the shore. It had stopped raining, and the moon had come out from behind the clouds. Their eyes were accustomed to the darkness and they saw much better than they had thought likely, but this also meant that they could more easily be detected. So they bent down and advanced even more slowly. Then suddenly Peter found the boat, half hidden under branches and leaves, tied to a wooden peg on the bank by a rusty chain. It was a very old boat; it had probably been abandoned years ago, and it leaked. There were no oars, which made it virtually useless. They went to look for some poles or sticks to direct the boat to the other shore, but could find only branches. They looked at their watches; it was two o'clock, they could not afford to wait any longer.

They threw their rucksacks into the boat, jumped in and pulled at the chain, which gave way. They tried to steer the boat but it was quite hopeless; the current carried them rapidly along the German side however hard they tried to direct it to the opposite shore.

Then they lost their branches and sticks, and for a moment it seemed that they would be carried back to Saeckingen. There were rocks in the water, some hidden and others clearly visible; there were currents in various directions and even whirlpools. Suddenly the boat changed direction and carried them towards the middle of the stream, then it went into a spin, and after a few seconds crashed against a rock. What a strange end to a long journey, Peter thought, as the boat capsized.

He came up almost immediately and saw the Swiss shore only a few yards away. The water was unbelievably cold. He called 'Erich,' but there was no answer. Then he saw his brother and reached him in a few strokes. Erich was only semi-conscious, and there was blood on his face. Swimming on his back Peter pulled Erich towards the river bank. Another yard and he was on firm ground. He was numb with cold, but fright kept him from collapsing. He stumbled and was about to fall when he felt a hand on his shoulder; someone shone a torch in his face: 'Who are you? Hands up!'

Two Swiss border guards had been on night patrol and witnessed the last act of the drama. When they saw that one of their captives was hurt, and the other about to collapse, they put away their revolvers. They gave them brandy from a flask; one of the guards stayed with them, while the others cycled to nearby Laufenburg to fetch an ambulance. The one who stayed with them cleaned Erich's face and rubbed the upper part of his body; he told Peter to keep moving about so as not to freeze. But Peter could hardly lift his feet. When the ambulance arrived, they undressed Erich and covered him with blankets; Peter was also put on a stretcher, and they were taken to a first aid station. They were given tea with a little rum, and soup; a doctor came and said that Erich had been badly bruised; he could not say whether he also suffered from concussion. They were not to be moved for the next three days.

Then, in the early hours of the morning, a police officer arrived and said that they had been very foolish and very lucky. Never in his life had he heard of anyone trying to cross the Rhine at this point at night in an old wreck without oars. He interrogated Peter at length. At first he took copious notes, but later pushed his notebook aside; it was not that his interest was flagging – he had apparently decided not all this extraordinary story had to be part of the official record.

When he had finished Peter asked whether they would be sent back to Germany again. 'What gives you that idea?' Peter mentioned their unfortunate experience a few months earlier. The officer said that there was no need to worry, the situation had changed, no one had been returned for weeks. He wished Peter a good night's rest and left the room.

When Peter woke up the next morning the sun was shining into their room, which was overlooking the river. He looked out of the window and for a moment he thought he was dreaming, or that his vision had suddenly been impaired: there were two little cities, one on each side of the Rhine, looking exactly alike – the church, the houses, the trees on the other bank all had their likeness on this side. These were the twin cities of Laufenburg, connected by a bridge on which two little trees had been planted to make the symmetry complete. One of them was German, the other Swiss. The distance between them was a hundred yard, perhaps less. It had taken the boys almost four months and many detours to travel these last hundred yards.

They stayed for three days in Swiss Laufenburg, and they could not have been treated more kindly. Laufenburg is a small town, and the news about their arrival spread quickly; curious people peeped through doors and windows, and they received a food parcel and newspapers from the Workers Samaritan Association. But what touched them most was a little brown bag which was handed to them containing two apples, a little bar of chocolate, and a handwritten note to the effect that the children of the fifth form in the local school had heard about them, and wished a speedy recovery to Erich and the best of luck to both of them.

On the third day a young man in a leather jacket appeared. He introduced himself as the representative of the rescue committee in Zürich. He had a long session with Peter, and took copious notes about how to contact the illegals in Berlin, about Singen and Ramsen and the approaches to the border. He congratulated the two; and before he went he said that they did not want any more crossings of the Rhine in November if it could be avoided.

Erich had fully recovered by the third day, even though it was many weeks before he could remember what had happened after the boat had capsized. On the fourth day they were taken to one of the many absorption camps for refugees. There was a debate among those responsible for their future welfare as to whether they should be taken to a children's camp, for they were under-age. After a short debate a resolution was passed that a children's camp was not appropriate in this particular case.

In late January 1944, we received the following short letter, postmarked Berlin:

Dear Parents,

We are taking this opportunity to let you know that we are well. We are sorry that you did not hear from us for such a long time, but this was not really our fault. The trip proved to be more complicated (and took much longer) than we had thought. One day, we shall tell you all. Nor are we sure that we shall be able to write again soon, the opportunities to send letters are not frequent. We are living very near a high mountain plateau, and since we have free time at weekends our skiing has made great progress. Work is not difficult but somewhat monotonous; in our spare time we concentrate on learning languages. Two of our old friends joined us here last week and we hope that the others will eventually come too. So much has happened since we saw you last, it is too long a story to be told in a letter. We think a great deal about the future, our own, and that of the world, and we think of you.

Love – and kisses to mother.

Three weeks later someone contacted me and told me that he was about to leave for Zürich and that I could send a letter to Switzerland on condition that it was couched in the most general terms, and that names of persons and places were not mentioned. Peter and Erich had never been great letter-writers, and I had impressed on them many times that at their age I had sent my parents letters that were both much longer and more substantial in content than their scanty notes. I was going to show them that with a little goodwill one could vastly improve on their performance even in the most adverse conditions. I sat down and wrote several pages about the crocuses and the snow-drops in the garden, about books I had recently read; I made subtle allusions to the probable future course of the war and our own delicate position. But then I realized that my Aesopian language was not at all easy to understand, and I tore it up and instead wrote the following:

Dear Children,

Your letter was the best news we had had for many years, or are likely to have for some time to come. You will be unable to appreciate this now – you may one day, once you have children of your own. Nothing much has changed as far as our situation is concerned. Mother is not at all well, but there is no cause for immediate concern. Your letter was the best medicine she could have had; she has been sleeping much better ever since it came. Her one wish now is to see you again, as it is mine – will it be this year or not till next?

With much love. . . .

The Survivors

The total quiet that has descended on the city after a crescendo of thunder which lasted for weeks seems almost equally frightening. The sirens no longer wail, bombs are no longer dropped, there are neither cars nor trucks, and the few people walking in the streets do not talk loudly. It is 5 May 1945 and the war in Berlin has been over for three days. Hitler committed suicide last week. It is the day so many millions of people have been longing for, but now that deliverance has come there is no overwhelming joy in one's heart in the face of so much devastation: whole cities have been reduced to rubble, and even if there is still life in the ruins, it will take a long time, much effort and a great deal of suffering before life returns to normal.

In the midst of the devastation, however, human beings are beginning to move again, emerging from the holes in which they have been hiding, full of suspicion at first, not yet accustomed to the absence of danger. Many of them have lost their homes and their belongings and are destitute. But a few years hence they will again have little apartments of their own, and later on perhaps a bigger one or even a house; they will have proper clothes, a car, and as much food as they want. Such visions seem preposterous at this moment, but they are in fact almost certain to materialize, for great is the power of human inventiveness and persistence: give the people five or ten years of peace, and there will be no limit to the amount of material goods they will produce.

These wounds will be healed, much quicker, in fact, than most now believe. But there are others that will never heal. Among the millions who now emerge from their shelters, unaccustomed as yet to the light of day, there are many who have lost husbands and wives, parents and children, lovers and friends. There is hardly anyone who has not suffered some bereavement and there are many who have lost everyone dear to them. During the last few weeks of the war the frightening noise and the rain of bombs and shells had drowned out even the mourning. Only now in the great calm the numbness will be replaced by acute pain.

A man in a black suit makes his way slowly from his home in Dahlem to nearby Grunewald; this was his usual walk for many years, though for months he has not been here. He did not leave the house because his wife was dying and because the battle for Berlin made it impossible to do so. It had never been in doubt that Elizabeth would die; it had been a miracle that she had survived so long. Their sons had been gone for almost two years, and while she missed them every day, the knowledge that they were safe had given her great comfort. But her husband was still in danger, a danger that grew as German's military situation deteriorated. Hitler and his acolytes became more desperate: if they went under, they would take everyone with them. Her cousin the general had been arrested, and though it could not be proved that he had participated in any conspiracy, he was kept in prison. The Gestapo, the SS, even the most lowly local representatives of the party had the right to take the law into his own hands, and if he could summarily execute 'defeatist elements' he had, of course, the right to liquidate a Jew who had somehow been overlooked in the general elimination of his race.

For more than a year the end of Nazi rule had been in sight, but the grand finale had been long, noisy and destructive. There had been countless air raids and, towards the end, massive artillery bombardments. There was less and less food, and the public services worked fitfully and eventually came to a standstill. He had been lucky because his house had been spared a direct hit; his money had run out, but then there was hardly anything to buy in any case, and by selling a few valuables he could afford the few rations which were still distributed. Life had become very cheap in every sense.

During the past year he had been cook and nurse to his wife; no outside help was available, and since he had little else to do he had done it gladly. She did not need much care; there was no dressing to be replaced, only an occasional injection to be administered. He was in her room for many hours of each day talking and reading to her from her favourite books.

In the last week their house had suddenly become very popular in the neighbourhood. The Russians were about to arrive, and surely he could extend his protection to others? Former colleagues from distant parts of the town had called on him, neighbours had implored him to put up their families just for a night or two. He had offered Otto hospitality when his friend had lost his home in one of the last air raids, and there was also another family which had behaved decently to them throughout the war. The house had been too large in any case, and though it was a little inconvenient to have to share the kitchen and bathroom, he preferred this to the utter loneliness.

On 4 May, Elizabeth died. The end had not come suddenly, nor was it painful. She was conscious up to her last hours; her husband had told her about the collapse of the Third Reich. She was glad, she had never doubted that it would end this way. But she was by then in a state in which outside events, however important, no longer mattered. What did matter was that her children and her husband were safe, and though she never said that she could now die in peace, this was probably what she thought, when she fell asleep for the last time.

He had just come back from the funeral. How easy was it these days to die, and how difficult to get buried – in later years people would find it incredible. One needed a coffin, which was very difficult to obtain, a pushcart or wagon, for there were no vehicles to be hired, and lastly a cemetery which was still functioning. The cemeteries were among the few public utilities operating in Berlin almost to the end, but during the last weeks the grave-diggers too had gone home. Otto had taken over: somehow he found a coffin and a pushcart, and through his friends in the police he got the address of an old grave-digger who, very reluctantly, and only after payment of a substantial sum of money, had agreed to dig a grave at nearby cemetery.

Early in the morning they had left the house, Otto helping him to push the cart and steer it in between the holes, the heaps of rubble, the abandoned cars and the barricades which had not yet been dismantled. There were Russian soldiers in the streets, but they paid no attention. Helped by Otto he lowered the body into the grave; he drew a little map for himself, since the provisional label which had been affixed would no longer be readable in a few weeks. As they left the cemetery another small group of people arrived; there were no clergymen to be seen. It was a warm spring day, the sun was shining, the trees were breaking into leaf, and wild flowers were growing in all corners. It would be a good year for wild flowers, he thought.

He was still in his dark suit, as he went for his walk. As he walked among the trees of the Grunewald he realized fully for the first time that he need no longer be afraid that at any minute he would be arrested and deported. On the contrary, he would now be more in demand than ever. The Russians would perhaps want him to help organize the restoration of medical services in the capital; his American friends would remember him – sooner or later a major or a colonel would appear in a jeep at his front door, hand over a food parcel and letters, and perhaps also a tempting offer of work. If he was still his old ambitious self, he now had a good chance to become a director general of something or other, perhaps even Minister of Health. For sooner or later there would again be an administration and a government.

But he did not feel tempted. He had just lost the person closest to him. His children were safely abroad, they no longer needed him. Who, in fact, did need him? He was not an old man by modern standards, but he suddenly felt very lonely, and he knew that success in one's work was no satisfactory cure for this affliction. He would come home after a long day in his office or clinic, and he would be alone. Perhaps he was too pessimistic: he would after all go out again, meet men and women, perhaps he would marry again one day. But it would not be the same; not because Elizabeth had been the only possible wife for him in the whole world, but because he was no longer the same. He was fitter physically now than he had been for many years, but the war years had taken their toll; he was mentally tired and emotionally exhausted. While the danger was ever-present he had not even been aware of this.

Peace had come, but it was very different from what he had expected. Once he had thought that he would be able to pick up the pieces, to make a fresh start and to succeed. All this now seemed to be his for the asking, but some of the pieces had been broken or lost irretrievably and he would not get as much satisfaction as he had once thought from the new life that was just about to begin. For him in the years to come there was to be

> Life in dark houses in unlovely streets
> Doors, where my heart was used to beat
> so quickly, waiting for a hand,
> a hand that can be clasped no more....

When he reached home again, Otto told him with some excitement that while he had been out a big Soviet car had driven up and an officer had come into the house, behaving quite politely and speaking tolerably good German. The Russian general wanted to see the doctor urgently; he would call again later in the evening.

His reinstatement in the world was about to begin, but all he felt was a great emptiness.

The war in Europe formally ended with the surrender of the German army in two parallel ceremonies: with the Western powers in Rheims on 7 May, and with the Russians in Berlin the day after. In Paris there was dancing in the streets and millions joined General de Gaulle as he walked to the Arc de Triomphe; in London Big Ben, Buckingham Palace and many other public places were floodlit for the first time in six years; there was a joyous roar from an immense crowd; there were dancing, songs and fireworks. In Moscow the news was received at two in the morning. One hour later, the streets and squares of the inner city were thronging with people as never before. There were salvoes from a thousand guns and perfect strangers were toasting, kissing and embracing each other.

The seventh of May was not a public holiday in Switzerland. The country had been neutral, after all; there was no victory to be celebrated. But in Switzerland too there was great relief; at long last the nightmare was over, hundreds of thousands of young men would be demobilized, the borders would be opened again, conditions would become more normal. There were no official festivities but there was no man, woman or child who did not feel that this day marked the end of one historical epoch and the beginning of another.

Among the crowd leaving a suburban train in Zürich's central station were two tall young men in their Sunday best who had taken the day off to have their own small private celebration. They had good cause to do so, for there had been a time in the not too distant past when they had every reason to believe that they would not live to see that day.

Peter was now almost twenty, Erich would be nineteen before the end of the year. A great deal had happened to them since they had crossed the Rhine near Laufenburg in November 1943. They had been sent first to a transit camp; later they had worked for a while in Davesco, a training centre for gardeners; they had been in camps in Engelberg and Zuerichhorn, and of late they had been on their own in a little town not far from Zürich, doing work which the authorities deemed sufficiently important to release them from a camp.

There had been difficulties at times; the population in these camps was very mixed, and there had been friction because most of the others had been considerably older. The fact that the two had stayed together all this time had made it easier. There was a man with the Red Cross at Geneva who had kept a watchful eye on them from a distance; they had never actually met him, but they knew of his existence. On one occasion he had helped to open doors which seemed closed, on another occasion, when they quite clearly misbehaved, there had been a short sharp letter: he regretted very much that their father (whom he happened to know) was not at present in a position to exercise his parental duties. For he had no doubt how their father would react if he knew about the most recent transgressions of his offspring. They were duly ashamed and promised to behave. A week ago they had volunteered to go with Red Cross missions to former German concentration camps such as Bergen Belsen; their friend in Geneva had just written that he greatly appreciated their gesture – which, he was sure, was not just a gesture – but in view of the fact that they were not Swiss citizens, it was uncertain whether they would qualify.

They walked along the Bahnhofstrasse and then crossed the Limmat. There were no sudden dramatic changes in Switzerland as there were in almost all other European countries: there were no cities in ruins, and in Zürich the shops were well stocked, at least in comparison with other countries. The newspapers had been predicting the total collapse of the Third Reich for a long time. They had also reported on Auschwitz, Maidanek and Treblinka and the murder of millions of Jews. Peter and Erich bought the evening paper and read that Truman, Churchill and Stalin had exchanged messages of congratulations upon the conclusion of the war.

They went to a little restaurant on the Limmatquai, as they often did, but today it was fuller than usual and they had to wait until one of their favourite tables near the window became free. They had been mere boys for whom life had been an exciting game when they had left Berlin; they were now young men, surprisingly serious and responsible for their age. They knew that from now on it would depend on them, and only on them, to make their way in the world. During their childhood and for years after there had always been the family to fall back on; later on they had to face grave dangers but a good fairy seemed to have protected them. When Peter now thought of their often reckless behaviour during and after their escape from Berlin he became afraid even in retrospect.

Their parents could not help them any more; they had not heard from them for more than a year. They knew that their mother was seriously ill, and that many people had perished in the air raids and during the last battle for Berlin. Had their father been deported during the last mad convulsions of Nazi rule? They wanted to make one more effort to establish contact, and this was one of the reasons for their trip to Zürich: within a week or two they hoped they would know.

The last years, they often thought, had been lost years as far as

276

their future was concerned; they had not learnt anything that could be of use later on. This was not, strictly speaking, quite correct, for they had made good progress in French and English, and in the camps they had picked up some Italian and Spanish. But since (as Erich used to say with some disdain) they had no intention of becoming night porters in a hotel, such knowledge seemed to be of only marginal importance. But even in their hours of dejection it occurred to them from time to time that, all things considered, they had been very lucky: how many of their contemporaries in Europe would not come back from the war, or would return crippled for life? And how many of their Jewish contemporaries had survived at all?

Of late they had been thinking about their own future quite often. Obviously they would not stay in Switzerland after the war. Peter wanted to join one of the kibbutzim, the collective settlements in Palestine, once connections were re-established. Newcomers would be needed more than ever after the terrible blood-letting the Jewish people had suffered in Europe. He had been in touch with a group of young people, refugees in Switzerland like himself, who had similar plans. They had met a few times and hotly debated whether to join one of the existing settlements or to found a new one. There were good reasons for and against either plan, and so the debate continued, and was likely to be decided only on the spot in Palestine.

Erich too wanted to go to Palestine, but he also wanted to study, and since there was only one technical university there, in Haifa, and since it did not teach the subjects he wanted, he had written to Caltech, to MIT and a few other such institutions in the United States. They had replied promptly with very nice, very understanding, very sympathetic letters, but conveyed to him that his problem would not be easy to solve. On one hand it would be for the best if he came as soon as possible after the war, for within a year or two they expected a major influx. But on the other hand, if they understood him correctly, he did not even have a high school certificate. They fully understood that the situation in Europe had not been quite normal of late, but he would still have to satisfy them that he was up to American standards before they admitted him.

But Erich, as the reader of this story will have realized by now, was not a young man who was easily deterred. He had gone to the United States legation in Berne, where the attaché who received him and to whom he relayed his request in heavily accented but correct English had been more than a little puzzled by the request – in the middle of a war – for American senior high school and college textbooks. The attaché had wanted to know a bit more about him; and when Erich had told him his story, he became pensive and said that he would try to help. The two had met again and almost became friends; the attaché had a brother who taught at an institute of advanced technology, less prestigious and less well endowed than MIT or Caltech, but still perfectly respectable. He mentioned the case to him, and had a reply which held out some promise.

Peter and Erich had their usual cup of coffee and single portion of Bircher Muesli which they shared. Outside, in the street, they saw a group of students celebrating noisily. Peter said that in view of the occasion they should have a drink. But Erich reminded him that their financial situation, as so often, was extremely critical, and that alcoholic drinks were unfortunately very expensive; Peter had to admit that his brother's logic could not be faulted. However, the proprietor solved the problem for them: he too had been watching the students celebrating outside and he announced that there would be free drinks for all.

Peter burst out laughing; their old luck had not deserted them. They gulped down their vermouth (which they did not really like) after having toasted first their parents then the friends whom they had left behind and then 'the future', having reached unanimous agreement that an uncertain future was greatly preferable to no future at all.

Postface

Thirty years have passed since the events that I have related – clumsily no doubt, but I believe truthfully. Those who were boys then are now middle-aged men; they are fathers, and soon, what with the early marriages customary today, they will be grandfathers. And I am now quite definitely an old man, though perhaps not old enough to put down my pen for ever. 7 May 1945 is a date which for many reasons was a watershed in my life as in that of so many others. But it is not the end of the story. I shall not deny that what I first regarded a tiresome burden gradually became a labour of love, and if I have the strength I shall perhaps continue this story one day.

If this were a novel of the old-fashioned kind, I should perhaps look back at this stage for the last time before closing the pages. But since I may one day continue my story I shall only say that some of my contemporaries mentioned at the beginning of this book have since died. Some are still very much in the public eye, and their activities are widely commented on; others guard their privacy, and I respect their wishes. Robert, who encouraged me when I was about to give up, has suddenly resumed work on his own magnum opus and I recently heard that he may finish it soon. Egon is now retired; he lives in a country house in Sussex and, believe it or not, is growing roses. He moved to England after the war and when I listened the other evening to the World Service of the BBC – a Second World War habit I cannot shed – I heard a most interesting little lecture by Sir Egon, delivered in his usual high-pitched voice and slightly mocking style, about the perils of world inflation.

I have not been back to Mariabronn, but I have been told that Pater Borromaeus died many years ago. He is still remembered among his flock as a model of what an upright clergyman should be. Once a year, around Christmas, I send a postcard to the young lady from Mariabronn who later became a doctor. She answers promptly in handwriting which is still that of the girl I once knew. Otto, my dear, my only friend in Berlin during the most difficult years, became politically active again after 1945; for ten years he represented the Social Democrats in the local Berlin parliament, and for two years he served as mayor of one of the suburbs. He has been dead for some years now, but I frequently think of him, and always with deep gratitude.

Elizabeth's cousin, the general, survived Nazi imprisonment and after the war published an interesting book on military history. The other day I had a visit from a very German-looking, very correct young man who is studying at Columbia – this was his grandson, a delightful boy. His politics, about which he talked dogmatically and at great length, were those of the extreme left. The old man would have taken a less lenient view than I did.

Leo Baeck survived Theresienstadt; he later lived in London, and then taught at the Hebrew College in Cincinatti almost up to the time of his death in 1956. His biography has been written. Paul Eppstein became mayor of the Theresienstadt ghetto soon after his arrival; this was of course a position of no influence whatsoever. But apparently he told the people around him that deportation meant certain death, and may even have suggested resistance. He was arrested on 27 September 1944 and shot the same day. Even those who had bitterly criticized him agree that he died with dignity.

Dr Lustig, who was the head of the Jewish hospital in Berlin, the only remaining Jewish organization after 1943, survived the war, but not by much. Some say that he helped as much as he could, considering that he had no freedom of action; others have judged him more harshly. He was arrested by the Russians a few days after the end of the war, and there has been no news of him since. Rosa Sterner and her young man were also arrested after the war, first by the Russians and later by the Western Allies. The case attracted some attention at the time. But they have been out of prison for a long time now, and I do not know whether they are still alive, and if so, where they live.

Dr Rothmund, head of the Swiss police and terror of the refugees, resigned his post after the war. Once omnipotent, he became suddenly a controversial figure, and in the last years of his life he was virtually ostracized by many of his fellow citizens. As the facts became known (in the 'Ludwig Report' for instance) it was realized that the period between August 1942 and September 1943 had not been a glorious page in Swiss history. Perhaps it was wrong to single out Dr Rothmund and make him the scapegoat for the indifference and faulty judgment of a great many people in public life.

One of the reasons for Peter and Erich's flight from Berlin was the wish to find an escape-route for the illegals whose position became untenable. A few followed in their footsteps during the winter of

1943–4, but most preferred the known risks of staying to the unknown dangers of crossing into Switzerland. Three or four were caught, but most of them miraculously survived underground.

The man whom I called Michael, the girl Ilse and some of the others live in Israel; some are in the United States. They do not like to talk about their underground days. They do not look at all like the heroes of popular imagination; if they were to tell their story now, their own children would not believe them. Their parents are so innocent, indeed such helpless people, that the very idea that they could have outwitted the security forces of the Third Reich for two years seems grotesque.

And so they have kept silent, and sometimes I am not sure whether I should not have kept silent too, for it seems to me most unlikely that those who were not there will ever understand.